THE
BOURNE
INITIATIVE

ROBERT LUDLUM was the author of twenty-seven novels, each one a *New York Times* bestseller. There are more than 225 million of his books in print, and they have been translated into thirty-two languages. He is the author of *The Scarlatti Inheritance, The Chancellor Manuscript*, and the Jason Bourne series – *The Bourne Identity, The Bourne Supremacy*, and *The Bourne Ultimatum* – among others. Mr Ludlum passed away in March 2001. To learn more, you can visit Robert-Ludlum.com.

ERIC VAN LUSTBADER is the author of numerous bestselling novels including *First Daughter, Beloved Enemy, The Ninja*, and the international bestsellers featuring Jason Bourne: *The Bourne Legacy, The Bourne Betrayal, The Bourne Sanction, The Bourne Deception, The Bourne Objective, The Bourne Dominion, The Bourne Imperative, The Bourne Retribution, The Bourne Ascendancy* and *The Bourne Enigma*. For more information, you can visit EricVanLustbader.com. You can also follow him on Facebook and Twitter.

ROBERT LUDLUM'S™

THE BOURNE INITIATIVE

THE NEW JASON BOURNE ADVENTURE BY ERIC VAN LUSTBADER

HEAD of ZEUS

First published in the USA in 2017 by Grand Central Publishing,
a division of Hachette Book Group, Inc.

First published in the UK in 2017 by Head of Zeus Ltd

9 7 5 3 1 2 4 6 8

A catalogue record for this book is available from the British Library.

ISBN (HB) 9781786694232
ISBN (XTPB) 9781786694249
ISBN (E) 9781786694225

Printed and bound by CPI Group (UK) Ltd, Croydon, CR0 4YY

Head of Zeus Ltd
First Floor East
5–8 Hardwick Street
London EC1R 4RG
WWW.HEADOFZEUS.COM

For Victoria, my one and only,
my everything.

THE
BOURNE
INITIATIVE

Prologue

THERE IS SOMETHING *about a man on his knees,* Keyre thought, *that stirs my very heart.* Keyre, the Somali magus, a Yibir whose lineage stretched back through time to the days of the Ajuran Empire, predating all the subsequent failed sultanates, stood on the hard shingle twelve feet from the soft rumble of the Indian Ocean. He breathed in the salt air, the familiar scents of the sere desert behind him, the sun-baked brick of houses destroyed by bazooka blasts and rocket fire. But all these clean scents were at the moment overwhelmed by the stink of human sweat, excrement, and terror.

Ah, but terror is what Keyre fed upon, lapped up like mother's milk since he was a child of eight, in the aftermath of his first kill. The first taste of blood was always the sharpest, but, for him, the blood didn't matter as much as it did to his compatriots. But then they weren't Yibir, weren't steeped in the Stygian darkness of his family's ancient sorcery. Their nostrils dilated as the fresh blood flowed from the newly dead. But for Keyre, the blood was an adjunct, as necessary as shooting dead the man who, on his knees, waves the white flag.

It's the white flag, you see, he told himself. *The white flag stinks of fear.*

I want to inhale its scent, savor its taste before I put a match to it and set it afire. Where he stood now, on the shore of Somalia, between the desert of destruction and the Indian Ocean on which he often enough plied his particular brand of terror, he was immersed in the stench of death.

Before him thirteen men knelt, backs bowed, heads bowed further. Some stared in stony silence at the shingle on which they knelt, its shifting layers slicing like razor blades into their knees. Others wailed their fear in pitiful ululations. One or two had tear streaks along their dust-caked cheeks. None of them murmured a prayer—further confirmation, if any was needed, of what Keyre already knew.

He was a tall man, cadaverously thin, all muscle and bone, with a long, triangular face and a saturnine countenance. He was both as athletic as a swimmer and as graceful as a dancer—not only strikingly handsome but possessed of a charisma gifted to very few. He had dedicated himself to many things, not the least of which was creating a dazzling smile that fooled everyone.

Thirteen men, on their knees, bowed down, wrists tied behind their backs. In Keyre's left hand a large German Mauser restored to all its World War II glory. *Who was its original owner? A member of the Gestapo, or the Abwehr, maybe, their mortal enemy. What did it matter anyway?* Keyre asked himself; it was his now, unlocked and loaded.

Stepping up, he placed the muzzle of the Mauser against the back of the first prisoner's head and pulled the trigger. The sound of the hammer falling was as loud as a thunderclap. As one, the line of men flinched. But there was no detonation, no bullet. Stepping to his right, Keyre placed the muzzle against the back of the second man's head. When he pulled the trigger, the man's head exploded, and what was left of him pitched forward, sprawled awkwardly onto the shingle.

Blood, the stench of it rising up to mingle with a terror that, to Keyre's heightened senses, was palpable. Above, black birds wheeled, calling to each other, dinner bells announcing another feast. High above them, the vast sky rippled with clouds, like a weight lifter flexing his muscles.

Another step to the right brought him to a spot directly behind the third man in line. Keyre shot him, with more or less the identical result. In all, there were twelve corpses lying facedown on the bloody shingle when he reached the end of the line. That left the first man. Keyre had reloaded two-thirds of the way down the line; his Mauser was still itching to inflict more death. He could feel the sensation run up the nerves of his left arm, like the output of a live wire. His hand twitched briefly in just the way a female lion's paw twitched when she was dreaming of running down an okapi or a gazelle. Jaws at the throat, clamping down, blood and viscera overrunning her teeth as the males loped up to feed.

Keyre took his time returning to the one remaining kneeling man. He stood in front of him, staring down.

"Look at me," he said. He could see the man shaking. "Look at me!" he said more sharply.

The man's head came up. Keyre locked his eyes onto the prisoner's. "I know who you are," he said, his tone conversational now. "I know what you and your kind have been up to. Their death sentence has been carried out, as you can see." He crouched down so suddenly the prisoner flinched. He was a thin man, short in stature, but with plenty of upper body strength. He was dark of skin, his nose long and sharp. His brown eyes were set close together. His lips were chapped, the skin flaking off as if he'd been out in the sun too long.

He's been here with me too long, Keyre thought. *That's for certain.*

He stared hard into the other's face as he said, "Here, your death sentence will be carried out in the blink of an eye." There were smears of dried blood on the prisoner's cheek; he stank of sweat and terror, and there was about him a certain fecal stench. "But for you, my friend, that death sentence can be commuted. Your life can continue." Keyre left it there; it was time to keep silent.

The prisoner's jaw muscles worked spasmodically. His tongue, gray as ash, appeared, then slipped back between his teeth. "H . . . how?" he asked in a thin, reedy voice, and Keyre knew the man would tell him what he wanted to know.

Despite the miasma the man wore like a cloak, Keyre leaned in and said in his ear, "What I want to know is this: who do you work for?"

The prisoner's mouth worked as if he was trying to summon up the courage to answer or enough saliva to speak clearly.

Before he could say a word, Keyre said, "His full name and position. Nothing less will save you."

The prisoner swallowed hard. His eyes flicked from one side to the other, as if frightened of being overheard, even out here in the Somalian wilderness. "Not out loud."

Keyre nodded, giving him permission to lean forward. He placed his lips against the opening of Keyre's ear and whispered six words.

Those words—the identity of the man who trained these thirteen to infiltrate his cadre—caused a profound change in Keyre's demeanor. His face darkened, his lips compressed, his eyes seemed to cross. Then, in a flash, he turned his head sideways and with his open jaws and his bared teeth, he ripped the man's throat out.

Part One

MEME

1

MORGANA ROY WALKED briskly to work at precisely 8:36 in the morning. As a creature of habit, she always walked a mile from the public parking garage to her office in the rear of a half-derelict building, on the flyblown main drag of Bowie, Maryland. Bowie was just southwest of Fort Meade, where the black-glass NSA colossus rose seemingly out of nowhere. As usual, she had arisen at six in the morning, driven to the dojo where she had been a member for seven years, and worked out vigorously with masters of two different martial arts disciplines for more or less forty-five minutes each, before showering and changing into her work clothes.

Her apartment, twenty miles southwest of the office, would seem to an outsider like a perfectly sterile environment: apart from appliances, there were two or multiples thereof of everything—sofas, chairs, lamps, coffee and side tables, laptop computers at two different workstations. On the dining room table stood two vases, each equidistant from the center. Six chairs. Everything was symmetrical. She lived a compartmentalized life; order was important to her. Chaos made her uneasy, though the truth was she found the concept intriguing.

She made this walk in all seasons, all kinds of weather, without fail, and at a speed that would make most others huff and puff and clutch the stitch in their side. There was about this walk something of a challenge, so grueling in summer heat and winter sleet, that those who occasionally had to walk with her privately called it the Bataan Death March. It was a joke, of course, but a decidedly grim one.

Morgana Roy worked in a small suite of offices hard by a gymnasium, and those new to her unit were assaulted by the smells of stale sweat, underarm odor, and worse, which insinuated themselves through the baseboards of the wall that separated the offices from the gym. Twice a week these would be temporarily overpowered by the acrid stench of Lysol and bleach. Morgana seemed unaware of these odious smells, or perhaps she had become accustomed to them.

Using a magnetic key card, she passed through the door marked with a small, discreet sign: MEME LLC, printed on a sheet of plain white paper. It looked as unsettled as Morgana's state of mind, and in bad weather it had to be replaced almost daily. Still, there was no plan for anything permanent to take its place. Across the street was the smallest post office Morgana had ever seen, a tiny brick building with a sadly draped banner, RENT A P.O. BOX TODAY, hanging off the iron railing of the cement handicap ramp.

At Morgana's entrance, a heavyset young woman of twenty-three in a distinctly non–government issue gabardine suit got up from behind a desk, said, "Good morning," and went to fetch them both cappuccinos.

"Good morning, Rose," Morgana said when Rose returned.

Beside Rose's desk a rubber plant's leaves shone as if polished daily. To the right was a cabinet, closed and locked, that, in fact, contained nothing at all. To the left stood a row of three chairs that had never been sat on, a low table on which were scattered copies of *Vanity Fair* and *Wired*, never read but nevertheless kept current. There were never any visitors to Meme LLC, ever.

At thirty, Morgana was the oldest member of the crew. She had seven people working for her in the office, seven more out in the field. All of them were young and ruthless; they had, to a person, lean and hungry looks, which was just the way she wanted them.

There were two doors in the wall behind Rose. The one on the right led to a break room, complete with a refrigerator-freezer, a two-burner stove, a sink, food cabinets, a coffee bean grinder, and the cappuccino-espresso maker. Farther along lurked a warren of store-rooms that eventually led to a basement.

The left-hand door was locked with a retina-recognition system. Morgana, cappuccino in hand, looked into the display, opening the door. She took a judicious sip of her cappuccino before stepping across the threshold.

She entered a large, windowless room. Across the left wall was a mosaic of LED flat-panel screens, but instead of showing feeds of CCTV cameras in airports and street corners in cities around the world, or images of desert encampments relayed from various drones, these screens contained images from computer terminals, hard drive data folders, dynamic malware firewalls. The images kept changing, often so fast they became a blur. Most of the writing on the screens was in Russian Cyrillic or Mandarin Chinese, but there was one in Persian, others in Hebrew and Arabic, still another in Urdu, a final one in Pashto.

The right-hand wall was a 4K video loop of aerial footage of the Swiss Alps. An hour from now, it would be scenes shot from a boat prowling the Maldives, and the hour after that, the crowded streets of midtown Manhattan. And so forth. No one ever complained about the lack of windows; no one looked up when Morgana strode in, which was just the way she liked it. Her cadre of six had eyes and minds glued to their laptop screens.

There were no partitions between workstations. Thick cables rose from each station to tracks hung just below the ceiling, which allowed Morgana's staff to move around at will, huddle together for impromptu conferences, exchange vital information in real time. Everything on the flat-panels was in real time. Real time meant everything to the operators of Meme LLC; being current was their currency. Morgana fostered a cluster method of cryptanalysis, hence the screens. All Meme's projects were collaborative efforts. This led not only to one success after another but to a close-knit comradeship among the team impossible to achieve inside the federal government's myriad clandestine services.

Morgana passed through a narrow door set discreetly in the far wall. There was no nameplate beside it. This was Morgana's sanctum. From here, she could monitor everything that went on in the outer room. She also had the freedom to turn it all off, and in the semi-darkness contemplate algorithms and her future.

Setting her cappuccino down at her workstation, she removed her jacket, slung it over the back of her ergonomic task chair, sat down. The moment she did so, the screen on her laptop flared to life. Her thumbprint was scanned, and she was in.

There was the usual slew of email messages waiting in her in box, but there was also one that was flagged.

Uh oh, she thought. *Black Star.*

She knew what Black Star meant, and it wasn't usual in any way, shape, manner, or form.

She clicked on the icon. Instead of opening the message, she was taken directly to the office of General Arthur MacQuerrie. His wind-burned, time-lined face filled the screen. His baby blues stared out of the screen as if he were Dr. Strange, who, along with Wonder Woman, was one of her favorite comic book heroes. The analogy was apt. Her boss at NSA was something of a magician. How he kept her unit secret from the mandarins floating at the top of the governmental alphabet soup—NSA, CIA, DIA, FBI, DOD, DHS, you name it—was a complete mystery to her. And that was only the top layer of his legerdemain. Meme was well funded—there wasn't one thing Morgana had ever asked for that the general had ever refused. They had bleeding-edge technology to the point where all their equipment was upgraded twice a year. Obtaining vast sums of money from Marshall Fulmer, former senator and head of the Joint Armed Services Appropriations Committee (JASAC) who had just been confirmed by Congress as the incoming president's national security advisor, without letting on what the funds were for, seemed an impossibility. And yet the general managed it.

"Morning, Mac," she said, as she took another sip of her cappuccino. "What's up?"

The general was possessed of a wide brow and beetling eyebrows. One could tell a lot from those eyebrows, which were the most mobile aspect of his diamond-shaped face. "It seems our old friend, Boris Il-lyich Karpov, has climbed out of the grave."

"General Karpov is dead," Morgana said. "His throat was slit from ear to ear, in Moscow last year at his wedding."

"And yet, he keeps bedeviling us." The general shook his head. "As you are well aware, Boris Karpov trod a fine line between doing the Sovereign's bidding and working for himself. That is more difficult in Russia than it is anywhere else in the world, save North Korea. It seems that in the months before he was killed, Karpov was working on several clandestine initiatives."

Morgana's screen split. MacQuerrie remained in the left half, while the right half was filled with a rain of vertical lines of computer code so complex they took her breath away.

"What in the name of holy hell is that?"

"No idea," MacQuerrie said. "Which is why I've brought it to you."

"We'll get right on it."

"That's just what you won't do," MacQuerrie said. "This is for your eyes only. No one is to see or even catch a whiff that this code exists. Got that?"

"Of course, but what do you think it is?"

The general seemed to age a decade before her eyes. He ran a hand across his face, and to her horror, she noticed a slight tremor in the fingers.

"My best guess: a cyber weapon, something so sophisticated that it's far beyond anything we've seen—or even dreamt of—before. For some time, this *thing*, this weapon, was a rumor, nothing more. But because some of the stories attributed fantastic powers to it, I kept my ear to the ground, collated even the most outlandish of the rumors.

"And, then, out of the blue, an hour ago, this shard appeared in the wild. My people found it quite by accident while trolling the dark web for intel on a certain arms dealer we've been after for years, but have yet to pin a single misstep on, let alone a crime. When leads do surface, the people behind them vanish as if into thin air. We never even find a body."

"What's this arms dealer's name?"

"Keyre. He's a Somali pirate—or was, anyway, until we took Viktor Bout into custody." She knew Bout was the most notorious illegal arms dealer of the last decade. "That left a giant hole in the illegal arms trade, and Keyre was first into Bout's territory, killing off whoever was left from the Russian's own network, replacing them with his own people.

"Keyre has proven himself to be smarter, better connected, and far more slippery than Bout ever was. The story goes that his network is larger, more far-flung, and, most crucially, contains contacts inside governments worldwide. Bout had customs and immigration people in a dozen countries in his pocket. By contrast, Keyre's network makes Bout's look like a kindergarten class.

"Whether that's the emmis, I don't yet know, but it's this cyber weapon that's giving me a migraine for the ages. You need to make sense of the fragment and you have to find the rest of the code."

Morgana sat back, absorbing the information Mac was throwing her way. Something was nagging at her, and she voiced it: "Mac, have you thought about why this fragment suddenly showed up on the dark web?"

"What d'you mean? There are any number of ways—"

"No, there aren't. Not something of this level of sophistication. No, Mac, my guess is that it was released on the dark web deliberately."

"But what for?"

"I think it's a strong possibility that whoever took possession of the cyber initiative following Karpov's murder is putting it up for auction."

"Auction?"

"What better way to whet potential buyers' appetites, and drive up the bids, than to let them take a peek behind the curtain, so to speak."

"Christ, I hadn't thought of that." MacQuerrie was sweating now, droplets forming at his hairline, rolling down the sides of his cheek.

"Could this Keyre be running the auction?"

"Possible. Even likely. Somalia is just the place for such things." The general frowned. "But I'm thinking he's only the conduit. Someone else is the mastermind. And knowing Karpov as I did, it would have to be someone he trusted implicitly as well as explicitly."

"That rules out just about everyone in the Russian government, doesn't it?"

MacQuerrie nodded. "Yes, it does."

"Someone from within the initiative itself, then."

"Again, knowing Karpov, he wouldn't trust anyone like that with the big picture. His operations were meticulously compartmentalized. That was his first rule of keeping his work absolutely secure. No one could betray him if they didn't know what was really going on."

"In that case, I'm willing to bet several people wrote this code, each one unaware of what the others were doing. Could Karpov himself have stitched all the pieces of code together?"

"The general was a man of many talents," MacQuerrie said. "It's possible, I suppose, but, frankly, not very likely."

"Well, no programmer could direct Karpov's initiative as a whole. The best ones are like idiot savants: they know their stuff backward and forward, but that's all they're good for. They couldn't direct themselves out of a paper bag." She pursed her lips. "So again, I have to ask, who is running the operation now?"

MacQuerrie did not answer right away. It seemed to Morgana that now they had come to the nub of the matter, his face had gone even grayer. Perhaps it was the lighting in his office, but she doubted that. His right eyebrow twitched, which meant he was under extreme stress. *What could cause such a thing?* she asked herself.

"One thing before we go any further, Morgana."

She said nothing. Even for her, who was more or less inured to such things, waiting for the second shoe to drop was a mighty unpleasant experience. This was General Arthur MacQuerrie, not some fatuous NSA type who didn't know his ass from his elbow.

"I have no doubt that Karpov's operation is aimed squarely at the United States." He paused to wipe at a growing film of sweat on his upper lip. "It could be the national electrical grid or even, God forbid, the president's bank of nuclear missile codes."

"What? But that's impossible. The code data is buried so deeply behind a phalanx of firewalls . . . and then the codes are changed hourly."

"All true. But Karpov's operational language is so obscure, so utterly unknown, I and my people believe the nuclear codes are its target."

"If the Russians access our nuclear codes . . ."

"You see the nature of the extreme danger we're in."

Morgana stared at the lines of code, cascading down her screen. *Good God,* she thought. *What we have here is the ultimate weapon of mass destruction.*

Black Star. No wonder.

"This is a superworm," she said. "A form of malware no one's ever encountered before."

"Tell me something I don't know. This is catastrophic. You had better come up with the answer, *stat.*"

Morgana didn't like the tone that had set into his voice. This had happened more than once before, when Mac started treating her like a low-level gopher, his voice hard and threatening. She bit her lip, but bile built up in her stomach, churning, as if a whirlpool had opened up inside her.

"Horrifyingly, there's more," Mac was saying.

She tensed even more as the code vanished, to be replaced by a grainy black-and-white photo, obviously taken with a telephoto lens. A surveillance shot, then. Men in tuxedos, women in fancy floor-length gowns, jewels and beading glittering. Over their heads an ornate crystal chandelier, spilling light down on them.

"Moscow." MacQuerrie gave her a date from last year. "On the occasion of Boris Karpov's wedding."

"I see Karpov," Morgana said. "In the center."

"D'you recognize anyone else? He has his arm across the shoulders of the man to his immediate right."

"Yes."

"Do you recognize that man?"

She leaned closer, zoomed in a bit, but not too much; the images would become too vague to accurately glean features and expressions. "I'm afraid I don't, Mac."

The general sighed. "Well, I suppose I shouldn't be surprised."

She felt the whirlpool congeal into an icy ball. She wanted to vomit it up and throw it at Mac. Instead, fighting to keep her cool, she said: "Karpov looks genuinely pleased to be with him. But, as you've told me, he didn't have any close friends in the Russian hierarchy."

"That's correct."

Now she was sure that MacQuerrie was in serious distress; his eyebrows were knit together in a dreadful expression of anxiety.

"That man isn't a Russian, Morgana. He's one of ours—or at least he was. You're looking at Boris Karpov's best friend, the only one he would trust to continue his operation in the event of his demise.

"The man Karpov is embracing is Jason Bourne."

2

THE AEGEAN SEA was a pure cobalt blue in the late afternoon sunlight. The boat plowed through the waves, on its way west. *Nym*, Boris Karpov's hundred-foot motorboat, whose captain and crew were Greeks and Cypriots, was the only asset of the late FSB general that hadn't been confiscated by the Russian government following his murder and the death of his new bride. The only reason it hadn't been confiscated was that Boris had wisely kept the boat in international waters, out of reach of even the Sovereign's avaricious clutches.

These thoughts were uppermost in Jason Bourne's mind as he stood amidships, leaning on the polished port railing, staring at the smudge on the horizon that even at this distance he recognized as the island of Skyros. To the northeast and days behind them was the Sea of Marmara and, beyond, Istanbul, where they had briefly anchored to take on supplies, fuel, fresh food, and water. Istanbul was no longer a safe haven for Westerners. And yet he knew so many people in and around the city that he, rather than the captain, did all the bartering.

From Skyros, he had no idea where he would go. At the moment, he was content to be at sea, to feel the salt wind in his hair, to have it cleanse him of Boris's horrific murder and its exhausting and perilous aftermath. Boris had been involved in a myriad of strategies, initiatives of which neither the Sovereign nor his comrades in the FSB were aware. Perhaps they would all unravel now, or even had already died along with the spymaster who had conceived them. It was a relief not to have to think of tomorrow, of ticking clocks, of countdowns toward one catastrophe or another, of outrunning life or deadly deadlines.

His best friend was gone, had left him the boat as a remembrance. In truth, he had no use for this huge boat. Nevertheless, here he was. It was a matter of honoring both his friendship and Boris's memory to accept the gift, to use it as he saw fit. Boris trusted him to do that; he had every intention of respecting that trust.

Behind him, too, was the Russian Federation. Last year, he had fallen so deeply into a nest of vipers he'd be quite happy never to set foot in Russia again. All this brooding about the past—the part of it he could remember—was making him melancholy. But what else should he feel? Every time he thought he'd had enough, that he should return to the professorial life of David Webb, the person he had been before the Bourne identity had been imprinted on him by the people running Treadstone, he knew it was useless. He'd tried that—twice, in fact—only to become bored within weeks. He was who he was now. He couldn't outrun it; senseless to try.

The *Nym* slowed to quarter speed. Captain Stavros appeared out of the wheelhouse, descended an outside ladder, and approached Bourne. He carried a bottle of chilled vodka, two glasses, and a pepper shaker.

"Berth or anchorage?" he asked in his typical shorthand.

In the days since Bourne had come aboard *Nym,* the two men had come to know each other, as much as two strangers in close quarters can know each other. They ate their meals together, drank together, afterward exchanged stories about the boat's former master, for whom Stavros had a deep and abiding affection. Despite his formidable personality, his studied cruelty, Boris had often been astonishingly genial. Despite his dark and brooding Russian soul—or perhaps because of it—he had loved good food, fine drink, and laughter. Lots of laughter, the perfect anodyne for the bleak profession he had carved out for himself.

Boris had felt things deeply, made friends for life, would do anything for those friends. These qualities, mirrored in Bourne, had formed the basis of their abiding friendship. Even though they often found themselves on opposite sides, many were the times they helped each other out, finding common enemies to defeat. Bourne would miss their camaraderie, but he missed the heightened experience of shared danger most of all.

"Anchorage." Bourne gave him coordinates, and Stavros nodded. He was used to being told the minimum about where his master was headed and why.

Handing Bourne one of the glasses, he gave them both generous pours of the vodka—a very fine Russian brand, Bourne noted. Before they drank, Stavros dotted the surface of the liquor in each glass with pepper. He grinned at Bourne, who returned the expression. This was a silent tribute to Boris, an old-school Russian, if ever there was one. Back in the day you always used pepper before you drank your vodka. Often, the liquor would contain fusel oil, a product of poor distillation; the pepper would bind with the oil, sink it to the bottom of the glass. The word *fusel*, Bourne knew, was German for "bad liquor."

"To our great general!" Stavros cried, holding his glass high. His voice was a deep basso, clotted by years of too much drink and cigarette tar.

"To Boris Illyich." *Long may his memory live on,* Bourne thought.

"We will never forget him!"

They clinked glasses, downed the vodka in one.

Above them, the sky was an inverted porcelain bowl, light-blue and white, the colors of the boat's master stateroom. Gulls wheeled and called plaintively, having flown out from the island's rocky cliffs on the eastern shore to beg for food.

"Will we be staying in Skyros long?"

"Several days," Bourne said evasively, and the captain nodded, understanding: it was none of his business.

He refilled Bourne's glass, then took his leave, heading back up into the wheelhouse to guide *Nym* the last half mile to the anchorage two hundred yards offshore. The water was quite deep on this side of the island.

Bourne moved toward the bow, the better to watch the craggy cliffs and the curved shingle coming into focus. Details, he thought. Everything was in the details. So many of his foes had forgotten to take care of the details; so many had lost their lives because of that lapse.

Bourne called for the speedy runabout with its overclocked dual diesels. As he descended the accommodation ladder, he saw the captain staring down at him.

"Sure you don't want one of the crew with you, sir?"

"Positive."

Stavros held up a Steyr M automatic pistol in a sign of query.

"Thanks, but there's no need."

"You never know." Stavros grinned. "The general used to say that."

True enough. Bourne raised a hand, caught the Steyr, then made his way down to the waiting runabout. The captain had dropped anchor at the precise coordinates Bourne had given him. Bourne had been to Skyros only once, and that under extreme conditions. But in light of what was about to take place he supposed his return could be considered a homecoming of sorts.

The crewman who had been preparing the runabout for him leapt up onto the accommodation ladder and cast off. Bourne fired up the outboard engine and headed to a spot just left of the headland that jutted out into the Aegean like a questing nose. Gulls peeled away from the boat, circled him for a while, then wheeled away, calling their disappointment.

When he was close enough for the runabout to enter the shadow of the looming promontory, he steered it farther left. By this point, the headland was between him and the *Nym*. No one on board could see what he was doing or who was waiting for him.

She was sitting on a rise on the shingle, smoking a cigarette, watching him beneath half-lowered lids as he cut the engines, dropped anchor, and leapt into the shallows.

She made no move to help him, stayed where she was, giving him that peculiar sideways glance of hers as he picked his way up the shingle to her. She wore a revealing swimsuit of a metallic plum-colored fabric. She was turned so that he could see the ugly scar that ran along the outside of her right calf all the way up to her hipbone. It was clear the wound had been inflicted in many stages, a form of torture. He knew what had been carved into her beautiful back.

Her magnificent legs were very long, her waist thin. A scattering of freckles dusted the bridge of her nose. Her eyes changed color with the light—either midnight-blue or black. In all, she was staggeringly beautiful.

"Do you think what I'm wearing is appropriate?"

"For the beach, you mean."

She smiled a thousand-watt smile. They were more or less repeating their lines from last year, when they had met in Nicosia. Before that, Bourne hadn't seen her since he had spirited her away from Keyre's camp in Somalia. She had been younger then, no more than a girl, but Keyre had spent months torturing her, indoctrinating her as dictated by his Yibir traditions. What he had meant to do with her, Bourne had no idea, and if she knew she had never told him.

Her name was Mala Ilves, an Estonian by birth. No one but Bourne called her Mala now; few even knew the name. These days she was known only as the Angelmaker.

"For what we are here to do," she said.

"How can I answer? I don't know why you asked me to come here, to such an out-of-the-way place."

She turned her face up to the lowering sun. "It's peaceful here, isn't it?" That sideways glance again. "But it's also bloody."

"That was a long time ago, Mala."

"Not for me, it isn't." She ran her fingertips down the length of the scar. "It's only yesterday."

Bourne came and sat down beside her. "I don't believe that." She smelled of licorice and the sea and clean sweat. A far cry from the stench of blood and rotting flesh that rose off her when he had brought her here from Somalia.

She ran her hands through her thick hair. "I've never lied to you, Jason."

"How many times have you wanted to?"

She wet her lips with the tip of a pink tongue and laughed softly. "I cannot count the times."

He waited a moment before he spoke again. Sunlight glanced off the waves, spreading the last of its warmth toward them. A cormorant vanished from sight, returned to the surface a good three yards away with a silvery fish in its beak. Lifting its head to the sun, as Mala had, it swallowed the fish whole.

"So tell me, why have you brought me here?"

"Are you in such a rush? Do you have somewhere to go? Or someone to see."

The last was not a question, and a tiny curl of warning reared its head in the pit of his stomach. How much did she know about his recent life? Perhaps everything. He knew he would have to begin with that assumption and work his way back to the truth. One thing he would never do is underestimate her; everyone who had made that mistake was dead.

"No," he said. "I'm all yours."

That sideways glance and a sly smile. Did she believe him, or was she as wary of him as he was of her?

"You belong to no one, Jason. Not even the Israeli."

So she did know about Sara. He was angry; it felt like a violation of his private life. But he was not surprised. There had never been anything about Mala that honored privacy. All of that had been systematically stripped from her by Keyre. Lacking her own boundaries, she observed none in others.

"Is that why you brought me here, out of jealousy?" His tone was bantering; nevertheless, his question contained a sub rosa strata of intention.

"Would that be so bad?" She leaned against him, her skin warm, the pulse of blood beneath like a song. "But then I'm a bad girl. No one knows that better than you."

"The ones who knew that better than me are all dead."

She laughed. "Yes. I suppose that's true." She slid her leg against his. More warmth as the sun began to melt into the western horizon. "There is no time but time."

He knew what she meant by that. Time was what you made of it, how you apportioned it, what you trained yourself to remember. And to forget. Is that why he couldn't remember any further back beyond the point when he'd been shot and pitched into the black Mediterranean? He had almost died then. Or was there an incident far worse—so dreadful that his mind had blocked it out of self-preservation? Something even worse than what Mala had been through? What if he never knew? What if it was better for him not to know? But not knowing was a purgatory in and of itself.

"Poor Jason, a man without a history," she said, as if reading his mind. "At least I know who my parents were."

"And how much has that helped you?"

"Ouch. Right. Needling each other is not such a good idea, after all."

"Then why start?"

"Because I'm the scorpion."

She meant the old story: a scorpion found itself on the wrong bank of a river. It asks a frog to carry it on its back across the river. The frog wisely says, *But you'll sting me.* The scorpion replies with perfect logic: *Why would I do that? If I sting you we'll both die.* Frogs being logical creatures, it agrees. But halfway across the river, the scorpion stings the frog. As they're both about to drown, the frog cries piteously, *Why?* And the scorpion replies with perfect logic, *I'm a scorpion. It's my nature.*

Mala shrugged. "But what d'you care? You're no frog."

The failing light seemed to have congealed, and, strangely, the island they were on seemed to shrink into the oncoming darkness, the night being dominated by the black sea, the high brittle dome of stars, the rising of the moon, lanternlike low in the eastern sky.

They rose, Mala leading him up the steepening shingle and over a hummock of rock where she had stashed her hiking boots, her striped beach bag, and a midnight-blue cover-up, which she shrugged on as they began picking their way up and over the rock face.

"Are you hungry?" she asked.

"We could eat on the boat," he said. "There's a fine chef."

"I already made a reservation." Which hardly seemed necessary on this isolated spot in the Aegean; Skyros was not a particularly popular tourist destination.

A packed earth path appeared before them, wending its way over a rise and down. Soon enough paving stones heralded the advent of what passed for civilization here.

The tavern, when they came upon it, was lit up with strings of electric lights crisscrossing its cement patio, where tables and chairs were strewn as if at random. A smiling Greek greeted them with glasses of retsina and showed them to a table at the lip of the patio. From the edge, the fall-off was steep, and they had a picture-perfect view down past the promontory on their right to the cove off which the *Nym,* lights ablaze, lay at anchor.

"That's some legacy your friend left you," Mala commented as she settled into her chair. "He must have had many millions of petro-dollars stashed away."

Bourne stared at her. Was she deliberately baiting him again, or was she just making idle chatter? Either way, he didn't care for the topic. Food came, lots of it. Presumably she had pre-ordered. Everything was sea-fresh and delicious. She did not look at him while they ate, staring out at the mysterious night as if waiting for a communication only she could hear.

As it turned out, she was momentarily at a loss as to how to broach a subject she knew would be delicate, would raise any number of red flags for him. She waited until the plates had been cleared, coffee and more retsina served, and they were once again alone in the night.

"Your friendship with the late General Karpov has caused consternation—not to mention anger—in a number of quarters."

He stared at her, silent, wondering where this was going. Fireflies danced in the shrubbery, moonlight turned the rocks a metallic silver. The crash of surf against the shore was a dim rumble, running up the hill toward them.

She smirked, reached into her beach bag, drew out an eight-by-ten blowup, which she placed before him. "You never should have accepted Karpov's invitation to his wedding. There you are, for all the world's clandestine organizations to see, with the general's arm slung across your shoulders. Bosom buddies, that's the phrase, isn't it?" She laughed. "The Japanese would say 'huckleberry friends.' But they get all these odd translations from American pop songs." She meant, in this case, "Moon River."

"Jason, in all seriousness, this photo has caused a hornet's nest of angst within your own secret services. And as for the FSB, now that the general is gone, now that Timur Savasin discovered you made off with Ivan Volkin's ill-gotten gains, the first minister is also out for your blood."

"Someone's always out for my blood."

"And what about your Israeli inamorata?"

Bourne briefly thought about not answering her, but then realized that might be just what she wanted. "She met Boris, several times."

"Enemies...or friends?"

"Boris Illyich was not like that. If you knew him—"

"Little late for that, isn't it?"

He was about to go when she put her hand over his. "Sorry." She looked him straight in the eye. "Really." Still he remained half-risen. She lowered her voice: "You know every wound, every scar...you know how hideous my body is."

Bourne sat back down. "Which is what makes me sad."

"You see," she flared. "I knew it!"

"Mala, you misunderstand me. What Keyre did to you, the rituals he performed on you. You became his. But that doesn't have to be. You're stronger than that."

"But, as you see, I'm here with you. Now. Jealous of your Israeli who, I am certain, possesses a flawless body."

Bourne was determined to say nothing more on this subject.

She sighed. "I suppose I feel possessive of you. Our history. And then there's what you've done for Liis."

"Then the two of you have spoken at least."

Mala shook her head. "I tried, but Liis won't speak to me."

"What happened? She was hoping you'd make one of her performances."

"I did. I was in New York in the winter, when she performed at Lincoln Center."

"And you didn't come backstage to see her?"

"We're not cut from the same cloth. I'm death to her. I won't come near her."

Then he understood: that was when she had seen him with Sara. He frowned. "How long have you been surveilling me?"

She pursed her lips. "I strive to know as much about you as you know about me."

"But you never can."

"It doesn't stop me from trying." Then she tossed her head again. "Oh, come on, I have no evil designs on your Israeli."

Sara. Her name is Sara, Bourne thought. He had met the Mossad agent five years ago, had saved her life in Mexico City, had worked with her on and off since then. Last year, she had been falsely accused of murdering Boris. The idea of speaking her name in Mala's presence, of hearing her say it, seemed intolerable. These were two separate areas of his life. Instinct told him that bringing them together in any form was a recipe for disaster.

"Who *do* you have evil designs on?" he said, wanting to steer the conversation in another direction.

"The people who are now out to terminate you with extreme prejudice. And I do mean *extreme*."

"It's been tried before."

"I know, but this is different."

"How?"

"The Americans and the Russians are coming after you simultane-ously. If you're not careful, they'll have you in a pincer movement, west and east converging on one target."

He considered this for a moment. "So you brought me here to warn me?"

She nodded. "Partly. And partly to—"

At that instant, the *Nym* was consumed by a series of oily fireballs. The rolling thunder of the detonations reached them seconds after the boat was engulfed.

And then its fractured components spewed high in the air, an infer-nal fountain.

3

HAVE THEY FOUND ANYTHING?"

"Nothing, sir."

First Minister Timur Savasin, second only to the Sovereign himself, stood on the grounds of Boris Illyich Karpov's dacha, in the dense woods north of Moscow, hands on hips, sucking on a cigarette stuck in the corner of his mouth. In front of him a squad of men were digging, burrowing, banging on walls and floorboards, checking for false backs in cupboards, secret niches under the stairs, in other words tearing the interior apart. Off to his left, a bulldozer sat idling, while its operator smoked a cigarette. Behind that was the huge flatbed that had transported the machine out here from Moscow.

"No money, no log books, no lists? Not a fucking thing?" he asked in a voice made brittle by frustration.

"No, sir."

He was answered by Igor Malachev, a Kremlin *silovik* who was his second-in-command. Karpov had muscled his way to become the head of both the FSB, the successor to the Soviet KGB, and FSB-2, the anti-narcotics organization. Never again would one man wield such power;

the Sovereign had purged all of Karpov's people from the nine FSB directorates. He had named Konstantin Ludmirovich to head the FSB. As for FSB-2, that posting was still vacant. The appointment had come as a shock to Savasin. He had not spoken to Konstantin in five years. Perhaps this was the Sovereign's attempt at a path to a rapprochement. On the other hand, it was just as likely the Sovereign's way of pointing out to both men who really pulled the strings in the Russian Federation. General Karpov had gotten far too powerful right under the Sovereign's nose; clever Karpov had found a way to game the system. That kind of clandestine disobedience would never happen again, the Sovereign's action had made that perfectly clear. Either way, having to deal with Konstantin on an almost daily basis returned to Savasin the old, ugly, and humiliating nightmares. However, with the Sovereign's blessing, Savasin had elevated Colonel Alecks Volodarsky to head of *spetsnaz*, the FSB's Special Forces.

"All right. Go ahead and bulldoze the fucker."

"Really? It's such a beautiful dacha."

Savasin laughed under his breath. Malachev was so transparent— one of his assets, as far as Savasin was concerned: *"Keep the reins tight on your horses; feed them only oats you grow yourself,"* his father had taught him; the old man might have been cruel, might have loved his vodka a bit too much, but he was no one's fool. It was a good lesson for Malachev to learn: seeing the dacha he coveted leveled, and he himself giving the order for its destruction.

Afterward, in the plush backseat of the armor-plated limousine transporting them back to Moscow Center, Malachev said, "Sir, what was it exactly you were looking for?"

Savasin sat back, thinking that if it were Karpov sitting next to him, after having searched a rogue general's dacha, he would already know the answer. But then Karpov was nobody's lapdog, not even the Sovereign's; that sonuvabitch did whatever the hell he pleased, including marrying a Ukrainian with dissident ties. Clever people like him had no business wielding so much power in the Federation; they were far too dangerous.

He sighed now, staring out at the blurred landscape, which was becoming more muscular with Brutalist buildings shoulder to shoulder like staunch Russian soldiers the closer they got to the ring road that girdled the metropolis.

"It seems that the general had any number of secret initiatives he was commanding before he died."

"Without the Sovereign's knowledge?"

Malachev seemed shocked, but was he really? Savasin asked himself. "Precisely. I am assured we've dismantled them all."

"Why do I sense the other shoe is about to drop?"

"You're right," Savasin said smugly. "General Karpov's best friend, the American Jason Bourne, was in country several times over the last year."

"He was at the general's wedding, I recall."

The first minister nodded. "Indeed. But he returned later on, around the time that Ivan Volkin died. I have no doubt Bourne murdered him, and took with him an enormous amount of money I believe Karpov had stolen from who knows where."

"So Bourne is ground zero for answers," Malachev said, finally getting with the program.

"There is no question in my mind." Savasin shifted from one buttock to another to ease a cramp in his calf. "Which is why I would dearly like to dispatch a Vympel *spetsnaz* death squad to take Bourne out—if we only knew where he was. With his termination we will finally be able to bury the last of Boris Illyich Karpov."

"That's Volodarsky's bailiwick," Malachev pointed out. "I've warned you about him."

"Stop." Savasin had taken out his mobile. "Volodarsky has assured me he's close to pinning Bourne's location down." He began to text as they arrived at their destination. "But just in case, Igor, I wish you to make your own inquiries. Discreetly, of course."

"Always," Malachev said, letting himself out.

Savasin did not miss the wolfish smile on his second-in-command's face.

Françoise Sevigne heard the knock on the hotel room door and, with one last emoji, sent her last text before dropping her mobile into her oversize handbag. Françoise came away from the window overlooking the marina in Kalmar, Sweden. Kalmar was in the southeast of the country, with easy access to the Baltic, via the Kalmar Strait, a narrow body of water separating the Swedish mainland from its largest island.

She opened the door for Justin Farreng, a slim, sandy-haired man with a perpetually harried expression. He slipped into the room, and she closed the door after him, double locking it. He was on her in an instant, his need overwhelming. She welcomed it as a mother welcomes the need of her child, as a totality, as something only she can assuage.

He took her up against the wall, as he often did, a breathless time when they made love like war, their clothes rucked, the fabrics rubbing skin to red welts, their voices rising and falling like a tide. The second time was in bed, naked, comfortable and comforting, slower but also fierce, in the way they threw each other around, like wrestlers grappling. Then rest. Perhaps twenty minutes of deep sleep for him, a letting go of the anxieties he carried around as a salesman clutches his samples case. The third time was languid, warm water cascading down on them from the showerhead. He lifted her as easily as he would lift a child, hands cupped against her buttocks, their heat rebuilding itself from glowing embers, heating the water as well as themselves. Steam enveloped them.

Later, reclining on the bed, propped up on one elbow, she watched while he dressed. "You're leaving early."

"I have a tight schedule."

She laughed softly, scrambled over the bed, sat at the foot, legs spread, thrilling to how instantly his gaze was magnetized.

"Stay," she said.

"I can't. I'm meeting—"

She spread her thighs further. Their insides were still wet. "A man like you..."

Half dressed, he came toward her, close enough for her to unzip his trousers. She pulled him down on top of her, guided him into her.

She stared up into his eyes but saw nothing of interest. Weeks ago, she had realized there was nothing but shiny surface frosting. What lay beneath was nothing—nothing at all. Justin had been born into poverty. His father took six weeks to die from a factory accident that took his leg and part of his hip. No one could be bothered to reduce his pain, let alone try to save his life. As a consequence, Justin had one holy mother of an axe to grind with the world at large. He was a very determined man; this made him incautious, even reckless. Foolish, in other words, though there could be no doubt that in matters of getting his revenge he was smart as a whip.

When they were done, she rolled him off her. Stretching full length, she reached under a pillow. Farreng had good reason to feel harried; he was wanted in a number of countries for publishing damning documents hacked off government, corporate, and institutional servers. These leaks had already caused consternation and chaos across the world—hence Farreng's status as a wanted man. LeakAGE, Farreng's organization, was proudly reliant on third-party whistleblowers, whose identity it protected with the ferocity of a lioness with its cubs. The trouble came in vetting the LeakAGE sources, of which Françoise Sevigne was one. He'd never give her up, she knew that even before the first time she had slipped her arms around him and pressed her body against his, felt his instant arousal. That was six months ago, and nothing had changed. His ardor for her burned just as bright.

Smiling, she handed him a thumb drive filled with files painstakingly manufactured expressly for him by agents of First Minister Timur Savasin.

4

THEY REACHED THE runabout at breakneck speed. Neither of them had said a word following the *Nym's* violent demise. Mala climbed into the runabout first, began to bring up the anchor. Bourne took the helm, started the engines. As soon as the anchor cleared the water, Bourne went full throttle. If Mala hadn't been braced she would've been tossed head over heels.

The sky above where the boat had been was a livid bruise. They could smell the aftermath of the explosions. The stink of marine fuel was in their nostrils. The moon and the stars had vanished into the spreading cloud of smoke and debris blown apart into what amounted to nothing more than grains of sand.

"Jason, what are you doing?" Mala asked as soon as she realized Bourne was heading directly toward the area of the disaster. "You can't believe anyone could have survived those explosions."

"No," he said grimly. "No one's survived."

"Then why are you—?"

"Quiet." His gaze was fixed on the way ahead. "Just be quiet."

She stared at him for a moment, shook her head, then, with a shrug, directed her attention to the debris field. She tried to see what he was seeing, without success. This journey was a mystery to her, and this made her uncomfortable.

They came up on the landward perimeter of the debris field quickly. Bourne still had the outboard at full throttle. Their eyes began to burn from the residue in the air. There was still a good deal of heat; at one spot the water appeared to be boiling, but the smoke made it difficult to see anything clearly. It was like entering a low-lying fog bank.

Mala could see debris bobbing all around them, most of it unrecognizable, until they passed a human arm, twisted and blackened, all the hair burned off. And then a foot, bones poking through. The stench was momentarily sickening.

Bourne plowed through all this at high speed. The instant they breached the far side of the debris field, they saw the patrol boat, lying to, motionless several thousand yards from them.

"Why are they still here?" Mala asked no one in particular. "What are they waiting for?"

"The last diver," Bourne said, cutting the engines.

Guiding her behind the wheel, he handed her the Steyr. Stepping to the gunwale, he removed his shoes, jacket, and trousers. Pulling up one of the cushions, he opened and felt around in the storage cabinet and removed a flying gaff, used to bring large fish up onto the boat. Pulling the hooked head off, he filled his lungs, then dove into the water.

Beyond the debris field, the smoke had risen, then dissipated in the freshening wind driving westward. Shimmering silver light from the full moon slanted down through the water. Almost immediately, he saw the piercing light emanating from the forehead of the diver as he headed away, toward the boat rocking gently on the surface. Bourne had rightly figured that divers had attached explosives to the hull of the *Nym* under the waterline. It was the most logical route to destruction; it was the one he himself would have used. Plus, no one had come onto the boat when they had briefly docked to resupply in Istanbul; he'd taken care of that himself. The process of elimination had been short and to the point.

Powerful swimmer though he was, the diver was too far away for him to make it without fins. He was about to kick up to catch some air rather than catch the diver, when a dark shadow appeared below him. It was as if the sea floor were rising toward him. A ripple of great wings told him all he needed to know. He waited as the creature rose, then he reached down and grabbed onto the upper part of the reef manta ray's mouth. The manta jetted forward with such speed that Bourne's arm was almost pulled out of its socket. Like its close cousin, the shark, the creature was all muscle. He could feel the power of the ray rippling the currents around it, sending patterns outward like a rock thrown into a lake.

Bourne's lungs ached, but he had been repeatedly waterboarded as part of his Treadstone training; his lungs held air as well or better than most free divers.

As if sensing its passenger's mission, the manta put on even more speed. The diver's silhouette bloomed in front of him. He was very close when the diver, feeling the pressure of the manta's approach, turned toward the disturbance. He saw the manta first and jerked in shock. That was when Bourne let go of his perch, pushed himself upward, and slammed into the diver.

The diver already had his knife out, and he slashed at Bourne wildly, disconcerted by both the ray and Bourne's sudden appearance. With a froth of bubbles, Bourne swept the diver's mouthpiece off, jammed it into his own mouth. He felt the serrated blade slide down his chest, opening a wound from which blood drifted. He grabbed the underside of the diver's mask, ripped it off. The diver flailed at it, and Bourne drove the hooked end of the gaff into the meat of his right arm. He let go of the knife in an automatic gesture to cover the wound with his hand.

The diver was done. Bourne turned him, grabbed him around the neck, dragging him back toward where Mala was standing watch on the runabout. He surfaced farther away than he had calculated, then saw that Mala had wisely backed the runabout into the debris field to keep herself hidden. A few more powerful strokes brought him to the side of the runabout. He spat out the mouthpiece, drew in the rich night air.

Mala ran to the nearside gunwale. Setting the Steyr down, she knelt to help keep the diver against the runabout while Bourne unhooked the diver's oxygen tanks and other scuba gear, which he hoisted into the runabout.

Mala heaved the diver aboard, and Bourne followed, launching himself out of the water and over the gunwale. She saw his chest wound first, but he waved her away toward their prisoner.

"Just a scratch." He put one hand over the diver's mouth, then wrenched the gaff out of his arm. The man's shout was muffled to a deep grunt.

Meanwhile, Mala was examining his wet suit and equipment. "American government issue," she said. "Part of a CIA hit team, I would imagine."

"Not necessarily." Bourne pulled off the diver's neoprene cap, stared down at his unfamiliar face. The man seemed to be going in and out of consciousness. Bourne slapped him hard across the face, then again when the diver gave no sign of coming around.

His eyes opened; he stared up at Bourne, and said, "Where the hell did you come from?" In the same instant, he drew a thin-bladed knife from inside the cuff of his neoprene sleeve and jabbed it upward toward Bourne's throat.

There was no time to pull away, but Mala interjected her forearm, her scars so hard and tough the knife point, driven fast but, owing to the diver's position, without much energy behind it, glanced off them. Bourne drove his fist into the diver's face, fracturing his nose. Blood fountained. Bourne snatched the knife away, threw it across the width of the runabout.

He glanced up for a moment, caught Mala looking at him. He took her arm, checked. Not even a scratch to her scars. He nodded and she smiled. Then she jammed the same forearm against the diver's throat. He looked up at her and laughed, spitting out blood pouring from his ruined nose.

Mala didn't like that. Scrambling over the deck, she retrieved his knife, brought it back to where he lay, Bourne pinning him in place.

"Time you told us who you work for," Bourne said.

"Some nerve." The diver's voice was thick and half-strangled by blood. He had a Tennessee mountain accent.

"Reconsider."

"Fuck you and the bitch you rode in on."

Mala liked that even less. With one swift, practiced motion, she slit the diver's neoprene suit lengthwise. Reaching down, she plucked at delicate things like a fisherman about to gut her catch.

The diver's eyes flickered. His face had gone unnaturally pale in the smoke-hazed moonlight. "What's happening?"

"You killed my captain," Bourne said. "You killed my crew."

The diver spat pink. "It should have been you."

"But it wasn't." Bourne leaned closer. "I'm still here, and you...well, you know where you are." Closer still. "But not what's going to happen to you."

"What is—?"

His voice was cut off by a scream. Mala had made an economical but very deep horizontal cut. She held her prize up for the diver to see. "I don't like being called a bitch," she said with remarkably little malice in her voice. "This is how much I don't like it." She threw the bloody sac overboard.

The diver shuddered and shook. Soon enough, Bourne knew, he would go into shock, and then he'd lose the opportunity that had been afforded him. Mala should never have cut off his balls. He suspected that making a preliminary incision would have been enough. But this was the Angelmaker, not Mala. He had to keep that firmly in mind going forward. Whatever she had been, the person he had saved, tended to, had been warped beyond all recognition by Keyre and his Yibir rituals.

The diver was starting to convulse. Bourne had only a matter of minutes before he passed into unconsciousness and, unless they could stop the bleeding in his nose, arm, and between his legs, which he thought unlikely, he'd bleed out in a matter of fifteen or twenty minutes at the most.

Pressing down hard on the diver's shoulders, he said, "You know my name. What's yours?"

"Smith..." He tried to laugh, blew blood bubbles. "Or Wesson."

Using his name would help focus him, keep him in the here and now. Who knew, maybe delirious as he was becoming he'd think he was among compatriots.

"Who do you work for?"

His eyes, red-rimmed and dull with pain, peered up at Bourne, as if through a hailstorm; it was impossible to tell who or what he was seeing. "Go fuck yourself." His voice was a reedy whisper.

"Who sent you after me? Who gave the termination order?"

The diver arched up. His eyes were going in and out of focus. He produced a macabre grin; his gums were bloody.

"Tell me. Who's your boss?"

"Right, yeah." Smith's eyelids began to flicker. His eyeballs were rolling up.

"Smith. Smith!" Bourne slapped him hard across the cheek. "Stay with me."

"Right."

"Can't do that until you give me the name of your—"

A froth of blood bubbled from between Smith's lips. "You'll never..." One shuddering breath. More blood. Then everything stopped, most significantly Smith's heart.

5

MARSHALL FULMER DID not like Sweden—too namby-pamby for him. The Swedes had no backbone, in his not-so-humble opinion. Cowards, all of them. And he liked Kalmar even less than Stockholm, where he could never get his bearings. It wasn't like a real city, let alone the capital of a country, but perhaps, he reflected during a lull in the meeting, it was just what the Swedes deserved.

Kalmar was nearest the Baltic States, nearest the western tip of the Russian Federation, which, Fulmer supposed, was why it had been chosen by NATO to hold the Baltic Alliances Conference. As national security advisor, it was incumbent on him to monitor this high-level conference hastily assembled to form a strong and united response to Russia's increasing bellicosity toward the Baltic States, and to offer support as part of the American contingent that included a four-star general from the Pentagon and a mandarin from the DoD, amusingly masquerading as a military attaché about seven levels below his actual pay grade. Well, that was the way the DoD worked, manifesting mysteries and obfuscations all over the ranch.

Fulmer, seated between the Pentagon general and the DoD mandarin, kept his own council. He was from Western rancher stock—Montana, to be exact. He continued to maintain his family ranch outside Bozeman, and over summer recess spent his time out there riding, herding cattle, hunting, fly-fishing the stream that ran through the north side of the property, and genuinely unwinding.

With his leathery skin and wind-crevassed face, Fulmer looked the part. Mounted on a horse, he could have passed for any number of renowned cowboys out of history. And he had built a reputation inside the Beltway of being a bit of a cowboy. Which meant he shot off his mouth almost as often as he shot his collection of sidearms at his gun club range. Out on the Bozeman ranch he was a crack shot with a scoped rifle.

His colleagues put up with his shenanigans, his media-hogging sound bites primarily, because of the power he had accrued throughout the right corridors in Washington. He was friends with all the right people, all the movers and shakers, left wing as well as right wing. He, better than anyone else, had honed the spectacularly difficult art of walking the political tightrope between parties. He certainly knew how to twist arms when he had to, but he could also charm the pants off just about anyone whose vote he needed.

Now, as the joint session was about to resume, his mobile buzzed. Not his official office mobile—the other one he switched out twice a month. Removing it from his pocket, he looked down at the screen as he held the phone below the table.

A time and a local address. He glanced at his watch. The time was twenty minutes from now. He gathered the papers laid out before him, which he'd barely glanced at, and stuffed them into his slim calfskin briefcase, pushed his chair back, and asked the men on either side of him to carry on while he attended to business back in D.C. They nodded their understanding. Both of them had business back in D.C. from time to time. It was business as usual.

Max, his bodyguard, was at his station just outside the door to the conference room. Naturally enough, he started to dog Fulmer's tail as

Fulmer headed for the private elevator that whisked attendees directly to the floor the conference had taken over.

"Stay," Fulmer said, as he punched the down button.

"But, sir—"

"This is Sweden, not Syria."

The elevator doors slid open, and Fulmer stepped in.

"Make yourself useful," he said, dismissing Max. "Go check to see that the Russians haven't tossed my room or something."

Outside the post-modern, anonymous building at which the meeting was being held, he paused to take several deep breaths. The security was duck-ass tight; not a creature was stirring that wasn't connected via wireless earwig to central station trucks just past the human perimeter. Fulmer ignored them all—they had become such a part of his life he scarcely noticed them.

By far the worst part of his job was the endless meetings he was obliged to attend, not to mention chair. Meetings were a waste of time, period. They were the sinecure of the indecisive and the weak-minded. And yet, he was more than willing to put up with the constant irritation in order to reap the myriad benefits of his powerful position.

What would his simple rancher father make of the place his son had carved out for himself in the world's most potent seat of power? Probably wouldn't have believed his son until Marshall toured him around his domain. Sadly, that was impossible; Marshall's parents had died in a barn fire twenty years ago. They'd both rushed into the barn to save their prized horses; neither horses nor his parents had made it out alive. Were their deaths a testament to the high esteem in which they held their horses or to their foolishness? Marshall had never been able to figure that out.

He waved off his car, set off to the west at a brisk pace. Using the GPS on his burner mobile he made his way to the Baronen Köpcenter, a vast mall near the water. Inside, he checked the directory for Stars and Bars, a sports café on the second floor. He took the escalator up. He saw the open entrance to Stars and Bars right away, but he turned on his heel, heading in the opposite direction. For the next seven or eight minutes, he wandered in and out of shops and storefronts. Inside each, he checked every person who entered after him, looking for individuals who repeated. He saw none.

Certain that he hadn't been followed, he retraced his steps, entering the café within thirty seconds of the time sent to him. He prided himself on being a man of promptness—something else his father wouldn't have recognized in his adult son. On the ranch, chores got done, but no one looked at their watches.

The young woman sat with a straight back and a certain sense of herself that Fulmer found extremely attractive. She was sitting at a table by herself, sipping at a cup of coffee into which she periodically poured what appeared to be a clear liquid—possibly vodka—from an old-fashioned glass. For long moments, he stood, transfixed, regarding her with curious concentration. Then, as if making up his mind about something, he strode through the crowded café, sat down in the molded plastic chair opposite her.

His face creased in a smile. *"Bonjour,* Françoise."

She wrinkled her nose, set her cup down with no little energy. "How many times have I asked you not to mangle my native language," Françoise Sevigne said.

"Vous ne voulez pas la façon dont je parle français? Comment provincial!"

"You're laughing at me in terrible French!"

"What of it?" His smile broadened. "Are you so thin-skinned?"

"You know that I'm not."

He nodded. "Indeed, I do."

"Then why do you do it?"

He grinned. "Try as I might, I cannot help myself." He spread his hands. "You French. I can't help thinking of the Maginot Line: what you considered impregnable the Germans turned to paper."

Her expression hardened. "You think this is amusing?"

"Mademoiselle, that is history. On a more personal front, what we

have here is so far from amusing I find I must joke about it in order to keep my mind on an even keel."

This response seemed to mollify her—even give her food for thought. Pouring the rest of the liquor into her coffee, she stirred it with a spoon, then pushed the cup across the table to a spot between his two hands. Before she could withdraw, he traced a tiny circle on her forefinger with the tip of his.

"I think it best our relationship remain professional, Mr. Fulmer."

Fulmer's expression remained placid. "As you wish, Françoise. But I thought the French…" He shrugged. "Never mind." He raised the cup to his lips and drank it down in one.

He cleared his throat. "So," he said in his best congressional hearing voice. "How is your friend?"

"That one is no one's friend," Françoise said shortly. "Especially mine."

"Yes, yes. I know all about what he does to little girls."

"I don't think you know the half of it," she said. "Otherwise you wouldn't be doing business with him."

Fulmer inclined his head. "And you?"

Françoise shuddered visibly. "I'm a go-between."

"To interface with anyone."

"I go where the money is."

Fulmer pursed his lips. "You see, that's the difference between us. I go where the power is." He regarded her from under hooded eyes. "Do you really believe your road is higher than mine?"

She turned away, her eyes searching past the customers coming and going. A young woman entered pushing her baby in a pram; three men in suits, all staring into the faces of their mobiles, sauntered slowly out. Beyond, the agglomerated sounds of the mall, echoing as if they were underwater, filtered into the café between the shouts of those at the bar. The flat-screen was showing a football match between Real Madrid and Manchester United.

Since it seemed clear Françoise had chosen not to answer, Fulmer opted to push on. "Back to our—to Keyre."

Françoise swung her head back toward him. "Everything's on schedule. But there are new players in the field. Circumstances have dictated a higher price."

His eyes narrowed. "How much higher?"

"Double."

"That's nosebleed territory."

It was her turn to shrug. "I don't set the price, I just report it."

"Tell him I agree. But that's the limit. Tell him he's hit the ceiling. I'm done negotiating."

"Don't worry. I'll make him see your point of view."

"That's what I'm paying you for." He pushed the coffee cup away. "Now I have another job for you."

"I'm full up."

Fulmer extracted a small leather-bound notepad from his breast pocket, wrote a figure down with a Mont Blanc pen. Tearing off the sheet, he pushed it across the table to her. "Half of that is already in your Gibraltar bank. All that's required is a phone call from me to have it transferred to your account."

Françoise crumpled up the paper, stuck it in a plastic ashtray, burned it. "Pretty sure of yourself, aren't you."

"I make it a point to know the people I hire."

"*Bien*," she said softly. "What's the assignment?"

"I want you to find out where Justin Farreng is getting his recent leaks."

Françoise sat stock-still. After a long, agonizing moment, she regained her ability to think clearly. "I'm a go-between, not a detective."

"From where I sit, knowing what you've accomplished for me, there's scarcely any difference."

"Still..."

He shrugged again. "If you don't want the money, I'll find—"

"I didn't say that." Her fingertips turned the ashtray around and around.

"Too much money to leave on the table. So much this could be your last score. You could get out of the game, lie on a beach in Bali or Phuket. Attract the muscled surfer boys. Sleep to your heart's content."

She licked her lips. "Why do you want to know...Farreng's source?" *Good God,* she had almost said "Justin."

"LeakAGE has always been a pain in our asses," Fulmer said. "But as of late Farreng has been spilling open some unpleasant business regarding Reade and Dunlop."

"The law firm in Panama." She regarded him carefully. "Are you a client?"

He shook his head. "But one of my shell companies uses another Panamanian firm."

"Name?" When he hesitated, she said, "I can't help you if I don't know their name."

"Musgrave-Stephens."

"Have you had any indication that Musgrave-Stephens has been hacked?"

"No, but I'm figuring it's just a matter of time."

"Then get your shell company out."

"Getting the company out is a snap. But then where to?"

"I suggest Fellingham, Bodeys."

"Never heard of them."

"That's the point, isn't it," Françoise said with a sly smile. "They take very few clients; they're extremely exacting, conservative to a fault."

"Sounds like just the ticket."

She produced a gold-edged card with raised lettering in a flowing script, handed it to him. "Tell them you're a client of mine."

"Is there anything you can't do for me, Françoise?"

"I seriously doubt it."

He laughed, putting the card away.

"I have another suggestion."

"Fire away."

"You want to be the presidential nominee in the next election, yes? I want to be sure you're not derailed."

"And how would that work, exactly?"

"Dirt, Mr. Fulmer. Have you brought the dirt?"

He grinned. "As we discussed." Slapping his briefcase on the table, he opened it, felt around for the hidden compartment, took out a thumb drive and held it up for her to see.

"And where are you getting the material from?"

"The deep, dark web." Fulmer laughed shortly. "That's strictly need-to-know." He twirled the thumb drive between his fingers. "What I want, what you need to tell me, is how you intend to use this."

Without hesitation, Françoise plucked the miniature drive from his fingertips. "I will have Farreng's source feed LeakAGE this material detrimental to your enemies. In no time, you'll be sitting pretty as the obvious next presidential candidate."

There was something greedy about Fulmer's smile. He made the call transferring her fee into her account, exorbitant as usual, but worth every penny.

"Nous avons toujours fait comprendre mutuellement," he said, murdering both the grammar and the pronunciation, as was his wont. *We always did understand each other.*

Françoise's loathing for Marshall Fulmer knew no bounds. On the other hand, she was determined to take as much of his money as she could lay her hands on. This conflict—emotion on one side, practicality on the other—was not unknown to her. Still, she needed to consider each episode as it arose. The conflict was uppermost in her mind as she made her way out of the Baronen Köpcenter and onto the docks.

It was a fine day. The sun shone brightly down on her, small puffy clouds floated by. Boats, skiffs, and ships drifted past. She might have been in a scene from a cartoon or a children's book. However, the life she was living was strictly X-rated. She went to the rail overlooking the harbor, leaned on it with her elbows. One of the clouds looked like a lamb, which reminded her to make a dinner reservation for tonight at Aifur Song, a new buzzy restaurant. Even Kalmar hadn't been left out of the latest culinary wave sweeping around the world.

Perhaps twenty minutes later, a young man with dark hair and even darker eyes came and stood near her. He held an expensive Hasselblad with which he was taking what appeared to be professional photos of the harbor. Despite his age, he already had the spidery red cheeks of the inveterate vodka drinker. He was known to Françoise. His name was Nikolay Ivanovich Rozin. Back home in Moscow, a city she had not seen in ten years, she knew him as Niki. Here, outside the Federation, he was Larry London, a freelance photographer for Global Photographics.

"Time," Larry London said as he clicked away on his Hasselblad.

"I don't like to be kept waiting."

"He knows that."

Without uttering another word or waiting for a reply he knew wouldn't come, he strode away, ostensibly to find another perspective on the harbor and its inhabitants.

Françoise waited for more time than she should have, then turned, went through a waist-high metal gate that led down to the marina itself. She felt the wooden slats shifting slightly beneath her feet as she made the transition from dry land to water.

The boat was at anchor three-quarters of the way down the dock, on her left. It was blue-and-white, a motored sailboat with the name *Carbon Neutral* painted across its stern. It had beautiful lines—sleek and trim—a pleasure boat rather than one made for fishing.

No one welcomed her as she stepped aboard. The deck was clear, but as she neared the cabin she heard music. As she closed on the hatch, which was pinned open, she heard Edith Piaf singing and made a face.

"You've dated yourself, I'm afraid," she said as she descended into the cabin.

"I thought the French music was a fine touch."

"I'm more a Mylène Farmer fan."

He grunted, waved her to an upholstered bench that would turn into a bunk this evening.

"Bourne," he said. "Have you found him?"

"He's on the Aegean."

"The Aegean Sea is a very big body of water."

"Not for everyone. The Americans blew up General Karpov's boat."

He raised his eyebrows, thick as hedgerows, expressive as his late father's. "Did they now? Which Americans?"

Françoise laughed shortly. "Dreadnaught."

He laughed with her. "And Bourne was on board?"

"No idea."

"Those Americans." He shook his head. His hair, dictated by the latest fashion, was thick and shiny along the top, shaved close to his scalp on either side. "Can't count on them being the least bit useful. Bad as the British, these days, and that's saying something."

"Turn off that awful caterwauling, if you please." Françoise crossed her long legs. "Something more appropriate."

The man hit a button, then spun the wheel on his iPod mini and the Junkie XL soundtrack to *Mad Max: Fury Road* pounded forth from the surround sound speakers.

"No listening device yet devised can hear us through this," Gora Maslov said. He had taken over from his late father, Dimitri, as head of the Kazanskaya *grupperovka*, the Russian mafia family that ruled Moscow. In Dimitri's day, the Kazanskaya had majored in drug-running and black market cars. These days, under Gora's rule, the family trafficked in the final frontier territories dominated by stolen cyber weapons, virtual currency, organ harvesting, and humans.

"Well," Gora said, "it seems that being away from Mother Russia continues to agree with you."

She laughed, her white teeth showing briefly. "I've been off to see the world."

"And how is the world treating you?"

"Like an empress."

"Impressive." He grinned. "What would the Sovereign think?"

Françoise rose, fetched herself a drink from the built-in across the cabin, since it was clear that Gora wasn't going to do it. "You know, I think he would approve." She splashed vodka over ice cubes she grabbed from the half-size fridge. "I mean, he's also off to see the world, isn't he?"

She took a long swallow, went and stood before him. Then, without any warning, she slapped him across the face.

"What the fuck?" A red mark blossomed on his cheek, but he seemed unperturbed.

"Keeping me waiting."

"Business."

"Bullshit."

"You take everything too personally."

She shook her head. "I'm disappointed. For someone who's ostensibly part of the new wave, you can be disconcertingly old-fashioned."

"I take after my father." He watched her with glittering gimlet eyes.

She almost hit him again, but knew hot anger wasn't the answer. "You've been watching too many American gangster films." She took a sip of the chilled liquor. "*Scarface* is your favorite, if memory serves."

"That's right," he said tightly. "Keep at it."

"Or is it *Wall Street*?"

He stood up abruptly, and she saw the bulk of him, the gym rat physique, the violence that sheathed his muscles just under his skin.

"One day you'll push me too far."

She looked up at him from beneath long lashes. "That will be a very bad day for you, Gora."

His face went tight. "Is that a threat?"

"It's a promise."

His hands curled into fists. She knew he longed to incite her, which was why she stayed where she was, calmly sipping her vodka. To use the terms of one of his obsessions, he often reminded her of Sonny Corleone: quick to temper, a beat-down never far from his mind. Also, his Neanderthal Rat Pack attitude toward women—meant to be used, fucked, then thrown onto the scrap heap. But not before he delivered a good thrashing or three.

She'd witnessed that happen over and over again with all his girl-friends, even one-night stands, observing at a remove. The last few years, when she had been away from everything Russian, she had received her intel on him through third parties. His behavior kept repeating without letup; Gora was incapable of change. He was who he was—but then that was true of so many people it might as well be part of the human condition.

"Brother, sit yourself down," she said in Russian.

"Don't call me brother, Alyosha."

"My mistake, Gora." Having wound him up as revenge for keeping her waiting, it was up to her to get him to throttle back, to defuse the situation. He'd never be able to do it on his own.

As he sat, she poured some Coke over ice, handed him the cooling glass. As he drank, she placed her hand on his meaty shoulder. "There's room for both of us," she said softly and felt the muscles beneath her fingers lose their tension.

He drained the rest of the Coke and set the glass down, leaned his head back, and sighed. "There are days," he said, "when it doesn't seem so bad being away from home."

"Home is lonely, Gora." She sat down beside him, maintaining physical contact. He'd never had that growing up. "I know you miss Dimitri."

"It was that shit Karpov who gunned father down. In a barber shop!" His eyes flashed. "Let me tell you, Alyosha, all debts will be paid."

She shook her head. "Karpov is dead, Gora."

"Until his best friend, Jason Bourne, is dealt with, my debt to father will not be paid in full."

Françoise had to laugh at that, but not to his face. "Is that what all your recent maneuvering is all about?"

"To that end, maybe you could help me. It would mean returning to Moscow."

She shook her head. "I like it out here. I'm never coming home, Gora."

"So you think that wise?"

"Wise?" She cocked her head to one side. "I can't say. Perhaps I no longer know what wise is. But I know I have to stay here."

"Why?" he asked. "Haven't you killed enough people yet?"

She snorted. "What is that, a joke?"

"I've never killed anyone in my life."

"No, you just order other people to do it," she said acidly.

"There's a difference."

She looked at him as if he were insane. But what was she to say? There was no rational response to an irrational statement, so she returned to the previous topic. "The guise of a go-between is perfect for me, Gora. Which is why I've no intention of returning."

"You disappoint me, Alyosha."

She stood, preparatory to leaving. "What else is new?" She'd had enough of him.

6

THE FOG OF death and destruction clamped them tight, kept them safe as Bourne and Mala, using the emergency oars clamped to the inside of the hull, rowed their way forward, away from the island of Skyros, toward the vessel holding the rest of the kill squad. The vessel had switched on its searchlight, which was aimed at the water. It was past time for "Smith" to have surfaced and swum back to his boat.

Reaching the outer perimeter of their cover of smoke, they shipped their oars momentarily, hauled Smith's corpse over the side, guided him toward the bow, then sent him off into the black water ahead of them. Then they rowed backward just enough that they were hidden again, but not so far that they couldn't see beyond the smoke field, which, in any event, was slowly but surely dissipating.

They could see "Smith" floating faceup, moving away from them on the currents. Bourne had been sure to keep him faceup, after he'd filled his lungs with air to keep him floating long enough for his comrades to spot him. Without his tanks, regulator, mouthpiece, and mask, he would keep afloat even longer.

"Will they find him?" Mala asked as she crouched beside Bourne in the bow.

"Wait for it." He pointed to the spot where Smith's bare feet, blue-white, veined as marble, drifted into the edge of the beam.

"There!"

The shout rushed at them across the water, and the beam swung wildly across "Smith," then past him, before swinging back, correcting. Bobbing in the low waves, he became a kind of metronome, his rhythm in tune with the sea.

The boat moved toward an intercept course. Beyond the searchlight's beam, it was lit up like an airport runway. They counted five men, including the driver. The hull struck the corpse, whirling it away for a moment before it was brought back alongside with a long-handled gaff.

"Christ," they heard someone say as "Smith" was hauled on board. "What the hell happened to Stone?"

"Caught in the blast?" someone else opined.

"His suit isn't shredded," a third voice broke in. "And where the fuck's his equipment?"

"Get ready," Bourne said, handing Mala an oar, taking up the other one himself.

"It's like he was stripped after he was killed," the first voice said.

Bourne and Mala were already rowing backward when the searchlight's beam extended outward, scanning the water between the vessel and the debris field. Reaching farther, the beam hit the smoke, reflecting backward as car headlights will in dense fog.

"The smoke won't keep us hidden for much longer," Mala whispered.

"With luck, it won't have to."

The searchlight beam kept reaching out, closer and closer toward them. But the closer it got, the more diffuse it became, the more the light was reflected back into the hit team's faces. The vessel began to inch forward.

"Here they come," Mala whispered.

"We hold our position."

"But they'll—"

The vessel came on, slowly but surely. They were close enough to make out one man straining to scan the debris field with night-vision goggles. But again the smoke refracted the spotlight's beam into his eyes. He was, in effect, blind.

Abruptly, he held up one fist, and the vessel came to a halt. Then he lifted a forefinger, circling it. The boat's engines engaged with a deeper sound, and with a roar, the boat made a neat one-eighty, its wake bright in the moonlight.

"Okay," Bourne said. Mala shipped the oars while he moved to the helm, fired up the engine, which would not be heard over the larger vessel's roar. They took off after the hit team, all running lights extinguished, the glow from the instrument panel masked by a towel.

Luck was with them: the lowering moon had been occluded by a bank of thickening clouds within which, every so often, flashes, like jagged shards of glass, winked on and off, semaphoring an oncoming storm.

The wind had picked up; it was against their faces. The chop increased. In their wake, the smoke had vanished. The night was clear, the last of the *Nym* gone to its watery grave. Somewhere back there, dorsal fins would be cleaving the wave-tops. Sharks would be circling.

Bourne's face was grim as he followed the hit team's vessel as it made a wide, sweeping curve to port in what he now believed would be a semicircle heading back to Skyros.

The Americans' pursuit reminded him that the purge of Boris's friends, colleagues, and family was still under way, both in Russia and the U.S. It wouldn't be complete until all signs of him and his affairs had been eradicated, his past achievements credited to others in typical Russian revisionism fashion. In Bourne's heart only would the real Boris Illyich Karpov remain alive.

A change in pitch on the boat they were following knifed through his sorrow. Immediately, he cut the engine on the runabout, listened to the sea and the night. The rising wind was now at their backs; the runabout wallowed in the deepening troughs. Behind them, the first throaty rolls of thunder could be heard. The night was now very dark as storm clouds continued to overrun the starlight.

Bourne could make out the looming cliffs of Skyros, blacker than black, sensed their solidity as the wind struck them and lifted off them. Now he had no doubt that the hit team was headed to the island, rather than to a ship lying to. Anyway, the team had had no time to mobilize a ship, as it had no idea where the *Nym* was headed; even the captain hadn't known until almost the last moment.

Their runabout, having a smaller engine, couldn't hope to keep pace with the hit team's vessel, but that wasn't Bourne's objective. All he needed was to ascertain where the boat was headed. Whether he got them there before or after the team debarked was immaterial.

And, indeed, by the time he guided the bucking runabout into shore, the vessel was deserted, lying to at anchor. The team was on dry land. A sudden gust of wind turned the runabout broadside, nearly shoving it against the sharp-toothed rocks, outliers of the cliff wall. Bourne restarted the engine, confident that it would not be heard over the wailing of the wind and the crashing of the waves. Surely, the larger vessel would bear the brunt of the storm and be smashed to pieces on the jagged teeth. Possibly that's precisely what the team wanted. If so, they had another means of egress off Skyros.

Bourne guided the runabout around the narrow headland, which would act as a natural barrier to the storm. The water was now shallow enough for Bourne to jump out, bring the runabout in via the nylon bow line. Water, pushed by the approaching storm, rushed up his thighs, over his waist, before momentarily being sucked away again. He made the line fast around a rock, hoped that thus protected leeward the runabout would survive.

Back in the runabout, he checked through all the cleverly concealed cabinets under the seat cushions, found fishing rods and rolls of lines, hooks, a scaling knife, which he jammed into his waistband. He stuffed all the rest of these, except the rods, into a well-used waterproof canvas bag, zipped it up. Then he went down on one knee, fiddling with a black box that depended from the bottom of the instrument panel.

"What are you doing?" Mala asked, but he made no reply.

Now both of them were in the churning surf, then onto the slippery rocks, picking their way to what passed for dry land in this inhospitable area of the island; there wasn't even a thin line of shingle to distinguish sea from land.

They ascended the cliff, finding hand- and footholds where they could. They rose into the wind, which, in no time at all, would seek to tear them off the rocks. The rain hadn't yet hit, but, like the pounding hooves of a charging cavalry, it was coming. Bourne knew they had to reach the cliff's summit and find shelter behind its peaks before that happened.

Mala was lighter than he was, which made her faster, but also more prone to being dislodged by the storm. Bourne struggled to keep up with her, prepared to catch her if she slipped or fell. They were nearing the top when the first raindrops, fat and far between, struck his back. The rock face, already slippery, would soon enough become impassable.

Sure enough, in the next instant Mala's anchor foot slipped as her other leg lifted upward for new purchase. Reaching out, Bourne grabbed her ankle, held her foot steady as she found a handhold above.

The raindrops became smaller, more numerous, until they were like needles trying to penetrate the climbers' sopping clothes. Bourne and Mala continued their assault on the cliff unabated; to slow or falter now would be fatal.

With her left hand, Mala grasped a vertical finger that jutted out from the body of the cliff. Using it as a fulcrum, she swung her body to the right, drawing her knees up to her chest just enough to miss crashing into a trio of rocks. Bourne followed her, grasping the rock finger higher up to accommodate his taller body, then swung himself as hard as she had.

He found himself in a small, triangular crevasse, a fault line near the apex of the cliff, pressed tightly up against her. If he reached up, extending his arm to its limit, his fingertips could just about grasp the cliff top. A violent gust of wind threatened to blow him sideways, the way it had the runabout, and a machine-gun burst of rain peppered his face and chest, for a moment blurring his vision. They had to risk moving to a safer spot. The weather was bad enough now, but the storm had not yet reached its full fury. As it did so, it would become more unpredictable.

He turned to see Mala watching him. By the expression on her face he knew she was thinking of another time, another place, another storm as violent as this one. Its ferocity was one of the things that allowed Bourne to rescue her out of the sacred place where Keyre "initiated" his girls, as he termed it. Bourne had been commissioned to fetch her, to bring her back from the "pits of hell," as her father termed it. He had told him that she and her younger sister, Liis, had been abducted by Somali pirates. During the aftermath, in talking to Liis while Mala was still feverish and in and out of consciousness, Bourne had discovered the father's treachery. His business in tatters, his debts run wild, he had sold his daughters into slavery. Delving deeper, information had come to him that their father had done all this in order to abscond with the money, leaving his old business partner and his irate debtors in Estonia behind, to forge a new life for himself.

After Mala was safe, after Bourne had seen to her many wounds, after he had secured for her and Liis a place to stay where they would be fed and protected and loved, he had, without telling them, dealt with their father. Had he really wanted his daughters to join him? Bourne hadn't given him the chance to lie again. Now it seemed as if storms had followed him halfway across the world, like the shrieking of the damned.

A burst of rain slammed them back against the walls of the crevasse, and Bourne knew it was now or never. Nodding to Mala, he waited for a brief lull in the wind-driven rain, rose on tiptoe, reached up as far as he could and grabbed at the highest part of the rock face. His fingers slipped as he tried to put his weight onto his right arm. He spun, feet off the ground like a hanged man, before Mala grabbed him around the waist, steadied him. He drove himself farther, got a firmer grip on the rock, hoisted himself up.

A vicious gust of wind caught him as he was about to roll over the top of the cliff. For perilous seconds he rocked back and forth, scrabbling for purchase as the wind tried its best to suck him out into the black void. His heart beat fast in his chest as he drove all extraneous thought out of his mind, narrowing his focus. Nothing existed save for the ridge of rock on which he vibrated and shuddered like a tree limb. Then, with a superhuman effort, he hurled himself over the ridge, down to a surface of rock rubble. Now the peak served as a kind of parapet, rising over his head, protecting him from the brunt of the storm.

But there was Mala to consider. Rising up over the parapet, slicing rain against his cheeks and in his eyes, he reached over and down. He called to Mala, but the howling of the storm tore his voice from his lungs, flung it far away. Still, she had had her hand up, waiting for him, and now she took him in a Roman grip—fingers grasped around wrist, and inch by agonizing inch, he lifted her out of the crevasse. In the last moments, one of her feet found solid rock, and with his help, she vaulted the rest of the way, landed, crouching beside him on the other side of the parapet.

"Are you all right?" he asked, over the wind.

She nodded. "You remember, right? When you took me and Liis." She could see in his eyes that he did. Her mouth moved, but for a moment nothing came out. "I didn't want to go. I wanted you to take Liis and leave me. With him."

"You fought me."

"Even bleeding all over, I fought you." She swiped the rain from her forehead but it was a losing battle. "But I didn't hurt you." She smiled, touched his cheeks with her fingertips so lightly it took him a moment to realize that she was mapping the configuration of his bones. "You can't imagine what happened."

"There will come a reckoning. One night when the moon is down."

"But not tonight." She blinked rain out of her eyes. "Tonight we have the American kill team to deal with."

"But not in the way you think," Bourne said, and seeing her brows knit together, he laughed softly. "I have a better idea."

7

MEME LLC'S STAFF did not like to see their boss angry, but this evening Morgana Roy was good and pissed. Her personnel in the field had relayed intel concerning the botched mission to terminate Jason Bourne with extreme prejudice. They could not identify the team, but Morgana had a gut feeling it was part of Dreadnaught Section, what her guys blackly referred to as SAMS—a special action murder squad, which is what the Nazi SS called their kill teams. Her people were an irreverent lot, which was just the way she liked it.

Although Meme LLC was an off-site, way off-the-books organization that was in no way connected to the U.S. government, it was still nominally a division of Dreadnaught, what she privately called "Arthur's Acres"—the untouchable domain he had carved out for himself within the clandestine services. Which was why Dreadnaught was allowed to have a black ops SAMS team.

After trying and failing twice to reach Mac on his encrypted mobile, she muttered, "Fuck it," and raced out of the office. The heated, muggy air drained all promise from spring. Belatedly, she realized that she was in too much of a hurry to return to where she'd parked her car. Back inside the office, she had Rose hand her the keys to one of the company cars. Moments later, she slipped behind the wheel of a Ford sedan parked on the street. She fired the ignition, cursed as a blast of hot air exited the vents.

Morgana liked MacQuerrie as a boss—he pretty much left her to do her own thing in the manner she felt best. That was a major perk of being off-site and so deeply blacked out from the rest of the government's acronymic agencies, who spent much of their time butting heads and snooping into each other's territory to make sure they weren't getting scooped. What a briar patch.

At that moment, she received a three-word text. She bit her lower lip, nodded to herself. She pulled out and raced down the street, heedless of what amber lights might come.

And then there were days like today when she felt run over, betrayed, marginalized, and totally out of the loop. After informing her of the über-secretive Karpov cyber initiative, after putting her in charge of stopping it, after informing her that Jason Bourne had taken it over from his old pal, MacQuerrie had gone out and ordered Bourne terminated.

Bourne's death is the last thing I want, she thought. *The very last thing this shitstorm calls for.*

She shook her head as she overtook a truck, accelerated into the left-hand lane. She had a heavy foot. In the long hours since Mac had given her her new brief, she and her team had parsed the vertical code he had sent her without even an iota of success. All they could tell her—and this she confirmed herself—was that the code delivered to them was a piece of the whole; a very small piece, indeed. Not nearly big enough to be the Rosetta stone to unlocking the full computer code.

As a consequence, she'd had a couple of her team members scour the web, monitoring chatter from the Russian Federation and their known affiliates, hackers lurking in their dark web dens, known purveyors of cyber weapons. They had turned up zero. She was beginning to consider the possibility that they would fail in their mission. That they wouldn't be able to decipher the code at all, and therefore wouldn't be able to stop it before it was deployed.

Two possibilities has occurred to her. One, the code was not yet complete. Two, it was complete but was being held in abeyance for some unknown reason. Bourne, had he been brought in alive, would have provided the answer to that vital question as well as the key to shutting this unthinkable weapon down for good.

Sure, Mac had told her that he was initiating new protocols to keep the nuclear codes safer than they already were. But who was to say those new protocols would be enough to stave off Karpov's cyber weapon? None of them could take that chance, least of all Mac. She had tried to make that crystal clear to him, but for some reason she had failed—or, more likely, he had failed to take her arguments seriously enough. People like Mac, career officers in the intelligence community, had blinders. They heard what they wanted to hear, they acted as they wanted to act, sure in the conviction that they knew best. This was particularly true when it came to ignoring intel on the ground that didn't fit their perception of the situation. She'd seen it happen again and again, aghast that no one learned from past mistakes. The old boys' club rules were rigidly—even obsessively—enforced to ensure hegemony, even when they ran counter to the rapidly changing situation in the field. They had invested themselves in a quasi-religious belief in the rightness of their iron-bound laws.

"Call Mac," she said to her Bluetooth-connected mobile. But, as before, the call went straight to voice mail. This time she didn't bother leaving a message. What was the point?

She raced along Route 175, headed toward NSA headquarters. She swerved around the vehicles in front of her, not caring how far over the speed limit she was pushing the car.

She knew she was spoiling for a fight. Part of her understood why Mac hadn't read her in to what he was doing: Mac was just doing his thing the way he always did his thing. But the fact was, the moment he had revealed that Bourne had taken up Karpov's mantle, he had involved her.

The bulk of the vast NSA complex loomed up before her, forcing her to finally slow down. But instead of heading to the perimeter, she veered off to the left, heading down narrower streets.

OTTO'S FINE EUROPEAN TAILORING, the stenciled lettering on the front window proclaimed. The building had once been painted white, but the pockmarked stucco façade was in dire need of multiple repairs. At cursory glance it looked abandoned, which was more or less the point.

Pushing through the front door, she passed into the tailor shop, where Otto, a balding man in his sixties, sat behind a waist-high counter, chalking up a suit jacket on a dummy. His own suit jacket was on a hanger hooked over the top of a full-length mirror. His shirtsleeves were rolled up to the elbow, revealing powerful forearms. His vest held his tie close to his chest. The air smelled of cloth sizing and sour pickles. A half-eaten pastrami on rye lay on its waxed paper at his right elbow. No one else was in the shop.

Otto glanced at her through dust-speckled glasses and nodded as she went through the swinging door in the counter and down a narrow, ill-lighted hallway, through to a room at the rear of the building.

A figure sat in a chair behind a desk equipped with a laptop and several other pieces of equipment. A wide pool of light from the desk lamp fell across the face and hands of the shadowy figure.

"Hello, Morgana." A well-modulated female voice with perhaps just a touch of an indeterminate foreign accent. "Thank you for coming."

"I did debate with myself, Soraya."

"Understandable. You live a remarkably ordered life." Her beautiful profile was typical of Egyptian women but at the same time utterly unique.

There was no place for Morgana to sit, so she remained standing.

"And yet you're here."

"It seems my desk is not as comfortable as it used to be," Morgana said.

"Well said. Feel like stretching our wings a bit, do we?"

"An offer like yours . . ." Her voice faded out. Their eyes locked; there seemed no reason to finish the sentence verbally.

There was a photo of a beautiful girl, age six, Morgana knew, on the desk. It was turned so that she could see it, deliberately, she supposed.

"How is Sonya?" she asked.

"Adjusting to life in America." There was a slight pause. "She doesn't remember her father. I am obliged to show her photos of him, but I'm not sure it does any good."

"I'm so sorry."

"Thank you. She would have loved him as surely as I did." Then, more brightly: "She misses you."

"We'll have to remedy that." Morgana cleared her throat. "Afterward."

"You have a concern?"

"Not exactly, but I'm so new at this."

"One of the things that makes you perfect for this particular brief." She used the British word for *assignment*.

"All right, then." Morgana nodded. "What would you have me do?"

"Go with the flow."

Morgana frowned. "Go with . . . ?" For a moment her alarm showed on her face. "Chaos."

Soraya inclined her head. "In a manner of speaking, yes." Her large, luminous eyes would not let Morgana go. "The brief is still of interest to you."

It didn't seem to be a question, nevertheless, Morgana answered. "It is."

"Saying good-bye to your very ordered life."

"I'm feeling claustrophobic. In a manner of speaking."

"Also frustrated, I imagine."

Morgana blinked. "I beg your pardon?"

"The bit of code General MacQuerrie sent you."

Morgana opened her mouth to ask how Soraya knew about the piece of the cyber weapon but thought better of it. That she knew, reinforced Morgana's decision.

"Frustration, too. Yes."

Soraya favored her with a smile. "Then it's settled."

"Okay, but . . . go with the flow." She shook her head. "I don't get it."

"Not at this point, at any rate," Soraya said. "But, trust me, to tell you more would be a mistake."

"All right." It wasn't all right, but what else could she say. "I do trust you."

"Or else you wouldn't be here." Another slight pause. "Events will be moving quickly now. No matter. Do whatever you have decided to do. Do not alter a thing."

"I understand." Morgana cleared her throat again. "Is that all?"

"Just—"

"Go with the flow." Morgana smiled now. "Got it."

As she made to leave, Soraya said, "One more thing."

Morgana raised her eyebrows. "Yes?"

"It's highly likely that at some point you'll think I've thrown you to the dogs."

"But you haven't."

"Further along, you'll be able to judge for yourself."

There was a distinct note of finality in the comment. The interview was over.

Ten minutes later, Morgana showed her credentials to security. She might not be government, but there were enough occasions when she was required to be at HQ that Mac had had a Dreadnaught clearance created for her. No one inside NSA had ever heard of Meme LLC, and that was just the way both she and Mac wanted it. NSA was PURINT, pure intelligence, meaning surveillance was done from the remove of satellites, wires, remote chatter interceptors. No one in the field. Whereas the CIA dealt in HUMINT—human intelligence—agents in the field reporting back to their controls. Mac believed in PURINT; otherwise he wouldn't have been in NSA. But he also believed in enforcement and interdiction intervention, hence his creation of Dreadnaught neatly hidden inside NSA. She was waved through, directed to park the car in Mac's designated section of the lot.

Morgana was stopped at another security post just inside the front doors. Then she was required to put her handbag through an X-ray and to pass through a metal detector. Even after that she was patted down by a muscular, grim-faced woman who seemed to be channeling a prison guard.

When the woman's hand rose to her crotch, Morgana said, "Try it" with such ferocity the woman froze. "Go on," Morgana said. The woman shrugged, backed off, turning away as if she had more important things to do than fondle Morgana.

The vast lobby was deliberately intimidating—high-ceilinged, hard-walled, and filled with people on missions far more important than yours, whatever that might be. Morgana laughed to herself as she crossed to the bank of elevators.

Yet another security checkpoint reared its ugly head as soon as she stepped off at the fifteenth floor. Passing through without difficulty, she went down the thickly carpeted corridor, passing doors with only inscrutable designations in a number-letter code. Like an aircraft carrier, you had to know your way around the place in order not to get hopelessly lost.

Righteous fury was a deadly thing, she knew this. It was more likely to defeat you than to bring you victory. Nevertheless, it was righteous fury that had brought her from her station at Meme LLC to Dreadnaught's door—designated NCN-113, for who knew what arcane reason.

Now, at the threshold, she paused not only to slow her heart rate down but to give equal consideration to rational thought. *"Collect your thoughts,"* her father used to tell her when she was a kid and would get flummoxed at school. *"Put 'em all in a basket, then rummage around in there until you pick out the best one."* Damn, if it didn't always work. But then everything her father taught her was of use to her later on as an adult. He was a twice-decorated former Navy SEAL. Everything he knew about guns, about knives, about hand-to-hand combat he taught her as furiously, as completely as if she were a boy. *"I love that you take to your training like a fledgling to the air,"* he said to her one balmy spring evening. And so did she. What would he think of her now? she wondered. Would he be proud of her or disappointed that she hadn't taken the steps necessary to become a field agent? She'd never know; he'd died ten years ago in a fiery multiple-vehicle accident on the New Jersey Turnpike. Her mother lasted six weeks without him before something inside her—possibly her will to live—failed. Morgana was an orphan; nothing between her and the grave.

With the image of her father as teacher vivid in her mind's eye, she collected her thoughts and drew out the best one, knowing that striding into Dreadnaught half-cocked—or, the way she had been feeling, fully cocked—was definitely not the way to get what she wanted.

And then another voice entered her consciousness: *Events will be moving quickly now.*

Taking a deep breath and letting it out slowly, she turned the knob, pushed the door open, and found herself inside Dreadnaught.

Not that it looked much different than what she imagined any other office inside NSA would be like: there were programmers, analysts, many, many computer terminals, the massed whirr of small fans, like moths fluttering against a windowpane, and the hot, metallic smell of electronics firing away at full throttle.

No one spoke—all communication in this place was made through emails, IMs, texts—even in this day and age when, as Morgana knew better than most, all electronic communication was among the most insecure. NSA personnel maintained absolute faith in the imperviousness of their firewalls and anti-malware software. It was naïve, even childish, in Morgana's view, but that was what came of investing yourself in quasi-religious beliefs. It was their hubris; she had no doubt it would be their downfall.

Heads popped up when she appeared. Nerds these guys might be, but they weren't neutered—not yet, anyway. A young man rose from his workstation to intercept her. He was blond, blue-eyed, square-jawed, and as magnetic as a movie star of the fifties, a time of pink flesh and innocence. She imagined the smell of the corn husks he must have been born into. He didn't disappoint her.

"Lieutenant Francis Goode. How may I help you, ma'am?" he inquired in that flat Midwestern accent she knew well.

Flashing him her creds, she said, "I have an appointment with Mac."

"Who?"

"Ah." That's right; he wouldn't know. "Your boss, Arthur MacQuerrie." The blank face remained, affording her a moment of amusement before she pitched herself into the fray. "The general."

His eyes narrowed, which made him look like a kid. "And what would your business be with General MacQuerrie?"

"I'm afraid that's above your pay grade, Lieutenant. What are you, a GS seven?" She saw that she had struck pay dirt. "Far, far above."

He scowled, which made him seem more handsome. But she could see that he was also intimidated. "Above your pay grade" was a trigger phrase that never failed to strike fear into the hearts of GS eights and below.

And then she thought, *Why am I pissing on this guy? He's been nothing but polite to me.* So she smiled until his scowl melted like ice in sunlight. "My apologies, Lieutenant Goode, but need-to-know is need-to-know. I should have phrased it another way."

He grinned hugely. "No problem, ma'am."

She matched the wattage of his smile, making it more than a veneer. "Call me Morgana."

"I don't think I can, ma'am."

She ducked her head. She could be coquettish as well as the next doll—probably a whole lot better. She regarded Goode from under sooty lashes; men liked that. "Not even between us?"

"Well, I suppose . . ." He gave her a goofy grin, as if it were a present.

"What is it, Lieutenant?"

"May I ask you a question?" And he hastily added, "It's not about your appointment with General MacQuerrie."

"Of course." She nodded. "Fire away."

"Do you really call the general 'Mac'?"

She caused her laugh to be high and fluty, like a teenager's. "Yes, Lieutenant, I do." She raised a finger in mock warning. "But that's only between you and me. If I go before a Senate subcommittee I deny all knowledge of the nickname."

They chuckled together. He was on her side now.

"Hold on a moment," he said. "The general has been in communications all day. I'll let him know you're here."

Morgana nodded as he turned away. Luck was with her. Mac could have been at the Pentagon or Capitol Hill or anywhere else, but he was right here where she needed him to be. And now she knew why he hadn't answered any of her three calls.

It was only several minutes later that Goode returned and, with that innocent smile of his, ushered her back to Mac's inner sanctum. He was going to see her even without an appointment—a sign of her worth to him, even though she had never been here before.

He was sitting at the far end of what looked like a football field, but that might have been an illusion caused by the eerie violet lighting that was part of the electronic security net that enclosed the space.

The lieutenant vanished as soon as Morgana stepped across the threshold, closing the door soundlessly behind him. Halfway to Mac's imposing desk, which surely wasn't government issue, was a conversation area, complete with matching leather sofas and easy chair and an inlaid glass-topped coffee table, also not government issue.

"Morgana," Mac said, smiling and extending a warm, dry hand. "To what do I owe this visit?"

Someone must have cleaned up the remnants of the meeting or else it had taken place elsewhere, as the conversation area was spotless enough to eat off of. Mac gestured for Morgana to sit, which she did on one of the sofas. The general chose the easy chair. He sat back, crossed one leg over the other, showing off the knife-edged crease down the center of each trouser leg.

"I tried calling you, but—"

He spread his hands. "I wasn't available." And smiled. "But I am now. I'm all yours."

"I appreciate that, Mac."

"How are you coming with the Bourne Initiative?"

"You mean the Karpov Initiative."

"The general's dead, as we've discussed," he said flatly. "It's Bourne's now."

She nodded. "Right. Of course." She swallowed, appalled to discover her mouth was suddenly dry. It was one thing talking to Mac over their private line or having lunch with him at one out-of-the-Beltway venue or other, quite another to be sitting in his office in the middle of the NSA wasp nest. She didn't like it here; she didn't like it one bit. She felt as if she were about to break out in hives at any moment. She scratched at her forearm.

"The fact is it's Bourne I'm here to talk to you about."

He frowned. "I don't understand. How does Bourne concern you?"

"First, I want to know if you have even linked Bourne with Keyre."

MacQuerrie grunted. "We have, and it's simple enough. He was spotted last year in Moscow with a female operative known only as the Angelmaker. She's a deadly assassin."

"And?"

"And, the Angelmaker was made a freak of nature by Keyre, then Bourne somehow got hold of her and put the finishing touches on her assassin's tradecraft. Just in the last five years, she's been linked to the deaths of no fewer than eleven businessmen, politicians, and the like. A board member of a multinational in Munich, a diamond tycoon in Joburg, a warlord in one of those constantly fomenting African nations, a rising right-wing pol and his two mistresses in Paris, a reclusive cyber-billionaire in Manaus, in the fucking Amazon, no less. Then there was Palermo, where she took out twin brothers, one a Mafia don, the other his high-powered lawyer—that was a doozy. And let's not forget the murder aboard a billionaire banker's yacht off the beaches of Ibiza. How she pulled that off . . . Well, you get the idea. She's a fucking menace and another reason Bourne needs to be eliminated." He cocked his head. "Is there a second reason Bourne concerns you?"

Morgana ignored the hint of sarcasm in his question. "So far we have been unable to crack the code you gave us."

Mac's frown deepened. "That's not good news."

"No, it's not." Her forearm was itching again; she resolved to ignore it. "Which is why I want to interrogate Bourne."

The general blinked. "I beg your pardon."

"It's now the Bourne Initiative. You said it yourself, Mac. He's the only one who can give us access to the—"

"Let me stop you right there." MacQuerrie held up a hand. "Morgana, you're a terrifically talented software engineer. The cyber weapons you've devised for me, the ones you've managed to dismantle before they carried out their nefarious missions, are legion. You're at the top of your field. But that field is a narrow-beam affair, do you understand me?" He went straight on, not waiting for a reply; she would have to be an idiot not to understand him. "Your expertise in one field does not qualify you as expert in any other."

"I understand that, Mac, but—"

"This clandestine service—any clandestine service—is, by definition, highly compartmentalized. You understand why this must be."

"Of course I do."

"Then let me say you are not qualified to understand what Jason Bourne would or would not do. So allow me to enlighten you. A man like Bourne—if, in fact, we were ever able to capture him, which is highly problematic—would never give us the secret to this cyber weapon. Even if we used the most extreme forms of persuasion, even if we waterboarded him for—"

"Good God, Mac." She was shaken to her core. "I would never encourage anything like that!"

He smiled thinly. "Of course you wouldn't. And neither would I."

"I'm relieved to hear that."

He regarded her for a moment, as if he was in the process of reassessing her. "What you are asking is quite out of the question."

He hadn't yet mentioned the termination order he had given. Could she no longer trust Mac? Had they become adversaries in a weird form of cold war? Only one way to find out.

"I know."

Mac shook his head. "Know what, precisely?"

"That you sent a team to kill Bourne—"

"What?"

"That the team blew up the boat he was on, only he wasn't on it."

"Morgana, I don't—"

"Bottom line, Bourne is still alive. I want him."

Color had rushed into Mac's face. "You don't know what you're talking about."

"I need him, Mac. *We* need him if we're to crack the Bourne Initiative, as you call it."

"Morgana, I don't understand. I did not order anyone to blow up a ship anywhere in the world."

Her eyes narrowed. "Are you saying that you have not put out a termination order on Jason Bourne?"

He spread his hands. "Why is a cyber jockey like you talking about termination orders?"

"You didn't answer my question, Mac."

The general sighed. "This is eyes-only intel, so . . ." He made a pained face as if he had a sweet in his mouth that had an unexpected sour core. "It was a Russian team that blew up the boat. General Karpov's boat. Out of sheer bloody-mindedness, I shouldn't wonder. Nothing whatsoever to do with Bourne." He seemed to swallow the sour taste. "Now. Stick to your patch of the woods, Morgana. That's my advice to you."

"You made Bourne my patch of the woods when you gave me my marching orders for this cyber weapon."

"Then you misunderstood me." He shrugged. "These things are bound to happen from time to time."

He said this in such a condescending tone that she sat perfectly erect, as if coming to attention while seated. Her entire body tensed like a pulled bow string. She took a beat to reset. "You gave me the impression that this cyber weapon—the so-called Bourne Initiative—is your highest priority."

He nodded. "And so it remains."

"Then you can't tie one arm behind my back. You have to give me all the tools I need to—"

"I *have* to? I don't *have* to do anything." The thunderclouds arrived with frightening swiftness. "Have you forgotten to whom you're speaking? Not to be overly melodramatic, but, dammit, I set you up in your job, I made sure you got every damned piece of equipment you asked for, even your Italian coffee thingy."

"Espresso maker," she corrected foolishly.

He glared at her. "I can take it all away, including your fucking *espresso maker*."

"And who will that hurt the most, General? Me or our country?"

"Morgana, Morgana, Morgana." He shook his head, his expression now mournful. "It's clear to me now that you have risen too far, too fast. You've reached the sun; your wings have melted. I gave you freedom. You mistook that freedom for power. You have no power, not now, not ever. Do I make myself clear?"

"Crystal clear, General."

He rose, turned his back on her, returned to his seat behind his desk, picked up his phone and began to dial. "Get this done, Morgana," he said, putting the receiver to his ear. "Or I'll find someone else who will."

Her tongue seemed stuck to the roof of her mouth. Her hands were shaking, her knees felt like Jell-O, and her heart was on fire.

There is no one else, she wanted to tell him. But of course, this wasn't true. There was no one else he knew of—but that wasn't the same thing.

Outside, the good Lieutenant Goode was waiting to escort her to the elevator.

"How was your meeting, Morgana?" he asked genially.

"Ducky," she said with a wooden smile. "Just ducky."

At least I didn't get shirty with him, she thought grimly.

8

LIGHTNING ILLUMINATED HER face, bone-white and dark-eyed. Her clothes clung to the shape of her body, revealing as much as they hid. The rain continued to pelt down. The air seemed subtropical, and the sky was low and virulent. Wind whistled over the rock face, the fluting now and again sounding like voices in a hellish chorus.

Bourne wanted to move inland, but in the blinding rain and pitch darkness it was far too risky. He had a flashlight he'd taken from the runabout, but using it would only alert the kill team of an unknown presence they would be obliged to investigate. The remaining members had a personal grudge against him now; he'd killed one of their own. That was an offense they would neither forgive nor forget.

The only saving grace of the storm's ferocity was the fact that the team couldn't move, either. How far ahead they might be was impossible to guess, but Bourne figured they had no more than a ten-minute head start. That could not put them too far ahead. They would have had to seek immediate shelter. He didn't know if coming to Skyros had been their original plan or a spur-of-the-moment decision once the *Nym* had anchored there, but for sure, they had to stay there now to find Stone's killer, which they undoubtedly suspected was Bourne.

"What are you thinking?" Mala asked over the incessant noise of the storm.

"Turn around," Bourne said.

"What?"

Hand on her shoulders, he turned her. The movement was gentle; she did not resist. When she was sitting with her back to him, he pulled off her outer garment. The rain turned the bathing suit black, like a partial suit of armor. Her back was exposed to him. Bourne placed his fingertips at base of her neck, the apex of the complex patterns of scars Keyre had inflicted on her over nine months, the period of time dictated by the Yibir laws of sorcery to complete the patterns.

Multiple flashes of lightning all at once threw the scars into livid relief—dark, ropy runes on an alabaster field. A chiaroscuro of agony.

These weren't just scars; they were written incantations. Spells woven into the fabric of Mala's body to bind her soul to Keyre. After reuniting with her on Cyprus last year toward the end of his previous mission, Bourne had spent hours every day and night learning as much as he could about Yibir sorcery, an almost impossible task, even for him. The problem was that there was an immense amount of disbelief in sorcery in the modern world, and in Yibir sorcery most of all. So little was known about it, and what few practitioners had come to light were, at heart, terrorists, pirates, reavers, and ravagers of those who did not view the world as they did. Keyre was one such terrorist—the worst of the lot—the smartest and the cleverest, who commanded absolute obedience from his followers and absolute loyalty from his clients to whom he sold prepackaged coups, complete with the latest weapons and the best trained soldiers. The caveat, which he never mentioned beforehand, was that these well-trained soldiers were absolutely loyal to him and no one else. Any form of skimming, withholding, or reneging on a deal ended one way and one way only: the client never saw another sunrise. So fearsome was

Keyre's reputation that such betrayals happened less and less often, until now they were virtually unheard of.

These thoughts passed quickly across the scrim of Bourne's mind as he traced the runes, one by one, and in the proper order—that is to say, the order in which they were inflicted upon Mala's flesh. Rather than horizontally, they were read vertically, like original Chinese or Japanese. But these runes looked nothing like Asian ideographs—or like any other language, for that matter. They possessed their own inscrutable meaning, their own grammar and syntax, their own logic, if one might call sorcery in any way logical.

Mala turned her head, so that in the next lightning flash he saw her in profile. "What are you doing?"

His fingertips continued to move down her back, his hands parting momentarily to trace the runes on either shoulder blade.

She flinched. "Please don't. I hate those things. I hate that they're a part of me." She had drawn her knees up to her chest. Now she laid her forehead on her forearms. Her back arched like a bow. "You can't do anything, Jason."

He was finished now, the so-called incantations memorized via his fingertips. He wanted to know them because they were lies. But her belief in what Keyre had done to her was what kept her bound to him. He had seen her at her lowest ebb, when she had come so close to death he could feel its chill breath on the back of his neck. He had brought her back from that brink; all the while she had spoken to him as she spoke to herself. He knew she hated Keyre, but at the same time the dreaded Stockholm syndrome had insinuated itself into her mind with each runic cut of his knife. He had led her to a place where hate and love existed side by side, like the most intimate of lovers; in this sinister manner he had made her his creature. Bourne knew that if he was to save her he would have to break the spell she was convinced she was under. If he couldn't, he harbored no doubt whatsoever that one day she would turn on him and, under Keyre's explicit orders, kill him when he least expected it. For these reasons he had determined to keep her close, to follow wherever she led. He would never be truly safe otherwise.

"Thank God you saved Liis before he could start on her."

"Your sister is safe," Bourne said. "I've made sure of that."

"But is she happy?"

"I've set up a trust in her name. She has her career, about which she is passionate. But beyond that, is anyone happy?"

She turned then, to place her mouth on his. Her lips were slightly parted, the tip of her tongue entered his mouth. She sighed against him, her hard athlete's body melting. He felt himself respond, even knowing she was at her most dangerous when she appeared most vulnerable. Unlike her younger sister, untouched by Keyre, Mala was incapable of vulnerability. If she had ever had it, it was clear to him that Keyre had excised it with the point of his sacred knife.

"Don't talk that way," she whispered into his mouth. Rain struck them out of the turbulent night. "If I thought you'd ever become like me I'd die."

Alarm bells went off in Bourne's head. Mala was not prone to over-statement, to embellishing a moment, wearing a ruffled blouse when she could don a T-shirt. If she said this terrible thing, she meant it. The thought rocked him; he'd been unprepared for such a raw and naked statement.

"Such morbidity. It doesn't suit you."

She shook her head, her solemn expression holding something deeper, darker. "You took me away from him," she said. "But you didn't save me from him."

"You mean the incantation—"

"This has nothing to do with that," she said sharply.

"What has it to do with?"

"When you took me away from Keyre," she said into the drumming night, "I left a part of me with him."

Bourne's throat had gone dry. *This can't be happening,* he thought. But it was.

"I had a child with him," she went on, each word seeming to be squeezed out of her guts. "A daughter. Giza."

She turned to him, and he saw the tears rolling from her eyes, down her cheeks.

"Her name is Giza, Jason. He keeps her locked away."

He recalled her fighting him, his strong sense that she didn't want to leave. She had begged him to find her sister, Liis, but never mentioned Giza.

"And please don't ask why I didn't tell you at the time," she continued, as if reading his mind. "I didn't know where he kept her then, and I don't know now. After you took Liis and me away...after that night...I've never seen her." Her shoulders began to tremble. "He holds that possibility out like a carrot, if I do what he commands."

Like a plague, the sins of the Somali continued to multiply exponentially: human trafficker, illicit arms dealer, broker between tin-pot despots and fanatic jihadists, brutalizer of girls, torturer. Extorter of the worst deeds from the tenderest and most intimate of emotions. These were the thoughts that swirled around Bourne's mind as he held Mala's shivering frame, wrapping his arms tightly around her. The worst thing in the world had happened to Mala. Her scars were as nothing compared to separating her from her daughter.

"He'll never let you see her," he whispered when she had quietened. "You know that, don't you?"

"I have to believe..." She passed a hand across her eyes. The blue light from a lightning flash struck her, passing like a theatrical scrim across her face. "My mind says one thing, but my heart says the opposite."

He understood her a bit more, but, frankly, it didn't help much. She was someone he'd saved, brought out of the fire of Keyre's encampment. In the aftermath, he had helped to nurse her back to health. And how had she repaid him? He was grateful that she had told him what she surely had never told another soul, but for him the cost was too high. He had been obliged to remove her and Liis from an intolerable situation. Now, in divulging her secret to him, she had obliged him to return to Somalia, find her daughter, and rescue her. She knew this; it was the reason she had engineered this meeting. Her secret was not Giza; it was with velvet gloves coercing him into killing Keyre—something she herself could not, or would not, do. Because, so far as he could see, the only way to pry Giza out of Keyre's clutches was through his cold, dead fingers.

He let go of her before it was too late, before she insinuated herself into him, made him forget completely that she was the Angelmaker, that death was always clinging to her shoulder, that unless he could save her from herself she already had one foot in the grave. He saw now that merely going after Keyre and killing him wouldn't make much of a difference, if at all. The Yibir would have control of her even from beyond the grave. Bourne suspected that the pain and suffering Keyre had inflicted on her had remade her, reconnecting axons, rewiring her brain to his demonic wavelength. For, make no mistake, Keyre was a demon made manifest in the body of a human being. Bourne had been to his camp; he'd seen with his own eyes the depravity he visited on human souls.

The storm had finally exhausted itself, the rain reduced to a drizzle that, without wind, fell vertically. After the last hours of the attack it felt almost pleasurable.

"We should be heading inland," he said, rising. He wanted to be done with this place, with its secrets, its sinister shadows. "The faster we discover where the kill team has bivouacked the more secure I'll feel."

"We should attack them while it's still dark," Mala said, shrugging on her wrap. Her skin was goose-fleshed, but she gave no sign that she was chilled. That was not her way. "But you said you wanted to hold off."

"I said I had a better idea."

Her eyes glittered. "What could be better than slitting their throats?"

And there it was, the extreme peril that lurked behind her beautiful facade. The Angelmaker killed for money. Worse, she lived for death, craved it as others craved food and water. Was there, then, no hope for her?

Pushing this question aside, Bourne moved them out, down the high ridge that had been their shelter. The last of the clouds, racing inland, shredded, revealing a star-strewn sky glittering with newfound luminescence. With the starlight leading the way, they soon enough came across a narrow path, the glistening rocks still shedding water. The passing of the storm had brought a lowering of the humidity and, with it, cooler temperatures that rapidly dried their clothes.

Almost immediately the path turned steep, passing between two massive boulders. Pines sprang on their side, gnarled and twisted by the wind, adding to the sense of claustrophobia. At one point, he had to stop them. They were faced with a treacherous rock fall, impossible to navigate. Anything could set it off again.

He moved them off to their right, finding another way down, always cognizant of the unstable rock fall to their left. As they descended, he kept a lookout for a break, to give them a broader view of their locale and, possibly, pick up the glint of movement presaging the appearance of the kill team.

"You said you have a better idea than taking them out," Mala whispered in his ear, mindful that their voices would carry over the rocky terrain. "What could possibly be better?" she asked again.

Bourne halted them. He pointed off to the right, where a break in the pines offered them a view inland down the slope. "There," he said. "There they are."

A fire had been lit, three tents surrounding it. Now and again they could discern in the glimmering starlight the movement of a human being, a quick, dull wink of an AR-15 assault rifle as light from the fire slithered down its barrel.

Bourne signaled silently to her, and they crept forward along the path, breaking off it when they were just above the bivouac. They were

close enough to hear voices but were completely hidden from view behind a dense copse of pines.

"Have you made contact with MacQuerrie?" one said.

"Not yet."

"Fuck, you'd better."

There was a pause. "Frankly, I don't want to be the one to tell him."

"About Stone or Bourne?"

"Bourne. He won't give a shit about Stone."

"You're right. He's a fucker. Well, you'll have to do it, and the sooner
the better. There's nothing to be done for the poor devil but to bring him
back home. Bourne, on the other hand, we can do something about.
He's got to be somewhere nearby. The storm must have pinned him
down just the way it did us."

The first one made a call, reluctantly enough, on a military-grade sat
phone. When he was finished, he wiped sweat off his brow.

"That bad?" the second one asked.

The first one shook off his question. "Break out the night-vision
glasses. He won't be able to see us, but we sure as hell will be able to
see him."

They heard the rustling as the kill team strapped on their night-vision
goggles. The agent was right: the goggles would pick up their heat sig-
natures. There would be nowhere to hide.

"Jason..."

Mala's soft voice pulled him out of his silent session with himself.
His short-term tactics were settled; it was the mid-term strategy that
still had to be worked out.

The American kill team was coming, heading up the slope because
they must figure Bourne had made landfall somewhere close by. This
part of the coast was forbidding, and there were only a few places to
come ashore safely.

Bourne moved them back to a more strategic position. Rocks and
water were their only friends now, the only natural configurations
that would block their heat signals. The soft pines, no matter how

closely clustered, could not be counted upon to keep them hidden for long. Even the slightest move or alteration in their position would leak a signature and give them away. They'd be effectively pinned down.

"Come on," he whispered. "There's a lot of work to do and little time to do it in."

9

JASON BOURNE. WHERE the hell is he?"

Faced with his boss's towering wrath, Igor Malachev trembled. "We don't know, sir."

Timur Savasin, First Minister of the Russian Federation, turned a withering look on him. "What do I have you for, Igor Ivanovich, except to keep an ear and eye out on *spetsnaz*?"

Malachev stiffened. "I do the best I can, sir. But Special Forces is a paranoid group."

"Everyone in Russia is paranoid, Igor Ivanovich. It goes with the territory." He raised a hand, fluttered it. "Find out where Bourne is, and don't return until you have the answer." Malachev was almost to the first minister's office door when Savasin said, "And, Igor Ivanovich, while you're at it, fetch Alecks Petrovich for me."

Alecks Volodarsky. Savasin could have, of course, picked up the internal phone and summoned the new head of *spetsnaz*, the FSB Special Forces, himself, but his ire was such that he had decided to turn his second-in-command into a lowly gofer. He resisted an urge to order him to bark.

Alone in his vast office inside Moscow Center, Savasin stuffed his hands into his trouser pockets, fuming so hard it was a wonder smoke didn't puff out of his ears. *That boat, Boris Illyich's fucking boat,* he thought. *The fucker might have been a traitor six ways from Sunday, but he had goddamn good taste.* He stalked back and forth across the gray tweed carpet like a caged tiger. *I wanted that boat. It was mine. The Sovereign said I could have it. And now we've blown it to kingdom come. I didn't order the boat blown up. Who the fuck did?* He went and stared out the window at Lubyanka Square. Directly across was the forbidding façade of Detsky Mir, Children's World department store, which reminded Savasin that one of his grandchildren was having his seventh birthday next week. He resolved, as further punishment, to send Malachev over there on his lunch hour to buy a suitable present.

"Come," he muttered in response to a crisp knock on the door. And then louder, a second time, "Come!"

Malachev or Volodarsky? He watched an old man on the square, lost in a greatcoat that might have been manufactured during World War II, struggle with a recalcitrant dog. The dog was almost as big as the old man. Savasin felt a quick stab of compassion for the dog's master. The visitor behind him cleared his throat. Savasin didn't turn around.

"Igor Ivanovich said you wanted to see me, sir."

For a moment Savasin said nothing. He was tempted to send one of his men outside to help the old man with his willful animal, but then reflected that would only shame the old man, who might very well be a war veteran, and that would never do.

"Tell me, Alecks Petrovich, have you found Jason Bourne?"

"Uh, not yet, sir."

"But you're close."

"Yes, sir."

Savasin finally turned around to face the man he had appointed as head of *spetsnaz.* "Volodarsky, if you lie to me a second time, I will personally frog-march you downstairs to the cellars." The cellars were where all the myriad terrors of the infamous Lubyanka prison resided.

People who were brought down there were never seen alive again. "Is that clear?"

Volodarsky swallowed hard. "Quite clear, sir."

"Now, shall I ask my question again?"

"No, sir. We haven't as yet acquired the specific whereabouts of the target."

The old man, as stubborn as his dog, reminded Savasin of his father, a man—a veteran of the war—whom Savasin had revered all his life. He'd never had enough time with his father, and every moment of their time together was of immense importance to him. When Savasin had finally laid him to rest, he had not spoken for ten days. He had gone away to the Kamchatka Peninsula, where his father had sometimes— not often enough!—taken him to fish. The glittering ice and softly fall- ing snow seemed like paradise to the young Savasin, and later, after his father was dead, he'd think of those times as if encased in a snow globe, a world sealed off, that only he and his father inhabited. He went there in his mind when his duties became too overbearing or the exigencies of his life went against the grain.

"Alecks Petrovich, I told you not to lie."

"But, sir, I haven't—"

"Really?" He sighed. "Alecks, we grew up together, didn't we?"

"Yes."

"We attended the same classes, university and all that."

Volodarsky nodded.

"We break bread together every Friday evening, do we not?"

"We do."

"And get roaring drunk on the best vodka." His voice turned icy. "Then please tell me why you haven't found Jason Bourne. He was the late, unlamented General Karpov's closest friend, though under what circumstances that came about fairly boggles the mind. Though I have learned not to put anything past him."

"No, indeed. We're all learning that."

A knock on the door deterred the first minister from doling out further verbal torture. But that was okay, for this was only the warmup to the main event. His mouth began to salivate, anticipating Malachev entering. Seeing Volodarsky still there, Malachev would no doubt blanch.

Malachev and Volodarsky did not like each other. It was still unclear to Savasin which one feared the other most. The relationship between the two was heavily reminiscent of the one Savasin had with Konstantin. Not for the first time it occurred to Savasin that he had deliberately set these two together in an attempt to get the better of Konstantin.

"Igor Ivanovich," he said as he turned around, but the sight of the tall, elegant man standing where Malachev should have been stopped him in his tracks. "Konstantin Ludmirovich," he said.

A thin smile curved the other's lips. "Close your mouth, brother. You're apt to swallow the flies on this floor." Konstantin Ludmirovich Savasin glanced around the office with obvious distaste. He sniffed, his delicate nostrils dilating alarmingly. "You really ought to have a cleaning crew in here more than once a month."

Savasin ground his teeth in fury but did not rise to the bait. Instead, he said with a maximum amount of sarcasm, "What brings you into the lion's den?"

"Is that what this is? Oh, well." He shrugged. "For one thing, it's my day for slumming." His laugh was like fingernails on a chalkboard. "For another, you've summoned a high-ranking FSB officer for what appears to be a dressing down."

"If that's what it is," the first minister said, "then you can be sure it's well deserved."

"Can I?" Konstantin circled his brother. "Can I, really?" He shook his head. "The fact of the matter is that Alecks Petrovich knows nothing about the *Nym*."

Volodarsky swallowed. "The what?"

The new head of FSB's smile was as sharp as a razor blade. "You see, brother, he doesn't even know what we're talking about."

Savasin lost it for a moment. "Colonel Karpov's boat, you idiot," he shouted at Volodarsky.

"That's an FSB officer you're yelling at. One you yourself appointed, brother."

"First Minister to you, Konstantin, as well as to everyone else. I can yell at anyone, even you."

Konstantin shrugged, shook out a cigarette, lit it, took a good, long inhale. The hiss of indolently expelled smoke grated on Savasin's nerves. Konstantin was handsome in an odd, saturnine way. His long face dominated by large, liquid eyes that, like their mother's, were set too close together. He had her skin, as well: pale, almost translucent.

Savasin glared at Volodarsky. "You're of no use. You don't even know what your men are doing. Get the fuck out of my office."

Volodarsky glanced at Konstantin, but the other wasn't about to meet his eye.

"Don't look at him. He'll be of no help to you, take my word," Savasin said shortly. "Just get out."

When the two brothers were alone, Konstantin said matter-of-factly, "The Americans blew up Karpov's boat."

Savasin stared at him as if he had grown another head. "Are you sure?"

When Konstantin delivered a withering look, he went on, "Do you have any hard evidence?"

"The Americans are smart enough not to leave anything behind that could be traced back to them. Let the Sovereign make propaganda hay; he's good at that. As for us, pursuing that line will only lead us down a path that never ends. Which is precisely what the Americans want."

"Nevertheless, the boat—a part of the Federation—has been destroyed by a foreign power."

Konstantin glanced around again, and, with the grace of a dancer, stepped to one of the upholstered chairs in the office, inspected it vigilantly before seating himself. He glanced down, admiring the perfect creases of his imported trousers as he did so. "Oh, come off it, Timur.

You don't give a shit about that. It's the boat itself that has your knickers in a twist." He looked up at his brother, a sardonic look in his eye. "I know you coveted it."

"The Sovereign promised it to me."

"Oops."

Konstantin continued to draw in tobacco and let it out in aromatic clouds when his lungs had become saturated with nicotine.

"You'll kill yourself with that filthy habit," Savasin observed.

"Don't you wish."

Konstantin tapped ash into a crystal ashtray thick enough to crack a skull open with one blow—at least that was Savasin's thought in the moment.

"Was Jason Bourne on the *Nym* when it left Istanbul? Or was it heading to a rendezvous with him?"

Konstantin shrugged.

"Bourne was Karpov's closest friend. There's a good chance he left the boat to him."

Konstantin lifted a bit of tobacco off the tip of his tongue. "What do I care."

"I don't believe you."

"That's certainly your prerogative, *First Minister*."

Konstantin had the ability to completely exasperate him, just like when they were kids. The fact was, Savasin loved and hated his brother. He also feared him, always had. Perched on the corner of his desk, he folded his arms across his chest, regarded his brother from beneath heavy-lidded eyes.

"As long as we're talking prerogatives, I don't like Volodarsky." Konstantin plucked a bit of lint off the supple fabric that covered his kneecap. "Volodarsky is your appointment."

"Yes."

"That's what you get for elevating old friends. He doesn't know his zipper from his shoulder boards. I mean, face facts, he can't even find Jason Bourne. But I have. He was on General Karpov's boat."

"What?"

"No, no, no." He waited a beat and, picking his way light as you please through Savasin's glare, added, "You should ask *why*, Timur. *Why* didn't your man know that?"

Savasin was still trying to recover from the news that the *Nym* would never be his. Maintaining an iron façade, he said, "And you maintain you have no interest in Jason Bourne."

"My dear Timur Ludmirovich, you're the one who hated Karpov with a—how to put it best?—a maniacal, near-religious fervor. I can only suppose that you feel the same way toward his best friend." He shrugged. "As for me, I couldn't care less whether Bourne lives or dies." His eyes glittered with mischief. "He hasn't gotten under *my* skin."

He ground out the butt of his cigarette and rose. "Now, if we're clear on the matter..."

A knock sounded on the door.

"It's like the Kazansky railway station in here today," Konstantin observed with one raised eyebrow.

"Come!" Savasin said, somewhat louder than was necessary.

Malachev advanced into the office, but he was brought up short by the presence of the elder Savasin. After a moment's contemplation during which Savasin could virtually see the cogs in his head spinning dizzily, he soldiered on, one eye on Konstantin as if at any moment the head of FSB would take a bite out of his thigh like a rabid animal.

"I have confirmed that Jason Bourne was on Karpov's boat when it left Istanbul."

Savasin gave his older brother a savage glare. "And was he on it when the Americans blew it up?"

Malachev spread his hands. "Unfortunately, First Minister, I don't—"

"He doesn't know." Konstantin broke in. "No one here knows." His scimitar smile seemed to extend from ear to ear. "Except me, of course."

Savasin felt a headache coming on. He dismissed Malachev with a curt wave of his hand. When the brothers were alone again, he said, "Well, what are you waiting for?"

"I'm waiting, little brother, for you to meet my price."

Savasin felt his blood pressure threatening to go through the roof. Still, he held himself in check, replied evenly, "And what would that be?"

"I want you to fire Volodarsky."

Relief was just a word away. "Done. He's proved eminently incompetent."

"Jettisoning your childhood pal. Just like that." Konstantin sniffed. "Well, I suppose that says something about you."

"I'll be more judicious when I appoint—"

"Oh, no. I want my own man heading up Special Forces. As head of FSB it's my right."

He should have known firing Volodarsky was only the beginning. "As first minister, I can veto any appointment you make."

"You could," Konstantin said. "But then you wouldn't find out about the disposition of Jason Bourne. Is he dead? Alive? And if still alive, where is he?"

Savasin felt as if he were standing at a waterline, the sand washing out from under his feet. "You said you didn't know—"

"I said I don't care. I don't. But you do." Konstantin flipped another cigarette into his mouth, lit it with his oversize steel lighter. "I am aware of *how much* you need to know, little brother," he added in a rush of smoke. "So . . ." He shrugged.

Savasin continued to struggle for equilibrium. Maybe this wouldn't be so bad, he told himself. After all, Volodarsky was clearly the wrong choice to head up *spetsnaz*. Konstantin was frighteningly intelligent. It was entirely possible that Konstantin's pick would be a good one. In that frame of mind, he said, "Who's your man?" The instant he said it, he knew he had capitulated. He realized his mistake. Whoever his brother had in mind would be his man through and through, which would, by definition, make him Savasin's enemy. Konstantin was also frighteningly clever.

"Nikolay Ivanovich Rozin."

"What?" Savasin raised his eyebrows. "Rozin is a field agent."

"Undercover. Yes, he's perhaps the best field agent we have."

"Huh. He's also something of a loose cannon, so maybe taking him out of the field is a wise choice."

"Who said anything about taking him out of the field?"

The disorientation returned. Damn Konstantin to hell. "Then how will he—?"

"I mean to break the mold, little brother. I *want* him in the field." He sniffed. "In my opinion, the *spetsnaz* officials have gotten too complacent, too comfortable milling around Dzerzhinsky Square. That requires a revolution, or don't you agree?"

The damnable fact was that Savasin did agree. Konstantin was dead on in his assessment of Special Forces. It was a problem Savasin himself had been meaning to address. Konstantin had beaten him to it. Nothing new there, he thought bitterly.

"As it happens, I do agree." He bit off each word as if they came from a bar of soap. He nodded. "All right. Elevate Rozin and let's see where that leads." He lifted a hand. "But know that he's on a short leash. If he steps out of line—"

"I'm the wrong person to threaten," Konstantin said. "Have you forgotten so soon?"

Savasin was so angry he almost lacerated his tongue. "I forget nothing," he said thickly.

"Better." Konstantin regarded the glowing tip of his cigarette. "As it happens, your Bourne boarded the *Nym* even before it put in to Istanbul." His eyes flicked up to engage his brother's. "By all rights, he should have been on the boat when the Americans blew it up."

"I thought you had no interest in Bourne."

"Insofar as you do, I have a great deal of interest."

"You wanted to deny me the satisfaction of taking his life."

"Correct."

"But the American team missed him. So he's still alive. Where?"

"In the eastern Aegean. The island of Skyros, to be exact. We have picked up a coded distress call."

Savasin's brows drew together. "Coded?"

Konstantin offered an unsavory chuckle. "Leave it to General Karpov. It's his signal." He beamed. "As it happens there's a *spetsnaz* team ready and waiting in Istanbul. It's only a short flight to—"

"I want control of the *spetsnaz* team," Savasin said, shaking off this latest specter of their shared past.

Konstantin shrugged. "Have at it, little brother. I've got what I came for."

10

NIGHT WAS DESCENDING into the shoals of a glimmering dawn.

"I don't like this," Mala said.

"You don't like anything."

The sea was ahead of them. The closer they came to it, the higher they ascended, until they were above the treetops down below. The harsh salt wind lashed what foliage remained into dwarfs, limbs painfully twisted as if from long torture.

"They're gaining on us," Mala whispered.

"I know."

"We ought to increase our speed."

"And risk exposing ourselves to their night goggles?" He shook his head.

"But at this rate, they're bound to catch up to us before we make the coast."

"Maybe. Maybe not."

She gave him a sharp, sideways look. "What d'you have up your sleeve?"

"It may not work," he said. "I don't want to give you false hope."

Her eyes flashed. "That's what you gave me when you took us out of Somalia."

He couldn't argue with her there.

He led her off the rough track they had been following, and they began climbing the cliff face, clawing for foot- and handholds. The problem of always keeping large enough rocks between them and the kill team added an extra degree of difficulty.

After setting the last of the traps, using the fishing lines and hooks, they reached a declivity in a massive rock formation, in the lee of the wind coming in off the sea. They were approximately halfway up the cliff wall on the other side of which was the Aegean and the boats, theirs and the kill team's.

She let out a small puff of air. "I particularly don't like this sitting here, waiting for the Americans to catch up with us."

"This crew isn't CIA."

"No? Who, then?"

"They mentioned MacQuerrie."

"Yes, I heard."

"General MacQuerrie is in charge of his own piece of turf within the American clandestine services. His group is known as Dreadnaught. His people do a lot of very dirty wet work."

"Isn't all wet work, by definition, dirty?"

"Maybe. But Dreadnaught's is pitch-black filthy."

"All the more reason why you should want to get up close and personal. Tooth and claw." She gave him a particularly piercing look. "Don't you have a personal stake in killing them?"

"Do you?" he said.

"Yeah, they blew up your friend's boat thinking you were on it. Instead, they killed the captain and crew. Now they're hunting both of us."

"They don't know you exist."

She grunted. "That's what this is all about, isn't it? You're testing me. See if I'll abandon you to your fate?" She shook her head. "Our fates became entwined the moment you entered Keyre's camp. The moment—"

"Don't say it, Mala. I'm warning you."

"Someone should have warned your friend."

The most terrible thing about being with her was that it was like looking into a mirror—somewhat distorted, but nevertheless the fact remained that they were both killers. Her unbridled bloodlust, the fierce joy in killing she had learned at Keyre's knee conjured up the spirits of all the people he had killed, no matter the reason. Each life you took diminished you, of this he was certain. Would there, then, come a time when there would be nothing left of him to keep alive? She also engendered in him this nihilism, these black questions that ate at him, not at the edge of darkness, but during the interstices of life in the shadows, the moments of idleness, few though they might be.

"Jason, I need you to know that things are different now with Keyre. These days, he runs a business, everything online: expenditures, profits, transfers to and from accounts held by a mare's nest of shell companies in Switzerland, Gibraltar, Caymans, Bermuda, Iceland, Lichtenstein, who knows where else? Domiciles don't matter, except on paper—and even paper doesn't exist anymore. It's all in cyberspace, all in ironclad clouds." She took a breath. "You wouldn't recognize the place."

"No pools of blood? No heads on spikes, shriveling in the sun? No incantations over guts pulled from the living?"

She said nothing.

"I'll recognize Keyre. There's a face I'll never forget."

She looked away for a moment, her hair streaming out behind her until she lassoed it with her fingers. She seemed to be listening to a sound only she could hear. It was very far away, coming off the sands of Somalia like a mirage.

When she turned back to him, her eyes seemed enlarged, as if she had ingested a drug. Maybe she had, Bourne thought. Maybe that drug was Keyre himself.

"You know," she said in an altogether different tone of voice, "there was a time when I loved you. A time when you were my entire universe."

"You were very ill," he said, not wanting her words to sink in, knowing that she might very well be laying a trap, that he absolutely could not trust her, no matter how much he might want to. She was still very much Keyre's creature, despite all his efforts. It saddened and angered him in equal measure that he had freed her body, but not her mind. He wished to convey none of this to her. "I nursed you back to life. It's only natural. Transference."

"That's one word for it."

"What word would you substitute?"

She eyed him, searching for any flicker of emotion. She was as expert at pulling emotions from people as a fisherman drawing his catch out of the water. She shook her head. "But, you see, Jason, what I learned is that love is beyond your ken. When love knocks on your door you re-main deaf, dumb, and blind."

She was talking about herself, of course, but what she said made him think of Sara, of all the time they spent together, how well they knew each other—and yet, Mala was right, he always kept a part of himself hidden, locked away, set apart from even the few people he was closest to: Sara, Boris, Soraya Moore. He loved all three of them in his way. But that was the problem: *in his way*. What was that, ex-actly? Was he really and truly incapable of loving someone, of giving all of himself? Had living in the shadows, inhabiting all the most per-ilous fringes of the world damaged him beyond repair? Had all the betrayals, the paranoia of future betrayals made him more weapon than human? No answer presented itself, only a blank wall even he was incapable of scaling.

Mala's voice was like a scarf of purest silk winding around him, im-possibly soft, impossibly strong. "I held you and Keyre, one in each hand"—she lifted both hands, cupping them—"balancing the two of you like the scales of justice."

"Keyre and the concept of justice are incompatible."

"So you think, Jason. But you're wrong. Justice is paramount to Keyre—it always has been."

"You have found some good in him, is that what you're telling me?"

She bit her lip. "We're—all of us—capable of great good and great evil, don't you think?"

The night, slipping away, was gradually being replaced by predawn light, dirty and wan.

"Right now I'm thinking it's ironic that light is better for us than darkness. Those night-vision glasses are better than the human eye in picking up and homing in on prey."

"You don't really think the traps will injure them?"

"They might—once. After that, no." Bourne moved them to their left, positioning them squarely at the head of the rock fall they had bypassed on the way down. "But it doesn't matter; that's not their purpose."

———

The first tripwire Bourne had set caught one of the Dreadnaught agents at thigh level, the fish hooks puncturing his trousers and flesh. As he reared back in reaction, they tore chunks of muscle out of both thighs. He grunted in pain as his legs went out from under him. The rest of the team abandoned their positions, grouped around him.

"Fucking Bourne," said the lead, a man with a long indentation down one side of his bald skull. He was about to cut the fishing line with his knife when he looked around. Then he put the knife back in its sheath. "Okay, this can't be the only one. Be on the lookout. And don't cut the line. There's no telling what that will trigger. We're dealing with a very clever and resourceful sonuvabitch. You see here a perfect example. He must've seen that we had night-vision goggles, exceedingly fine for picking out living creatures in the night, but of no use at all seeing trip wires."

The man on the ground was writhing in agony. The leader glanced at him briefly. "Give him something."

"He's bleeding like a stuck pig," said another and pointed. "One of the hooks must've torn open an artery."

The wounded man started to scream as the real pain set in. The leader clamped a hand over his mouth. "Give him something to shut him the fuck up," he said.

"We're just going to leave him here?" asked another.

"This isn't the marines. We don't exist." The man dug into a first-aid kit, extracted a hypodermic needle, and drove it into the man's biceps.

As the wounded man calmed, closed his eyes, the leader nodded, then stood up. "Bury him deep, where no one will find him. Then let's move out."

Afterward, they returned to their positions, more or less, trying as best they could to compensate for the loss of their comrade. With two down, there were three of them left: the leader, the boat driver, and one other, the man who spoke up. Their spread was of necessity more compact, covering less territory. That could not be helped, and, as it turned out, it didn't matter, since as they encountered more of the trip wires they were forced to move closer together.

This was the purpose of the trip wires' placement as Bourne conceived of them: to create a funnel along which the Dreadnaughts were forced forward. He did not want them spread out when he sprang his lethal surprise.

———

It took them longer to come into Bourne's view than he had expected. Then, as he counted their number, he understood. The first trip wire must have caught one of them because there were three, not four. He glanced to right and left, but this was inhospitable terrain for a flanking maneuver, plus they couldn't be sure where he was.

That would change in a moment.

Ready? he mouthed, and she nodded. She was ready.

They had briefly discussed how to get the rock fall moving most efficiently. They separated now, growing dim to each other in the ghostly light. Sea birds had awoken, calling and crying as they circled overhead.

He welcomed the raucous noise; the clatter as the rock fall began would easily be confused with the clamor of the birds.

They were each now on separate parts of the rock fall, their butts on solid ground, their boots hovering inches above the layers of precariously balanced rock shards. Ignoring each other, they looked to the movement below them as what was left of the Dreadnaught team entered the defile into which they had been herded, beginning the steepest part of the ascent.

Bourne pushed himself back, stood up, fired his pistol at them. The report caused the rock fall to tremble, that's how fragile its stability was. The three men below scrambled as best they could, but the defile afforded them scant cover and, in any event, at that moment, Mala ground her boot heels into the shards with a powerful double kick. The rumble began.

Bourne lowered himself, gave his own mighty double kick—once, twice, the third time in exact concert with another from Mala, and the entire rock fall gave way. The avalanche picked up speed at once, and, as it did so, its sound deepened, widened, became palpable, like an intense atmospheric disturbance, rushing, tumbling, roaring down the defile with such demonic energy all three Dreadnaughts disappeared from view.

It was only afterward, in the stifled peace of the rock slide's aftermath, that they heard the sound of the rotors and, looking up, saw the military helo diving toward them.

11

MORGANA WAS WAITING behind the wheel of the car when Lieutenant Francis Goode exited the NSA complex. When Goode got in his car and fired the ignition, she followed him out of the vast parking lot that surrounded the black edifice like a castle moat.

He took the highway, headed deeper into Virginia. She turned off with him at the Odenton exit, tailed him through local streets, watched him park in the lot attached to the Long Range, a local firing range, and enter the building. Five minutes later she followed him through the front door.

The big guy behind the counter in a red SHOOT FIRST T-shirt looked at her askance until she waved her ID in his face. Then he was all smiles and what-can-I-do-for-yous. She paid for an hour, chose her weapon, and was rung up.

She was given a 9mm Glock, ammunition, and a set of sound-dampening headphones. She entered the range itself, trolled through the row of shooters, looking for Goode.

The lanes to either side of him were occupied. She was on the verge of taking a free lane down from where Goode was firing, but the shooter to his left stopped firing, pressed a button on the partition, and watched as his target headed back to him. Striking it down, he took it and his handgun, and brushed past her as he left. Morgana stepped up into his spot, clipped a new target to the wire, sent it hurtling to the far end of the range. Then she loaded the Glock, took her stance, aimed and squeezed off six shots in rapid succession. She pressed the recall button, but she already knew what she would see: six holes dead center. Having been trained by her father when she was still in her early teens, she had developed into a crack shot.

She was staring at the target when Goode tapped her on the shoulder. She turned, the look of surprise blossoming perfectly, and smiled.

"Hey," she said, taking off her earphones. "Lieutenant Goode, right?"

He nodded, clearly pleased that she remembered his name. "Ms. Roy!"

"Morgana, remember?"

"Ah, yes, of course."

He had a horsey kind of laugh, which meshed perfectly with his corn-fed looks. She wondered whether he'd say "Aw, shucks" if she complimented him. That'd be a hoot and a half.

"What are you doing here, Ms. . . . er, Morgana?"

"Working the Glock, same as you."

"Now there's a coincidence."

"A happy coincidence, I hope."

Here comes the "Aw, shucks."

"Gosh, well, it is for me."

Good enough, she thought with an interior grin.

His gaze slid reluctantly from her face to the target she was holding. "Hello! That's some nifty shooting."

"Thank you, kind sir."

He blushed and grinned, but for the moment seemed to have run out of compliments to give her.

"Well . . ." She picked up the Glock she had set down when he tapped her. "Nice running into you. Gotta get back to my routine."

She started to move away, thinking, *Is he going to bite, or not?*

"Uh, Morgana."

There's my good boy!

His voice trailed after her. She took two more steps, then paused, turning back. "Yes, Lieutenant?"

He came after her, just like a puppy dog. "If you don't..."

She stood her ground, waiting for him to come to her.

Obedient to her will, he took another couple of steps toward her. "If you don't mind me asking, are you almost finished?—with work, I mean."

She gave him a rueful smile. "Sadly, I'm only about halfway through." She cocked her head. "Why d'you ask?"

"Oh, well." His face fell; it was so pathetic. "I only meant, it's getting to be dinnertime. Mine, anyway. I have early mornings."

Oh, goody, Goode. Her smile brightened. "So do I."

"Well, d'you think you could...you know?"

"Could what?" Such sweet torture for him.

His cheeks were flaming. "Make an exception and come have dinner with me."

She looked around as if trying to decide. "I don't know. I..."

He was right in front of her, eager and terrified. "Please say yes."

"I did skip lunch today, so I am kind of hungry." She nodded. "And I guess I can catch up tomorrow morning."

He didn't hesitate at all. "Really? That's super."

"Frankie. I wish you'd call me Frankie," he said. "All my friends do."

"I like the sound of that," Morgana said. "Frankie." She watched his cheeks color again. He was so transparent, like all men when you engaged their reptile brains.

They were ensconced in a back booth of a jam-packed steak house not far from the shooting range. The restaurant, clearly one of his local haunts, smelled of charcoaled meat and beer. At the bubbling, full-up bar an early season baseball game was playing on a TV screen. The oversaturated colors made her retinas throb. It was odd and vaguely disturbing, she thought, how the screen drew your eye no matter where in the room you sat.

They were drinking beers. Their server set plasticized menus in front of them, then slipped away without a word.

"So, Frankie, how d'you like working at Dreadnaught?"

"Are you involved?"

She smiled. "Not married. No boyfriends."

He laughed, relaxing, as she had hoped. "No, no. I meant involved with Dreadnaught. I mean, you call the general Mac."

"Oh, that." She shrugged, keeping her voice offhanded. "I run an off-site enterprise for him. Deep data analytics."

He frowned. "Isn't that what NSA itself does?"

She smiled, took a sip of her beer. "What we do is a bit more specialized."

"Well, that tells me a whole bunch of nothing."

"Uh huh." She set her mug down carefully. "And you never answered my question."

"I can't talk about Dreadnaught." He appeared concerned. "You understand. You can't talk about yours, either."

"No." She waved her hand. "Of course. You're a good soldier, Lieutenant Goode."

"Frankie."

She cocked her head, gave him a quizzical look. "That was a joke."

"Huh? Oh . . . oh, yeah. Sorry."

"Never apologize, soldier."

He gave her a salute. "Yes, ma'am."

She dropped her eyes to the menu but didn't read it. She was thinking that she had already caused him to drop enough clues as to how he liked his women. "What's good here?"

"The New York strip."

"I'm partial to the tomahawk rib eye." She lifted her eyes to him. "Ever had that?"

"Uh uh. I always order the same thing."

Sure, you do. "How about we share the rib eye? It's big enough for two."

"Sure." He grinned. "Why not?"

It was crystal clear he liked the idea of sharing his meat with her. She laughed silently at the double entendre.

She slapped the menu. "It's settled then. You choose the fixings." She was betting with herself that they would be potato skins, loaded, and creamed spinach. The waitress drifted by, he ordered, and she won a million dollars.

"Well, one thing's for sure," she said, when they were alone. "We're in the same business."

"What business is that?"

"Secrets."

He nodded. "I hear you." Tilting his head back, he drained his mug, licked his lips as he looked at her. "So I know you'll get it." He sighed, rubbed a hand across his face. "It's so hard, you know. Keeping the secrets."

"The secrets set you apart. Who can you get close to, right? You can't even hold a decent conversation with most people."

He let go a deeper sigh, relaxing all the more. "You got that right."

"Unless it's with an insider. Someone who keeps as many secrets as you do. Maybe more."

"And even then."

Their steak arrived, along with the potato skins, loaded with butter, sour cream, bacon bits, chives, and creamed spinach, which she despised. They spent the next forty minutes sharing the tomahawk, which was surprisingly good. Frankie thought it had too much flavor, which made her mouth twitch in a sardonic smile. What a plain vanilla guy he was. While they ate, they spoke of things of no consequence to her: where he was raised, went to school, how he became interested in intelligence work while he was in the army. He had two brothers and a sister. He told her where they were and what they were doing, but that information went in one ear and out the other. She reciprocated with her own background. She drew enormous enjoyment from fabricating it on the spot: small family, home schooling, an abusive father—that was a must with this guy; men like Frankie were dying to fix females with broken wings.

"I see you're not plying me with liquor," she said, lifting one eyebrow, "like most men."

"I'm not like most men."

Oh, yes you are.

She laughed softly, throatily. His sincerity was almost heartbreaking. "I'm beginning to get that impression."

———

Afterward, in the parking lot, with chorus lines of traffic snaking by, he told her he wanted to see her home, as if they were sixteen-year-olds. That was a no-go. She didn't want him to see how far away from here she lived, she didn't want to raise any red flags about why she was at his shooting range.

"My place is being repainted; it stinks to high heaven." She gave him a judicious look. "But, you know, Frankie, I'd like to see where you live."

"Really?"

They were striped in shifting vehicle headlights. A semi's air horn trumpeted a mournful sound, dopplering away.

She nodded. "Really." Just a bit shy now. "Unless you don't want me to."

Of course he wanted her to; his eyes were glazed with the thought of her.

His home was in a concrete block building, low-rise, painted a pastel blue, one of many on a street lined with dusty chestnut trees. To her it looked like limbo, lost in the mists between urban and suburban. As they got out of their cars, a teenage kid in a high school varsity jacket bicycled past. He raised a hand to Frankie, who called, "Hey!" after him. Somewhere a dog barked, mournful as the semi's air horn.

"Well, this is it," Frankie said, opening the door to his second-floor apartment.

A bachelor pad, for certain. The living room was dominated by an enormous flat-panel TV. A sofa and easy chair were plunked in front of it with no thought to placement. Opened bags of potato chips and Cheetos shared a low table, cheap and scratched, with an oil-stained pizza box, one forlorn slice, cheese congealed like icing, lying within. No rugs. No pictures or photos on the walls, only posters for *Metal Gear Solid V* and *Call of Duty: Black Ops*. Military video games.

"My goodness," she said, turning slowly in a circle, "this could use a woman's touch."

Frankie flushed. "Sorry. But, well, my job gives me no spare time."

"Except for the shooting range."

"Huh. That's part of my job." He stepped toward her. "Here, let me take your coat."

It was the first time she felt his hands on her. They trembled just a bit right before she let her coat fall into his waiting arms.

"And what about weekends?"

He shrugged. "Weekends I treat myself to a big Waffle House breakfast after I hit the shooting range."

Waffle House, she thought pityingly. *That's his big treat.*

He watched, mouth half open, while she unzipped her dress. It slid down and pooled around her ankles. Very carefully, she stepped out of it; she did not take her high heels off. Men liked their women in high heels, especially with nothing else on.

He seemed to have stopped breathing. Then, as she walked him backward into the bedroom, his breath started to come in little wheezes, like he had asthma. When the backs of his knees pressed against the bed, she shoved him down, climbed on top of him.

"I can't believe this is happening," he said thickly.

"Shut up." She put her lips over his, her breasts pressed against his fluttering chest.

She undid his belt and trousers because his hands were trembling too badly, but when they touched her bare flesh they were terribly gentle, terribly romantic, if hands could be said to move in a romantic fashion, so that she felt some inner cog slip in the machinery of her plan, just for a moment, she felt the dissonance, the potential for change, and then it was back in place and everything was as it had been.

The act was purely physical for her, but not for him. And like the best escort she made it real for him, made him believe what he wanted to believe, helping him wish it into existence. There was an eruption of violent motion, of sweat and intimate moisture, and then it was over. It ended abruptly, and more than a little sadly. But then these things always did, she had found.

She had once seen a film of a cheetah running down a baby Thomson's gazelle while its mother hightailed it. The cheetah had used every last ounce of energy to reach the small gazelle, grab it by the throat, and kill it. For a long time, it crouched above its fallen prey, watching for larger predators, chest heaving mightily until it slowly brought its breath back into itself.

This is how Frankie seemed to her now, his chest rising and falling just as if he had run a great distance. She was still on top of him, thighs spread, hands gripping his shoulders.

"My God, that was good." She looked him right in the eye when she said this, which was the only way to lie successfully. She had learned that particular lesson a long time ago.

"Wow," he replied. "Just wow."

She laughed her soft, silken laugh, and, putting her lips against his ear, she told him how she had felt when he did that to her, and that, and that. She felt him stir beneath her.

"Frankie," she said.

He stroked the base of her spine. "Mmm?"

"I want to tell you something."

"Okay."

"I want to tell you what I do."

"But I thought we—"

She pressed a finger against his lips. "I'm trusting you, yeah? I need to. I've got no one else."

He stared up at her, as mesmerized as he had been at dinner, but for a different reason. Then again, maybe not.

So she told him about Meme LLC, about what they did there, and, saving it for last, about Mac giving her the impossible task of deciphering and intercepting what had come to be called the Bourne Initiative.

"I never heard of the Bourne Initiative," he said. "You sure that's what it's called?"

"Of course I'm sure, and here's why: Mac claimed he didn't send a Dreadnaught field unit to terminate Bourne."

"Well, I know the Russians have a kill team in place."

"That's what Mac said."

"Right."

"I don't believe it. I need Bourne. I want you to help me find him."

"Wow." He lifted her up, moved her aside, rolled to the edge of the bed. He stood up, looked back at her. "As usual, the general was right."

"What?" She experienced the sudden onset of free fall. "What did you say?"

His demeanor had altered radically. The dazzling marquee lights had shut down; the carnival of pink flesh and innocence had left town. His smile was a little sad, but mostly pitying. And that pity—now it was he who was pitying her—was in the instant possibly the hardest outcome of this failure for her to endure.

"You know what a honey trap is, I take it?"

His eyes were alight with a dark and sinister energy. But at the moment she was too shocked to feel fear.

Jesus Christ, she thought.

She wanted to say something, anything, but her tongue seemed glued to the roof of her mouth. She could not move or breathe. An unbearable weight pressed down on her, forcing the air out of her lungs.

What the fuck is happening? She knew; of course she knew. But her brain refused to process the information.

Her consciousness, lifting out of her body, flew far away. Once, when she was a teenager, her father had taken her hunting up in the Yukon. They had gone hunting for what? Deer, elk? She couldn't for the life of her remember now. It was snowing when they'd come upon the wolf. Its left forepaw was stuck in one of those awful steel traps. It turned, looked at them with eyes that she could swear spoke to her. Then it put its head down and started to gnaw at the trapped leg just above the steel jaws. *"Oh, hell,"* her father had muttered just before he shot the wolf dead.

Lieutenant Goode opened the shallow drawer on his bedside table, took out a pair of real handcuffs. There was a pistol in there, too—a 9mm Glock—which he expertly slid out of its stiff leather holster. Both gestures carried grave portent.

"You're a bad girl, Morgana. Very bad." He pointed the Glock vaguely in her direction. "So this is where you find yourself. I'm the honey, this here's the trap, and there's no fucking way you're getting out of it."

12

IT WAS MEN, not machine-gun fire that came down out of the dawn. The helo disgorged four men, jumping out of the open bay as the helo hovered over the rocky slope. To a man, they tumbled, unable to hold their initial balance, but soon enough they were up and bounding like mountain goats across the rocks, heading straight for Bourne and Mala.

"At last," he said. "*Spetsnaz* has arrived."

But that wasn't all. Three figures emerged from out of the dust of the rockslide as it began to settle. The Dreadnaughts weren't buried; they were very much alive, and like a nest of wasps that had been swatted they were mad as hell.

"We have no choice now," Mala said. "We have to fight them." She looked from one group to the other. "But we're just where we shouldn't be, caught between them."

Bourne squeezed off one shot at the *spetsnaz* unit.

"That was a lousy shot," Mala muttered.

Turning, Bourne squeezed off a shot at the advancing Dreadnaughts.

"Missed again," Mala grumbled. "What the hell's the matter with you?"

Grabbing her, Bourne crab-walked, picking his way through the spaces between the rocks, moving as quickly as he could out of the line of fire that had just started up between both sides.

And then Mala shut up, because she understood at last what he had meant to do all along. Following his lead, she slid on her backside, careful not to dislodge any loose rocks, making her way by staying completely in his shadow as he advanced along the cliff. The newly risen sun, tearing open a fiery rent in the pinkish dawn sky, was directly ahead of them. Behind them the two warring groups increased their combative fire.

Far enough away from the fray, Bourne slowed them, then halted altogether. They remained flat on their backs, staring up at wisps of cloud reflecting on their undersides the tender colors of the new day, while fusillades of submachine gun fire ripped apart the tortured soughing of the wind.

They lay in a little hollow, completely blind to the action, using their ears in a vain attempt to follow the battle. Beside him, Bourne felt Mala's muscles twitching spasmodically and knew she was itching to bang some heads together—American or Russian, it made no difference to her. Her nostrils flared to the scent of fresh blood. Hearing the moans of the dying, Bourne sensed it was all she could do not to leap up and join the killing.

She started when his fingers wrapped around her wrist, and she turned her head. A sorority of disparate emotions darkened her eyes to midnight-blue. Rage, frustration, and, yes, love swirled in those eyes. Her lips were half open, as if she were about to reveal something terribly intimate, but if so, it never emerged.

Silence. The sea wind regained sovereignty. The gunfire had ceased as abruptly as it had begun; the calling of the gulls resumed, tentatively at first, then, as a sense of normalcy returned, the morning righting itself, the cries became more plaintive as the gulls appeared over the crown of the rock face.

Just above where they lay, the crest of the cliff began a downward sweep, leading to the lowest ridge to the east. Bourne felt the waves of restlessness in Mala and, turning to her, mouthed, *Wait.*

Why?

Listen. Just listen.

Both were stilled, then, as if they were among the corpses littering the rocks to the west. Their eyes were turned in that direction, as well, which is why they didn't see the lone survivor of the crossfire, a *spetsnaz* assassin, who had circled around to come at them from the east. He held a knife in one hand, his other weapons having emptied themselves during the withering firefight. He was big, muscular, bald of pate, animalistic of eye.

Baring his teeth, he leapt onto Bourne, drove the knife toward him. He meant to rip open his neck, but at the last instant Bourne twisted enough to change the strike point to his shoulder. Mala whipped up and around, one arm swinging wide to catch the Russian on the chin. This was a Special Forces member, hard-trained, wet-trained, with neither conscience nor room for remorse. He withdrew the knife blade, slashed it across Mala's chest, biting through the scarred skin, into the flat muscles between the hollow of her neck and the sharp rise of her breasts.

In the first few seconds, that seemed to be a mistake. The attack allowed Bourne the time to slam the edge of his hand into the side of the Russian's neck. The strike should have temporarily paralyzed him, but he only grinned—more a grimace, a hard surface, revealing nothing, reflecting everything.

As swiftly as the rock-fall avalanche, he crashed against Bourne, driving him backward. Sharp rocks bit into Bourne's back. Using the point of his knife, the Russian opened the shoulder wound he had inflicted, twisting the blade, until Bourne, lips drawn back in a silent snarl of pain, wrapped his hand around it, the edge scoring a line of blood in his palm as he wrenched the blade out of the muscles of his shoulder.

The Russian jammed the heel of his hand against Bourne's chin, pushing his head back until Bourne was effectively blind to what he was doing. Twisting Bourne's hand back on itself he created a fulcrum of pain in Bourne's wrist so acute that Bourne should have been forced to let go of the blade. Instead, Bourne used his free hand to pinch the Russian's carotid artery, temporarily cutting off blood flow to his brain. The Russian grunted and, in that instant, Bourne took charge of the knife blade, pushed the point into the Russian's face.

The point struck the ridge bone just below the Russian's left eye. Because of the upward angle, it slipped off the bone, tore through skin and flesh, burying itself in his eye. He gave out with a bellow, jerking back, giving Bourne full control of the knife, which he pushed in deeper, past the eye, into the Russian's brain.

Françoise awoke, as she always did, in a strange kind of purgatory, neither here nor there, but elsewhere. Possibly she hadn't slept at all, although there were intimations of the Swedish dawn sidling through the drapes. In the bathroom, she knelt as if to pray, and vomited up the memory of her abominable meeting with her half brother, Gora.

Françoise, with her face drowned beneath the cold water flow from the sink, heard the opening bars of "Bad Habits" by the Last Shadow Puppets from her mobile's speaker. It was a special ringtone she had edited and installed for only one person, and she lifted her head, crossed the hotel room without toweling off, snatched up her phone from the bedside table. Because of her insistence on dinner at Aifur Song, on squeezing out whatever amount of experience she could from this excuse of a city, she had had her guts mangled. *Oh, well,* she thought. *It's part of the price of doing business.*

"Auntie," Morgana said into her ear, by which code word she knew Morgana was in trouble.

She sat on the edge of the bed, back as ramrod straight as a sentry's, and said slowly and precisely, "What flavor of trouble are you in?"

"Licorice." The worst.

They both hated licorice.

"Where are you?" Knowing the severity of the trouble, there was no point in asking Morgana details.

"NSA HQ. Under armed guard. They allowed me one call, and I—"

"Stop." Françoise knew she needed to get off the line before NSA had a chance to realize they couldn't trace the call and started in on Morgana. That wouldn't do at all.

"I'll take care of it," she said, and broke the connection. Immediately, she opened her mobile, removed the SIM card, crushed it with the high, sharp heel of a shoe. Just in case. After inserting a brand new SIM card, she pressed a speed dial key.

There was hollowness on the line, along with a number of clicks like insects or electronics communicating with one another.

"Yes," the male voice said.

"It's happened," Françoise said. "It worked. Just as I predicted."

"That is gratifying news," Marshall Fulmer, the national security advisor, said, as if he had just heard the local weather report. "Where are they holding her?"

Françoise told him.

"I'm more than halfway back to D.C.," he said. "I'll make a call freezing everything in place."

"She's my friend. I don't want her harmed in any way."

"I promised you that she wouldn't be. Just keep her out of my hair, okay?"

"No problem there."

"You still sound nervous. Have faith, my dear."

"In an American national security advisor?"

He laughed at that. "I like you. I really do. You have what we call true grit back in the old country." He chuckled again. "Sit tight. She'll be with you shortly."

Françoise tossed the phone onto the bed, crawled between the sheets, and slept like a baby until Justin Farreng knocked on her door with the breakfast he had had delivered to his room two floors above.

She opened the door nude.

"Good morning." He looked her up and down appreciatively. "What would've happened if I'd been housekeeping or the night manager?"

"They would've had a helluva story to tell." She let him into the room, closed the door behind him.

He set the tray down on a table.

"Coffee first," she said. "Black." As he filled cups from the silver carafe she regarded him from beneath hooded eyes. He was not a bad-looking fellow, smart, funny at times, slightly crazy, like all the best people. And his lovemaking was more than adequate. It was a minor wonder to her that she felt nothing at all for him. He might just as well have been a slab of raw meat hanging in a butcher's locker.

He smiled at her when he handed her the coffee, and she smiled back, even while her mind was elsewhere—with Morgana. Had Fulmer arrived in D.C. yet? Had he freed her, set her on a plane to Stockholm? Was she on her way here? Now that she was awake, the caffeine kicking in, she felt on edge, in an entirely different way than last night, waiting for Morgana's call, which, she had had to admit to herself, might not come.

"Toast?" Farreng asked, holding up a freshly buttered triangle of whole grain.

"Revelations?" Françoise replied, holding out the thumb drive Fulmer had given her.

"So soon?" Farreng's eyebrows lifted as they made the exchange. "How good?"

"It will give even you pause," she said, dunking her toast into the coffee, then ripping off a bite between her even, white teeth. She had inserted the drive into her laptop's USB port, using the security code Fulmer had made her memorize, the moment she had returned to her room and before she dressed for dinner. The files therein were real eye-openers, especially the ones pertaining to General MacQuerrie. *Good Lord, what these people get up to,* she had thought while showering off the day's sweat and sticky particulates. Everything online, buried in servers protected by layers of firewalls and malware busters, and yet vulnerable to attacks so sophisticated the cyber weapons morphed exponentially every week, if not daily. *Nothing's safe anymore,* she thought, *unless it's a hard copy locked away in a vault buried in the concrete foundation of a massive office building. And even then... Back to the future, right?*

"Is that so?" He grinned, tumbling the drive between his fingers like a prestidigitator. "I'll be eager to see what your sources have unearthed this time."

"Make sure you're sitting down when you do."

His eyebrows rose again. *Don't do that,* she thought. *It makes you look like a clown.*

"It's not like you to oversell your product, Françoise."

"That's right." She bent, taking another slice of toast. "And this time alert me before it goes live. I want a front row seat at the freaking firestorm."

———

Mala hauled the Russian off Bourne, unwrapped Bourne's fingers from the knife. "Shit," she said, staring at his bloodred palm, "I can see clear to the bone." She looked at him. "Does it hurt?"

"Don't feel a thing," Bourne said. "Same for my shoulder." But his eyes were going in and out of focus.

Using the knife to make strips out of the Russian's trousers, she fashioned compression bandages by wrapping the strips around his palm and over his shoulder under his armpit. "Not the most antiseptic, but what the hell."

Waving off Mala's help, he got to his feet.

"We've got to get out of here," she said. "Right now."

Bourne nodded. "We'll take the powerboat."

The climb up to the crest taxed neither of them, but the way down to the shingle and the curling combers was dauntingly steep for Bourne in his condition. Nevertheless, they began their descent without hesitation.

Despite the difficulties, their progress was easier than the night before in darkness and the beginnings of the storm. The wind had lapsed to the lightest of breezes, the air was still night-cooled, and the way was sunlit.

Bourne did not give the slightest indication of the level of pain he was in, now that his body's trauma defenses were wearing off. There was no option other than to keep moving.

Nevertheless, two-thirds down, he was obliged to pause. Despite the still, cool air, sweat ran down his face, trickled along his spine and from under his arms. The throbbing in his shoulder and hand was a palpable thing, spiking his heart rate. Black spots danced before his eyes. He realized his breathing was coming in shallow gasps; he slowed it down, taking deep, even breaths, reoxygenating his lungs.

Mala, realizing something was wrong, paused below him, turning an inquiring gaze back at him.

He made a shoveling motion with his good hand, indicating she should continue on. This she did without another word, and, relying on his second wind, he followed close behind.

An eternity of pain accompanied him, during which nothing existed beyond the next hand- and foothold, the search for the best path, bypassing deadfalls, perilous crevasses or cracks, and loose rocks. Following Mala made all this easier and more difficult at the same time. She was lighter than he was by a good margin; sections that held her might not hold him, which made him doubly cautious. On the other hand, this intense concentration kept his attention from the pain, which was so excruciating he was only partially successful in compartmentalizing it.

But, at last, even eternity must end. He slid the last three feet to the shingle, keeping his knees bent as if he were a parachutist landing, in order to cushion the shock to his feet and legs. They were several hundred yards to the east of where the boats had been left. They seemed to have weathered the storm better than he expected.

He and Mala set off at once, with him taking the lead. Mala did not protest. In fact, she had said nothing at all since their brief conversation while she was jerry-rigging his bandages and binding his wounds, both of which were deep, bloody, and angry. He'd need expert medical attention, the sooner the better, in order to stave off infections that would put him in the hospital, weak and vulnerable.

They were a dozen feet from the powerboat when he collapsed. Mala ran, knelt beside him, and gasped. The wound in his shoulder had bled right through the thick cloth, soaking it. His entire right side was dark and sticky with blood. The wound must have punctured the brachial artery.

She lifted the lid of one of his eyes, said, "Shit," wasted no time in a vain attempt to revive him; it would take too long, and time was now in short supply. She understood the extreme peril Bourne was in. Reaching under his armpits, she dragged him directly into the water, kept him afloat as she swam to the port side of the powerboat. Grabbing on to his bloody shirt with one clawed hand, she levered herself over the gunwale, then, feet firmly planted on the deck, hauled Bourne up and over, onto the deck.

For a moment, she stared at his face, pale and bloodless. Despite her efforts at field dressing, he was still bleeding. In fact, now that she had a chance to study him closely, it was clear to her that he was dying.

Part Two

Keyre

13

AS JASON BOURNE lay slowly bleeding out on the deck of a water-swilled powerboat, purchased by a cutout offshore middleman for Dreadnaught, a veritable shitstorm was exploding in the face of General Arthur MacQuerrie, head of that most secret of government entities, in the form of the latest LeakAGE bombshell, a hacked trove of eyes-only documents from the NSA's very bowels. They revealed that, in the first place, NSA, that most august, feared, and reviled surveillance division of the American clandestine services, which prided itself on its SIGINT, electronic and satellite spying, and turned its nose up at the CIA and its outmoded HUMINT, boots-on-the-ground form of intelligence gathering, had on its blackest of books its own HUMINT division code-named Dreadnaught. In the second place, that Dreadnaught was heavily and, needless to say, illegally, funded from various named sources, none of which, apparently, existed. In the third place, that said Dreadnaught was in the business of targeting enemies of the American homeland—controversial, gray-area entities, to a person—and terminating them with extreme prejudice, without the knowledge, never mind the consent, of Congress. In the fourth place, that these bloodletting assignments were decided upon and meted out solely by one General Arthur MacQuerrie without any kind of oversight whatsoever.

And in the fifth place, and most damning for MacQuerrie, were a raft of files spewed out into cyberspace documenting the eye-opening amounts of money salted away by the aforementioned General Arthur MacQuerrie in a briar patch of shell companies in the Caymans, Panama, Argentina, Gibraltar, and Cyprus. As an adjunct to this perfidy visited upon the federal government and the American people was the treasonous way these shell companies appeared to rub shoulders with those known to belong to certain high-level officials and billionaire oligarchs of the Russian Federation.

The flurry of documents was released at three in the morning, Eastern Daylight Time. Before first light in D.C., emissaries of Homeland Security, accompanied by a contingent of heavily armed military personnel, confronted a sleep-bedazzled MacQuerrie on his front doorstep. Moments later, under the teary gaze of his wife, he was handcuffed, hustled down his McLean walkway, past prize azaleas and rhododendrons, ushered with only a modicum of courtesy into the back of one of three gleaming black Chevrolet SUVs. Four minutes after they had arrived, the modern-day caravan was gone, leaving only faint bluish exhaust fumes that dissipated even before the distraught Mrs. MacQuerrie closed the front door and dialed their lawyer's home phone number.

Meanwhile, the ominous caravan made its next stop at the home of Lieutenant Francis Goode. Goode, having received advance warning of the intentions of the long arm of the federal government, had tried to do a runner, but too late. As the SUVs hurled themselves around the corner to his street, he sprinted back into his house and barricaded himself inside. A fierce firefight ensued, in the midst of which the good lieutenant, having determined beyond a shadow of a doubt that there was no way out, put the muzzle of his pistol into his mouth and blew his brains out.

At around the same time as the LeakAGE barrage began, Fulmer, having deplaned at the VIP side of Dulles International, and true to his word, deployed the full flower of his influence, gaining Morgana her freedom from NSA custody. As dawn broke over D.C., she was aboard a military transport on her way to Stockholm and thence, via a far more comfortable commercial flight, to Kalmar, where Françoise was anxiously awaiting her arrival.

Not many things gave Françoise anxiety; doing nothing but waiting was one of them; meditation was not her thing. Of course, as recompense, she experienced the delightful diversion of watching the LeakAGE shit-bomb light up the Internet like a line of napalm detonations. The speed at which LeakAGE stories went viral still astonished her, but this one, as expected, flashed around the globe at what seemed light speed. And why not? Not only was an American general implicated in nefarious dealings, but the NSA itself—everyone's favorite whipping boy since Snowden—was caught with its pants down. As she had foreseen, everyone wanted a piece of that action. And, not so incidentally, the pressure on Fulmer's own not so very kosher interests domiciled in Panama was lifted. This story was so big it would defy the usual mayfly-short news cycle; it would build and build, and then linger for months. More than enough time for Fulmer to leave Musgrave-Stephens and reassign his interests to Fellingham, Bodeys.

Which reminded her. Hunched in front of a laptop shielded from ISP snooping, she began the long, laborious process that would ensure her another airtight get-out-of-jail-free card to play should the necessity arise.

———

The Angelmaker was reluctant to leave Bourne alone on the rocking powerboat, but there was no help for it. Slipping over the gunwale, she swam the short distance to where the shingle came up to meet her just before the creaming surf, if that's what you could call these laughably small waves. But that's what you got in what was essentially a land-locked sea.

Picking her way across the prickly shore as quickly as she could, she approached the area where she had been waiting for Bourne as he drove toward her in the *Nym*'s runabout. Down on her knees at the base of the cliff, she dug beneath the surface, extracting a neoprene waterproof bag, which she unzipped. Inside were a mobile and a sat phone, two different caliber handguns, extra ammo, a serrated knife in a thick rubber sheath, a coil of nylon rope, and a first aid kit in a long red plastic box. After assuring herself that it hadn't been disturbed and that everything was there, she made an encrypted emergency call on the sat phone, not trusting to mobile service here. Then she put back the phone, zipped the bag, and returned with it to the powerboat.

Back on deck, she placed the bag next to Bourne, pressed her fingers against his carotid. Relief flooded through her: he was still alive. Then she opened the bag, took out the first aid kit. First, she applied tourniquets to stop the bleeding. Then she cut off the bloody field dressings and commenced to clean the wounds, first with an antiseptic solution and then with a powerful antibiotic powder. Lastly, she bound them with Elastoplast, sealing them temporarily. Still, there was nothing she could do about the blood he had lost, and that was a real worry.

She sat back on her haunches. Bourne's blue-white face looked like a three-day-old mackerel. It made her sick in the pit of her stomach. Bending over from the waist, she placed her lips against his. They were cold as ice, as if he were already dead. She opened his mouth with hers, breathed warm air into him, as if this were a fairy tale, as if she had magical powers and she could breathe life into him. Why not? She had done everything else she could think of to save him.

Fuck those fucking Russian fucks, she thought. *Their day will come, and when it does I'm going to use their guts for balalaika strings.*

A moment later, she heard the deep, rumbling sound of the heavy diesels, and the ship came into view. On the elevated rear deck of the ship was a helo, which airlifted them to Skyros Island International Airport. There, a newly minted Bombardier 8000 long-haul private jet was ready and waiting for them. Customs and immigration had been arranged following her call, and they wasted no time in taking off. The Bombardier 8000, the company's newest flagship jet, cost nearly $69 million, cruised at a speedy Mach 0.85, and was as comfortable as could be.

Preparations had been made for Bourne to be transferred onto a locked-down gurney. Every conceivable blood type was available. As soon as the surgeon on board had determined Bourne's blood type, his nurse commenced the first of what would no doubt be a number of transfusions. A saline drip was arranged on Bourne's other side, to deal with his dehydration. By that time they were six and a quarter miles high, the sky was a shell of bright purple-blue, and the Angelmaker could finally relax. For a time, from the aspect of her cushy leather seat, comfortable in dry clothing, she drank bottle after bottle of water, observing the surgeon, who looked very grave indeed, and his nurse expertly attending to Bourne. When it was that her eyes closed and she dropped into the arms of sleep she could not, afterward, recall.

It was just over 2,688 miles from the Skyros airport to Somalia. The Bombardier 8000 touched down just over four hours after it had taken off, one of its passengers still more dead than alive.

14

BOURNE, LYING INSENSATE in a spotless room near the center of Keyre's camp, hung suspended between yesterday and tomorrow. The camp, riding the Horn of Africa, still on the shores of the Arabian Sea, would have been unrecognizable to him. Since Bourne had made his first nocturnal visit, it had grown into something resembling a medium-size village, complete with its own airfield with runways long enough to accommodate jet planes even larger than the Bombardier 8000, for cargo shipments were constantly being flown to and from the camp, executing Keyre's arms traffic. Thanks to extensive dredging, the area was now a deep-water port for cargo ships, which came and went with the same purpose as the air traffic. Too, the tents Bourne had encountered when he snatched Mala and her sister had given way to sunbaked brick buildings. Cranes rose into the air, bulldozers, and all manner of earthmoving equipment rumbled and thudded, as more and more buildings were constructed. Cart paths had been widened and paved, altered here and there to form a semblance of a grid within the perimeter of the village, which was protected, like military bases the world over, by high fences, barriered gates, and three shifts of armed sentries. There was even a radar tower, along with a pair of anti-aircraft missile launchers.

But all of this bristling modernization was at present unknown to Bourne. His mind, teetering on the verge of an abyss with no bottom, had returned to the Somalia he had known. To the pitch-black night of an AWOL moon and stars, filled with the ominous rumbling of what would rapidly develop into a monstrous thunderstorm. As if in a grainy film he saw himself planting the two incendiary bombs on the north end of Keyre's tented camp. Detonators set for six minutes, he threaded his way through the darkness, passing up at least three opportunities to break the necks of sentries; he wanted no evidence there was anyone near the camp except in the north.

In the days previous, he had made a map of the camp during a series of clandestine forays at dawn and twilight, when daylight was at its weakest. Mounting the heights slightly inland of the camp, he sighted through powerful binoculars, taking mental notes of the comings and goings of everyone within the camp. Occasionally, he saw the girls, and he determined, sadly, there were too many for him to free them all. He saw the line of wooden spears upon whose sharp tips were jammed severed heads, some fresh, others reeking beneath their crawling carapace of flies, still others meatless, dark and leathery from sun and salt wind. Bony cattle roamed through the compound, heads down, in a vain attempt to forage scraps amid the pyramids of plastic bottles.

One dawn he observed a contingent of jihadists firing machine pistols at a cracked and bullet-pitted Western toilet, lying on its side in an open space of dust and porcelain shards. The next morning, assaulted even at this remove by the horrific stench of rotting flesh, he bore witness amid the wreckage of the ruined toilet to five wooden stakes to which had been crudely bound five headless corpses. The same contingent fired their machine pistols at these targets, making them dance as the bullets struck them. The jihadists laughed obscenely.

The morning before his planned raid, he observed Keyre using a crude but enormous machete to sever a man's head. His men kicked the head around like Aztecs at their ball game before hoisting it onto an available spear. During his twilight recon, Bourne was unfortunate enough to see one of the girls being dragged out of the communal tent. It was not Liis—he had been given portrait photos of both sisters by their father. To his horror, the girl could not have been more than twelve. Perhaps she had been recalcitrant, perhaps she had spat in Keyre's face, or tried to escape. In any event, she now faced the ultimate punishment. Quitting his position, Bourne sprinted as fast as he could manage while keeping himself hidden, but he was too far away to come close enough to do something to save her—though precisely what that might be without getting himself killed he could not say. And yet it was impossible for him to stand by and do nothing. But, apart from attacking the compound with a company of well-armed soldiers, there was nothing to do. And this knowledge pierced him deeply and completely.

The poor girl's death, barbaric and inhuman as it was, served to confirm every horror story Mala and Liis's father had told him about Keyre and his jihadist cult of personality. Feeling helpless in the face of such evil was one of the worst moments in Bourne's life, a nightmare that would stay with him for years to come. There was no good way to bear witness to such an atrocity, except for him to promise himself that the people responsible—especially Keyre—would pay with their lives. And in the here and now, he knew the best thing he could do was to save Mala and Liis from such a monstrous fate.

———————

Even in the dead of night he knew where every tent was and who or what resided inside each. Most important, he knew where Keyre spent most of his time and where his girls were kept. For reasons he had yet to determine, Mala was stashed in a separate tent next to Keyre's, perhaps for easy access. But her sister, Liis, was in with the other girls. It made things awkward—more difficult, but not impossible. It didn't help to see how much other death lay around the camp like so much fallen snow; it made it worse. He wanted nothing more than to rid this camp, this spot of beautiful coastline, of torture and death-dealing. But virtually the whole of the Horn of Africa was an abattoir, a cesspit of tribal warfare and bug-eyed revolutionaries, maddened by their own religious zeal.

The night had come, the darkness around the tented camp absolute. The incendiary explosive devices were in place. Less than ten seconds to go until the twin detonations, causing panic, shock, and chaos.

Seven, six...

"What the hell is going on?" Morgana said when Françoise met her as she entered the small, neat-as-a-pin arrivals hall, after deplaning. "Nobody told me anything." It was clear she was equal parts incensed and frightened from her brief though surely scary incarceration. "I'm sitting on both flights biting my nails, looking over my shoulder, waiting for the NSA to drag me back to holding."

"Forget the NSA," Françoise said, kissing her on both cheeks, then taking the crook of her arm in hers. "At the mo-mo, they have more on their plate than they can handle."

Morgana halted them both, and in the middle of the echoing arrivals hall, Françoise dragged out her mobile, fired up a browser, and showed Morgana the CNN site. Morgana grabbed the phone out of her hand, greedily reading and scrolling down at the same time.

"Good Christ, all hell's broken loose."

Françoise nodded. "MacQuerrie has vanished down the fed rabbit hole, possibly never to return." She grinned. "Ding dong, the wizard is dead."

Morgana looked up into her friend's face. "This is real?"

"Uh huh."

"Wow," Morgana breathed. "Just...wow."

She went back to reading the adjunct articles as Françoise steered her outside, where a hired car was waiting. She managed to get Morgana inside, then slid into the backseat beside her and closed the door. The driver glanced at her in the rearview mirror, and she nodded.

"It's good to have you here," she said as the car pulled out into the exit roadway. "With me."

Morgana, finished reading, for the moment anyway, handed back the mobile. "Did you have something to do with this?" When Françoise shrugged, the grin still on her face, Morgana said, "I don't know what to say."

"I told you I would help you if you ever got into real trouble."

"I know, but..." She took a deep breath, let it out slowly. Relief brought her shoulders down from either side of her neck. "I don't know how to thank you."

"Oh, I'll think of something," Françoise said with a twinkle in her eye. "But first, we take you shopping. You look like Raggedy Ann." She took her friend's hand, squeezed it in a reassuring manner. "Then we eat. I know a great place. The last time I was there I threw up three hours later."

Morgana laughed. "That's a recommendation?"

"In this case, it is." She laughed. "Trust me."

"Always," Morgana said. "Always."

Tick-tock...*Boom!*

The entire tented camp was in a frenzy, revolutionary zeal temporarily submerged under the twin necessities of putting out the fires and finding the perpetrators. Under cover of the major diversion, Bourne headed in.

Moving fast and low, he threaded his way between the tents, taking as direct a route as he was able, considering all the running troops he had to dodge. Now, with an earth-shuddering roar, the sky cracked open and the deluge commenced. That was both good news and bad news. The thick curtains of rain added to the confusion and helped mask his progress through the camp, but it also went a long way to putting out the fires prematurely.

Inside their prison tent, a dozen girls stood perfectly still. They stood on their mean pallets, legs slightly spread as if they were on a ship rolling on the high seas. They were the only immobile people in the entire camp. Not one of them thought to take advantage of the opportunity to run, not after what had happened at twilight.

Someone had lit a kerosene lamp. By the inconstant light of its flickering flame, they stared at him out of emaciated faces with overlarge eyes, their bodies pale beneath tattered clothes. Once again Bourne's heart was rent. He wanted to save them all, but to save two he needed to leave the others behind. He'd never make it out with all of them in tow.

Stepping to Liis, he grabbed her hand, led her out of the tent, out into the deluge. Already the ground was a muddy morass. The rain was coming down so hard, even the sandy soil could not drain it away fast enough.

He endeavored not to let the girl's stumbling gait slow him down, carrying her under one arm when he had to. Like a waft of air, she weighed next to nothing. Arriving at the rear of the tent in which Mala was being held, he used a knife to rip open the fabric. With Liis in tow, he stepped through the rent to find the older sister.

She was not alone.

Bourne had expected a guard, perhaps two. The person standing between him and Mala was Keyre.

15

AND LIEUTENANT GOODE," Morgana said, as she sipped her dirty martini. "Ah, Lieutenant Goode."

Françoise, her hands cupped around a vodka rocks, said, "You know this man?"

"He was the one." Morgana took another sip, delighting in how the icy liquid turned to fire in her belly. "The one who MacQuerrie prepped to suck me in."

"A double honey trap." Françoise nodded. "Very clever."

"I was an idiot."

"We're all idiots once in a while." Françoise laughed. "Otherwise, how would we know we're human?"

Aifur Song was packed to the gills, an apt analogy given the preponderance of fish and seafood on the artfully designed menu. Since they had arrived a half hour ago, the noise level had steadily risen, until now it was a dull roar, like stormy surf heard at a short remove.

Their drinks finished, the waiter brought refills without being asked. Shortly thereafter, while the two women were catching each other up in a concerted attempt to restore Morgana's equilibrium, a young man with dark, probing eyes and straight dark hair, slicked back to reveal a window's peak, appeared out of the crowd, wending his way to their table.

"Ah, there you are," Françoise said, raising a hand. She made the introductions. "Morgana Roy, meet Larry London, a terrific freelance photographer."

Smiling warmly, Rozin, newly minted head of *spetsnaz*, briefly took Morgana's hand before sliding into a chair at their four-top. "Very pleased to meet you, Ms. Roy."

"Morgana, please."

He nodded. "Morgana. And you must call me Larry." He laughed. "All my friends do." His laugh was dry and easy to digest; it drew you to him without any fuss. Their waiter materialized at his elbow; Rozin pointed to Morgana's dirty martini. "I'll have what the lovely lady is drinking."

"Very good, sir," the waiter said, departing.

"Morgana," Françoise said, "you recall the photo of the mother and daughter Afghan refugees being pulled out of the water after their boat capsized."

"The one that won the Pulitzer? Sure. It was the centerpiece of the Global Photographics traveling exhibit a few years back. Everyone's seen it."

"That was Larry's work."

Morgana cocked her head. "Really?"

He shrugged. "Right place, right time."

Françoise scoffed. "He has no ego, this one. That was peak performance, Larry. Everyone knows that."

The anecdote served its purpose; the ice had been neatly broken. When Rozin's drink was set before him, they all toasted "better days," and swallowed the alcohol.

"And what do you do, Morgana?" Rozin asked, setting his cocktail glass down.

"Oh, no, Larry," Françoise cut in. "You mustn't ask her that."

"Mustn't I?" Rozin's eyes sparkled. He knew very well Morgana's specialty, having been read in by Françoise via text message while Morgana was trying on clothes. "How delightfully intriguing."

"Intrigue is just what we seek to avoid." Françoise picked up her menu. "Isn't that right, Morgie?"

Rozin made a face. "Oh, don't call her that; Morgana is such a beautiful name. One you don't hear very often. Welsh. From the compound *Morcant*—a circle or bright sea."

Morgana was impressed. "That's more than I knew."

"Oh, Larry's assignments take him to every corner of the globe," Françoise said, "where he absorbs knowledge like a six-year-old."

"Are you two lovers?" Morgana asked, looking from one to the other.

"Lovers?" Françoise burst out laughing.

"It's that funny?" Rozin exclaimed. It wasn't difficult evincing wounded pride.

"Larry's one of my messengers," Françoise said. "Receiving and delivering vital information." Her eyes flashed merrily. "Number one. *Ichiban*, as the Japanese say."

Rozin shot her a dark look, as if with her bantering she was cleaving too close to a kernel of truth. But Morgana was too entranced by the lighthearted byplay that included her as an instant friend—part of this family, one might say—to notice. Fun was to be had here, and a secure place to rest her still-spinning head, safe and protected from the dreadful events of the last twenty-four hours. Her unwinding had begun when Françoise had taken her shopping. It continued now, at a faster pace, running downhill like water to the ocean. And, oh, it felt so good to finally let her guard down.

That was when the shakes started. She looked up helplessly at Françoise, who understood that her friend was going into delayed shock. Jumping up, Françoise took Morgana by the hand, steered her through the restaurant as quickly as she could.

They made it into the ladies' room just in time. Françoise held Morgana's hair back from her face as, bent double, she vomited up the gin and terror that had been roiling inside her, clamoring to be released. Periodically, Françoise lifted her head past the electronic eye, automatically flushing the toilet over and over.

"Jesus, Françoise." Ripping squares of toilet paper off the roll, Morgana wiped her mouth with shaky hands. "Jesus fucking Christ." She was shaking like an addict in withdrawal. "I'm not cut out for this life."

Françoise cradled her shoulders gently. "None of us is, darling. I'm afraid there's a steep learning curve."

Morgana stood up, but, still shaky, she leaned against the stall's left partition. "Was it the same with you?"

Françoise nodded. "Of course. But, you know, it was Larry who taught me a lot."

"Larry. Really." Morgana allowed herself to be led out of the stall to the line of sinks.

"Uh huh," Françoise affirmed.

Morgana washed out her mouth, splashed water on her face, toweled off. "God, I look a fright," she said, staring into the mirror.

"Nonsense. You're one of those women who don't need makeup to look beautiful." She tilted her head, handed Morgana a tube. "Maybe just a touch more color on your lips."

As Morgana checked out the color, then applied the lipstick, Françoise said. "You know, now I think about it, maybe Larry would do the same for you."

———————

Like the tent that held the other girls, Mala's tent was lit by a kerosene lantern—two of them, in fact, one on each side of the tent. Their light revealed a cheap tribal rug covering the rough ground, a small propane ring on which hunkered a squat iron kettle, beside which were a handleless cup and a square tin canister marked as Russian Caravan tea. Next to that was, incongruously, a wooden rolling cart with six long drawers. One of the drawers was pulled partway out. Bourne could see inside, and his blood ran cold. An array of implements, all sharply bladed or pointed, some steel, but others iron or fire-hardened bamboo, each meticulously nested in its own lined niche. In the center of the tent stretched a curious contraption made of bentwood and dowels, stained almost black in spots, a framework on which a human body could be lain giving access to both front and back. The carpet beneath the thing was black, as well. Many layers of blood, dried one over the other.

At the head—or foot, it was impossible to tell—of this strange and sinister piece of furniture, stood Mala. Keyre was pressed up against her back, holding an instrument much like a scalpel, but with a wickedly curved blade, at her carotid, which pulsed with her terror. Liis, cleaving to Bourne as if he were a rock, gave a little strangled cry.

"Kill her?" Keyre said without preamble in Somali. "No, I don't think so." Was he addressing Bourne or Liis? Perhaps it was both.

The instrument moved down from the side of Mala's neck to a spot just underneath her right breast.

He caught Bourne's eye. "But one of these will come off now." He gestured with his head. "Unless, that is, you let go of the girl so she can be with her sister, where she belongs."

"The girls belong as far away from here as they can get."

"And that is why you're here, one guesses." He was tall but not a big man. Wiry and athletic, one muscle fitted into another without the interference of fat or excess flesh. His mahogany skin appeared to be stretched over muscle and bone with the form-fitting tightness of Lycra. His cheeks were shadowed, deeply sunken—or were they deformed by ritual scars? In the lantern light it was difficult to tell. His tightly curled hair fit like a cap high on his head, the sides and front shaven clean. His eyes radiated the fever-bright light of the fanatic. People like Keyre could not be reasoned with; they had to be dealt with on their own terms or not at all.

"Before anything gets out of hand—"

Keyre tossed his head. "It's already out of hand. Thanks to you."

"And yet here I am. I've got your attention. More than that, I have an audience alone with you." Bourne cocked his head. "How d'you suppose I could have gotten that otherwise?"

Keyre grunted. "You speak very good Somali, for an infidel."

"I'll take that as a compliment."

"Don't take it for fucking anything."

Bourne decided he needed to take a chance. Pushing the cowering Liis slightly away from him, he unwound her fingers from his. For a long, tense moment, Keyre did nothing. Then he lowered his instrument to his side, but kept it at the ready.

"Speak, then."

Bourne produced the deep sigh of a businessman who finds himself at the short end of the stick. "You're right, I did come here for the girls."

"Their father."

Bourne nodded.

"Their father's a shit. He sold them to people, who sold them to me."

It was easy to believe Keyre was an inveterate liar; the talent went with the territory. But this time Bourne felt certain he was telling the truth. "Nevertheless, I'd like to take them away."

"Impossible," Keyre said. "The process is in its final stages."

Ripping off her stained cloth shift, he pushed Mala forward with his chest and knees so that she came fully into the light. Liis's cry was like that of a baby bird witnessing her mother being crushed. Mala's skin down her torso and limbs was a reddened webwork of open cuts, angry wounds, and livid scars. She had been systematically tortured. This was Bourne's initial reaction, not yet understanding the maiming wasn't disfigurement at all—at least, not in Keyre's eyes—but a series of Yibir magical glyphs, whose lineage stretched all the way back to the ancient Ajuran Empire of the 1300s.

"Once it has begun," Keyre said in a frighteningly reasonable tone, "this process cannot be interrupted." He gestured with his chin. "Take the little sister if you must. I will name a price, you will pay it, here, now, and you will depart, never to return."

Bourne had been moving, ostensibly to gain a better look at the extent of the damage Keyre had inflicted on Mala. He stared into her eyes, which looked like depthless pools, dead at their bottoms, and he thought, *She's already lost*. But then the punishment he had witnessed, meted out at twilight to the little girl, returned to him with all the force of a hammer blow. An innocent caught up, like so many innocents, in the tribal warfare between fanatic religious factions. These days, jihadists came in every color of the rainbow, shedding blood and brothers over territory more than two thousand years old.

"Those are your terms," Bourne said, still evincing the businessman's attitude.

"They are."

"Let's see if we can—"

"*Final* terms," Keyre said flatly, and the instrument returned to the soft flesh beneath Mala's right breast. "Rejoice that I have given you any terms at all."

"Oh, I am," Bourne said. "Rejoicing, that is." And with that, he kicked over the lantern closest to him, which was why he had moved in the first place.

Kerosene spilled out of the uncapped reservoir and with a great *whoosh* of heat and light caught fire. The fibers of the rug were dry, perfect fuel for such a conflagration. Bourne pushed Liis backward through the rent with one hand, then, in almost the same motion, stepped through the flames, emerging on the other side like some avenging deity, a god of death.

16

THE NEW, IMPROVED, and far more powerful national security advisor Marshall Fulmer bestrode the D.C. Beltway like a colossus. As the person who had uncovered MacQuerrie's illegal incarceration of Morgana Roy and, by extension, the existence of Meme LLC, a black off-site cyber operation seemingly devoted exclusively to furthering the general's astonishingly far-flung interests, which might or might not sync up with Russian Federation business interests—even before LeakAGE released the slurry of MacQuerrie files—Fulmer received an unprecedented quantity of air time, photo ops, and interviews with the most prestigious of TV's talking heads. He was invited to the White House to meet with the president and his security staff, who solicited his opinion on how to ensure they would not miss even one of MacQuerrie's well-hidden tentacular organizations.

Since MacQuerrie had shut up like a giant clam, they also wanted to know just what the hell the general was up to. Was it simply greed? Or was there a more sinister purpose at work here?

At no time during these intense sessions did Fulmer mention the Bourne Initiative. Further, he felt confident that MacQuerrie would never, ever divulge the initiative's existence, let alone his almost obsessive interest in it. For Fulmer, since the time when he'd conceived of his plot to overthrow the general, was convinced that MacQuerrie had engaged Meme LLC to uncover where in the cyber-world General Boris Illyich Karpov had stashed the code to build the ultimate cyber weapon, one capable of punching through any firewall in its path and penetrating to the heart of America's final defense: the nuclear launch codes.

What MacQuerrie wanted to do with it was not quite clear—sell it, use it as ransom to scramble to the top of the federal heap, what? One thing Fulmer did know was that Meme LLC was Morgana Roy. It was her mind that ran the cadre; without her, Meme LLC was useless. In fact, as of last night, Meme LLC was finished. Its members had been let go, but not before signing a second document of nondisclosure on pain of being charged with treason and, without access to counsel, tried and incarcerated for the rest of their lives. They were little people; they didn't matter. Only Morgana Roy with her brilliant mind and knack for parsing the most mind-bending algorithms mattered. And now she was where she needed to be, with Françoise. Françoise had her orders. She'd soon put Morgana to work.

In the meantime, it behooved Fulmer to bask in the glow of his newfound notoriety. He had attained hero status. In the best vampiric Beltway tradition everyone wanted to include themselves in the halo effect. But he had been around politics too long to believe it would last. As Napoleon famously wrote, "Fame is fleeting, but obscurity is forever." Soon enough, another hero would come to the fore and be anointed by the press, and he would be forgotten, put on the shelf along with all the other sclerotic pols. Not so when he became president. Every day would be like this one, filled with spotlights and sound bites. He'd make damn sure of it.

One of Fulmer's beautifully self-serving traits was his ability to change course as the situation before him demanded. Difficult enough to do in the slippery business world, almost impossible in the sclerotic political arena, where you were eternally enmeshed in a web of back-room deals, bill riders placating insistent interest groups in your states, flexing moral muscles in the service of amassing a nest egg of favors from your enemies across the Congressional aisle. At this point in time, Fulmer had a larger nest egg than even Lyndon Johnson had had in his heyday.

As a result of this ecstatic flurry of activity, Fulmer found himself at the end of each long day both exhausted and exhilarated. And it was at this time, doubtless because of their ability, akin to the Nazi Gestapo's, to strike their target at the precise moment of maximum vulnerability, that the lampreys swam closest to him, looking to attach their suckers to his flesh without being immediately brushed aside.

Such a person was Harry Hornden, a freelance journo of no small note. He was peculiar inasmuch as he had no trouble straddling both the old and the new worlds of journalism. He wrote award-winning think pieces for prestigious monthlies, while also maintaining a snarky and, in Fulmer's opinion, somewhat subversive blog, read by more than a hundred thousand people, which meant, of course, an alarming number of crazies, idiots, cranks, and professional Internet trolls. That the blog appealed to both far-left anarchists and far-right white supremacists was, Fulmer supposed, some sort of victory, though over what he wasn't at all sure, and possibly didn't want to know. Except that Fulmer wanted in on everything, because if you weren't constantly vigilant, you never knew what might pop up and bite you on the ass.

And so it was that on the fifth day after the MacQuerrie shitstorm clogged cyberspace and even, for a time, overloaded the current LeakAGE site, which, for security's sake, changed ISP daily, Fulmer accepted the invitation to have dinner with Harry Hornden. Hornden himself called Fulmer instead of having one of his flunkies do it, which, to Fulmer's way of thinking, showed at least a working knowledge of political protocol.

And yet he wasn't above tweaking the journo's nose when he arrived at the corner table Hornden had booked at The Riggsby, a newish restaurant that had the feel of old Hollywood.

"Harry, how many times did you get called *whore's son* in college?" he said, sliding into his chair opposite the journo.

If Hornden was offended, he gave so sign of it. "That started in high school, actually." He grinned as the drinks arrived. "I took the liberty of ordering us a brace of Sazeracs. Good for you?"

"Always," Fulmer said, clinking the rim of his glass with Hornden's. He was intrigued; the journo hadn't picked one of the top ten power restaurants in D.C., so he must have something unusual on his mind; he didn't seem to care whether he was seen with the new hero or not.

Hornden was a largish, square-shaped individual, long hair still sandy, eyes still bright blue, but turned down at the outer corners, as if he were eternally mournful. He looked like a college athlete gone slightly to seed. He was on the wrong side of forty and as yet unmarried, Fulmer knew, having leafed through the jacket on Hornden his staff had assembled. There wasn't much to it, really, beyond schools attended. The text would have you believe that he was a genuine boy scout. No arrests, no girlfriends, or boyfriends, though he networked like a fiend. But his contacts were just that: contacts and nothing more. In fact, when you came right down to it, there was startlingly little background on him. This, also, Fulmer found intriguing.

"What shall I call you?" the journo said, ignoring the menus the waiter had left on the table.

"Just think of me as the pope," Fulmer replied.

"I hope you're not expecting me to kiss your ring."

"I'll let that pass." Fulmer held up both hands, free of rings of any sort. "Divorced. Twice."

"Condolences."

"My exes would lap that sentiment up with a spoon. As for me..." He shrugged.

The prelims over, they took up their menus as if in response to a call to arms. "I eat here all the time," Hornden said. "Michael Schlow's my favorite chef."

They ordered Caesar salads and the *côte de boeuf* for two, along with a fine bottle of Faust cabernet, an ironic choice if ever there was one, Fulmer thought with a wry smile. Small talk followed, continuing through the meal. Not one word of business, not a single probing question from Hornden. The conversation most closely followed the lines of two old colleagues at a reunion meal.

"I'd prefer to leave the desserts to the pigs and the kids," Hornden said when the main course plates and platters were cleared. "But I'm not averse to an espresso and an after-dinner drink. Averna, perhaps?"

The usual wolf pack of reporters was milling around the restaurant's exterior. A minor frenzy ensued as the two men exited, but Fulmer's driver, with his lineman's body and sharp senses, was expert at keeping the flies away from the meat. Not a word was uttered by either of the principals as they climbed into Fulmer's black SUV, which drove off down New Hampshire Ave, NW, as soon as Max swung into the front passenger seat.

"So," Fulmer said, shooting his cuffs, "what's on your little mind?"

The journo indicated with his chin. "What about the driver and the bodyguard?"

Fulmer pressed a button and sheet of bulletproof glass rose up to seal them off.

"Happy now?"

"Hardly." Hornden seemed to have grown a haunted look. "But then was I ever?"

Fulmer shot him a sideways glance, then looked away out the window. The last thing he was interested in debating was the existence of happiness—a state of mind so ephemeral it did not exist in the physical world. In his opinion, it was something concocted by the wolves of Madison Avenue in order to sell great quantities of useless and expensive crap to people who thought they needed it. Fulmer fervently wished he had come up with that scam. Well, there were always others; that particular magician's hat was bottomless.

"I want in," Hornden said without even a pretense of a preamble. It was go time.

Fulmer was still staring out the window, looking at nothing. His inner gaze was concentrated fully on what was happening as each moment ticked by. "In on what?"

"Whatever it is you have up your sleeve."

Fulmer evinced zero interest. "This is why you asked me to dinner?"

It wasn't a question; no reply was forthcoming.

"I'll say one thing, Hornden. The dinner was excellent. Thank you for that." He waited a beat. "Otherwise, you've wasted my time."

"If you let me in," Hornden said slowly and distinctly, "you get everything."

"I already have everything I want or need."

The journo's tone changed abruptly. "Listen, Mr. Fulmer, I know your fingerprints are all over that last LeakAGE release."

Fulmer grunted. "I don't even know Farreng. Never had any communication with him whatsoever."

"So you used a cutout. Come on, I know you're the origin of the leak that buried MacQuerrie and his team."

Despite his innate caution, Fulmer's head swung around. He tried to stare Hornden down, but the man wasn't giving an inch. "How could you possibly know such a thing?"

"The only way for you to find out is to let me in." Hornden's eyes glinted in the semi-darkness. "Then you get access to every one of my contacts—including the one who knows what you did last week."

The journo's trap had been laid out, baited, and sprung. *Oh, what a lovely night this turned out to be,* Fulmer thought. He took his time running through possible courses of action in his mind. First off, was Hornden bluffing? Had he triggered a lucky shot in the dark? What if it wasn't luck at all? What if he really did have an informant who knew that he was responsible for the leak? Fulmer had been dead careful, which is why he had set up the meet with Françoise in that little city in Sweden he'd already forgotten the name of. But he also knew that no matter how careful you were in this cyber day and electronic age, there was no such thing as airtight security.

He could dismiss Hornden's claims, kick him to the curb, go on about his business, and forget this meeting ever took place. It was certainly a tempting choice. But if Hornden's contact was real, if he, in fact, knew what was transferred at Fulmer's meeting with Françoise, then there was danger lurking in the long grass Fulmer could not afford to ignore. His new status and what it meant for him going forward would be put in jeopardy. The theft of government files was an act of treason, even if it uncovered wrongdoing. And then there was the NSA—those people would crucify him. He closed his eyes, counted to a hundred while watching the pulse of his heart on the inside of his eyelids.

When he opened his eyes, he had made up his mind. All possible decisions had fallen into line, leaving one at the head.

"I want the name of that one contact."

The journo had the grace not to smirk. "Naturally."

"Immediately."

"Just say the word, Mr. Fulmer, and I'll do better than that. I myself will take you to the source."

"Deal," he said, as much to himself as to Harry Hornden.

———

Flames leapt like a living thing from the cheap carpet, up Keyre's arm, turning his clothes to smoke and ash. He appeared oblivious. In fury, he hurled Mala to the floor, stamped hard on her forearm. Bourne heard the crack of a bone and saw the girl's face distort in pain.

Keyre or Mala: the choice was not a difficult one. Reaching down, he grabbed Mala off the burning carpet, slapping out the flames snapping at her bare flesh. His momentary focus on the girl gave Keyre all the opening he needed. Leaping at Bourne, he slammed his whitened knuckles into Bourne's right cheek, over and over. Something gave way an instant before the flames reached Keyre's face, climbing his left cheek. He gave them no mind until their tips cindered his eyelashes. Then he withdrew behind what was now a wall of flames.

Bourne, his face a bloody mess, dragged Mala to her feet. Whirling her around, he picked up the other lantern, threw it at where Keyre had been standing. Then he shoved her out into the night, where her sister was waiting, quaking in terror. The chaos gripping the camp was if anything more intense. The rain still pelted down, thunder rumbling down from the hills that had served as his observation garret. Gathering up both girls, he hurtled through the silvery downpour toward the south end of the camp, back the way he had come.

With a scream, Mala tried to break away, to turn around, return to her tormentor. She was so violent that Bourne was obliged to lift her off her feet, carry her beneath one arm like a sack of squirming snakes while he held Liis with his other hand. Blood sluiced off Bourne's cheek. Beneath the ripped skin, the bone was fractured. As for Mala, she was bleeding in too many places to count. She was holding her broken forearm in her cupped palm.

"I hate you, I hate you, I hate you!" she chanted over and over again, her eyes rolling wildly.

17

KEYRE DID NOT want to look at Bourne; it was the Angelmaker who looked in on him to make certain the doctor was performing his duties to the utmost of his abilities. Not that he had a choice; not that he would jeopardize his life by missing a trick in bringing Bourne back from the dead—or as near to it as you could get without passing over to the other side. The Angelmaker supposed that was why the doctor, whose name was Mure, hyperventilated every time he came near his patient. If she were of another nature, she would have murmured a word or two to calm the physician down. But she would no more think of doing that than she would inhale water in an attempt to breathe.

Keyre was not, however, above asking her, "How is the patient?" every time she emerged from the camp's surgery, no matter how many times a day that happened.

"The same," was her standard reply.

"Still unconscious?"

She nodded. He seemed anxious, and with good reason. He had tasked her with bringing Bourne to him, only not half dead.

"It's been five days." He roamed the sparsely furnished room like a caged tiger. He was naked to the waist; something he only was when they were alone. The same whorls and glyphs that he had incised into her back were weals, raised and hardened, on his own. He had filled out since his first encounter with Bourne. He had the shoulders and upper arms of an American linebacker. His left arm and the side of his face bore the terrible scars, white-blue, twisted like serpents as if with the imprint of each flame separately, of the kerosene fire. His eyelids had no lashes—once burned off, they had never grown back—and the lower lid of one was permanently withered, making that red eye water constantly. The fire, or perhaps the inhalation of smoke, had altered his voice. It was deeper in tone, darker, but at the same time paper thin, like the eerie, wavering notes of a bassoon.

"There should have been some improvement by now."

"There is," she pointed out. "He's no longer at the point of death."

Keyre spun on his heel; the six-sided scar on his chest, the glyph of a Yibir master, seemed to stare at her. "What use if I can't talk to him, tell him . . ." He broke off, wiped a dark hand across his forehead, his eyes, his mouth. The gestures were ritualistic, a Yibir prayer, or invocation, possibly even a spell, the Angelmaker wasn't sure.

"Time is running out," he said, and for the first time she understood fully how isolated he was, how utterly alone, even among his own cadre, even at the heart of this village of gold and diamonds and international legal tender he had built fostering a larger and larger percentage of the illegal arms and human trafficking trade.

He has no one, she thought now. *He's never had anyone.* For the longest time, she had assumed that was what he wanted, what he needed. But she had mistaken him, just as everyone who came in contact with him had mistaken him. And now, for the first time, with the advent of his extreme anxiety, she glimpsed the reason for the violations he perpetrated on the girls, including her. They were the same violations that had been performed on him as a child. He was searching for someone to douse his loneliness, his apartness. Someone like him.

To date, she was the only one who had ever fit the bill, even if it was imperfectly. This was the reason she was so precious to him, why he had fought tooth and nail to bring her back to him, why he always would. Before her he had always put himself first. With her, that had changed.

And yet, what was he to her? Warden, torturer, artist, collaborator in Yibir with her skin and the flesh just below. A totem, in other words. Something of this world and yet not of it. Something Other, for which she had no words, which, apart from the Yibir, did not exist in any vocabulary.

She took a step toward him, felt the heat from his glyphs, as if they were living things. "What do you want me to do?"

"I want him awake."

"Then use your magic." There was a mocking tone to her voice she knew was dangerous, and yet she would not shy away from it. It hit her, all of a moment, that being near Jason emboldened her, just as it had when he'd first invaded the camp.

"I hate you, I hate you, I hate you." Her own words reverberated in her mind. But what had she really meant?

"He responds to you." Keyre seemed to have ignored her comment. "You're the one to push the process."

"But—"

"No buts. You were the one who got him here; no one else could."

He stared her down, and like always, she acquiesced. "As you wish."

"As *we* wish,"—his eyes grew dark—"isn't it?"

She laughed, because she had to laugh—it was the only way forward now. She had taken only one step on Jason's path, and Keyre's uncanny Yibir antennae were already vibrating. She couldn't afford to make that same mistake again.

"Go," he commanded. "Do what has to be done."

"Whatever it takes?"

"Whatever it takes out of you, Angelmaker."

What do you do when you've a brother both older and smarter than you? More clever, too. A chess master who delights in outmaneuvering you?

These were the questions that had plagued Timur Ludmirovich Savasin virtually all his adolescent and adult days. How simple life had been, how happy, before Konstantin revealed his true nature. *Like a strange vampire, drunk on fucked-up nourishment,* Savasin thought, *Konstantin has drained all the enjoyment out of my life.*

From the backseat of his armor-plated Zil, Savasin stared morosely out the tinted window at the garbage-strewn streets, at the pedestrians, backs hunched against the cutting spring wind, shoulders up around their ears, hands jammed deep in the pockets of their flannel overcoats. Except the kids. They smoked, stood splayed on building stoops, hair stiff and glossy, arms tattooed like the evil-looking drawings in Japanese manga, and stared sloe-eyed at Savasin's long, sleek Zil, as if assessing its worth on the black market. Were they armed? Savasin wondered. Did the future belong to them? Not if the Sovereign had anything to say about it. In this, above all, there was no difference between the White Russian czars, the Red Russian Communists, and now the current regime. All used what was to hand, the Cheka, the OGPU, the NKVD, the MGB, the KGB, the FSB. Only the names changed; the orders from the state ministers remained the same.

Savasin, Moscow a blur outside his bulletproof windows, felt a welling up of disgust, not only for his own weakness in failing to find a way to deal with his brother, but for the city, the Federation itself, which was rotting beneath the soles of their expensive foreign-made shoes. The Sovereign would not countenance the truth, and everyone around him—Savasin included—was too terrified of him to clue him in. He still dreamt his dreams of a reconstituted Soviet Union without any thought of how his regime could govern such a far-flung empire when previous regimes hadn't been able to manage it before. Moscow couldn't even manage the Chechens, not to mention the other Muslim minorities, gorging themselves at the table of the worldwide jihad.

The chattering of his mobile fax startled him out of his increasingly gloomy thoughts. Tearing off the single sheet, he read through the text his office had sent. He was ten minutes away. What was this that couldn't wait until he arrived? Then he read it again. What was the Bourne Initiative?

The intel had been siphoned off of the leak inside Dreadnaught. The fax coughed to life again, spewing out a second sheet. This one had only one paragraph of text, according to which the Bourne Initiative was the designation the now disgraced General MacQuerrie had given to his search for a supposed über cyber weapon a cadre of Russian dissidents had been working on under the supervision of—He now had to break off a moment, pressing his thumb and forefinger against his closed lids in a vain attempt to forestall that tension headache rising like a poisonous toadstool from the hellish depths of wherever it hid itself.

His head throbbing, he took his fingers away, stared down at the four words at the end of the single paragraph: General Boris Illyich Karpov.

Savasin's stomach gave a great heave. Had he not been told that all of Karpov's initiatives had been eradicated as completely as if they had never existed? Hadn't that been guaranteed him? And yet, here was evidence that at least the Americans believed this so-called Bourne Initiative was still alive. Savasin briefly consoled himself with the possibility that this could be a masterful piece of disinformation. But that didn't last long.

Apart from Bourne, the Americans knew next to nothing about Karpov. Why would they? The general was a mystery even to his own people, and, really, the Americans were idiots. So rule out disinformation. Which left the worst possible scenario: that Karpov had been running a rogue cyber workshop right under their noses, and Savasin's people had not unearthed it.

Savasin was incensed, as well he should be. He had a brief thought of informing Konstantin, but Savasin was still smarting from the news that the *spetsnaz* team he had taken over was, to a man, dead. And where was Jason Bourne? God alone knew, and surely God wasn't speaking to Savasin. Besides, using the FSB had never been the correct method of winkling out what Karpov was up to. There was a better way. More risky, yes, but, as the Americans said, no pain, no gain.

Savasin had barely been in his office two minutes when Malachev appeared. The fact that he had entered without knocking, that the upper eyelid of his left eye was twitching to beat the band, spoke eloquently of his extreme agitation.

Nevertheless, Savasin, whose brother had put him under a very dark cloud indeed, said, "What?"

Instead of being taken aback by his superior's shortness, Malachev grinned as he placed a mobile phone on Savasin's desk. "A short video just came in from one of your agents."

The first minister's ears pricked up like a hunting dog scenting game. *Your agents.* Like General Karpov, Savasin had his own cadre of agents in the field, each one on a specific assignment. "Is it the *right* agent, Igor Ivanovich?"

Malachev gestured. "See for yourself, sir."

Savasin did. In fact, he watched the surveillance video three times before he lifted his head to look at his second-in-command. Their gazes met like fireworks exploding. "You know what this means, Igor Ivanovich."

"Indeed, I do, sir. When are you going to spring it on him?"

"Oh, no, no, no. Nothing so straightforward." His fingers caressed the mobile's screen. "This calls for something…more elaborate, more byzantine." A crafty smiled curled his lips at their edges. "Igor Ivanovich."

"Sir!"

"An extra thousand in the Cypress bank account of the agent who caught this encounter on video."

"Right away, sir."

When Savasin was alone, he checked the directory on his second mobile, the one he used only sparingly. Then he took his Makarov from his desk drawer, checked that it was loaded, and, rising, grabbed his overcoat and headed for the door.

Back in his Zil, he gave his driver an address in a district a mile away from where he needed to go. The Zil could wait for him there. He wanted no one, not even his driver and bodyguard, to know his destination.

———

When the Angelmaker entered the surgery, she sensed a change in the atmosphere. Nothing she could put a finger on, but something was definitely different. The doctor rose upon her arrival. He gave her a disapproving face when she signaled him to leave her alone with the patient. Clearly, he didn't trust her. She couldn't blame him.

She stepped to the bedside, gazed down at Jason's face in repose. He had regained much of his color but—and here she reached out, moving her fingertips gently over his cheekbone—in this place where, years ago, Keyre had fractured the bone, the skin tone was slightly different, so subtly that if you didn't know what to look for you'd not even notice. But the Angelmaker did know, and she saw that the skin over the repaired bone was the tiniest bit paler, as if it belonged to someone else.

"Jason," she whispered. But all she heard in reply were the rhythmic beeps of the monitor to which he was still hooked up measuring his heart rate, oxygen level, and respiration. She watched the saline and antibiotic solution slowly drip into the vein in the crook of his elbow.

She bent over him, put her lips to his ear. "Jason, it's raining outside," she whispered. "Pouring. Thunder rumbling. You have Liis by the hand, you have me under your arm. We're both bleeding, both hurting. Behind us is the tent. Inside it's burning; the rain hasn't yet penetrated. Liis and I are drowning in a night of chaos. You move quickly and stealthily through the camp, avoiding the armed men. We can barely see what's ahead of us, the rain is so thick. But you know where to go, and I say, 'I hate you, I hate you, I hate you,' over and over and over."

She took his hand in hers. *I've thought about that moment... What did I mean by that?* She squeezed his hand. *I'm desperate to know, but I fear it's a question without an answer.*

And then, to her immense relief, she felt his hand squeeze hers in return.

She raised her head, looked into his face. "Jason, wake up." Then she kissed him, partly open lips pressed ever so gently to his.

Eyes opened.

"Jason."

"Where?"

His throat was dry, and she fed him several slivers of ice from a cooler at his bedside. His eyes continued to study her as he worked the ice around his mouth, helping the shards to melt. She watched him swallow. Such a small reflex, yet she found herself loving it inordinately.

Swallowing the last of the ice water, he said, "Where am I?"

She should have had a ready answer for him, a quick-draw explanation, but she found herself uncharacteristically tongue-tied. This frightened her, though fear was an infrequent visitor at her door.

"Are we still on Skyros?"

This she could answer. "No."

Something changed behind his eyes, a wall forming. She knew that wall, knew once it came down she'd never get past it.

"Tell me this isn't a CIA facility."

This made her laugh. It was a genuine laugh, one that made him laugh as well. *When was the last time I laughed?* she asked herself. At dinner with Jason overlooking the moonstruck Aegean before the *Nym* exploded. Time being more elastic than a rubber band, that seemed like a lifetime ago.

"No. No guards here, Jason."

"Just you and me."

"Not quite."

"No, of course, a medical staff."

She nodded. They were coming closer to a moment she now dreaded.

"A doctor, a nurse. Yes." Best to take baby steps now. "And, of course, the emergency team that worked on you while we were in the air."

His eyes regarded her, revealing nothing. She shuddered inwardly. His coldness, his complete apartness, as if he lived in another dimension she could not touch, let alone share, caused her real pain.

"How far have we come?"

And there it was. The question she could not dodge, and lying to him would only make matters worse. If, now, he didn't trust her, all was surely lost.

"We're in the Horn of Africa."

Again his eyes changed, and she felt a bit of life drain out of her.

"Somalia."

Her lips scarcely moved, her voice so low his head lifted off the pillow in order to hear her. "Yes."

18

I DON'T LIKE IT."

"Which part?" Hornden asked. "I mean it can't be the neighborhood." He gestured at the nighttime street. "We're in Dupont Circle." He grinned. "It can't be this beautiful Georgian townhome we're about to enter. You'd be hard pressed to find a tonier address in all of the District."

Fulmer glanced back at the line of Cadillac Escalades and more prosaic limos lined up at the curb, their drivers reading the paper, drinking coffee out of paper cups, or resting their heads against the seatbacks, catching a few winks.

"None of the drivers are on their mobile phones," Fulmer said.

"A strict policy of the establishment their distinguished guests are only too happy to oblige."

A man of no small stature at sentry duty just inside the front door nodded to Hornden—he was very conspicuously known here—and they passed through the small vestibule, pushing through another door into the two-story entrance hall proper. A huge crystal chandelier hanging from the ceiling threw discreet lights every which way. Directly below it was an inlaid fruitwood table, polished to a glassy finish, on which stood a cut-crystal vase bursting with a professionally arranged profusion of long-stemmed flowers that looked like a fireworks display caught in mid-burst. Behind all of this was a grand staircase, curling upward to the second floor.

As far as Fulmer could tell, all the activity was on the ground floor. To their right was a grand salon, furnished with silk divans and love seats. The warmly lit room was devoid of chairs or proper sofas. To their left was a small salon, a library, in fact, with floor-to-ceiling shelves filled with books, no doubt all erotic classics, Fulmer thought acidly, for he had noted immediately that every single woman in both rooms was young, shapely, gorgeously dressed, magnificently jeweled, and coiffed to a fare-thee-well, confirming his suspicions about what sort of gathering he'd been brought to.

"I think I'll take a pass. My wife and kids are waiting for me, and tomorrow is Sunday; we always go to early worship."

But as he turned, Hornden caught him by the elbow, swung him back around. "No need to be alarmed. You won't be tainted here. On any given night half of the most influential men inside the Beltway unwind with appointments here."

And, indeed, it was true. As Fulmer's gaze moved from the female pulchritude so brazenly on display, it alighted on one representative and senator after another. There were a couple of men from DoD, another from the Pentagon, along with a handful of ex–administration appointees who had maintained or, in some cases, increased, their standing among the District's power brokers.

"You see?" Hornden said, "nothing to be concerned about."

Fulmer put his back to the crowd. "I don't want them to see me here."

As if he hadn't heard Fulmer, Hornden's smile broadened. "And here she comes."

Fulmer turned around to see a willowy woman in a simple black cocktail dress and exceptionally high heels approaching them. She matched Hornden's smile, revealing small, white, even teeth. Unlike the other women in the rooms, she wore only a modicum of greasepaint, as Fulmer called makeup. Her skin was flawless, clear and dewy as a child's. He was rocked by a sudden, unbidden thought: *She has the face of an angel and the eyes of a devil.* Those devilish tawny eyes regarded him with a straightforward interest, mixed with a certain curiosity. They were so light they gave her skin a burnished glow.

"National security advisor Marshall Fulmer, meet Gwyneth Donnelly. She's the genius behind this place."

"Stop it, Harry," she said as she held out a perfectly manicured hand. As Fulmer took it, she said, "Call me Gwen." She cocked her head. "And what shall I call you? Mr. Fulmer? No, too formal. Marsh?" Her laugh was like the tinkling of small bells. "No. I think not, judging by the horrified look on your face."

Fulmer cleared his throat. He felt a bit dizzy. Was it overly warm in here? "Mr. Fulmer will do quite nicely."

Gwyneth nodded. "As you wish." She lifted a well-toned arm. "This way, gentlemen."

She led them through the library, where their passage went totally unremarked. One of the hallmarks of the place was that every one of the clients kept his eyes on the women. Each to his own, self to self, could have been the business's motto.

Thus heartened, Fulmer crossed to the far side of the library. They looked to be heading toward a wall full of books, until Gwyneth released a hidden latch and a door-size section of the wall swung inward. The three of them went through.

Down a wood-paneled corridor, lined on either side by Audubon lithographs of tropical birds, at the end of which was a door Gwyneth opened. The room was capacious, decorated not as an office but as a den. Lamplight only, turned low, gave the place a nestlike aspect. Oversize easy chairs covered in tobacco-colored leather, an abstract pattern rug under their feet, a glass coffee table, a small sofa upholstered in the same material as the chairs, between them a low cocktail table with a shiny, mirrored top. The papered walls were hung with Currier & Ives prints. In all, it felt like stepping back in time, into a men's club from the nineteenth century.

"Please make yourselves comfortable," Gwyneth said as she crossed to a sideboard holding a dozen or so bottles of liquor. "Mr. Fulmer?" she said over her shoulder.

"It's late. Nothing for me."

"Harry? Your usual?"

"Perfect."

Gwyneth brought two glasses, handed one to Hornden, sipped at the other as she settled herself in a chair directly opposite Fulmer.

Is it my imagination, Fulmer asked himself, *or did she take an extra few seconds crossing her legs?* Either way, he glimpsed more of her than he had before. He liked what he saw, but was loathe to admit it to himself. Instead, he stiffened his spine, like a good soldier preparing for inspection.

"Harry," Gwyneth said, a small smile playing about her lips, "be so kind as to remind me why we're here?" She was looking directly at Fulmer, which she had done since she sat down.

"The national security advisor would like you to answer a question," Hornden said.

"Just one?" That smile, less enigmatic, more playful now. "Oh, dear."

Hornden cleared his throat. "Fulmer would like a bit of clarity as to who told you that he was responsible for the latest LeakAGE debacle that brought down General MacQuerrie."

Before Gwyneth could answer, a repeating noise sounded, growing louder, like an approaching police car, causing Fulmer to start, only to relax as Hornden drew out his mobile. Gwyneth's brows knit together.

"Dammit to hell, Harry, how many times do I have to tell you—"

"Sorry, Gwyneth. Mr. Fulmer." He rose. "I have to take this." And he exited the room without another word.

"Honestly," Gwyneth said, clearly irritated, "I don't know why I continue to tolerate that man."

"Perhaps because he's a good source of income," Fulmer said, feeling more in control than he had since he'd stepped foot inside the townhome.

Gwyneth seemed to consider this for a moment while regarding Fulmer over the rim of her glass. That tinkling laugh rose again. "A pity you're not a drinker."

"I didn't say that."

She graced him with a sly curve to her lips. "You know, late at night, when most of the city is asleep, is the best time to drink, the best time for conversation, the best time for reviewing what went before and planning what is to come."

"For that, I require a clear head."

She drained her glass. "Liquor clears my head."

"Then I salute you."

Leaning forward, she put her glass down on the mirrored table, and Fulmer was treated to the sight of her full, creamy breasts. He was startled to realize she wasn't wearing a bra. Didn't every woman wear one?

"Harry warned me that you were no fun," Gwyneth said, straightening up, but none too quickly.

It took more effort than he would have liked to keep his eyes from bugging out. "Harry knows very little about me."

That smile again, returning to the enigmatic. *When did enigmatic become so erotic?* Fulmer asked himself.

"Don't you ever let your hair down, Marshall?"

He was about to correct her, then decided to let it go. He liked her calling him by his Christian name. "I can't afford to."

"Then what good is living?"

Fulmer felt the ground giving way under him again. "Tell me who told you I was responsible for supplying LeakAGE with...I assume it was in the course of pillow talk."

"It's true," Gwyneth said. "Men like to unburden themselves after sex. One intimacy leads quite naturally to another."

"I wouldn't know, but I'll take your word for it." He sat forward. "Who blabbed?"

"Your bodyguard, Max."

"What?" Fulmer winced as if he had been stuck with a needle. "Don't be ridiculous."

"I pride myself on never being ridiculous."

"But it can't be. Max has been with me for years. He's a loyal—"

"Even guard dogs get fed up with their masters, especially if they're treated poorly."

Fulmer was about to deny that he had done any such thing, when he cast his mind back to how dismissive he'd been to Max in Kalmar. But, really, now he thought of it, that was only the tip of the iceberg. The fact was, he treated Max as part of the familiar furniture that was always with him. Except when he needed to be alone. And speaking of Kalmar, who knew what Max had got up to when Fulmer had dismissed him outside the conference room. What if he had followed Fulmer, witnessed his meeting with Françoise? Max leaking his secrets? It was possible, but…

"How d'you know for a fact it was Max?"

"Because it was me he told, directly."

Fulmer's eyes opened wide. His complexion had gone waxen. "Afterward?"

That smile, more knowing than enigmatic now, but even more erotic, if that were possible. "Say this for him, the man's got good taste."

Fulmer slumped in his chair. He passed a hand across his brow.

"Betrayal's a bitch, isn't it, Marshall?"

———

"So you've brought me back." He heard nothing in reply; his mind was clearing. "That was the plan all along, why you reached out to me, why you set up the rendezvous in Skyros."

"The rendezvous saved your life," she reminded him gently. "Understand, Keyre despises the Russians. He's at war with them." She watched for a beat, taking the temperature of his reactions. "It's why he asked me to bring you to him."

"I don't believe you."

Steady on, she told herself. *Even the hint of a lie and all will be lost.* "But you do believe me. I know you do."

He thought about this for some time. His sudden bark of a laugh startled her. "Are you telling me that Keyre wants my help?"

She said nothing; there was nothing to say. The situation spoke for itself.

"This is too rich," Bourne said. "Too damn good. Keyre is asking for a favor."

Still, she said nothing. All at once, even knowing how dire the situation with the Russians had become, she felt ashamed at her part in what could only be called an abduction. She knew now what she had known before, but had doggedly pushed away: her position between these two men was destroying her from the inside out. But perhaps that was her fate. She had endured too many indignities, too many insults to her mind and her body to ever be what she would once have been. She was what she had been made into, a product of inhumanity. Like Jason. In fact, precisely like Jason.

Bourne struggled to sit up, and she pressed a pedal that lifted the top third of the bed until he was in a comfortable position. He gave a glance at the IV in his arm, the beeping monitor's eye. "I want to get out of here."

"Not yet."

"I don't care."

He reached to pull out the IV. She said, "You've been unconscious for six days."

That gave him pause, as she knew it would, brought home to him the severity of his wounds.

"You lost a ton of blood," she added.

He let go of the IV needle, lay back against the pillow, but it was clear he wasn't happy about it. "You haven't said another word about Keyre."

"I have nothing left to say."

"I doubt that. What's he want me to do?"

"That's for him to say."

"But you know." It wasn't a question; he knew her too well. Of course she knew; she was being the good soldier, waiting for the general to deliver the marching orders. "Tell him I won't do it."

"You don't know what it is."

"It doesn't matter."

A certain silence threw up its spikes between them. The air they breathed was stretched with tension.

"Listen to me," the Angelmaker said at length.

"Now you're going to tell me he isn't evil."

"Oh, no, Keyre is evil, all right. But the fact is, he's battling a greater evil."

"By selling arms to fight the infidel."

"A case could be made for that, yes."

Bourne shot her a skeptical look. "And how is he fighting the infidel by trading in human trafficking?" He took her wrist; his voice was a raspy whisper. "You and Liis were part of that."

"There is no good side here," she said tersely. "No angels in residence."

"Tell him I want Giza. Tell him to let your daughter go."

She shook her head sadly. "He'll never agree."

"He must if he—"

"No. Don't you understand? He wouldn't let me go. He would never have made that bargain. You forced it. You're in no condition to force anything." She looked away. "Besides, Giza is his daughter, too."

He let go of her wrist. "You shouldn't have brought me here. You know that."

"I had no choice."

"You were only following orders." His voice mocked her.

Her face fell, all pretense gone. "Only one man has the key." Her voice cracked. "How I wish it were otherwise." She turned away abruptly, ensuring he wouldn't see her eyes well up.

"Mala..."

"It's no good." She shook her head. "There's no exit for me." She took a breath, turned her head back to him. "You're right. I shouldn't have brought you back."

"Then help me get out of here."

"That won't be necessary," said Keyre, filling the open doorway. So rapt were they in their conversation, neither had heard him open the door. "Nor is it desirable."

He stepped toward them, his eyes burning like coals, and involuntarily, the Angelmaker moved back to stand in the semi-darkness beyond the monitor. Her eyes were blank; her expression revealed nothing. It was as if their intimate conversation had never occurred.

"Look at me, Bourne, not her," Keyre said with silken smoothness. "You're with me, until I say otherwise."

———

After almost a week, Morgana was growing used to Kalmar—the breakfasts of thick, sun-yellow yogurt, dark bread spread with Kalles kaviar out of a tube, the strong coffee that seemed to burn its way through the lining of her stomach, the ubiquitous muesli, to which Larry London insisted on adding crushed flax and sesame seeds, the open smoked fish sandwiches for lunch. Even the Proviva, a juice drink said to ensure digestive health, which had nauseated her the first day, was now palatable. But the profusion of fresh berries—many of which, like cloudberries, she had never before heard of—took no getting used to at all. She had also become inured to the sonorous bells from the spires of the Kalmar Cathedral and Lutheran churches ringing at all hours. But she never forgave Larry and Françoise for serving her *filmjölk*—the fermented milk Swedes are so fond of—without first warning her.

"The look on your face," Françoise had cried as she and Larry doubled over in laughter. "Priceless!"

Actually, she did forgive them. How could she not? Françoise had saved her from incarceration—and possibly worse—and Larry treated her like an old friend, trusting her completely. In fact, within days of her arrival, the three of them, having swung easily into a routine, were acting as tightly as a family unit. This was particularly gratifying to Morgana, coming from a broken family with a mother and a sister who wanted no part of her.

But of course this was an integral part of the plan Françoise had devised for Marshall Fulmer. Or was it for Gora Maslov? Well, in this case it was for both, though only her brother was aware of it. There was something about working both ends of the block that appealed powerfully to her—a woman brought up with a strong, willful father and brother, who, consciously or not, undercut her at every turn. Their bullying necessitated her building a series of personae, strong as brick-and-mortar edifices, to hide her true identity. This process had begun so early in her life and gone on for so long that she had become lost behind the walls she had erected, until she no longer knew who she really was. Nor did she particularly want to know. This could be viewed as a flaw in her character, perhaps even a weakness. But since no one had yet breached her defenses, certainly not Gora, whose personality dictated that he be attuned to taking advantage of situations rather than people, it was hardly a danger.

Morgana's routine consisted of spending days with Larry London and evenings with Françoise—dinner once or twice with both of them. Larry was smooth without being obvious about it; he knew how to draw her out, to set her at ease. It was a gift, a great one at that.

"You're a photographer," she said the first day they were together. "Why are you interested in cyber-sleuthing?"

"Ah, well," Larry London said. "You have me there."

They were sitting next to each other in what passed for the business center of her hotel, a small windowless room bare apart from task chairs, a fax, and a pair of computer terminals on an unsecured wi-fi so riddled with malware and keystroke loggers Larry wouldn't touch them with a six-foot Cossack. Guests came and went, checking email, logging into their airline accounts, opening themselves up to credit card or identity theft.

"Morgana . . . Françoise said I could trust you with a secret. Is she right?"

"Françoise and I know each other quite well."

A slow smile crossed his face. "Very well, then." He scooted his task chair closer to hers, looked over his right shoulder, then his left, leaned in and whispered: "My job as a freelance photographer is a cover."

She frowned. "A well-documented one."

"What good would a cover be if it weren't? It was created by the best professionals." Now he drew back, his expression one of sudden doubt.

Morgana leaned toward him to maintain their close proximity. "What is it?"

"I'm not sure this is a good idea."

"Why not? I thought you said you trusted me."

He reflected a moment, then nodded. "You're right." His voice lowered even further. "Actually, I work for the Company."

Of course she knew that meant the CIA; the putative enemy of the NSA. The two agencies were eternally at odds on how to gather intel.

He allowed her time to digest this bit of information.

"Honestly . . ." she began.

"Yes?"

"Any American agency antagonistic to the NSA is okay with me."

He laughed softly. "Françoise said you'd say that."

"Did she really."

"Well, something like it, anyway." He opened up his laptop, booted it up, then opened an app that provided him with a military-level shield, a bogus ISP that could not be traced. "Okay," he said, rubbing his hands together. "Let's get the ball rolling."

And that's how, five days ago, Morgana's hunt for the initiative continued. Of course, Morgana was under the impression that she was schooling Larry London in looking for other pieces of the cyber weapon on the dark web, and in a sense that was correct. But it was also correct that he was schooling her, in the sense of getting her used to working with him beside her.

In the evenings, Françoise played the perfect friend—empathetic, solicitous, strong of opinion and the strength to fight adversity.

"We can't expect to succeed," she said over their late supper in a small, ramshackle seafood house near the water, "until we've failed at least once." She extracted a bit of pink langoustine flesh with the tines of her tiny fork. "It's a cliché, I know, but in my experience it's true enough."

"It's happened to you?" Morgana cleared away a piece of shell to get at more of her langoustine's delicious meat. "Failure, I mean."

Françoise laughed shortly. "More than once." Playing Morgana's friend wasn't difficult. For one thing, they had been friends for years, having met in Paris, at the Musée D'Orsay, admiring Édouard Manet's *Le Déjeuner sur l'Herbe*, and, after discussing the painting in the most positive terms, spending the next forty minutes strolling through the museum. Thereafter, they repaired to lunch, where, over salads niçoise and a bottle of a commendable Sémillon, she had presented herself as a business advisor to the rich and famous. At the end of four hours together, they had struck up a lasting friendship. For another, Françoise genuinely liked Morgana. She was smart and quick; Françoise found her naïveté charming. That Françoise was at some point able to use that naïveté to her advantage was an unexpected bonus. If she felt any remorse at using her friends, it was pushed to the sidelines, where it languished unnoticed in the shadows.

"Give me an example," Morgana said.

Françoise considered for a moment, tapping her lips ruminatively with a forefinger. "*Bien,* well, to be honest, I failed as a sister. My brother is a shit." All true. "But as the better person I should have found a way to maintain a relationship with him." Like hell. Also, a lie. But she was considering Morgana's sister, who had cut Morgana off because Morgana did not want to revisit the pain her parents' bitter divorce had caused her. "He, well, you know, he made life impossible for me, so..." Her hand lightly fluttered. "Pffft!"

"I'm sorry."

Françoise smiled. "Don't be. I'm not."

Morgana, abandoning her langoustine for the moment, leaned forward. "You said that you had more than one failure."

"Yes, well, but I'd rather not—"

"Oh, come on. You know all my secrets."

"Not *all* your secrets, surely."

Morgana reached out, squeezed Françoise's hand. "Besides, what are friends for?"

Françoise gave a little chortle. "Since you put it that way." She took a breath. "I made a mistake with Larry."

"Larry London?"

"The very same." Françoise put down her fork. "When we met I fucked up. I came on like an army tank, but that was the wrong approach. It took me six months to mend that particular fence. But the point is I learned, from both the failures. You can't use the same strategy with everyone. Assessing the playing field before deciding on how to act is essential."

"That sounds so cold, so clinical." Morgana's eyes narrowed. "Is that what you did with me?"

"What, no. Oh, my God, Ana, no." Ana and Franny were their secret names for each other, never to be used when there were others around. "I was speaking of business, not friendship. My God, if I was reduced to doing that with friends—with you, of all people—I'd be on antidepressants."

Morgana, with her hand still on Françoise's, turned her friend's hand over, tapped the blue vein on the delicate flesh of the inside. "I'm glad to hear that."

Françoise's sudden laugh was like the sun breaking through clouds. "Speaking of dear old Larry, how's your search coming? Is he being helpful?"

"Larry's been a help." Morgana withdrew her hand, set it in her lap, as if embarrassed by its intimate gesture. "But I still don't know where the locus is."

Françoise frowned. "The piece is still online."

"Yes, and another just showed up, but it isn't helping me much. It's like a jigsaw puzzle with no clues."

"Then we've got to redouble our efforts to find it."

"Larry and I already agreed on that. We've split up assignments. While I'm working on decoding the algorithm, he's using his sources worldwide to track the locus."

She smiled. "He's closer than I am. In fact, he's very close, which is good because this algorithm is like nothing I've ever encountered before."

"Yes, but we still have no idea when it's scheduled to be deployed."

Morgana took a breath, let it out slowly. "Actually, we do now. One thing I've been able to decipher is that the new algorithm has a built-in Day Zero trigger."

"What does that mean?"

"Ten days from today, the cyber weapon will be deployed, and the American president's nuclear codes will be vulnerable. Bourne or whoever is directing the team will be able to set off a catastrophic event of unprecedented proportions."

"Armageddon."

Morgana nodded. "And as it stands right now, nothing will be able to stop it."

19

KEYRE, THERE IS no way I'm doing anything for you."

"No hasty decisions, Bourne."

"Nothing hasty about this one."

Keyre smiled like an uncle indulging a willful and ignorant adolescent. The two men were sitting in facing rattan chairs with cushions of a tribal pattern typical of coastal Somalia. Between them was a wooden table carved in the intricate Arabic style. On it was a beaten bronze tray on which sat a large pot of tea, two handleless cups, three small plates, one each of dried dates, hummus, and wedges of unleavened bread. A solid concrete floor, rather than beaten earth, beneath their feet, solid walls, lamps lit by electricity provided by a pair of large generators. The room was a far cry from the soiled tents of his first visit.

The Angelmaker stood at some remove. Beside her was a small table on which was placed a buff-colored folder and an army or marine surplus walkie-talkie. She inhabited a spot precisely between the two men, as if in an effort to appear neutral, which Bourne knew perfectly well was an illusion, tempting though it might be to consider.

"I must have missed the line of tanning heads on my way in," Bourne said now.

Keyre kept his smile in place. "Beheadings are part of the past." He gestured with an open hand. "You should eat. You need to build up your strength."

Bourne ignored him, lifted his head slightly, nostrils dilated. "The air smells fresher, too. Is target practice on headless corpses a thing of the past, too?"

Keyre's smile was stretched now, a veneer that Bourne was determined to crack.

"What we have here now is a business," Keyre said. "We even have a CFO."

"A chief financial officer," Bourne echoed. "What's next, a listing on the stock exchange?"

"A lucrative idea." Keyre reached for a date, held it on the tips of his fingers and thumb. "But I'm afraid it's still imperative we fly under the radar."

Bourne grunted. "I can imagine."

At this point, the Angelmaker stepped forward, slathered a triangle of bread with hummus, handed it to Bourne. He waited a moment before taking it. Their eyes met for a moment before he popped it in his mouth, chewed slowly. Keyre ignored her as she returned to the spot of her vigil.

"So . . ." The date disappeared into Keyre's mouth. He ate it, pit and all. "Time to get down to business."

Bourne stared at him. "We have no business."

"So you say." Keyre's hands, fingers intertwined, lay in his lap, as if to emphasize his calm. "But the fact is, there is business between us— business you *will* want to discuss."

Leaning forward, Bourne dipped a triangle of bread into the hummus, ate it as slowly as the first, while regarding Keyre with a neutral expression.

Keyre now lifted a hand as if he were carrying a tray. This must have been a signal; the Angelmaker turned, took the folder off the table and placed it in his hand before returning once again to her original position. He left it there, for a long moment, then plucked it off with his other hand. Opening it, he held up an eight-by-ten head shot, the features flattened, indicating it was taken with a long telephoto lens.

"This man is known to you."

It was not a question, and Bourne didn't take it as such. "Is he known to you?"

At last the tiniest crack appeared in Keyre's carefully constructed façade. "Gora." He could not keep the disgust out of his voice.

"Yegor Maslov, known to his friends as Gora. Son of the late Dimitri Maslov, head of the Kazanskaya."

"The fucking Russian mafia, yes. A thorn in both our sides."

"General Karpov took care of Dimitri."

Keyre took another date. "You know Gora has taken his father's place at the summit of the Kazanskaya."

"I do."

Plucking another eight-by-ten from the folder, he handed it over. This one was not a head shot. It showed a young woman from the waist up. She was dark-haired, light-eyed, an intense expression on her face as she turned a three-quarter profile toward the telephoto lens. She was very beautiful, in an aggressive, almost warlike manner.

"How about her?" Keyre said. "Also familiar?"

As Bourne looked from the photo to Keyre, the ghost of a smile could be seen in the Somalian's expression. Bourne did not know the young woman, but he sensed an unpleasant surprise coming.

"No?" Keyre cocked his head. "The woman you can't identify, Bourne, is none other than Alyosha Orlova, Dimitri's illegitimate daughter, Gora's half sister. She refused to take her father's name, or he forbade her. Possibly both. They had a naturally contentious relationship, but it was nothing compared to the one Dimitri had with Alyosha's mother, Ekaterina Orlova."

"So Alyosha, as well as Gora, has come to your attention."

Keyre delivered the briefest of grins. "The Maslov clan holds intense interest for me—as it does for you, Bourne. You see, we do have business to discuss."

"No, we—"

"Business beneficial to both of us."

"Keyre, I cannot imagine how the stars could be aligned to allow that to happen."

"And yet they are aligned in this curious pattern, Bourne. Of this you can be assured."

"Tell me, then."

Keyre nodded. "As you wish." He took back the photo of Alyosha Orlova, ran his fingertips over the glossy surface of her features. "There is something about a man on his knees that stirs my very heart," he began in a softer, more contemplative tone. "It's the white flag, you see. The white flag stinks of fear. I enjoy inhaling its scent, savoring its taste before I put a match to it and set it afire."

Silence in the room. They could all have been deep within the bowels of the Lubyanka prison for all that the outside world made itself known. Bourne's eyes were locked with Keyre's.

"I sense how much you hate me, Bourne. I can feel it on my skin like an army of ants."

"Pleasure comes in such odd packages these days."

Keyre delivered a curious smile. "Two weeks ago, thirteen men knelt not a thousand yards from where we sit. I put a bullet in the head of each of them, one by one, going down the line. Then my men buried them. But they weren't erased; the memory of them lingers like the taste of spoiled food in the mouth."

"That's because these thirteen men were Somalians co-opted by the Russians. And not any Russians, mind you." Now he held up both photos, Gora Maslov in his right hand, Alyosha Orlova in his left hand.

"Why would Gora and Alyosha want to attack you?"

"That's the question, isn't it?" Keyre's eyes gleamed eerily. "And it's made more curious considering I have a highly lucrative business arrangement with Gora."

"He's turned on you."

Keyre rustled the photo in his left hand. "Let's not forget about Alyosha. To do so would be a grave error in judgment."

"Maybe she persuaded him to seek a better deal elsewhere."

"Half right, Bourne. You see, the thirteen didn't set out to attack me. They infiltrated my cadre."

"They were looking for something you have."

"Also half right. Because I don't have what they were sent to fetch. I believe it was Alyosha who persuaded her brother—excuse me, *half brother*—to risk his business arrangement with me to steal this item."

"This item must be highly prized."

"Oh, it is, Bourne. It's so highly prized that everyone who knows of its existence—a handful of people, but that's more than enough to ensure extreme danger, I assure you—wants it. They would do anything and everything to get their hands on it."

Out of the corner of his eye, Bourne saw the Angelmaker stir uneasily. "And what exactly is this item?" he asked.

"I've no idea what it was originally called—possibly its only designation was a letter-number combination. But that's of no import. It's come to be known as the Bourne Initiative."

Bourne gave a start. "What?"

Keyre continued as if he hadn't heard Bourne's interjection. "The name given it by someone high up in a division of the American NSA known as Dreadnaught."

"I've never heard of Dreadnaught."

"Of course you'd say that," Keyre said silkily.

"And I have no idea why an *Initiative*—whatever that might be—would be named after me."

"That's easy enough to answer," the Angelmaker said, stepping forward. "The initiative was the brainchild of your late friend, General Boris Illyich Karpov."

Keyre's eyes narrowed. "You *were* good friends, weren't you, Bourne. *Close* friends."

"What of it?"

"Karpov willed you his boat."

"Again."

Keyre placed the photos back in the folder. "Did it ever occur to you that the Americans who were sent after you wanted to make sure that your friend's boat was destroyed?"

Bourne sat very still. Frankly, in the crisis of the moment, it hadn't occurred to him. Now he kicked himself for not considering the possibility. "There was nothing on the boat," he said flatly. "I searched it from stem to stern."

"What were you looking for?" Keyre asked.

Bourne shrugged.

"You see, there you have it." Keyre gestured for Bourne to continue eating. He poured him more tea. "You had no idea what you were looking for." He tilted his head. "But I must ask you: Why did you search Karpov's boat in the first place?"

Bourne, eating his hummus, said nothing at all.

Keyre supplied the answer. "Because you knew your friend better than anyone. You suspected he left something for you other than the boat itself." Keyre did not smirk, or even smile. His expression was perfectly serious, as befitted one businessman talking to another. "Your friend was like that, wasn't he?"

"You don't know anything about Boris."

"Enough, Bourne. I know enough."

"Tell me about him, then."

Keyre shook his head. "This is not the correct trajectory of this meeting."

Bourne laughed. "*Meeting?* Interesting choice of words."

Keyre gave him a pained smile, the smallest one Bourne had ever seen. "Back to the Bourne Initiative."

"Which doesn't exist."

"Oh, it exists all right," Keyre said.

"In the minds of very small men."

Keyre lifted a forefinger, shaking it. "You know, Bourne, I never realized you had a sense of humor."

"Frankly, I'm surprised you're able to recognize it."

"The Bourne Initiative." Keyre held up a hand. "Please. It does exist. It's a cyber initiative cooked up by General Karpov. No, don't interrupt. The reason the very small circle of people who know about it either want it or want to destroy it is because it's a cyber weapon capable of penetrating the American government's many firewalls and malware-killers to open up the codes to the country's nuclear arsenal." He sat back with the kind of self-satisfied air that made him insufferable. "What do you think of that, Bourne?"

"I think it's bullshit," Bourne said. "In fact, I know it is." He watched Keyre's self-satisfaction slowly slink away into the shadows at their feet. "Boris would never, under any circumstance, countenance creating such a cyber weapon."

"So everyone is wrong except you."

"That's right."

"I wonder. Would you stake your life on it, Bourne?"

"I would, indeed."

"Well, get ready, because that's precisely what you're going to have to do."

20

AFTER A BRIEF stop at a shop in the Arbat, Savasin's driver drew the Zil to the curb at the address Savasin had given him, a gray, nondescript office building in a gray, nondescript *raion*, as Moscow's districts were called. Ordering the Zil to return in three hours, Savasin exited the car, passed inside the building, which smelled of stale sweat and fear, and called a *bombila*, one of the city's fleet of taxis so run-down they deserved the nickname, bomb.

Twenty minutes later, he was deposited in Kapotnya, twelve miles southeast of the center of Moscow, hard up against the MKAD, the Moscow ring road. Savasin was a native Muscovite. Still and all, there were any number of *raions*—especially the seedier ones, where trash lined the streets, the gutters stank of urine, and where in the brutal winters, people froze to death huddled in shallow doorways and beneath parked cars—he had no clear knowledge of, let alone had visited. Kapotnya was one such *raion*—the worst in Moscow, in fact.

It was a crime- and drug-infested district, overstuffed with migrants best ignored by the government. Twenty-seven thousand souls were crammed into a shit-box of crumbling low-rise brick buildings dating back to the fifties and seventies, overshadowed by a monstrous oil processing plant. Not a metro station nor a municipal bus route dared come anywhere near Kapotnya. As a result, the streets and surrounding roads were clogged around the clock with vehicles spewing diesel particulates into the already oil-polluted atmosphere.

After only twenty seconds in the famously foul air, Savasin started coughing. Another twenty and his eyes began to burn, thirty more and his throat felt raw. Pulling a woolen scarf out of the pocket of his overcoat, he wrapped it around the lower half of his face, as if he were passing through a fire. Not much help, but it was something. In his right hand he carried his loaded Makarov, in his left the bottle of a green liqueur he had purchased in the Arbat. He might have been safer on the streets if he had chosen to wear his military greatcoat with the general's shoulder boards, but that surely would be a mistake at his destination. As for his Makarov, his mood, pressing hard against the border of giddiness, gave way to a pressing desire to fire it. And just like that, as if he'd conjured it out of thin air, an opportunity reared its head four and a half blocks from where the *bombila* had dropped him. Three young toughs hanging out across the street with nothing to do but drink beer, smoke cigarettes, show off their tattoos, and generally act like cartoon versions of Mick Jagger perked up at his approach. They called to him in the nastiest manner possible. *Wait,* he thought. *Let them come to you.* When he ignored them, one of them smashed his beer bottle on the stoop, swinging the jagged-edged remainder menacingly. Another slipped out a switchblade. Spewing a chain of epithets his way, each one more obscene than the last, they crossed the street, slipping between vehicles, heading directly for him. Savasin raised his Makarov and shot the leading tough through the heart. He went down between two cars stalled in the traffic. His mates, giving Savasin looks of shock, pulled at their friend as if he were a slab of meat, hurriedly carting him off without either a word or a backward glance.

Savasin continued on his way as if nothing untoward had occurred. Irresolute in the offices of the Kremlin and Moscow Center, he was by every measure assured on the streets of the city. The simple fact was that he wasn't cut out for bureaucratic work, which he found dull and extraordinarily tedious. He harbored the suspicion that the Sovereign had appointed him to the post of first minister for the sole reason of blocking Konstantin from the post. Konstantin, whose mind, like that of the fictional Mycroft Holmes, was perfectly suited to bureaucratic brilliance, and so considered an ally. The Sovereign had already been down a treacherous road with Boris Karpov, too smart by half; he wasn't going to make the same mistake twice. The Sovereign couldn't care less that Savasin muddled along. In fact, it suited him, since the first minister was neither expected nor allowed to administer any important decisions. Any advice he was foolish enough to offer the Sovereign was duly ignored with a smile of such condescension it set Savasin's teeth on edge. So he stopped, which was the point.

The first minister proceeded on, light of heart and, for the first time in a long while, optimistic about his future. The sky above Kapotnya, what he could make out, anyway, was a sickly, sulfurous yellow. Visibility was low. Neither sun nor cloud could be seen. Fire and black smoke plumed from the multiple stacks of the oil plant. It was like being inside a vast man-made dome, which, in a sense, was true enough.

Everyone he passed had scarves wrapped around their noses and mouths. They scurried past him, shoulders hunched, eyes on the ground. Occasionally car horns blared, as if that would get the traffic moving.

After trekking for fifteen minutes through this mini hell, he came to the street he needed, turned left into what would, in brighter parts of the city, be an alleyway. Here, it was a side street. Concrete buildings in the Brutalist Soviet style shouldered the alley into insignificance. The street stank of garbage and human waste. A dead dog had been kicked to the curb. It lay there stiff as a board, its fur, what was left of it, standing up like porcupine quills.

That's me. A dead dog in the Kremlin gutter, Savasin thought in an unseemly spasm of self-pity. And then in another spasm, this time of glee: *At least, it was me.*

No numbers here—he had to count the buildings, fifth on the left, just before the street elbowed to the left. When he pulled the door open, he was attacked by a stench so vile he nearly vomited. He crossed the vestibule as quickly as he was able, then vaulted up the steep staircase. He wished he had had the foresight to bring gloves. The sounds echoing through the stairwell were more suited to a hospital ER or, on the third floor, an insane asylum: the unnerving noises of the human mind at the breaking point and beyond.

It was as if as he rose he was really descending into the pit of hell. But at last he came to the fourth and final floor, and it was like stepping from a mountain of trash into a serene garden. By some quirk of the building's acoustics, not a sound traveled up from below. Here, it was quiet, here the air was fresh and clean. This was beyond his ken until he saw that the hallway was filled with a profusion of plants and flowers in huge stone pots, breathing in carbon dioxide, breathing out oxygen. Depending from the entire length of the ceiling was a line of grow lights, artificial suns that bathed the foliage in warmth and energy.

A mountain appeared through the thickets, seemed to be heading in Savasin's direction. He came very fast—so fast, in fact, that he plucked the Makarov out of Savasin's hand before he had a chance to react. Not that he had any intention of shooting someone in here.

"You," the mountain said. He was a massive creature with a chest like a bull, legs like tree trunks, and arms like anacondas. His brow was low, his eyes small, his demeanor intimidating. "You," he repeated.

"Timur Ludmirovich."

"More," the mountain rumbled. He spoke Russian as a peasant would. He definitely wasn't a Muscovite.

"Savasin. Timur Ludmirovich Savasin."

The mountain regarded him, and for that moment Savasin felt as a field mouse must feel as an eagle swoops down on him from on high.

"Stay."

Savasin thought of the dog, dead and stiff in the gutter, as he watched the creature turn on his heel, disappear through a double door in the center of the hallway—a magnificently turned wooden door banded in iron—visible now through the foliage that was shockingly out of place in this dismal dump. With a start, Savasin noted the eagle bas-relief, wings spread, talons to the fore, in the center of each door. And now it occurred to him that the name Orlova was derived from the Russian word for eagle.

Moments ticked by. Savasin lifted the bottle, reread the label, hoping he'd brought the right gift. Time passed without any sense of whether he would gain the interview he sought or would be turned away by the movable mountain.

Finally, one of the eagle doors opened, and the frame filled with the gargantuan creature. He stared balefully at Savasin out of his raisin eyes. Then he raised a hand. Savasin's Makarov looked like a child's toy in his fist. The mountain gestured with the barrel of Savasin's own handgun, beckoning him on.

Unlike the rest of the dank, murky building, the interior of the apartment was awash in light. His gaze traveled upward to the immense skylight. Two clusters of halogen lamps hung from the ceiling like chandeliers. They were a corrective, their blazing illumination draining the natural light of its sulfurous hue. The apartment had been carved out of the entire top floor. Open doorways led left and right, but the vast space into which the mountain led him was the entire apartment's raison d'être. It was filled with yet more foliage, traveler's palms chief among them. On either side of the large, open room rose a pair of fruit trees, lemon on the right, fig on the left. An old man—apparently a gardener—was busy at the fig tree, pruning and fussing. He ignored the guest completely, as did the mountain, now that Savasin had been granted permission to enter the inner sanctum. In fact, the massive man was in the ungainly process of seating himself on a stoutly reinforced bench in front of a baby grand piano. His massive hands hovered over the keyboard, then struck the first chords of Maurice Ravel's heartbreakingly beautiful "Pavane for a Dead Princess."

Astonished, Savasin stood transfixed as the mountain played the

piece with consummate skill and a tenderness impossible to comprehend coming from such a hulking creature.

"I see you've met Cerberus."

At the sound of the smoky voice, Savasin tore himself away from the
transfixing scene and turned his attention to the woman who, having
stepped from behind a tree, now planted herself before a large artist's
easel. She held a brush in one hand, a palette in the other. Beside her
was a paint-spattered stepladder whose top was an open case filled with
tubes of oil paint and a can of turpentine, the time-tested old-school
thinner of oils.

Even in her mid-fifties Ekaterina Orlova was a beautiful woman—
pale, oval face, eyes of a blue akin to the deepest ocean, an aggressive
nose, and wide lips, which were now turned up in an ironic smile.

"Timur Ludmirovich. Shall I say it's good to see you? Perhaps it is,
perhaps it isn't." She turned to regard the half-finished painting of a
swimmer half submerged in what?—a pool, the sea? It was impossible
to tell. Possibly that was the point. The swimmer was in her element
and yet out of sight of land.

"The painting is lovely," Savasin said, partly because he meant it,
partly because he could think of nothing else to say. He had come all
this way, fended off an attack, risen through the stench of an abattoir,
and now what? He had conveniently forgotten how intimidating Ekaterina Orlova was. But perhaps that had been deliberate.

The artist, putting brush to canvas, said, "Tell me, Timur Ludmirovich, why have you come?" She wore a smock that once had been
light-blue but now displayed all the colors of the rainbow, and some in
between.

Savasin lifted the bottle. "I brought you a present."

She laughed, a guttural, utterly erotic sound that came from deep in
her throat. She turned. "Now I know you came to ask a favor."

"Just to talk," Savasin said, a touch too hastily.

That laugh again, making him feel things best not spoken of in the
area below his belt. She set her brush in a smeared jar of colorless liquid

and set the palette on the top of the stepladder. Then she crossed to the piano, where the mountain had placed Savasin's Makarov. Expertly, she ejected the magazine, checked the number of bullets. Then she sniffed the business end. "Whom did you shoot?"

"No one of import."

She smiled, her bared teeth like knives. "Your situation must be very, very bad for you to brave coming here, Timur Ludmirovich."

"Well, I suppose it is."

"Boris is dead."

Her voice had abruptly turned cold as ice, sending a shiver down his spine. Plus, she still held the Makarov.

"'The center cannot hold. The blood-dimmed tide is loosed. The best lack all conviction, while the worst are full of passionate intensity.'"

She was quoting Yeats, though Savasin was too ignorant to know it. Never mind, the words sent another, deeper chill through him.

"I'm afraid you're right, Ekaterina."

"You did nothing to save him." Her eyes flashed like warning lights. "You who had the means to stop—"

"No one could have stopped his murder." This he knew beyond a shadow of a doubt. "Not all his bodyguards, not all the FSB in attendance. Not even his best friend, Jason Bourne."

At Bourne's name, Ekaterina relinquished the icy rage with which she had been temporarily gripped. Unbuttoning the smock, she set it and the Makarov aside. She was wearing a pearl-colored silk blouse and black, wide-legged trousers of the same luscious material. Ekaterina had always known how to dress well. "Let me see."

Savasin handed over the bottle of absinthe. Ekaterina, having read the label, said, "How on earth did you get this, Timur Ludmirovich? Not at GUM, I'll warrant." She meant the central department store on Dzerzhinsky Square.

"The same avenue where you buy your clothes. A private source."

She nodded in acceptance. "Come," she said, indicating a curved sofa clad in deep-purple velvet.

As if being directed by telepathy, the mountain ceased his playing, rose, and brought to the table in front of the sofa a pair of cut-glass cordial glasses that looked very old and very expensive. Having completed this task, he returned to the baby grand, taking up the reins of another Ravel piano piece, not nearly as sad as the first.

Savasin watched Ekaterina put the bottle aside, pour out glasses of vodka. The toast and draining of the vodka having been accomplished with the minimum of pomp, Savasin set down his glass and turned to his hostess.

"Ekaterina," he said, "I've come to talk to you about Alyosha, your daughter."

21

THERE FOLLOWED A peculiar silence, the kind found in a grave-yard at night. It was broken by a laugh from Keyre, like the trumpet of an elephant. He slapped his knee in mirth; he was grinning from ear to ear.

"You see, my dear Angelmaker, I was right all along. The story put about that the Bourne Initiative is the ultimate cyber weapon is so much smoke. And here before us is the only living human being who can confirm my suspicion. Which he has done."

He leaned forward abruptly, elbows parked on his knobby knees. "Here is my second gift to you, Bourne. I've cleared up—well, one essential matter, anyway—why the Americans and the Russians are hot on your trail."

"Mala could have told me all this back on Skyros," Bourne pointed out.

"True enough." Keyre spread his hands. "But where's the fun in that?" He wagged his forefinger again. "You and I both know that we aren't done with each other; we were fated to meet again. But who could have imagined it would be under circumstances where we're in the star-crossed position to help each other."

Bourne turned to the Angelmaker. "I'd like something more substantial to eat."

She took up the walkie-talkie on the table, spoke into it briefly. No one spoke another word until one of Keyre's people arrived with a tray on which sat a bowl of stew and a round of unleavened bread with which to eat it.

Bourne took the bowl off the tray as it was being set down, sniffed it.

"It's goat, Bourne," Keyre said with a wry smile. "You won't find a morsel of human flesh in there."

As Bourne ripped off a piece of bread, scooped up the stew, and began to eat, Keyre said, "So here, in a nutshell, is what we are dealing with: you and I are both under attack because of something your friend, Karpov, dreamed up. Neither of us know what it is, let alone have possession of it. But we won't have any peace until we find out what the general was up to." He steepled his long, spidery fingers. "I think we agree on that, yes?"

Bourne looked up into Keyre's face, swallowed. "With your farflung network I would think it should be easy enough for you to find out."

"Normally that would be the case, more or less." Keyre sighed. "But these are not normal times, Bourne. Even I cannot infiltrate an American NSA black site."

Bourne stopped eating, put the bowl aside. "What are you talking about?"

"The gist of it is this: it was General MacQuerrie, the head of Dreadnaught, who dubbed this mysterious data the Bourne Initiative. He set one of his private people, Morgana Roy, by all accounts a cyber genius, to the task of decoding the data. The problem is we only have MacQuerrie's word for what this data is. Was he telling Roy the truth? We can't ask her because she's disappeared. Was he lying, and, if so, for what reason? No one knows the answer to that but MacQuerrie himself, and he's been arrested, due to a damning server leak disseminated by LeakAGE while you were in dreamland.

"So. It seems to me that we have only one way forward. We have to penetrate the NSA black site where MacQuerrie is being held and interrogate him."

Bourne gave a harsh laugh. "It's you who's in dreamland, Keyre."

Once again, Keyre chose to ignore Bourne's comment. "Only one man on earth can get to MacQuerrie, interrogate him, and get out alive. That's you, Bourne. The chameleon."

"Even I—"

"My people have discovered where he's being held, so part of your job has been done for you." Keyre sat forward. "Bourne, there's no other way out for us; much as you despise me, much as you want to see me dead, you know this to be true."

Bourne did. Much as he hated to admit it, there was a lot to be said for Keyre's plan. He kept his gaze fixed steadily on the Somalian. He did not look at the Angelmaker; did not want to see what she held in her eyes for him. There was nothing he wanted more than to be wherever Sara was, even if it wasn't a sun-splashed beach in Bali or Thailand. He missed her with an ache that penetrated to the very marrow of his bones. But they had realized that becoming attached in that way was a liability, too much danger for them both. In their line of business, love was the ultimate liability. Now that it had happened to them, it was better to live in denial than to allow the perilous truth to overwhelm them. But rationality did not diminish Bourne's ache for her.

But he wasn't with Sara, didn't even know where in the world she was. He was here, the present danger to him was acute, and a solution, though extremely treacherous, had been presented to him.

"Bourne, can you come up with an alternative?" Keyre prompted. When Bourne said nothing, he nodded, continuing, "I and my people will provide transportation and all the support you might need."

"I work alone."

"So I've heard."

Bourne rose, stretched his legs. He had already begun strenuous workouts. "Where is the NSA holding MacQuerrie?"

Keyre rose, studied Bourne for a moment. "Seriously, you won't believe it when I tell you."

———————

"My daughter?" Ekaterina had gone very still. "What have you to do with Alyoshka?" She jumped up, her agitation setting Cerberus into motion, like the mechanical creature of a clock about to chime the hour. "Do you have her in custody on some trumped-up charge? That's the Sovereign's way, after all."

Savasin held up his hands, palms outward, both to placate Ekaterina and to ward off an anticipated blow from Cerberus. "Calm yourself. Nothing of the sort has happened. Your Alyosha is as free as a bird."

Ekaterina made a gesture. Cerberus came to an immediate halt but, Savasin observed with no little trepidation, did not return to his place at the piano. He maintained his position, his baleful glare striking the first minister like a series of hammer blows, causing him to rise off the sensuously comfortable sofa.

"However," Savasin began.

"*However* what?" Ekaterina exploded.

"I'm afraid to inform you that Alyosha has put herself in grave danger."

Ekaterina stared at him for a moment, her anger causing her to tremble.

"Continue," she said when she had collected herself.

He gestured. "Shall we be seated?"

"I'd rather stand," Ekaterina said icily. "So would you."

"Indeed, yes." Oh, how this vexing woman cowed him, he thought in anguish. He wished he were back on the dismal streets of Kapotnya, Makarov in hand, like Gary Cooper in *High Noon,* about to settle old scores.

He spread his hands. "Well, here it is in a nutshell. Alyosha has got herself involved with some high-grade criminals, in an enterprise that—"

"Impossible!" Another explosion.

"My dear Ekaterina, for some unknown reason, your daughter has gone and hooked herself up with her brother."

"Alyoshka has no brother."

"All right, then. Her *half* brother."

Ekaterina's eyes opened wide. "Gora?" An emphatic shake of her head. "No, you must be mistaken. She and I see eye-to-eye on Gora: we both hate him."

"I assure you I'm not." He dug into his breast pocket. This gesture caused Cerberus to start into motion again until he withdrew his hand, held up the mobile phone so both Ekaterina and her giant minion could see. "I have the proof right here."

"Fuck you." With fists dug into her flaring hips, she said: "Show me."

With the mobile held in front of him, screen first, he activated a video. "We are in Kalmar."

"Where the hell is that?"

"East coast of Sweden. Close to Russia." He watched her face closely as the video showed her Alyosha moving along the docks to lean against a railing and, moments later, being joined by a man.

"Who's that?" Ekaterina said, squinting. "Who is Alyoshka talking with?"

"A man named Larry London," Savasin said. "Although that's a legend. His real name is Nikolay Ivanovich Rozin."

"Never heard of either of them."

"Information is my business. For the past ten years, Nikolay Ivanovich has been out in the cold, as we say in the trade. Deep undercover in the West. But my brother recently named him head of *spetsnaz*."

Ekaterina's indrawn gasp was audible. "What is she doing with him?"

"I'm afraid that's not the worst of it, Ekaterina. Please watch."

Her gaze was fixed to the screen as her daughter took her leave of the false Larry London and stepped down to one of the floating docks where strings of boats were docked on either side. Just before Alyosha stepped aboard a boat near the far end and the video ended, the camera was able to pick out its name, stenciled on the stern.

Ekaterina gave another, deeper gasp. "Yegor Maslov!" She put a hand to her mouth. "*Carbon Neutral*. That's Gora's boat."

"I'm very much afraid it is." Savasin shut down the file. "And there you have it."

Ekaterina, eyes glazed over, sank back down onto the sofa cushion. Cerberus returned to the piano. Taking this as a cue, Savarin perched beside her on the edge, all the while keeping an eye on Cerberus's profile. He had switched from classical to pop, was in the middle of a curious slowed-down rendition of Kate Bush's "Running Up That Hill." As a pianist he had a knack for bringing out the heartache in a melody.

Savasin filled his host's glass, handed it to her. She drank it as if in a trance.

"What are we to do, Timur Ludmirovich? Alyoshka has fallen into the wrong hands."

"First, we must determine how far she has fallen," Savasin said briskly, all business now that he had delivered his hammer blow. "Then we must determine how to extricate her."

He watched Ekaterina's dark-blue eyes turn toward him. "We are at a distinct disadvantage."

"Perhaps," he acknowledged. "But then again perhaps not."

"What are you babbling about?" Ekaterina snapped. She was coming out of her shock with almost superhuman alacrity.

"Don't you see? My brother has appointed a man to be the chief of FSB's special operations who is clandestinely in collusion with the head of the Kazanskaya mafia." He grinned broadly. "The whole thing is—I don't know, what's the right word—delicious!"

"I don't believe that would be *my* word," Ekaterina sniffed. "But I take your point." Then, turning, she addressed the old gardener. "Papa, did you get all this?"

When the old man stood up straight, Savasin could see that he was ex-military. He had steel-gray hair, cropped very short, and eyes of the same color as his daughter's.

"Every word," he said in a surprisingly strong voice. Without being beckoned forward, he crossed the atelier, bringing a wooden, round-topped stool with him, warding off Cerberus, who had leapt up in mid-melody in order to assist Ekaterina's father.

"What a world," he said, as he sat on the stool facing them across the low table. "I hope I die before it gets much worse."

"Papa, shush!" Ekaterina said in mock dismay. Turning to Savasin, she said, "He's always saying things like that. It doesn't mean he means it."

"Hah!" her father interjected, draining Savasin's glass of what was left of the vodka. He made a face. "Vile stuff. I don't know how you drink it."

Ekaterina shook her head with a small smile. Clearly, Savasin thought, she was used to indulging the old man's whims.

"Timur Ludmirovich Savasin, First Minister of the Russian Federation,"—her arm swept out—"may I introduce you to my father, Dima Vladimirovich Orlov."

Orlov sat with straight spine on the backless stool, crossed his arms over his chicken chest. "Such an exalted figure here in my daughter's humble atelier." He wagged his head from side to side. "The modern world moves in mysterious ways; its wonders to perform."

"I wonder," Savasin said, wanting to regain control of the situation before this dotty old man ran it off the rails, "do you think it wise to paraphrase the Christian Bible to me?"

Orlov regarded him a moment, a small, disconcerting smile playing about his lips. "Mr. First Minister, are you by any chance referring to the following quote: 'God moves in mysterious ways; His wonders to perform; He plants His footsteps in the sea, and rides upon the storm'?"

"Indeed, I am," Savasin said, feeling quite proud of himself.

"The verse is quite beautiful—moving even, is it not?" He cocked his head. "No, but I suppose to a Communist ideologue such as yourself the verse, in mentioning the power of God, is anathema."

"I can recognize the poetry in the Christian Bible as well as anyone," Savasin replied somewhat defensively.

"That's quite a statement, First Minister. Are you certain you want to stand behind it?"

"Why, of course."

"Well, as it happens that quote isn't found anywhere in the Christian Bible, whose poetry you purport to admire. It is from a nineteenth-century hymn written by the English poet and hymnodist, Richard Cowper."

Savasin's hands curled into fists at his side. He dug his fingernails into his palms in order to keep himself calm, cool, and collected. Having been led like a lamb to the slaughter by this curious relic, it wasn't an easy task.

"I'm wondering now," he said slowly and icily, "whether you and your daughter want my help in extricating Alyoshka from—"

"Please don't call her that," Ekaterina said.

"It's not your place," Dima Orlov said.

"My place?" This was too much. "I am first minister. It's my place to—"

"Yes, yes, I know who you are," the old man said testily. "However, I am now of the opinion that you are ignorant of who I am."

There now was a deathly silence in the atelier. Cerberus had stopped playing. Having detached himself from the piano bench, he took up a position within what Savasin considered striking distance from him. Beset on what seemed all sides, he did not like that at all.

Already regretting his decision to come here, he said, "You appear to have me at a disadvantage, Dima Vladimirovich."

"Appear? *Appear!*" Dima exclaimed. "There are no ifs ands or buts about it. Are there, Katya?"

"No, Papa, there aren't." She seemed curious and fascinated at the same time. "Your name rings no bells with the first minister."

"Should it?" Savasin said, equally testily. If not for the looming presence of Cerberus, he might well have stood up and made his exit.

Then he thought of the dead dog in the gutter and he remained in place.

"Well, you are the first minister, after all. You are privy to reams and reams of information about the citizens of the Russian Federation, not to mention your enemies. But not me." Dima was grinning. "But that's all to the good. It means my people have done their job."

"Your people?" What *people* could the old man have? Savasin wondered. In his mind, maybe. He glanced at Ekaterina, but it was like looking at a brick wall. She had nothing for him.

Dima's grin was widening. "Let me tell you what I believe is happening here, First Minister. You didn't come to see Katya to help her with our beloved Alyoshka. You came here to elicit my daughter's help in whatever scheme you have concocted to take your brother, Konstantin, down a couple of pegs." He unwound his arms to wave one hand. "I won't ask you whether I'm right, to give you the opportunity to continue dissembling. The three of us must now face the truth of the matter."

"What truth?" Savasin said, the sharp edge making his voice brittle.

"Patience, Timur Ludmirovich," Ekaterina advised.

But Savasin, having endured one humiliation after another, starting with that creep Cerberus, was in no mood to be patient. He leapt up and, keeping one eye on the moving mountain, pointed at them. "I've had it with you two. An hour from now I'll be back with a cadre of FSB agents. We'll see how clever you are when I start interrogating you in the basement of the Lubyanka."

Ekaterina looked up at him from out of damnably serene eyes. "Calm yourself, Tamerlane."

At the use of the name of the great conqueror for which Timur was interchangeable, Savasin tried to bank his fury.

"Gospodin Tamerlane," Dima said, "I am quite certain that you are familiar with the name Ivan Volkin."

"Of course I am." Savasin was confused by the sudden switch in topic. "He was an *eminence grise*, a kind of consigliere to a number of the *grupperovka* leaders."

Dima nodded. "That's right. Last year, Volkin was killed in Moscow by Jason Bourne."

"That is known to me," Savasin said in a calmer voice. "The American agent provocateur did us all a favor."

"He did what the FSB—even the Sovereign—could not do."

"What's your point?"

Dima lifted a hand. "Please sit down."

Savasin waited the requisite amount of time so as not to give the impression that he was following an order. When he was seated, Dima said, "As it happens, Bourne did me a favor, as well."

Savasin frowned. "How, precisely?"

"Ivan Volkin was a fucking pain in my side."

The curse coming out of the old man's mouth was initially startling, but then it got the first minister to thinking that he had sized up the situation all wrong. Sitting before him wasn't any old dotty man, indulged and put to use by his daughter as a gardener. Dima was the power here, not Ekaterina. Savasin almost slapped himself. Egged on by his superior position, he had been blinded by his hubris.

"Then we have something in common," he said in his most accommodating voice.

"That we do, Tamerlane," Dima said. "More than you know."

22

THE LATE HOUR was growing even later. The low lamplight was even lower. Harry Hornden had not returned. Fulmer sat very still, stewing in his own juices. On the one hand, he wanted to get out of here, find Max, and turn him over to Department of Homeland Security. On the other hand, and to his complete surprise, he felt a keen desire to stay here with Gwyneth. It had been a long time since Fulmer had found himself smitten the way he was with this woman. He was floored. How could his wife and children have so quickly come to seem part of another universe, existing as no more than photos in a drawer in a desk in an office belonging to someone he once might have known?

Gwyneth had her back to him. She was pouring herself another drink. His gaze was fixed on the taut globes of her buttocks, as visible as the arcing crease between them.

"Marshall," she said, "may I ask why you're still here?" She turned around. "After all, you have what you came for."

"What is that you're drinking?" Fulmer said, levering himself off the sofa.

"Absinthe." Gwyneth held up her stemmed cordial glass. The drink was emerald green. "The real thing."

Fulmer had heard vague stories about absinthe but he had felt no particular reason to give them his attention. He watched, fascinated, as Gwen placed a cube of sugar in a slotted spoon, placed the spoon over the glass, and slowly poured a thin stream of water from a chilled carafe over the sugar cube. The result was startling; the drink clouded up, turning a pale, icy green.

"It's a liqueur. French," she said, putting the paraphernalia down. "It was brought back here by the black expats who spent time in Paris."

"Well, then I definitely have no interest."

Gwyneth pursed her lips. "Who is it you don't care for? The French or blacks?"

"The French are idiots. The French love themselves. The French think they know everything about everything, and yet they can't even run their own country. I hate the French."

"And blacks?"

"The French took them in, didn't they? Accepted them as equals. I told you they were idiots."

"Here, try this." Gwyneth held out the glass. "Maybe this will assuage some of your hatred."

"Nothing's going to do that."

That smile again, the slight curving of those luscious lips. "As long as you're here."

She came and stood in front of him, so close he could feel the heat emanating from her. He had no choice but to inhale her scent.

"What's that perfume you're wearing?"

"Do you like it?"

"I do."

She smiled. "I'm not wearing perfume."

If Fulmer were capable of blushing, which he was not, his neck and cheeks would be aflame. To take his mind off his reaction to her, he took the proffered glass.

"You know, absinthe was made for late-night drinking."

He took a sip, experienced many flavors at once: licorice, a very distinct herbal undertone, and a certain bitterness, as if he had been gnawing on a root.

"What do you think?"

"It isn't terrible." He took another sip.

Gwyneth laughed. "It contains thujone, an essential component of wormwood, as well as a combination of powerful herbs. The mind is cleared, energizing the body, while the alcohol serves as a relaxant. Really, there's nothing else like it."

She regarded him from beneath long lashes. "And as for the French, they know how to have sex."

Fulmer engaged her eyes with his own. "I don't like that Max put his hands on you."

She sipped the absinthe while the glass was still in his hand. "Max paid for that privilege, Marshall. You, on the other hand—"

As he grabbed her around her narrow waist, the cordial glass fell to the carpet, spilling what was left of the absinthe on his shoes. Too wrapped up in closing with her, he scarcely gave it a thought.

As he felt her breasts and the heat between her thighs press against him, something was unlocked inside him, some bestial thing that had long been lurking, pacing back and forth in the deepest shadows of his soul, waiting for its chance to be turned loose.

Now was its time, and it reveled in it.

―――――――――

Gwyneth's office might have looked like a salon to Fulmer, but in fact it was kitted out with enough bleeding-edge eavesdropping gear, all cleverly hidden from view, to make it the envy of even TMZ.

And so while Fulmer's interview with Gwyneth morphed from friendly banter to a bit of business, to bantering flirtation, to full-on sex of a massive hard-core variety heretofore hidden deeply inside Fulmer's firmly buttoned-down psyche, all of it, from his foul-mouthed imprecations to his all-too-willing submission to the mistress side of his hostess, was duly recorded in high-fidelity and in living color, as was said by both Gwyneth and Harry Hornden.

Later, Harry would deem it "a sight to behold," and toast Gwyneth for peeling away the layers of tough skin that shielded Fulmer from his inner demon, which now belonged, lock, stock, and barrel, to them. At the time, however, Gwyneth was far too busy goading the Fulmerial demon into more and more outré forms of behavior that were nothing she hadn't experienced before, but would be "Holy shit!" unacceptable to the general public.

Within eighteen hours Bourne was airborne, in the belly of one of Keyre's transports. He studied the surprisingly deep dossier on General Arthur MacQuerrie the Somalian's network had assembled. When he had committed it to memory, he set it aside, put his head back, and fell into a deep and restorative slumber in which he dreamed of Sara. They were running along the sand on Beit Yannai Beach, and the sun was in their eyes. Sara took an abrupt right turn, crashing into the Mediterranean surf. He was right on her tail.

Diving through a wave, he found her on the other side and kissed her with a fierceness that drove itself all the way through his bones.

The Angelmaker was similarly in the air, heading for the same destination. As she stared out the Perspex window, she reviewed the final conversation she had had with Keyre before heading to his airfield.

"There's good reason why he likes to work alone," she had told Keyre.

His eyes narrowed, and he gave her the look she knew so well, the one that passed through skin and flesh and bone to lodge in her brain. "I'm not going to have a problem with you, am I?"

"What kind of a problem?"

"A Bourne problem." Keyre scrutinized every facet of her face with the exquisite attention of a jeweler about to cut a precious stone. "It has not escaped my notice that you have formed an unhealthy attachment to him."

"You know where my loyalty lies."

"Yes, Angelmaker," he said, putting heavy emphasis on each word. "I do." He had rubbed his hands together. "So. To the matter of Bourne's preference to work alone."

"I will shadow him," she responded firmly. Then her face clouded over. "Even into the NSA dark site?"

Keyre smirked. "What d'you think?"

The Angelmaker—or was it Mala?—did not sleep a wink on the flights' long legs to America. Instead, she watched the visions unspool behind her eyes. She saw herself as she might have been had her father not sold her and her sister into slavery. As she might have been had she not been taken into custody by Keyre, and he not initiated her into the exquisite horrors of Yibir, had he not incised his magic formulae upon her back, had he not bled her day after day, working on her to morph the pain he inflicted into a pleasure that ensnared her in its insidious web. Always pulled in two directions, she was on the verge of losing her self in the cauldron of Yibir when Bourne had arrived to extricate both her and Liis. What would she have become? A prima ballerina like Liis? She didn't think so. But something. Something other than what she was now: a puppet of man and magic. She no longer knew what was real, what was Yibir magic, and what was her own fantasy.

23

CROWCROFT, TWENTY-ONE ACRES lying ninety-five miles southeast of the Leesburg Pike, had a long and storied history stretching back hundreds of years. Originally bought by an English shipping magnate to house his son, who had impregnated a woman far below his station, it was turned into a tobacco farm by the wayward son, who, as it turned out, had a better head for business than he did for women. Or for politics, for that matter. Having sided with the South in the Civil War and having agreed to house Johnny Reb during those bloody years, he was, in his elder years, thrown out on his wide bottom. For some years afterward, Crowcroft was kept afloat by remnants of the son's ragtag progeny, but time after time it went bankrupt, preyed upon by northern carpetbaggers out to line their pockets as quickly and as unscrupulously as possible. Near the end of the twentieth century it went into foreclosure for the last time. For some years after that, it sat fallow and forlorn on the books of the local bank that had lent money to the unfortunate owners, who, as it happened, were thrown in prison for drug trafficking. The same isolated location, which was perfect for illegal activities at Crowcroft, served as a detriment to selling it to legitimate businesses. Until the U.S. government came along and took it off the bank's hands for ten cents on the dollar.

For the next eighteen months, Crowcroft remained uninhabited while contractors for the NSA made the required repairs and modifications. These modifications spiraled out from the huge Tara-like great house itself to the various barns, which were remade as barracks for the rotating contingent of federal agents trained to guard the property, and the sheds, which now housed multiple banks of electronic equipment, generators, and back-up generators. The old stone walls that demarked the limits of Crowcroft's fiefdom were reinforced on the inside by concrete muscle over a steel skeleton. A network of CCTV cameras was installed to complement the motion and heat detectors. Bomb-sniffing dogs on chain leashes patrolled the grounds day and night.

Arthur Lee, Crowcroft's manager, was the one holdover from the previous regimes, absent the drug pushers, who had summarily kicked him out. He had been vouched for by the bank and vetted by NSA nerds. For the current regime, he was a necessary but invisible member of the Crowcroft estate. He was a descendant of the shipping magnate's son and the African slave he fell in love with and elevated to live by his side in the great house. Many generations had come and gone since her only son was born. Though she subsequently gave birth to four daughters, only the son survived the war.

Arthur Lee was that man's great-great-grandson. He had been born and raised on Crowcroft, had been witness to the good, the bad, and the very, very ugly, all of which had rolled in, done its damage to the acreage, and then ebbed away. Through it all, Arthur Lee, part English, part Angolan, part Powhatan, and who knew what else thrown into the hopper, abided, standing tall. He thought of himself as a mongrel, half jokingly, half bitter. He was decidedly antisocial, suspicious of everyone, but when it came to the crunch, it was Arthur Lee who set the broken leg of Jimmy Lang after he took a header off his tractor one autumn afternoon.

Bourne had met Jimmy Lang through Lang's ties to the NSA, which were tenuous at best. Lang had a fifty-acre farm that abutted one side

of Crowcroft. With his wife ill, his children off in college with no interest in the farming life, and no buyer for his acreage, Lang had had to
use his brains to figure out how to make ends meet. What he hit upon
was the flock of strangers who had taken possession of Crowcroft. God
alone knew what they were doing there, but when Arthur needed his
help to keep up Crowcroft's appearance as a working farm, he called on
his friend; Lang was only too happy to take the extra money. Whoever
these strangers were, they paid damn well.

Bourne had come upon Jimmy when, after he had successfully ful-
filled the assignment for which the Bourne identity had been created,
he was tasked with figuring out what the NSA was doing with that
property so far from their HQ. The Treadstone powers-that-were harbored a pathological hatred of the NSA, and were delighted to take
every opportunity to undermine the agency, which was why Bourne
was given this particular brief. The Treadstone people were ruthless
spyocrats. They were aware of his extraordinary prowess, and they were
determined to ride him as hard as they could for as long as they could.
But none of them was smart enough or prescient enough to figure he'd
find a way to break his psychological shackles and drop off their radar
screens.

As for Crowcroft, at first it was assumed the NSA was using it to
debrief defectors, and perhaps in the beginning it was. But not when
Bourne first began snooping around nine years ago. It was Bourne's
practice to come upon a target indirectly, slip through an unexpected
interstice, and cut to the heart of the matter. This he did by befriending
Jimmy Lang. Of course, the basis of the friendship was related to
Bourne's assignment, but the two men genuinely liked each other, and
afterward he and Bourne remained friends.

This was why Keyre had said, *"Seriously, you won't believe it when I
tell you,"* when Bourne had asked him where the NSA had stashed General MacQuerrie.

How Keyre knew of Bourne's friendship with Jimmy Lang was yet another question about the Somalian for which Bourne needed an answer.

"How long has it been?" Lang asked when Bourne approached him in the field. He had swung off his tractor, stood beside it, wiping his hands on a rag he kept stashed in the back pocket of his old-school overalls.

"That long," Bourne said as he put down the small satchel he was carrying and locked hands with his friend.

Lang, with wide-set eyes, a shock of light-brown hair, and a jaw like a granite boulder, had a body built for the great outdoors. Bourne supposed that with the right training Jimmy could have been a WWE fighter; he didn't have the disposition, though. He was a hunter the way his daddy and granddaddy were hunters: to put food on the family table. He hated violence and inhumanity, which is why Bourne had told him the first time they met what the NSA was really up to in the remade and remodeled great house.

"What've you been up to?" Jimmy held up his hands, palms outward. "Stupid question. Don't ask, don't tell." He indicated with his head. "Shall we head up to the house? Got a rocking chair with your name on it. Plus, there's a bottle of corn whiskey idling away in the pantry just begging to be drunk."

"As good as that sounds…"

"Ah." Lang nodded. "A business call. I should've known. What can I do for you?"

"Crowcroft."

"Again." Lang looked off to his left, toward the thick line of trees that separated his property from the NSA black site. When his gaze swung back, he said, "I got bad news on that score. They dynamited the last of those tunnels, including the one you used to get in last time."

Bourne squinted in the deepening western light that elongated their shadows. "I've got to get in there, Jimmy."

Lang sighed. "Well, I sure don't know a way." He considered for a minute, then snapped his fingers. "But there's someone who just might."

"What's his name?"

"Arthur Lee."

"Crowcroft's manager."

"Right." Lang nodded. "He's a good friend of mine." He slapped his left thigh. "Ever since he fixed the leg I broke."

Bourne reflected for a moment. "You can introduce me. I can say—"

"Now hold on a sec. Art's a peculiar bird. For one thing, he don't like big city people, especially those like to snooping around his property. For another, he's a fistful of Prickly Petes."

In other circumstances Bourne might have laughed. "There's got to be a way," he said. "Tell me everything you know about him."

Arthur Lee squinted gimlet-eyed at Bourne when Jimmy introduced them. Jimmy had invited Art to his house for dinner, not an unusual occurrence; Art, an inveterate loner who didn't even own a TV or a computer had never refused.

"Who's this?" he said, standing in the open doorway. He had a face like a hobo's shoe—every line a crevice, every protuberance a boulder. Black eyes, glossy and wary as a crow's, scrutinized Bourne as if he were a piece of meat hanging in a butcher shop. "I don't know him." As if Bourne were deaf or invisible.

"Jason's an old friend of mine," Jimmy said easily. "Don't stand on ceremony. Come on in, Art."

Arthur Lee did not make a move to step over the threshold. From one fist dangled a bottle of mountain whiskey. "I think not."

"Oh, come on. I made your favorite—"

"Not a bit of it."

As Jimmy had said, the stubbornness in Arthur Lee stemmed from his background, stubbornness born of generations of fury.

"Arthur thinks of himself as some kinda freak," Jimmy had told Bourne while relating as much of his friend's family history as he knew. *"Well, it's more than that, really. He despises the English lord in him. Y'see, Jason, he's overseer and slave all wrapped up in one self-hating*

bundle. I sure as hell wouldn't want to be him. But don't judge him too harshly. Deep down, he's got a good heart; trouble is he often has a problem locating it."

Which was why, just after Jimmy had called to invite his friend over for dinner, Bourne used a pair of small scissors he found in Jimmy's bathroom to open up the stitches in his shoulder. Immediately, he started to bleed. When he had come out, blood seeping through his shirt, Jimmy said, "Damnit all, what the hell did you do?" And then his eyes lit up, and he grinned, tapping the side of his head with his forefinger.

Now, as Arthur Lee backed away, Jimmy said, "Hold on, Art, it's not that I didn't want your company, but...and Jason told me straight out he didn't want any help, but, I mean, just take a look..."

Lee hesitated, still suspicious, took a step back toward them.

"What now?"

"His shoulder. Here, take a look..."

Lee squinted. "Awful lot of blood there."

Jimmy nodded. "See what I mean. The boy's as stubborn as you, not wanting to take any help."

Lee took another step forward, studying the mass of blood soaking through the shirt. Then he glanced up at Bourne. "Son, I do believe you're lucky I'm here."

Then, handing Jimmy the bottle of mountain whiskey, he stepped inside, already taking over.

———

Arthur Lee cocked his head. "What did you say your name was?"

"I didn't," Bourne said.

"It's Jason—" Jimmy began before Bourne cut him off.

"Smith," Bourne said, with a quick glance at Jimmy. "Jason Smith."

They were sitting in the hallway just outside Jimmy's bathroom, where he had pulled up three chairs. Lee, leaning on his elbows after peeling off Bourne's shirt, pursed his thick lips. "That's some wound you've got there, Mr. Smith."

"Why don't you call me Jason."

"Why don't the sun crawl down from the sky." Lee addressed Jimmy without taking his eyes off the wound, rattling off a list of items he'd need. While Jimmy was in the bathroom hunting and gathering, Lee continued in a jaundiced tone. "Someone did a right nice job the first time around." He eyed Bourne. "What happened?"

"I live an active life."

Lee gave a little bark that might have been a laugh. "No city feller, huh?"

"I hate cities," Bourne said truthfully.

"Ach, don't get me started."

Jimmy returned with all the first aid requirements, and Lee set about his work. "Arthur," he said, "Jason is something of a linguist."

"Is that so." Lee concentrated all the harder on cleaning and disinfecting Bourne's wound. "I'll bet he doesn't know how to speak my language," he said, in Powhatan, an eastern Algonquin offshoot.

"I would be honored if you would address me directly, Powtitianna." Bourne replied in the same language.

Arthur Lee stopped what he was doing. With surgical thread and needle in his hands, he looked directly at Bourne, "I am no chieftain. But I do thank you for the honor."

As he began to put the needle to good use, Bourne said, "As far as I can tell, you are around these parts, Arthur."

Lee grunted, but he couldn't keep the smile of pleasure off his face. "Done," he said, after tying off the thread. He had returned to English, mainly because of Jimmy. "Keep your activities to a minimum for the next several days."

"I'm afraid that's not possible."

Arthur Lee sat back on his haunches. "What is it you said you do?"

"I didn't," Bourne replied. Then switching back to Powhatan, "I need the Powtitianna's help."

Arthur Lee, the very essence of stillness, regarded Bourne for several moments. "That's a mighty forward request, Jason." Then he broke out into a smile. "Nevertheless, I do believe I'll take it under advisement."

———————

Bourne was naturally eager to get inside Crowcroft, but in Arthur Lee's world all things presented themselves in their time. There was simply no use in being impatient; the man moved at his own speed. Over generous pours of the excellent mountain whiskey he had brought and the equally excellent meal Jimmy had prepared, Bourne followed Lee's lead, sinking into his deliberate pace.

"Where did you learn to speak Powhatan?" Lee asked, midway through the meal.

"In another life I was a college professor," Bourne said. "Comparative languages was my field. I have an instinctive ability to learn languages, the more obscure the better."

"Well, Powhatan sure is obscure." Lee nodded. "Leastwise, these days."

"It wasn't always like that."

Lee squinted at him. "You know?"

"The history of the indigenous people hereabouts? Yes, sir, indeed I do."

"Well, don't that beat everything." Lee pointed with a leathery fore-finger. "The decline and fall of civilization." He almost spat, such was his disdain. "And after the carpetbaggers, the industries, the conglomerates, and the criminals, what are we left with?"

"I divorced myself from all that years ago."

"Betrayal upon betrayal, right?"

Bourne nodded. "As it was with you, it is with me," he said in Powhatan which, as it happened, was a far more powerful and involving language than English.

They drank coffee laced with more mountain whiskey, and for once there was a silence pregnant with expectation around the table. Bourne said nothing; it was for Arthur Lee to approach the heart of the matter that had brought Bourne here.

Lee laid both forearms on the table, hands open, in the manner of the Powhatan at a parlay among equals. The open hands showed Lee's receptive intent far better than anything he could say.

"How may I be of service to you, Jason?"

No point in beating around the bush now, Bourne thought. "The men who run Crowcroft now have devious intent. They are beyond any border of civilization."

Arthur Lee watched him carefully but made no comment. Did he know about the NSA's doings inside the great house? Bourne wondered. The man gave him no outward clue. On the other hand, he was still listening.

"These people are holding a man against his will," Bourne continued. "I need to get inside Crowcroft to reach him."

"Do you mean to free him?"

Bourne felt the black crow's eyes on him like a weight. Arthur Lee needed an answer, and Bourne knew better than to lie to him about his intent. "No."

"Then why?"

"His mind holds the key to a problem that is otherwise unsolvable."

"This problem," Arthur Lee said, "it is of great importance."

Bourne reverted to Powhatan. "Powtitianna, a great many people are trying to kill me because they believe I have the answer."

One eye closed, the other seeming to increase its power of discernment. "Are you a federal agent?"

"Federal agents are among those trying to kill me."

Arthur Lee poured himself the last of the mountain whiskey while he deliberated. He swallowed the liquor, closed his eyes for an instant, savoring the flavor to its utmost. Then he smacked his lips and, addressing Bourne, said, "I understand your dilemma, Jason. Now you must understand mine.

"Apart from several dark years, I have worked at Crowcroft all my life. In that sense, it is more mine than any owner's—including the current ones. Loyalty is of extreme importance to me—as I believe it is to you—thus you will comprehend me when I tell you that my loyalty lies entirely with Crowcroft."

"We are both men of intent, Powtitianna. You know what transpires in the great house."

"Oh, not only in the great house, Jason. No, indeed."

Bourne glanced out the window. "It's dark now. It's time for me to go. Will you help me gain entrance to Crowcroft, Arthur?"

Lee spread his hands. "Jason, over the course of these hours breaking bread with you, we have become friends." His expression bore a sorrow beyond comprehension. "I know what is done inside the buildings of Crowcroft. Terrible things. Things which should not exist in this world. Things that belong to the time of the Southern slave owners and the Northern carpetbaggers who came after. There was little difference between them: both wanted to exploit us, to make their fortunes off our backs. Today is it any different?" He shook his head. "Which makes it even more painful to tell you that all the tunnels have been rendered impassible; every time I go in and out, every square inch of my car is inspected. Men with specially trained dogs surround the vehicle; I couldn't smuggle in a gram of weed even if I wanted to." He sighed. "There is no conceivable way I can sneak you into Crowcroft. I'm afraid your mission is doomed to failure."

24

THERE CAME A time in everyone's life when the innocence of childhood was punctured and the adult world, with all its hatred, betrayal, and sewage, was revealed. The break was often abrupt, shocking; it was always irrevocable. Such a moment came to Morgana Roy on a mid-morning like any other she had experienced since landing in Kalmar. She had awoken early in her hotel room, a floor below Françoise. It was barely light out. She performed her forty-five minutes of aikido exercises, ordered breakfast, showered, and was dressed in time to usher in the room service girl with her rolling cart.

She ate in silence while she watched the news on TV: one story after another about the increasingly warlike stance of the Russian Federation, its growing belligerence toward the United States. The president had called Russia a "regional power," enraging both the Sovereign and the Kremlin as a whole. The stories frightened and sickened her in equal measure. Her fried eggs and pickled herring lay in her stomach like lead shot. Switching off the TV, she pushed the cart away. The taste of fish in her mouth nauseated her further. She took a swig of coffee, washing her mouth out with it, spitting it onto her plate before taking another gulp, swallowing it this time.

As she had the day before and the days before that, she met Larry London in the lobby. Together they made the short walk to the building where Larry had his temporary office, riding up to the fifth floor. She wasn't comfortable there. If she were to be honest with herself, the entire fifth floor gave her the creeps. It was deserted when they arrived in the morning, was similarly devoid of life when they exited late in the afternoon or early evening.

The office itself was nothing to look at: bare walls painted battleship gray, wood floors, a minimum of Swedish Modern furniture—desks, a sofa, a pair of chairs, a low table, and two floor lamps, that was it. The space was as anonymous as a doctor's waiting room. In fact, with its spray of magazines on the table, that's precisely what it reminded her of.

Three hours of work trying to decipher the latest bit of code she had found led to nothing at all. After so many days both in D.C. and here of slogging through incomprehensible code, a suspicion had begun to grow that she was trying to put together a jigsaw puzzle with the wrong pieces: nothing fit together, no matter which way she tried to integrate the various bits. If there was a unifying algorithm, she had yet to discover it, which was a first for her. She was hitting her head against a wall so often it had begun to hurt.

Abruptly, she pushed her chair away from the laptop, stalked over to the window, stared down at the anonymous passersby on the anonymous street, while she put her fists just above her buttocks and arched her back, stretching hugely.

London, sensing her distress, said. "Time for a lunch break."

"It's your turn to go get it."

"So it is." He nodded. "What d'you want?"

"Anything so long as it isn't fish."

He laughed easily. "Tall order, but I'm sure I'm up to it." He grabbed his coat. "Back soon."

She didn't bother to answer him. She was in a dark mood. The shock of her sudden incarceration had worn off, leaving behind a dull ache, like a bruise on her psyche. Lately, though, she had realized that she was homesick. She missed D.C., missed her apartment, missed the people she had worked with at Meme LLC. Often now, she found herself wondering what had happened to them. With Mac taken into custody, surely Meme LLC had been disbanded. Where had her team gone? Scattered to the four winds, she supposed, which was a pity; it had been a long and painstaking process finding them, meshing them into a well-oiled machine.

With a spasm of disgust at her self-pity, she turned from the window, went back to her laptop. She sat down and began to work again, but her heart wasn't in it, so she left it behind, went out into the street, walking purposefully until she found a shop selling running clothes. She bought a pair of sneakers, set out on a ten-mile run, five miles out, five back. That was her lunch hour, and reconnecting with her body settled her, damped down her anxiety, made her feel more herself again.

Back in the office, she returned to work, feeling refreshed and optimistic. Surprisingly, Larry hadn't yet returned with lunch. Who knew what he was up to? For all she knew, he was having a matinee somewhere discreet. He seemed just the type.

She frowned, picking up where she'd left off on the latest packet of code. For the next ten or so minutes, she was immersed in trying once again to parse the code, and when, as usual, that didn't work, she tried to fit it into the mosaic of the previous bits she had stored on her laptop. The screen flickered; she paid it no mind—the electricity in foreign countries always seemed dodgy to her. Then it happened again, and it was like a mote in God's eye, a speck that had attached itself to her eyeball and was now making her eye water.

She turned her attention to the flicker, but it was gone. She waited, but it didn't return. But then something odd happened. She had gone looking on the dark web for more bits of the weaponized code, had widened her search, expanding into bands of the dark web she had heretofore not explored. A flicker like the shortest bolt of lightning ran down the edge of her screen. Was that the flicker she had seen just before? Her fingers flew over the keys. This time, inside the dark web, the flicker had left a trace of itself. She followed it back, further and further, deeper and deeper, drawing closer and closer to its origin. Which was how, when it appeared again, she was able to catch it—like trapping lightning in the bottle of her laptop.

It was a bit of code, but totally unrelated to the one she was working to decipher. At first, it appeared to be a dangling bit of code, but a few minutes of concentrated effort on her part revealed that it was only disguised as such. It was, in fact, a message—or part of one, the fourth part, if she was right and the three previous flickers were from the same source.

After so much time frustrated at not getting anywhere with the Bourne Initiative, she had begun to doubt her abilities. But her furious and brilliant work now in punching through the exceedingly clever electronic disguise renewed her faith in the abilities Mac called extraordinary.

She set about decoding the cipher. The first thing she discovered was that it had an authenticating marker. That meant the message was sent either by a large international conglomerate or a state-sponsored agency. But why had it come here into Larry's office space? It wasn't meant for her. In fact, she would never have seen it had she been working as usual; instead, she'd been on a local screen, trying and failing once again to put her malformed pieces of code into a coherent whole. If the message wasn't for her, then it must be for Larry.

There was a moment, brief though it was, of thinking she should just forget about the whole thing. If it was for Larry, which seemed more and more likely, she had no business reading it. But then that authenticating marker stuck in the corner of her eye, as the flicker had before, and she thought, *I won't read the message; I'll just take a peek at who sent it.* She shrugged. It was most likely from Global Photographics, the organization he freelanced for. But then why had it come in from the dark web; that made no sense.

So she copied the marker, sent it out into the dark web. What came back was this: Unit 309. What the hell was Unit 309? She'd never heard of it. She latched on to the site that had ID'd the marker, which led her to another site, and another, and still another, until she was deeper into the dark web than she'd ever been before—so deep that she began to feel uncomfortable. She'd heard stories of the very bad entities winging their way through this section of cyberspace.

Her line of inquiry at last dumped her onto a site selling all manner of armament—not simply handguns, semiautomatics, and the like. Those were a dime a dozen out here on the cyber frontier. No, this site was delighted to sell you missiles, flame-throwers, guided rocket launchers, tanks, smart bombs—the list went on and on.

And then her screen blacked out for an instant, to be replaced by an overlay that blared in large lettering: PLEASE ENTER YOUR AUTHENTICATION CODE in seven different languages. She didn't have one, so she backed out. Or at least tried to. Something had hold of her—a worm algorithm that was trying to find out her identity. It was a very fast worm, and if she hadn't installed firewalls that she had created that went beyond military grade she would have been a dead duck.

As it was, she was having difficulty staying ahead of the worm. As she worked rapidly and methodically she realized that she had encountered this very worm before while she had headed Meme LLC, and her blood ran cold. It was a Russian military worm, which, now that she had ID'd it definitively, she shut down in short order.

It took her less than ten seconds to remove herself from the dark web entirely. She was sweating through her shirt and her scalp itched. Her heart rate was elevated and her hands trembled slightly.

Unit 309 was an organ of the Russian state. Now that she knew that, she knew where to search to ID it. Less than a minute later, she had her answer: Unit 309 was a cyber-infiltration cadre under the command of *spetsnaz*, a division of the FSB, the state security agency.

Her mind had just registered this terrifying fact when Larry London waltzed through the door with their lunch.

"Guess what," he said jovially. "I brought you a cheeseburger and fries." He set the paper parcels on the table. "A nice little bit of home."

Only his name wasn't Larry London, he didn't just freelance for Global Photographics, and he was no undercover operative of the CIA. Of these things Morgana was now sure. Larry London was a Russian spy, and she had been aiding and abetting him.

Pushing her chair back, she excused herself, hurried down the hall to the ladies' room, where she vomited up the remains of her breakfast, which now seemed as tainted as if it had been a vile combination of a glass of vodka and a bowl of borscht.

"I found him near the edge of my property," Arthur Lee said.

The three guards who had stopped him at the front entrance to Crowcroft were dressed in jeans and checkered shirts. They wore Timberland ankle boots and matching gabardine jackets, which, if Lee didn't know it already, would have given them away as feds. He thought they were morons. Dangerous morons, to be sure, but morons all the same.

"Where?" one of the NSA guards said, peering suspiciously into the interior of Lee's vehicle as if they hadn't all seen him every day for the last three years. The guard was built like a heavyweight boxer.

Lee indicated with his head. "Trunk."

While the lanky guard checked the underside of his vehicle with a mirror at the end of a three-foot handle, the bald guard drew his service weapon, opened the trunk.

"He's not tied up," Baldy said, and Boxer, leaning in Lee's window, repeated the statement as if, he, Lee, were the moron.

"He's hurt," Lee said, keeping it smooth and servile the way they liked it. "Hurt bad."

"There is, in fact, one way you can get me into Crowcroft," Bourne had said, an hour before. *"As your prisoner."*

Arthur Lee had shaken his head. *"Absolutely not. I'm not going to abet your suicide."*

"I'm hurt, Arthur. They'll see that as soon as you point it out to them. They'll take me to the infirmary. A doctor will look at me."

"And then they'll start to interrogate you."

"Well," Bourne replied, *"I'm sure they'll want to."*

"He was out for a while." Lee said now. "In his shape he couldn't hurt a fly."

"Nevertheless," Boxer said.

Baldy went through a barely conscious Bourne's pockets, grunted disgustedly when he didn't find anything of interest. He whipped a plastic tie from his jacket pocket, manacled Bourne's wrists in front of him. Then he transferred Bourne to the backseat, slid in beside him, while Mirror Man stepped around the other side and climbed into the shotgun position. Boxer gave the all clear signal and Baldy said, "Okay, drive." He pointed. "That way." Just as if Lee were a kid caught with his hand in the cookie jar ten minutes before dinner. But then federal morons like these were known to have the compassion of a weasel.

"Where are we going?" Lee asked in the servile tone honed over decades of practice.

"The infirmary," Baldy said.

Lee suppressed a laugh; at least his heart was lighter.

Bourne did not look like Bourne. He hadn't needed to use much of what he had in the satchel he had brought; he was already haggard and thinner by five pounds than when he'd stood at the bow of Boris's boat, contemplating his coming rendezvous with the Angelmaker. But, among many other singular talents, Bourne was a master of disguise. The key was not to overdo it—a dab of makeup here, a prosthetic to change the shape of mouth and jawline, above all an altered gait, which was what most observers looked to first. It was a kind of magic, cues that nudged the observer's keen eye in another direction. It was, when all was said and done, a form of sleight of hand. He hadn't had enough time to dye his hair, but just enough to give himself a military high-and-tight hair-cut.

"We have him, yeah." Baldy was on his mobile. "No ID anywhere on his person. Military type, mebbe ex." He listened for a moment. "Right...Okay...Got it."

"We're almost at the great house," Bourne heard Lee say.

"Keep going," Baldy said.

"But the entrance to the infirmary is right—"

"Do as you're told, asshole," Baldy ordered. "Left past the big oak up there."

They drove past the great house, stately on the outside, rotting from within. The oak tree rose up quickly, blotting out the sky, then vanished as Lee turned down a rutted cart track.

"This is the way to the firing range." A quaver made Lee's voice seem like he was under water.

"Park over there," Baldy ordered.

Lee pulled over next to what had once been a horse barn and was now a storage area for his tractors and balers. The sharp odors of grease and oil were suddenly in the air.

"Don't move," Baldy said, as he slid off the seat.

Mirror Man grabbed Bourne and hauled him roughly out of the vehi-cle.

"Against the wall," Baldy said. "We'll do it military style."

"Old school," Mirror Man said, gripping Bourne tighter. "I like that."

They both laughed.

High overhead, a trio of crows stared down with cocked heads, claws gripping a branch of a maple. As Bourne was slammed against the barn wall, they took off like rockets, cawing indignantly.

Mirror Man, palm pressed against Bourne's chest, put his face so close to Bourne's their noses almost touched. Baldy was directly behind him, his sidearm out, standing at a safe distance.

Mirror Man flicked open a gravity knife, brandished the narrow blade. "We're gonna have fun with you, fucker, whoever the hell you are."

25

A SUDDEN BURST OF rain rattled the windows. Morgana looked up from her lunch. The sky was a dark bruise; the air pressure had plummeted far enough so that even here inside the building she could feel its effects. The room seemed to tilt as the air grew thick, weighing on her like a wool blanket. She felt unmoored, drifting in a limbo from which she could find no clear exit.

"Are you all right?"

London's voice made her start. She glanced down at the cheeseburger out of which she had taken a single bite in the twenty minutes since they had begun to eat. "I'm fine." Her stomach rumbled, but the sight of the burger grease made her want to gag. She put the burger down, wiped her hands on the wad of paper napkins that came with it.

"I want to get back to work."

"But you've scarcely eaten a thing," London pointed out.

"Morning sickness," she said, crossing to her laptop and sitting down in front of it.

London frowned. "You're joking, right?"

"What d'you think?"

"I think you got up on the wrong side of the web today." He came and sat down beside her. "That was a joke." When she didn't respond, he swiveled his chair to face her. "Hey, hey, what's up?"

"Hey, hey, what's up?" Would a Russian say that? she asked herself. And then she realized that if she suddenly started behaving so coldly with him he'd surely get suspicious. She put on her sad face, not so very difficult to do. She sighed. "The truth is, I'm missing D.C." She fluttered one hand. "I mean, I'm stuck here in the middle of nowhere, pretty much going back and forth between the hotel and this dump—no offense. And the only people I see are you and Françoise."

"I understand completely," London said.

What would it sound like if he said that in Russian? she wondered.

"But you've been sequestered, Morgana, for your own good. Things are still unsettled in Washington."

"From what I see on the TV things are unsettled all over—Washington, Moscow, NATO HQ. It sounds to me like the world's going to hell in an out-of-control handcart."

"Which is why Françoise has you here, safe and sound, where you can work undisturbed by outside forces."

Like Unit 309, the FSB, or spetsnaz, she thought sourly. But she put a reluctant smile on her face. "Truthfully, Larry, I need a break. I've been at this day and night for days and days."

"No one knows this better than Françoise," London said. "But, Morgana, we're under a severe time constraint here. You have to solve the mystery of what the Bourne Initiative is and how it's going to be deployed." He gestured with his greasy fingertips. "We're almost out of time, and, honestly, we're in your hands."

"Of course." She nodded, the good little soldier. "Forget what I said."

"That's the girl." He smiled broadly. "There'll be plenty of time afterward, I promise you."

She returned to her work—*her* work. She could feel him next to her, smell his woodsy aftershave. Did it remind him of his dacha outside Moscow? The fir trees and the snow? She shivered inwardly at these thoughts. What was his real name? Now she knew the truth, "Larry London" was such a ridiculous alias.

He and Françoise read her daily reports; they were always the same. No matter how many bits of the Bourne Initiative she unearthed, none of them fit together. That might be because each new piece was in some small or obscure way different than the last, almost as if the thing was a living organism that kept evolving. And yet the one thing each bit had in common was the zero-day trigger that was now six days away.

What she didn't put in the reports was her growing conviction that the cyber weapon was being assembled by people far smarter than she was. So many hours at this and she was still at square one when it came to defining the category of cyber weapon it might be. Was it an über-worm built to penetrate the firewalls that guarded the nuclear missile codes available only to the president, as Mac believed? Or was it a virus that self-replicated, creating a zombie army of botnets; was it a key logger that clandestinely transmitted a user's keystrokes to a third party? The code was nothing like Stuxnet, nothing like Flame or Wiper. Nor was it in any way akin to BlackEnergy, the latest and greatest weaponized malware program. So, then what the hell was it? Maybe Mac knew, maybe he didn't. In any event, he had now been taken off the board. No one could get to him.

On the other hand, at this moment, Morgana was less interested in reliving her daily frustration with the Bourne Initiative than she was in deciphering the section of coded message she had captured on her laptop before Larry had returned with lunch. While he noshed on her fries as he worked, she was simultaneously running three different programs she herself had created in order to break the cipher and analyze the results.

It was an unsettling project to be working on with London sitting right beside her. Neither could see the other's screen, but still she felt goose bumps come out on her skin as she worked or, rather, watched her programs do their thing.

The encryption Unit 309 used was masterly, but it wasn't up to defending against her programs. Eight minutes after she had sicced them on the enciphered message, she was able to read the words *en clair*, and a full-body panic knifed through her:

PKT4: out of time. She is now in your hands. Use her, then dispose of her. Kay

———————

Bourne kneed Mirror Man hard in the groin. As all the wind rushed out of him, Bourne whipped him around, found the knife blade, used it to slice through the plastic manacle. Mirror Man, recovering, jabbed Bourne in the ribs with his elbow. He saw what Baldy was up to, jerked himself free, putting Bourne in the line of fire as Baldy aimed. Bourne chopped down on the side of Mirror Man's neck, hauled him back in line, jammed his body against his as the bullets meant for him struck Mirror Man instead.

Grabbing the gravity knife as Mirror Man's knees gave way, Bourne flicked his wrist, and the knife shimmered through the air, sunlight winking off its steel. The blade buried itself in Baldy's chest. He staggered, knees buckling, then, recovering, launched himself at Bourne.

He fired once as he came, missed. Then he was too close for a firearm, reversed it, seeking to use the butt as a club. Bourne blocked it with the edge of his hand, then grasped Baldy's arm, pivoted back on his right leg, drawing Baldy in and down. With the back of his neck exposed, Bourne smashed his elbow into the first cervical vertebra. It was the smallest and, therefore, the easiest to fracture. It was also the closest to the skull, its disintegration catastrophic. And so it was with Baldy. He went down and stayed down.

Turning, Bourne saw Arthur Lee, staring at him, slack-jawed, from behind the wheel of his vehicle.

"Get out of here, Arthur," Bourne said, lifting a hand in a loose salute. "Stay away from the great house and everything will be fine."

He heard the engine start up, and Lee's vehicle rumbled away toward his small house near the western edge of the estate. Bourne stripped off his clothes, replaced them with Baldy's, zipping up the jacket to cover the bloodstain on the shirt. He found the electronic ID key card in the back pocket of Baldy's pants. Looking around, he saw only the crows, who had returned to their perch, regarding him with their glassy black eyes as he loped back up the track toward the great house.

———

There was a meeting in progress. Bourne could hear multiple voices bleeding out of the half-open door to the library. Someone was being teleconferenced in from D.C.—DoD or the Pentagon. Bourne could see at a glance that the layout of the first floor hadn't changed since he had last stolen inside.

Once, he had to duck away so as not to be seen by someone passing down the hallway. Reaching the locked door to the back stairs, he fitted Baldy's key card into the reader at the side of the door, pulled it open, and proceeded cautiously down the stone steps.

His previous reconnaissance had revealed the interrogation cells to be in the basement, where, in happier times, before the NSA got hold of it, the wine cellar had been; the air still held a whiff of wine must. In typical NSA fashion, the space had been recreated into a strictly utilitarian area with five "holding rooms"—like all government services, the NSA was hooked on euphemisms—all of which abutted observation chambers outfitted with one-way glass panels inserted into the common walls. Farther along was the "laboratory"—another euphemism for a very nasty section containing three rooms, each one equipped with the paraphernalia necessary for the kinds of articulated interrogation that was now illegal and which high-ranking members of the NSA swore before various Congressional subcommittees they absolutely, unconditionally no longer tolerated.

The NSA psych team assigned to Crowcroft had names for these three rooms: My First Experience, Nothing To See Here, and The Drowning Pool. In the first the uncooperative client, as the prisoners were called, was softened up with grueling sessions of incessant questions, interspersed with periods of unexpected explosions of static, a hundred voices talking over one another, death-metal rock shrieking, sudden bursts of blinding light or total darkness; in the second the client was subjected to sensory deprivation; in the third the waterboarding was the centerpiece, although by no means the only extreme measure available to the interrogator.

It was said that no one survived what was known as The Whole Nine Yards intact. Though that might well be the kind of hyperbole the NSA traded in, it was just as possible it came very near the truth.

Since the door was key-coded, there were no guards at the bottom of the stairs. Bourne did, however, have to be mindful of the psych staff, two members of which he spied on his way to the cells.

A quick recon revealed that General MacQuerrie had been graduated out of My First Experience. He must be in the sensory deprivation tank.

The connection corridor between the first and second interrogation chambers was so dimly lit Bourne had to pause to allow his eyes to adjust to the gloom. Once he did, he advanced to the closed door ahead of him and slid the key card through the reader. Opening the door, he hung back, waiting, looking for any movement of shadows, but there was nothing.

Stepping in, he closed the door behind him. Before him was a shallow float tank of perfectly calm water. He knew it would be set at precisely the same temperature as the client's body temperature. Peering through the dimness into the water, he could just make out the outline of a figure floating in the center, tethered, unmoving. A mask was over the general's face, fitted with a breathing tube. MacQuerrie looked like he'd already lost weight as a result of the shock tactics in My First Experience.

Shedding Baldy's too-tight shoes and gabardine jacket, which contained

Bourne's sat phone in one pocket and a thick wad of hundred-dollar bills in the other, Bourne slipped into the water, untethered the client. His hand was on the breathing mask, but before he could pull it off, the overhead lights blazed on, momentarily blinding him. When he could focus he saw the third guard, built like a boxer, the one he and Lee had left behind at the front gate. He held his 9mm sidearm out in front of him, pointing it at Bourne.

"Ed and Marty are MIA and you've been using Ed's key card all over the place, you miserable little shit." When he spoke his voice had a weird dead sound, devoid of echo, due to the state-of-the-art sound-proofing in all three rooms. His forefinger slipped inside the trigger guard, balanced on the trigger itself. "Now you're gonna pay."

26

HE MADE A deal with the devil," Dima said.

"Who?" Savasin asked. "Karpov?"

Ekaterina laughed, but her father's hand slicing through the air cut her off.

"No, not Karpov," Dima said with a glint in his eye. "Your brother, Konstantin."

The three of them—four if one counted Cerberus—had repaired to Ekaterina's large kitchen, where they sat around a central table while the moving mountain served them food and drink, silent as usual. The food was excellent and plentiful, the drink Iron Mountain black tea from the hinterlands far from Moscow. It was very strong and very good.

"My brother." Savasin set down a forkful of *karsky shashlik*, marinated in red wine and crushed bay leaves. "Do tell." The tender bits of lamb were bedded on wild rice, surrounded by baked tomatoes, string beans showered with slivered almonds. He steepled his hands. "Continue."

"Konstantin is in bed with Gora Maslov."

"The head of the Kazanskaya? That's mad."

Dima poured himself more tea out of the porcelain samovar. "It's the truth."

"Unlike his father, Gora is a weakling. Why in the world—?"

"Precisely *because* he's a weakling. Konstantin can control him."

"But that's only the tip of the iceberg," Ekaterina interjected.

This time, her father did not silence her.

"This also is true, Timur." Dima sipped, watching Savasin from over the rim of the glass. "You are aware of an agent abroad with the legend Larry London, real name Nikolay Ivanovich Rozin."

"Of course." Savasin nodded. "As I told your daughter."

"Little Niki," Ekaterina said with the ghost of a smile.

Savasin's brows knit together in growing annoyance. "What about him?"

"Has your brother mentioned Niki recently?" Dima asked.

Savasin hesitated a moment, then said, "You know he has. You just heard me tell Ekaterina that he's appointed Rozin as the new head of *spetsnaz*."

Ekaterina glanced at her father, then commenced laughing. She laughed so hard tears came to her eyes.

The first minister, glancing from one to the other, said, "What the hell is so amusing?"

Dima put down his glass. "Tell him, my dear."

Ekaterina wiped her eyes. "Dear, dear Timur. Your brother is about to fuck you well and good. Guess whose payroll little Niki is on?"

Savasin gaped at her, swallowed, and said, "Not Gora's. Tell me he's not working for Gora."

"Oh, but he is," Dima said. "And from what you've just told me, Gora's plans are further advanced than I had thought."

"So." Savasin stared down at his *shashlik* for a moment, trying to orient himself. Strange as it might seem, nothing that Dima or Ekaterina said surprised him all that much. He put nothing past his brother; his ambition, his lust for fame and fortune was unbounded. That's why he had hated Boris Karpov so much. The general had blocked his way in every avenue.

He looked up at Dima and Katya. "The most interesting thing about my brother is this: he fancies himself faster, stronger, and cleverer than he is." Savasin spoke slowly and thoughtfully. "But I now have to say this for General Karpov—he actually was faster, stronger, and cleverer than anyone else, including my brother, possibly even the Sovereign. And, unlike Konstantin, he knew his limits, and he never stepped across that line into the danger zone."

Ekaterina frowned. "We were under the impression that you hated Boris Illyich."

"Ah, well. It seems to me now that my hatred was merely a reflection of Konstantin's. I took on his hatred without really knowing why." Savasin placed his hands flat on either side of his plate. "But now you must tell me what the devil my brother is up to."

Dima lifted a hand, and Cerberus cleared the plates, replaced them with small saucers of sweetmeats before retreating to see to the dirty dishes. It occurred to Savasin that the running water might be deliberate and wondered whether even in the Orlov sanctum sanctorum there loomed the specter of hostile ears, electronic or otherwise. He ought to know if there were, no? But then he realized that he knew absolutely nothing of Konstantin's activities over the last year.

Savasin, in no mood for procrastination, said testily, "What about my brother?"

Dima's face clouded over. "Yes, well, we'll get to that in a moment. First, we must speak of Boris Illyich."

"I admit I've had a hand in erasing him and all he's done from the memory of the Russian Federation."

Dima spread his hands. "Timur, this is the trajectory of Russian history, is it not? Who among us has not had the opportunity to erase that which we do not like or find objectionable."

"But in General Karpov's case—"

"In his case, perhaps it was a necessary evil."

Savasin cocked his head. "How so?"

Dima held a saucer of sugar cookies out to the first minister, who silently declined. "Pity. Cerberus made them. They're really quite excellent." He plucked one, popped it into his mouth. "Circling back, we come to what you yourself said about Boris Illyich—that he never overstepped his limits." He licked powdered sugar off his fingertips, wiped them on a napkin. "Now I will tell you why—well, one of the reasons, anyway. Boris had a *stvol.*"

"A weapon," Ekaterina said. "A *secret* weapon."

"Even more than that, First Minister." For the first time Dima smiled. It was almost identical to his daughter's smile—midway between that of a dolphin and the Mona Lisa.

"Boris Illyich had a secret weapon *in plain sight.*"

Savasin shook his head. "I don't quite—"

"Bourne," Ekaterina said, leaning forward to put added emphasis on her words. "His best friend, Jason Bourne."

"You mean the general leveraged his friendship with Bourne to get things done he couldn't do himself?"

"No." Dima shook his head. "You misunderstand."

"What do you expect, father," Ekaterina said with open contempt. "He's first minister."

"I think it would behoove us all to be a bit more flexible in our thinking."

It was a clever way to gently admonish his daughter without pointing a finger at her, Savasin thought. Then he realized that Dima must mean him as well.

Dima smiled to soften the rebuke. "Listen, Timur. I knew Boris Illyich better than you. And as for Katya, she knew him better than both of us put together."

"He was a Russian, yes, loyal to Mother Russia," Ekaterina said. She was perched on the edge of her chair, her body so tense it found its way into her voice. "But, at heart, he was a humanist."

"Just as Bourne is a humanist," Dima said. "For them, their friendship transcended both politics and ideology."

"I don't get it," Savasin said truthfully; he felt that he had failed at something vital to what was happening now. "A Russian and an American—both spies. They should have been mortal enemies."

Dima tried not to express his frustration. "First Minister, if nothing else, you must understand this about them: they both hated politicians and ideologues, of every stripe. That's what brought them together; that's what formed the bedrock of their extraordinary friendship."

"Why must I understand this?"

"Konstantin wants everything," Dima said tersely. "He craves the unprecedented power General Karpov wielded over the FSB and the FSB-2. In his hands, that power would be, well, destructive to all of us. I still maintain my ties with the *grupperovka* old guard."

"And the money," Savasin replied. "We mustn't forget the money."

"Your cynicism does you proud, First Minister." Dima's mouth twitched upward in a sardonic smile. "Nevertheless, we are talking about your brother. He has the ambition of a Caesar. He knows the Sovereign will never give him your position, just as he would never have given it to Boris Illyich—far too dangerous, considering the personalities involved. The Sovereign's strategy with your brother is the same one he used with General Karpov—give him his head within a circumscribed area, keeping him happy and controlled at the same time."

"It wasn't working with Boris," Savasin said with a distinctly sour intonation.

"Indeed not." Dima nodded. "Boris Illyich had devised a number of workarounds, none of which were known to the Sovereign and his minions."

"I see. So my brother is seeking to do the same."

Dima nodded. "But while Boris sought an equilibrium between east and west, Konstantin craves the opposite. Like the Sovereign, he wants to destroy the West—particularly America, whose presidents have time and again insulted him and Mother Russia. He bridles every time Russia is termed a 'regional power' in the Western press, while the United States is known as the only true 'global power.'"

Savasin ran his hand across his forehead, finding it damp. "So he's going to destroy America."

"That is his goal, undoubtedly."

Savasin shook his head. "But how, specifically? Gathering power clearly isn't enough."

"No, it isn't," Dima said. Perhaps it was the changing light, as the day began to die, but he suddenly looked ten years older.

"The problem is we don't know what Konstantin is planning," Ekaterina said.

"We've tried and failed," Dima added. "What we need now—"

"Father," Ekaterina interrupted, "can we trust him?"

"My dear," he said mildly, "we have trusted him this far." He shrugged. "Besides, he has a personal stake in siding with us now."

Ekaterina took a deep breath, let it out slowly. Then, shooting Savasin a sideways glance, she nodded.

"What we need now," Dima continued, "and by *we* I include you, First Minister, is Bourne. We need him to be the tip of the spear. We need him to be our *stvol*.

"As I said, we have failed. Bourne won't. You, Tamerlane, are the only one who can get to him without your brother finding out and sending us straight into the bowels of the Lubyanka."

"What do you say, First Minister?" Ekaterina regarded him coolly. "As it turns out, you need us as much as we need you."

27

B Y THE TIME we get through with you, I fucking guarantee you'll wish you were dead."

Bourne popped the face mask off MacQuerrie. The body began to thrash, and Boxer took his eye off Bourne just long enough for Bourne to grab the coping of the pool with one hand, grasp Boxer's ankle with the other.

He jerked hard just as the gun went off, but Boxer was already on his way into the float tank, and his aim was high. Bourne grabbed Boxer's wrist, twisted so hard he was forced to drop the gun. Boxer bent double, then straightened up, the crown of his head slamming into Bourne's chin. His right hand balled into a fist, buried itself in Bourne's solar plexus, sending Bourne to one knee. The water lapped at his nose.

Disengaging, Boxer groped in the water for the gun, but it was nowhere to be seen. Hadn't it sunk to the bottom of the tank? Bourne blindsided him before he could hope to answer that question. Bourne jabbed him in the ribs, then smashed the edge of his hand into Boxer's rib cage. He heard a satisfying crack, and Boxer grimaced. But he was far from done.

Breaking away, he kicked hard, his heel making hard contact with Bourne's left shoulder. Had the water not slowed the kick Bourne's shoulder would surely have been dislocated. As it was, the burst of pain was followed immediately by a terrible numbness that traveled down Bourne's left arm, leaving a trail of pins and needles.

Taking immediate advantage, Boxer grasped Bourne's head on either side, slammed the back of it against the coping. Again and again. And then his forefinger jabbed at Bourne's eye. It never made it. Struck from behind with the butt of his own 9mm, Boxer fell to one side. Bourne could just make out a blurred shadow of MacQuerrie. He must not have had a lot of strength. He staggered backward in the water, the effort of the one blow having done him in.

Bourne, his head in a muddle, black spots crowding his vision, drove the edge of his hand into the side of Boxer's neck. Boxer's head rocked like a bobble-head. Spinning him, Bourne wrapped one arm around his neck, placed the heel of his other hand just below the ear. Boxer, frantic, struggled mightily, but Bourne kept his grip, gave a sharp twist that broke Boxer's neck.

He lay back then against the coping while Boxer's body floated facedown in the water. Despite the shallowness, the chop was as frenzied as if from a school of feeding sharks. Gaining his equilibrium, Bourne waded past the body to the opposite side, where MacQuerrie sat in the shallow water, trying desperately to hold on to the coping. With the lights on he caught his first look at the client; it wasn't General MacQuerrie.

Bourne, taken aback, said, "What the hell are you doing here?"

"Surprise!" the Angelmaker said weakly.

Bourne, arm around her shoulders, drew her away from the coping. Her face was pale, and there was a curious unfocused aspect to her eyes. "How long have you been under?"

"Long enough for it to make a difference."

"You owe me an explanation," he said. "But not now. We have very little time to get to General MacQuerrie and get out of here before we're discovered."

He pulled her out of the water, sat her on the coping before climbing out himself and snatching two towels from a pile in the corner. She swayed slightly as he dried her off. He'd been subjected to every form of interrogation technique during his Treadstone training. He knew what time in the floatation tank could do. At first you're sure you can hold out, but then in the blink of an eye your nervous system goes numb, and you've slipped away from yourself. It doesn't matter what other kinds of torture you've experienced, sensory deprivation is another animal entirely, one you cannot prepare for. Most methods of interrogation involve dealing with pain in one form or other. Techniques have been developed to handle pain, no matter how intense. They all involve carving out a private space for your consciousness that is inviolate and curling your essence inside that space while whatever is being done to your body goes on.

Sensory deprivation is different inasmuch as there's no pain. Instead, there is a cessation of all feeling. You're alone with yourself, and the lack of outside stimuli starts to distort your thoughts. Under these conditions, a private space is of no use, as your own thoughts make it porous.

This is what had happened to the Angelmaker. Whether her adolescent torture at the hands of Keyre made her more susceptible to sensory deprivation or it was due to a quirk in her personality was at the moment irrelevant: she had succumbed; her mind had detached itself from her body.

"Your clothes," he said with some urgency. "Mala, where are your clothes?"

He took hold of her jaw, pulled her head so that she was looking directly at him. Her eyes looked like those of a junkie—the pupils pinpoints, despite the bright light. They wandered over his face as if tracing a route on a map. But she didn't answer.

"Mala. Mala." He leaned in, pressed his lips to hers. They were cold, trembling slightly, as if being affected by electric currents under her skin.

Jason.

He felt her "speak" his name through vibrations transferred from her mouth to his, and took his lips away from hers. Her eyes focused on him.

"In the locker, there," she whispered hoarsely.

She pointed, and Bourne left her momentarily, though her torso was still rocking a little, as if she were someone who had been at sea a very long time.

He returned with her clothes, helped her into them. Then he toweled off and climbed into his.

"Can you stand?" He had helped her into her trousers while she was sitting down. He extended a hand, but she shoved him away.

"Cut it out."

He stood back, checking the door he had come through every few seconds, while she struggled to stand. He could see that her knees were rubbery, but she was as strong of will as she was of body, and soon enough she was up, stalking back and forth beside the tank, her strength flooding back with each stride.

"Ready?" he said, and when she nodded, he led her to the door that gave out onto the short corridor to The Drowning Pool.

This third room was smaller than the others. On one side, an array of standing heat lamps were lined up like birds with bulbous beaks, all directed at one spot. Filling a sweat- and bloodstained wooden butcher's table directly below them were a series of clamps, graduated from small to large, lines of files, scalpels, and a grouping of what appeared to be dental instruments, gleaming in the light from the ceiling overheads. On the other side, an industrial-size stainless-steel sink stuck out from the wall like the snout of an enormous hog. Beside it, a hose that could be attached to the sink's spigot, a galvanized metal trough, a number of cotton cloths through which the water was poured onto the client's face, and a table on which the client—in this case General MacQuerrie—was strapped.

"He's been the gamut," the Angelmaker said. Her voice was steadier now, sounding more like herself.

"The Whole Nine Yards."

"What?"

"That's how it's known here," Bourne told her. "The Whole Nine Yards."

"Lovely." She frowned. "What state is he in?"

Having stepped beside the table, he bent over it slightly so he could look directly into MacQuerrie's eyes. They were open wide, terror having taken up residence behind them. He was strapped down as if he were a mental patient prone to violent outbursts. Glancing up, Bourne signaled to the Angelmaker to keep guard on the door they had slipped through.

"General?" Bourne raised his voice slightly. "General! Can you hear me?"

MacQuerrie's eyes focused on Bourne, but his lips did not move. They were bluish as if he was chilled to the bone. He was wearing a sweat-stained undershirt and trousers. His hands and feet were bare, blue-white, utterly still.

"General, I'm not part of the NSA group. I'm not here to hurt you. Do you understand me?"

No response.

Bourne unstrapped him. "Do you understand me, General?"

After a long moment, MacQuerrie's lips moved. "Who?" It was thin, barely a whisper.

"Who am I?"

The general blinked. "Yes."

"Let me put it this way," Bourne said, slowly and carefully. "I'm intimately connected to what you call the Bourne Initiative, though, oddly, I don't know why or how."

The general licked his lips. "They tried to break me."

"What did they want from you?"

"I don't think they know. It's possible they didn't even care." He took a breath, blew it out his nostrils. "I'm a traitor."

"In their eyes."

"In here, that's all that matters." He grimaced as a deep shiver went through him. He coughed deep in his chest. "I would be grateful now to sit up."

Grasping him by one hand, placing his other behind his back, Bourne levered him into a sitting position.

"What's that smell? Never mind, it's me."

"We have very little time," Bourne said. "We've got to get you out of here."

"Not even easily said," the general said. He squinted, seeming in no hurry to go anywhere. "You're not Bourne, are you?"

"I told you as much as I can," Bourne countered. "I need you to tell me what the Bourne Initiative is, really."

MacQuerrie was still squinting at Bourne. His cough rattled his chest; he turned his head, spat blood onto the floor. "I've been under duress for . . . I've lost all track of time. How do I know this isn't all a part of the . . . that I'm not still under duress?"

Bourne stripped off his shirt, showing the general his wounds; the bruises he'd gotten during his fight with Boxer were just blossoming. "I've expended a lot of time and effort—not to mention pain—to get to you, General."

MacQuerrie grunted, nodded. "Point taken." He flicked his hand out, stared at the fingers trembling in midair, closed his eyes for a moment. "The Bourne Initiative is a weaponized cyber program started by Bourne's—or should I say *your*—good friend, the late General Boris Karpov, of the Russian FSB, to penetrate our defenses and winkle out the president's nuclear codes. Are you seriously telling me you don't know anything about that?"

"More than that, I can tell you categorically that Boris would never be party to such a program."

MacQuerrie lifted one eyebrow. "Really?"

"So either that's not the true nature of the Initiative, or you don't know what you're talking about."

"I *always* know what I'm talking about." He grunted again, but this time he expelled a gout of blood. "Ugh, what the hell?"

Bourne laid the general back down, palpated the areas over his vital organs. MacQuerrie screamed.

"What is it?" the Angelmaker asked. "What's the matter with him?"

"What isn't?" Bourne looked down at MacQuerrie. "No point in sugar-coating it, General. Liver, kidneys. As a result there's massive internal bleeding." He bent lower. "Tell me what you know."

"I don't—"

"You always know what you're talking about, General. You're not a liar, are you?"

"Jason, I hear footsteps," the Angelmaker said from her position by the door.

"Turn on the heat lamps," Bourne ordered.

"What?"

"Just do it, Mala. And take your SIM card out of your mobile."

She switched the heat lamps on, and immediately the temperature in the room increased.

"These things could roast the skin right off you," the Angelmaker said, palming her SIM card.

"What they're there for," the general said with an infinite weariness. He'd taken the Whole Nine Yards and was about to pay the ultimate price.

Bourne's eyes locked with MacQuerrie's. "Spill it. Now."

"I suppose it doesn't matter now. The Initiative is indeed a cyber program—a DDOS malware."

"Okay. We've already experienced a handful of distributed denial-of-service attacks. They've brought the Internet to its knees, like a power grid outage. Malware infects and then directs a huge number of DVRs, security cameras, Internet-connected cars and cameras—anything and everything that is an Internet-of-everything device—to create a world-wide botnet, a cyber-creature with one mind, which sends massive amounts of queries to any number of websites, crashing them."

"Right. But this one is as different from the botnets we've seen as VR is from the old Asteroids video game. It will slice right through the correctives like a knife through warm butter."

"What's the target?"

"You know your old friend, Bourne. He wasn't a political animal, not at all. In fact, he hated the Sovereign and all he stood for. No, this malware is meant to crash the sites of the world's biggest banks."

"Money," Bourne breathed.

"Yes, money. Of course money. Transferred out while the sites are frozen through a program piggybacked onto the malware."

It sounded right. Just like Boris. And yet, he had the sense there was something MacQuerrie wasn't telling him, or, more likely, didn't know. That also would be like Boris. "And you know this how?"

MacQuerrie tried to laugh, but another gout of blood was all he could bring up. Through lips stained red, he said, "Your pal Boris and I were partners."

With a deep-felt groan, he turned on his side. His face was deathly pale. His extremities seemed already devoid of blood. "Beautiful plan, Bourne, magnificent." He hawked up more blood, and something else that was black and viscid. "Problem is...someone hijacked the program, shortly after Boris was killed."

"Who?"

MacQuerrie shook his head once, then grew very still.

"General, who hijacked the malware program?"

"There's a third partner, a friend of Boris's." He gasped. "I never met him."

"Who?" Bourne leaned closer. "Who is he?"

"I went on Boris's word."

"General..."

MacQuerrie's eyes seemed to be dissolving in water; they had lost almost all the luster of the living. "His name is Dima." He gasped again, and fingers of one hand curled, as if grasping for something unseen. "Dima Vladimirovich Orlov."

Bourne glanced briefly at Mala. "I don't know of him. Do you?"

After a moment, she nodded, her face pale and waxen.

"Problem is . . ." MacQuerrie gave an animal grunt that brought Bourne's attention back to him. "The trouble is that Dima Orlov is free to use the program to attack anything he wants. Get me, Bourne? Any fucking thing. And there's something else . . ."

"General . . ."

But MacQuerrie was done, and, in any event, the Angelmaker said, "Here they come." She shot Bourne a glance. "I don't know what you're thinking, but we're never making it out of here."

28

'M NOT HUNGRY," Morgana said when she met Françoise for dinner. "This evening I'd rather walk."

The storm that had gripped Kalmar earlier had spent itself inland, leaving the sky clear and the air cool and refreshed. It was, in fact, the perfect evening for a long walk. Also, a long talk, which was Morgana's purpose in skipping dinner. She was far too nervous to sit still, let alone to eat a meal. There was a lump in her throat no amount of self-calming could clear. Her biggest worry was how her friend would take the news that she had been taken in, as Morgana herself had been, by the falsely named Larry London. She knew Françoise well enough to understand that she prided herself in her friends—they were, to a person, immaculately curated, trusted, and prized.

For a time, they strolled along the waterfront, until Morgana's nose was so filled with the stench of fish she felt her gorge rising. Everyone she passed looked strange, slightly off-kilter, vaguely sinister, even the two boys who snickered, seemed to eye her with evil intent as they kicked a soccer ball around. Shadows appeared to leap out at her from the narrow spaces between buildings. Doorways looked smashed down, windows crooked. The noises of the city, usually soft and gentle compared to D.C. or New York, threatened to overwhelm her.

As she turned them inland, Françoise broke the silence between them. "You look troubled. Is anything the matter? Is it the usual? Are you missing home again?"

"No, it's not the usual, though I am missing home, more than ever." Morgana replied so slowly it seemed every word was being pulled out of her.

Françoise took her hand. "Then what is it?" She halted them, so they could face each other. "Come on, you know you can tell me anything, right?"

"Right," Morgana said, though without much conviction.

Françoise smiled. "So come on, then. Let's hear it. I mean, how bad can it be?"

"Maybe you shouldn't ask that," Morgana said with a brittle laugh that ended abruptly. She stared into her friend's eyes. "I've found out something about Larry."

"What? He's fucking around, yes? While he should be working. It's okay, Larry's kind of ADHD, he's on and off everything all the time. It doesn't mean—"

"Stop," Morgana said, jerking her hand away. "Just stop, okay?"

Françoise nodded, frowning deeply. "Okay. What then? I'm listening."

"Françoise, Larry London isn't Larry London."

A look of disbelief crossed Françoise's face. She laughed and shook her head. "What? I'm not following."

"Larry London isn't his real name."

Françoise's eyebrows rose. "No? What is it, then?"

"That's just it. I don't know."

"Then how—?"

"He's a Russian spy."

Françoise's laughter rang out. "Oh, come on! That's ridiculous. Our Larry?"

"He isn't *our* anything, Françoise. He's not at all what he makes himself out to be."

"Really?" Françoise's tone turned skeptical. "Okay, then, show me the proof."

Now it all spilled out: the Internet flash-carrier band that had delivered a four-packet message to Larry—"or whoever the hell his real name is"—the fourth packet Morgana had managed to translate. She took a sheet of paper from her handbag, unfolded it carefully, handed it to her friend. Françoise scanned a hard copy of the message, reading it over and over. Then Morgana pointed to the line in the top in very small print that showed the message came from Unit 309 of *spetsnaz*.

"I don't know about you," Morgana concluded, "but I had to look up that word: *spetsnaz*. It's the 'special action' division of the Russian state police." She shuddered. "I've been marked, Françoise—as have you, I surmise."

Françoise found a stoop and sat down heavily, her eyes glued to the message fragment. "Calm down," she said, as if by rote.

"Calm down?" Morgana's hands flailed the air. "Françoise, this whole thing...I mean, my God, I'm working for the fucking Russians."

"Wow, I..." Françoise ran a hand through her hair. "Okay, well, let's think this through."

Morgana bent over her. "Hey, there's nothing to think through. I'm already guilty of treason. I want out, Françoise. Now. Tonight. Get me the fuck out of Dodge."

"And leave me here to deal with this clusterfuck myself?" Françoise looked up. "Thank you very much."

"That's not what I—"

"Well, that's what I meant when I said let's think this through. Give me that much credit at least. I mean, I'm as shocked as you are. More, really. I've known Larry a long time. Christ, what a nightmare. What was he hoping to get from me?"

"Besides me, you mean?"

"We met years ago. He couldn't have known—"

"What? We were already friends," Morgana said. "D'you honestly think your meeting was accidental? D'you really think you weren't vetted in every detail of your life—including your friends, associates and clients—before he made contact?"

"Oh, my God." Françoise put a hand over her mouth.

"I know, right?"

"How could I have been so blind?" Françoise crumpled the sheet of paper in her fist. "I should've seen..."

"How could you?" Morgana sat down beside her friend, enfolded her hand, and Françoise began to cry. "No one could have seen it. It was just a fluke—a lucky break—that I stumbled on that fragment."

"Morgana, what would I have done without you?" She wiped her eyes. "We've got to sort this out."

"What? No. This guy's a professional spy. Françoise, he's been ordered to kill me."

"Not until you're done decoding the cyber weapon."

Morgana reared back. "What the hell are you saying?"

Françoise looked down.

"What is it?"

Heaving a sigh, Françoise's eyes met hers. "I can't just cut and run. Larry knows too much about me. I have to figure out a way to—"

Morgana's eyes opened wide. "A way to what?"

Françoise shuddered. "You know."

Morgana uttered an incredulous bark. "Are you for real?"

Françoise's eyes were imploring. "Morgana, I can't do it on my own."

"You must be out of your mind."

"I wish I were, I really do." She squeezed Morgana's hand tight. "But I'm not." Her expression was intense. "Please, Morgana. Help me. Please, please, please."

"Jesus God."

Morgana weighed her intense desire to get as far away from Larry London as she could, as quickly as she could, against her obligation to her friend. It was Françoise who got her out of the NSA's clutches;

without her, she would still be in a locked room somewhere in D.C. Françoise had saved her life. She owed her friend big time for that.

"All right," she said at length. She had committed herself, though not without a deep sense of misgiving. "Let's see what we can come up with."

29

"QUICKLY, NOW!" Bourne gestured. "Your mobile. Drop it under the heat lamps."

A smile of understanding lit up her face. She dug the phone out, set it down in the center of the circles of heat, drawing her hand back quickly.

"I never liked that phone much, anyway," she said as she followed Bourne out of The Drowning Pool, through the door opposite the one through which they had entered.

Behind them, the lithium-ion battery that powered Mala's mobile heated up to an intolerable level, and, just as three NSA techs rushed into The Drowning Pool, it exploded in their faces.

Alarms went off all over the place. They sprinted down corridors, the Angelmaker following Bourne's every step. His eidetic memory had imprinted every nook and cranny of the great house. They hid in a utility closet as armed men rushed past on their way to the emergency in The Drowning Pool; they gingerly climbed an old, disused staircase with several rotten treads to gain the main floor; they escaped the confines of the house, not through any of the four doors on the main floor that led outside, which were doubtless being guarded, but by jumping out a second-floor window that overlooked a huge oak tree, down which they climbed.

They made their way past the huge tree, left down the dirt track. Bourne made sure they skirted the site of the shootings, hurrying them along through copses of oak and poplar, until they were in sight of Arthur Lee's small stone house.

Lee was waiting for them in his old rattletrap of a truck.

"Once I heard the commotion, I knew you'd either be coming through the woods or you'd be dead. One way or t'other the day had gone in another direction." He pointed. "Who's this lovely lady?"

"A friend," the Angelmaker said. "That's all you need to know."

"Sassy critter, ain'tcha?" Lee grinned. "My name's Arthur, but you, missy, can call me Artie."

"Arthur," Bourne cut in.

"Right." Lee hooked a thumb over his shoulder. "Under the tarp back there, situate yourselves between the bales of hay."

When Bourne hesitated, he added, "They check coming in, not going out."

"But with the alarms going off—"

"There's a fire now in the great house, but I'm guessing you know that already." Lee winked. "You just get covered up and leave the rest to me."

They climbed in the back, made themselves as comfortable as possible, being squeezed between bales, pulled the tarp over themselves, tied it down to hooks in the sides of the truck bed.

No sooner had they done that, then, with a protesting shriek of gears the truck rocked away from Lee's house, heading for one of the gates. Soon enough, it was clear that he was making for the eastern gate on the other side of the property, an excellent choice, since it was the one farthest away from the growing mayhem.

By the time they reached the gate, the wail of fire engines could be heard, and the guards, distracted by the noises, addressed Lee only long enough to ask him what was going on. It seemed as if everyone near the great house was too busy to contact them.

"Grease fire, far's I can tell," Lee said easily. "But, y'know, I'm not al-lowed inside the great house, so it's anyone's guess."

One of the guards grunted. "I'd fucking let you in," he muttered under his breath.

The other said, "Going for your usual evening hay run, Arthur?"

"To the Sizemore farm. That's about the size of it."

The gates opened, and he drove through, out into the darkling coun-tryside. The sun had set, splashing vivid colors across the western sky. Crows wheeled overhead, then made for their nests in faraway trees. A dog barked, then was still. Rabbits were at play in the fields, their heads coming up, their bodies freezing as the truck trundled past.

When they were far enough away from ground zero, Lee tooted his horn; it was a funny sound, like something you'd hear at a circus or a sideshow. Bourne and the Angelmaker scrambled out from under the fluttering tarp. Lee stopped just long enough for them to join him in the cab.

"Where to, missy?" he asked with a crooked smile.

"It's his show," she said, indicating Bourne.

Lee's head bobbed up and down. "Know that already; just bein' po-lite."

"I appreciate that," the Angelmaker said. "More than you know."

Seeming satisfied with the direction of the conversation, Lee put the truck in gear, and they continued their rumbling journey due east, away from Crowcroft.

"Second star to the left," Bourne said, "then straight on till morning."

"Shouldn't that be 'to the right'?" Lee said.

"Only if we're going to Never, Never Land," Bourne replied.

For a time, they rattled on in companionable silence. Bourne could tell Mala was depleted; she needed rest, but he had questions he needed to put to her.

"I assume you followed me all the way from Somalia," he said.

"That's right." She had her head back, resting on the seat.

"Keyre's orders."

"Right again."

"How the hell did you manage to get into Crowcroft?"

"I didn't." Her eyes snapped open, but they seemed to be looking at something only she could see. "I was stupid. I made a mistake. I under-estimated—"

"And they caught you."

"After a fashion."

"After a fashion?"

She smirked. "I got inside, didn't I?"

But at what cost? Bourne wondered, but said nothing, letting a brief pause mark the end of any further discussion of Mala's presence.

"What do you know about this third partner, Dima Orlov?"

"Not much. He's a shadowy figure flitting about the Moscow under-world. I never met him; no one I know has. He's like a ghost." She screwed up her face. "I heard once that he and General Karpov were childhood friends, they had a falling out as adolescents, but you know how deep the bonds run between childhood friends in Russia. The story goes they patched things up in adulthood."

Bourne wracked his memory, trying to recall if Boris had ever men-tioned Dima Orlov. But his memory was unreliable, and for the ten-thousandth time he cursed it. His eyes were closing; the motion of the truck, the low rumble of its engine, was making him drowsy. All the adrenaline had drained out of him. He was almost as depleted as Mala looked. It felt so good to see the open road ahead of them, the trees a blur of green, to hear the whistle of the wind through the open win-dows, feel the air on his skin. Just, for once, to relax.

But in Bourne's world that was a kind of joke. For someone who slept with one eye open, the concept of relaxation scarcely existed, and when, like now, that rare sensation crept over him, it usually had the life span of a mayfly. And, sure enough, this moment would be no exception.

The roaring of big honking motorcycles coming up behind them dis-solved the instant's peace like a pin in a balloon. There were four of them—German-style spiked helmets, grinning skulls emblazoned on

the backs of scarred black leather vests, fringes and long, stringy hair
fluttering like wounded birds. They rode new Harley V-Rod Muscle
bikes, the most powerful in the line.

They came up two on each side, muscled arms shining, as well oiled
as their machines. They moved in and out, coming just close enough
to rattle Arthur Lee. Lee, who had seen just about every atrocity man
could perpetrate on another, didn't seem to be the type to rattle easily.
But these big guys were armed with handguns. Two had sawed-off shot-
guns slung diagonally across their backs. One, on the passenger's side,
had his pistol cradled in his lap.

One of the four horsemen of the new apocalypse veered toward
Arthur Lee. Before Arthur had a chance to zip up his window, the biker
brandished a hunting knife with a thick serrated blade.

"Hey, you!" he shouted. "You, boy!" He swung the blade in a shallow
arc. It whistled through the air over the moaning of the wind and came
within inches of Lee's cheek. "Hey, boy, I have some boots for you to
shine! I have some grits to push into your pussy face!" He swung again,
Lee cringed away, and the truck careened out of its lane.

The leader laughed. "Careful, boy! Didn't your master teach you how
to drive?" Holding his knife high, he swung in again, this time with the
blade pointed directly at Lee's carotid artery. Lee turned the wheel over
hard, toward the two bikers on the other side.

Bourne had had enough. He was prepared for Lee's sharp swerve to
the right. Swinging his door open, he leapt at the biker brandishing the
handgun, knocking him clean off the saddle. The biker hit the ground
hard, shoulder first, then his head. His helmet flew off and, as he rolled,
the side of his head struck a stone outcropping.

Grabbing control of the Harley, Bourne made a screaming U-turn,
came at the second biker on his side. He was aiming his big Colt .45
at the spot right between Bourne's eyes. An instant before he squeezed
the trigger, Bourne dropped down below the level of the handlebars.
The bullet whanged over his head, and he kicked out with his left boot,
delivering a hard enough blow to the V-Rod to send it veering off the

road. He followed it as the biker struggled to regain control. To do that he had to holster his Colt. Bourne, executing another 180, rushed at the Harley from behind. He struck the biker in the kidney, and the biker winced; Bourne snatched the .45 out of its holster and shot the biker in the back, shattering his spine. The out of control V-Rod roared to a spectacular crash against the guardrail, its gas tank splitting open. Flames sprang up, engulfing the leather saddle and the man sitting astride it, followed by a blinding flash and a red ball of confusion.

Bourne revved the Harley, taking off after the truck and the remaining two bikers. Some distance behind him, a cloud of dust was rising rapidly, and he wondered whether guards from Crowcroft had finally gotten their act together and come after them.

Even so, first things first.

One of the remaining bikers had slipped his sawed-off out of his quiverlike sheath, was aiming it into the truck's interior while the leader came roaring back down the road directly at Bourne. A pair of legs shot out of the truck's open window, scissored around the biker's arm. The shotgun went off, tearing a hole in the truck's fender right above the gas tank. Some of the buckshot must have penetrated the tank because the truck began to leak gas like a sieve. Meanwhile, The Angelmaker, having consolidated her grip on the biker, drew him off his saddle with the astonishing strength of her thighs. As she brought his face close to her, she slammed her knuckles into his windpipe, crushing the vital cricoid cartilage. She released her viselike grip and the biker slammed against the curve of the truck's fender on his hard tumble to the tarmac.

That left the leader. Instead of aiming his shotgun at Bourne, he swung it behind him. He was staring at Bourne, a big, fat grin on his bearded face as he squeezed off a shot right into the heart of the truck's gas tank. Sparks flew, what was left of the ruined cap blew off, and flames shot from the open mouth. It was only a matter of time before the fire spread to the cabin, or worse, the truck exploded.

As the leader had correctly anticipated, Bourne swung around him, making for the truck, which was yawing back and forth in ever widening arcs. Inside the cab he glimpsed the Angelmaker struggling to regain control from Arthur Lee. He hoped she was grinding the gears into neutral in preparation for turning off the ignition. She knew they had to get out of the cab before it became an inferno, trapping them inside.

Just as Bourne passed the leader's bike, he felt a flash of agony in the side of his head. The biker had thrown his sawed-off at Bourne, striking a direct blow. Black spots danced in front of Bourne's eyes; his hands went slack on the handlebars. One foot slipped off the rest, and he swayed, close to taking a fall.

The leader was coming at him, his Colt out and at the ready. He was close enough for the kill shot, but he was a careful man. Closer still, and even with the erratic motion of the Harleys, he couldn't miss. His forefinger, tightened on the trigger, began to squeeze, and then with a deafening roar his head exploded, drenching Bourne in brains and bone. The driverless V-Rod wobbled, then jumped the road, struck the top of the guardrail, flipped like a pinwheel going over.

Bourne didn't get to see the end result. He heard it, though, a great booming, a grinding of hot metal and scorched tires. Then out of the chaos, Jimmy Lang's vehicle appeared beside him. A strong arm grabbed him, settling him back on the saddle.

"You didn't think I was going to let you have all the fun," Jimmy said, grinning.

"Arthur's truck," Bourne said, still slightly disoriented.

"Not to worry," Jimmy said. "They're both out."

At that moment, Arthur Lee's truck went up like a screaming, rageful fireball.

Part Three

Dima

30

I T WAS AN ill-omened day in her life when Françoise was obliged to seek out her brother unannounced. She spent a fruitless but necessary twenty minutes surveilling the area in and around the marina, making certain it was clean. She was sure Gora's people had already done this, but years in the field had ingrained certain routines so deeply she performed them even when logic dictated they were redundant. Fieldwork had proved time and again that logic had little to do with being captured and either killed or put under articulated interrogation.

So it was that forty-five minutes after dawn on the morning after Morgana's dramatic revelation concerning Larry London, she found herself progressing down toward her brother's boat, which lay peacefully at anchor just as it had been when he had summoned her some days ago.

The wind plucked rigging like the strings on a double bass, tap-tap-tapping them against masts. Clouds scudded by overhead, and the new day's sunlight slanted in, warming the back of her neck. There was something jolly and at the same time peaceful about a marina—boats rocking gently in their slips, people going about their deck work with a particular serenity. No one hurried, no one ran, no one shouted. Often, as now, it was all but deserted. And yet the marina remained alive, moving to the pulse of the tide.

Two of Gora's men stood guard at the head of the metal gangway. One, who was new and therefore didn't know her, barred her way. But the other, Sigi, was an old hand, and he waved her aboard. She found Gora below, in the galley, in a silk robe. He was frying eggs and the kind of bacon you could only purchase in America. An aromatic waft of coffee came to her, making her mouth water.

A young blond woman, naked to the waist, was seated at the built-in table, a sheet twisted around her loins. She turned, startled at Françoise's abrupt appearance, but she made no attempt to hide her nakedness.

"Who's she?" she asked in Swedish-accented English.

"Get dressed," Gora said to her, turning the strips of bacon. "And get out of here."

The blonde pouted. "What about the breakfast you promised me?"

Gora threw a fistful of bills on the table, and said, "Go on. Beat it."

When she reached for them, he swept them onto the floor.

Françoise took a step toward the woman. "Gora, there's no need—"

"Keep still," he said in Russian.

The blonde, trembling, crouched to gather them up.

Brother and sister confronted each other warily. Not a word was exchanged until the woman hastily dressed, hopping on one high heel while trying desperately to slip on the other, and crossed the cabin. She shot Françoise a glare as full of hatred as it was of jealousy before flouncing out onto the deck, where Sigi took her in hand.

"Breakfast?" Gora said then, as if the woman had never existed. "It's one hundred percent American."

"So I see."

"Go ahead, sis. Pour yourself some coffee." He eyed her. "You look like you need it."

He lifted the bacon strips out of their own fat, laid them carefully on a sheet of paper towel; about some things he was meticulous. When she had a mug in her hands and had taken the first sip, he said, "I assume it's important."

"Urgent, more like."

His eyebrows rose like a pair of ravens lifting off a tree branch. Using a spatula, he transferred the fried eggs, two at a time, onto plates. Then he meted out the bacon in identical portions. Crossing to the table, which was already laid with two places, he set down the plates. No toast; he hated toast.

They both sat at the same time, facing each other, and began to eat with the same quick motions, as if they were identical twins.

After he had finished precisely half his breakfast, he looked up at her. "Tell me."

So she did. She told him everything that Morgana had related regarding the messages from Unit 309 to Larry London, or, as they knew him, Nikolay Ivanovich Rozin. "Now she knows Niki is a Russian spy. Now she knows she's been working for the Russians, and she's terrified. I had to talk her down from fleeing the country immediately." She tried unsuccessfully to interpret Gora's flat gaze. "How could *spetsnaz* be so careless?"

"*Spetsnaz*," her brother said, "and specifically Unit 309, have no knowledge of this girl you've brought to us."

"Morgana's a fucking cyber genius," Françoise spit out. "She's going to save you—"

"Maybe she is," he said, chewing on a bit of bacon. "Maybe she isn't." Grease lacquered his full lips. There was a spot of it on his chin. He picked up his last strip of bacon. "The point is, we are now saddled with a liability."

Françoise reacted instantly. "Oh, no. You're not going to harm a hair on her head."

"Alyoshka, did I say anything about doing her harm?"

"You said she's a liability."

Gora shook his head. "No, Alyoshka. I said we are saddled with a liability. My exact words." He looked over at her plate. "Finished?"

She made a contemptuous gesture. "Go ahead."

Picking up her plate, he set it down on top of his own. Then he drove the tines of his fork into the last remaining egg. The yolk ran every which way across the plate; he mopped it up with two of her bacon strips, cramming them in his mouth. He chewed reflectively for what seemed a long while. Times like these, he disgusted her. She wondered how it could be that they shared any amount of DNA. But she waited for him to continue; there was no use prodding him.

"What about you?" he said at length.

She shook her head, not following. "What about me?"

"She knows Niki is a Russian spy. You introduced her to Niki. You and Niki are friends. Does she suspect—?"

"Absolutely not."

"How can you be sure?"

"If she suspected me, Gora, she would have booked the first flight out of here. Instead, she came to me. She thinks Niki gulled me as well as her. We're friends; she trusts me."

"You'd better be right." He pushed aside both plates and gave her the cool, appraising look she hated. "Did it ever occur to you that she's been working you?"

"What? No. Not for a minute. I know her too well."

"None of us know anyone else. Isn't that the first lesson we learn in the field?"

She said nothing, folded her arms across her chest.

"Wait a minute." Gora struck his forehead with the heel of his hand. "How was I so stupid? How did I not see it?"

"See what?"

"You and this woman, this Morgana Roy." He rose from the table and stepped toward her, torso inclined aggressively. "You really *are* friends. You care about her."

"Don't be ridiculous." A ball of ice had formed in the pit of her stomach.

Her brother's eyes were gleaming darkly. "I know your secret now,

Alyoshka. The one you would never tell me. You've made the mistake all novice field agents are trained to avoid."

"You're babbling, Gora." But she felt a kind of panic rising up inside her.

"You've become involved with your mark."

She shook her head, a weak response, to be sure.

"You've come to see her as a *person*, you *care* about her well-being." He clucked his tongue against the roof of his mouth. "How you've weakened yourself. Sis." He raised a forefinger. "We shall have to do something about that. Otherwise..."

The cotton ball of panic had reached the back of her throat, and she almost gagged. "Otherwise what?" she managed to get out.

"Otherwise, you'll be of no use to me."

She felt the silence between them like a straitjacket. She found herself in a place she did not like, with no exit.

Gora tapped his lips with a finger, a quick pattern, like a silent song's beat. "Here's what we'll do." The glimmer of his smile turned her bones cold. "You'll get your *friend* to do it herself."

"Do what herself?"

"Don't be dense, Alyoshka. You'll get her to dispose of our liability."

"Who? Niki?" She was aghast. "He's the head of *spetsnaz* now, for God's sake. You're crazy."

Gora grinned. "Crazy like a Russian bear. Konstantin appointing him was simply a power play aimed at his brother. I know that. You know that. Every-fucking-body knows that. Just as they know that it's far too dangerous for the head of *spetsnaz* to be in the field." He shrugged. "Konstantin violated the rules of the game. When his chess piece gets taken off the board he only has himself to blame. We weaken Konstantin, we're free of blame, and we clear the field for you to slip into Niki's old position, make his contacts yours." He chuckled. "That is, *ours*."

"Huh. And how exactly am I to do that? I doubt Morgana's ever even held a gun."

"All the better," her brother said. "Niki will never suspect her until she pulls the trigger, and by then it'll be too late."

"You didn't answer my question."

Gora cleared the dishes, stacking them in the small stainless-steel sink. "Simple," he said, "you'll put her in a situation where she has no other option."

Just like me, Françoise thought in despair.

———

Everybody knows that in the field the best-laid plans are sometimes undone by the simplest of human quirks which, no matter how one tries, cannot be anticipated. Everybody knows no plan is airtight. Everybody knows it can all go sideways, but the plans are made nevertheless because in the field the dice are rolled and the chances are taken. There is no other way.

And so, what everybody knows, everybody conveniently forgets.

One of these unforeseen human quirks had occurred the previous night, when Morgana told Françoise what she had learned about Larry London. When they parted ways, both women to their hotel rooms, Morgana could not sleep. After switching off the light, tossing and turning on a roiling sea of anxiety, she relit her bedside lamp. When reading didn't help, she got out of bed, dressed, and stood by the window, looking out at the street below, just as she had as a kid when high fevers made sleep impossible. Watching the wind in the willows, the play of moonlight on the brushlike branches, soothed her more effectively than a cold compress across her brow. In this urban setting, the streetlights, the occasional passing car, the lamps blinking in mysterious conversation along the marina wharf, did the same. And she stood there, her mind starting to relax as the night staggered to its end and light returned to the world.

A short time later, she spotted Françoise hurrying out of the hotel. She crossed the street, heading toward the marina. Curious where her friend might be going at this ungodly hour, she slipped out of her room, ran down the stairs, and out the front door, following in Françoise's urgent footsteps.

She ducked behind the corner of a building as Françoise turned to look over her shoulder. For upward of twenty minutes Françoise appeared to do nothing but survey the area. Why then had she been in such a hurry? Morgana wondered. She hesitated, awash in guilt. What was she doing, following a friend, the woman who had moved heaven and earth to free her from the clutches of the NSA? And yet, she found her feet moving forward, as if of their own volition. *Curiosity killed the cat,* she thought. But it created a terribly strong impulse, one that wouldn't be denied.

At length, she saw Françoise heading along one of the wooden walkways. Boats rocked gently in their slips, rigging snapped, far off a buoy clanged. All soft sounds. Morgana, still partially in hiding, observed that Françoise stopped in front of the slip where a boat named *Carbon Neutral* was tied up. Two burly, rough-looking men with Slavic faces guarded the gangway. One of them barred her way, but the other appeared to know her, for he beckoned to her.

Françoise stepped aboard with the alacrity and confidence that could only come from having been on *Carbon Neutral* before. What in the world could she be up to? Something stirred inside her, a cool, slithery thing that raised questions along with its head.

Moments later, she saw the guard who had recognized Françoise escorting a young blond woman off the boat. Her hair was uncombed, her makeup smeared. Her ultra-short skirt and her ultra-high heels marked her out as a prostitute. With a little cry, she ripped her arm away from the guard's grip, turned her back on him, strode unsteadily away. Morgana marked her drunken progress along the walkway, and when she was almost at the end, where the wooden wharf met the concrete dock, Morgana decided on a course of action.

She waited until the blonde was out of sight of the two men guarding *Carbon Neutral*, then started on her trajectory. As she neared the blonde she increased her speed until, glancing fearfully over her shoulder, she ran right into her.

"Oh, my God, I'm so sorry," she said as she helped the blonde back onto her feet.

"Shit's sake! What's the matter with you, anyway?" the blonde all but snarled. "Idiot! Why don't you look where you're going?"

Morgana put on an apologetic face. "Well, I would have, except for the man who was trying to grab me."

As Morgana had calculated, this little tidbit immediately reversed the blonde's demeanor. "What?"

"It happened back there." Morgana gestured vaguely toward the streets. "I was on my way home after, you know, a long night with..." She cleared her throat. "A guy I met in a bar. I was drunk, not thinking clearly. I was almost at my hotel when this guy grabbed me. When he started to pull me into an alley I kicked him in the balls and ran like hell."

The blonde nodded, captured her unruly hair, which the sea breeze kept blowing into her face, deftly twisted it into a knot at the top of her head. "I know exactly how you feel." She unbuttoned her shirt halfway down so Morgana could see the deep bruise darkening between her breasts. "Something of the kind happened to me this morning."

Morgana squeezed her shoulder in sympathy. "I'd say what we both need is some strong coffee and a good breakfast. What d'you say?" She held out her hand. "My name's Morgana."

The blonde took her hand briefly but energetically. "Natalie," she said. "And, I don't know about you, but I'd love a jigger or two of liquor in my coffee."

———

Down by the marina, soldiers appeared in full camo, helmets, carrying submachine guns across their chests. They were members of the Skaraborg Armored Regiment and an odd sight indeed. Morgana asked Natalie about them, but she had no idea why they might be deployed.

The two women sat across from each other in a small, dark café near the water. It smelled of stale beer and staler sweat, but it was the only place open at this hour. Morgana did not want to take Natalie to her hotel restaurant for fear of running into either Larry or Françoise.

The door kept opening, fishermen coming in straight off their boats, reeking of the sea, scales making tiny rainbows on their slickers as they caught the light. Usually, the banter between the men was light-hearted and inevitably salty, punctuated with raucous laughter. But this morning, as if echoing Morgana's mood, the atmosphere was tight with tension. What banter began petered out quickly and morosely.

"His name is Gora, that much I know for sure," Natalie said. "And he's Russian. I know a little. He spoke to his guards in Russian."

Russian, Morgana thought. *Dear God.*

The smoked fish and thin triangles of dark bread Morgana had ordered were already half gone. The stink of fish no longer bothered her; she was adjusting to her new life.

Natalie stirred enormous amounts of sugar into her black coffee, the café's only substitute for liquor. "And the woman was Russian, too."

Morgana felt the muscles in her shoulders and neck tense. Her head came up like a pointer scenting prey. "What woman?"

Natalie made a face. "A woman came in while Gora was fixing us breakfast. Very beautiful. Gora's demeanor changed as soon as she appeared. He stiffened, became an iceman. He had no more use for me. He began to trash-talk me. Then he kicked me out."

These details rushed past Morgana like a runaway freight train. "You said the woman was Russian. How do you know that?"

"Gora spoke to her in Russian."

"But—"

"Morgana, I know enough Russian to understand. He spoke to her as one intimate to another, nothing formal about it."

Morgana's throbbing heart was already sinking in her breast, but just to make sure, she said, "Can you describe this woman?"

Natalie had a keen eye, that much was clear after only fifteen seconds.

But even if she hadn't, Morgana would have recognized Françoise from the description. Of course it was Françoise. Morgana had been watching; no other woman had gone anywhere near *Carbon Neutral*.

She needed not to think about Françoise for a moment, give herself a little time to recover from the stunned reverberations this revelation had caused deep inside her. She turned her attention to the subdued conversations around them. She still had only a bare-bones understanding of Swedish, so she asked Natalie to listen in and translate for her.

After several minutes of concentration, with her expression seemingly darkening each second, Natalie said: "Now I understand the military presence. The MSB—that's the Civil Contingency Agency—has ordered local governments countrywide to establish operations centers in underground bunkers, maintain a network of emergency sirens, and to coordinate with Swedish Armed Forces." She stared at Morgana. "We're being asked to prepare for a conflict with Russia."

Morgana's thoughts were in total disarray. She had hoped that taking her mind off her own problem would help settle her, get her over the shock. But now this. But whereas Natalie had to consider the bigger picture, she needed to concentrate on her own situation first, which was precisely this: Larry London wasn't Larry London. Françoise Sevigne wasn't Françoise Sevigne. How could she be so blind, why hadn't she seen that the moment Larry was exposed Françoise was suspect as well? The answer was clear enough: emotion. She liked Françoise. A lot. They had been friends for some time, shared intimate moments. They had laughed together, shopped together; they'd even, on occasion, shared clothes. *Good Christ,* she thought. *What have I gotten myself into?*

Natalie put down her coffee cup, placed her hand over Morgana's. "Your face has lost all color. Is everything all right?"

"I'm perfectly fine." Morgana smiled like the porcelain doll she'd adored as a child. "Never better."

31

THE TV, SET to CNN, was muted. Nevertheless, the scroll at the bottom told the breaking story of Russian military forces moving toward the borders of Estonia, Latvia, Belarus—with which the current Kremlin regime had an economic accord but no formal alliance—and already pushing farther into Ukraine. This in addition to the troops and war matériel inside Syria. Despite the Russian Sovereign's claims that all maneuvers were simply part of war games, all this bellicose activity was sending NATO into a frenzy, especially since the new American president seemed indifferent to the threat. Events that had been long simmering appeared to be coming to a head.

Mala turned away from her contemplation of the news. "Whatever the Bourne Initiative is, do you think it could be tied in to the Sovereign's far more aggressive stance?"

"I think it's highly likely, which is why we've no time to waste in getting to Dima. According to General MacQuerrie, Dima Orlov took advantage of the chaos following Boris's murder to hijack the cyber weapon." Bourne wasn't looking at the screen, but nor was he looking at her.

"You're angry with me," Mala said.

"I didn't say anything to that effect."

"You didn't have to."

"I don't know how you can do the bidding of a man who tortured you," Bourne said. "I don't know how you can keep doing his bidding when I saved you from him."

They were lying on a bed in a chain hotel room on the fringes of Dulles International Airport. Bourne had called his old friend, Deron. After sending him photos of Mala and himself, they were awaiting Deron's messenger with new passports. Bourne still had his prosthetics; he had cut Mala's hair and she had dyed it jet-black. They had checked into the hotel under the names Arnold and Mary Winstead, the same names that would be on the new passports; Bourne had paid cash, in advance.

The color scheme was ocher and brown, the room in dire need of refurbishing. Lights from the control tower periodically swept through the window, passing across the opposite wall. It was a depressing place, though both had been in far worse. For the moment, though, it was home.

"You took me away from him," she said softly. "But you didn't save me from him."

He reached around her, felt along the lines of the ritual scars on her back. "The incantation will only work if you believe in it."

Her eyes, lit with an inner fire, searched his face. "I do believe in it, Jason."

"Why?"

"I have no choice."

"There's always a choice. You still have free will."

She seemed to sink into herself, to ruminate deeply on the problem. As she did so, her countenance darkened. Rain spat against the window.

"You have no idea what I have, what I don't have."

"Then tell me."

She smiled, sadly, wistfully, ruefully. No one else he'd ever encountered could encompass so many emotions with a simple curl of the lips.

"No," Bourne said. "You're going to have to do better than that."

"Then you'll have to do better." She reached for him. "This is to be our lingua franca now, the currency with which we do business."

He held her at bay, shook his head. "Mala, don't."

She tossed her head. "Why not? I've dreamed of this moment, why should I not have it?"

"Why? Because I don't want it."

"It's the one thing you've withheld from me. And I want it."

He got up off the bed, moved away from her. He did not want her to touch him. "What you want is wrong, Mala. You must know that."

"I don't care," she raged.

"I know that." He said it calmly, softly, as if gentling her.

Abruptly, she turned away from him, but not before he saw that she was silently weeping.

Four Harleys by the side of the road, a man and a woman to ride two of them.

Hours ago, they had said good-bye to Arthur Lee and Jimmy Lang. Arthur had wanted to accompany them all the way back to D.C., but Bourne had reminded him that, considering the carnage, the best thing for both of them was to return to their respective homes as quickly as possible and resume their normal lives as if nothing had happened. Jimmy had concurred, and in the end, Arthur had conceded the point.

Bourne's next objective was to get himself and Mala into Russia as swiftly and efficiently as possible, while keeping so far under the radar they wouldn't be picked up by any clandestine organization; he was still acutely aware that both the Americans and the Russians were hunting him.

Keyre's transport plane was awaiting him, refueled and mainte-nanced, but the pilot and crew had orders to bring Bourne back to Somalia, so using it was out of the question. Bourne did not want Keyre to know where they were going, and while he couldn't be with Mala 24/7 to ensure she wouldn't contact the Somali magus herself, at least he'd had her destroy her mobile.

So while Arthur and Jimmy took the license tags off Arthur's truck, then climbed into Jimmy's vehicle, Bourne and Mala had taken possession of two of the motorcycles, the pairs setting off in opposite directions. On the way, Bourne had called Deron with his requests. Still in rural Virginia, he had withdrawn money from one of his many accounts under assumed names in banks throughout the world. They shopped for new clothes, and while Bourne purchased a pair of scissors, Mala chose the black hair dye color. Around three in the afternoon, he'd checked them into the chain hotel.

Bourne would buy their tickets as soon as he received their passports. The first leg was to Frankfurt. After a ninety-minute layover they would be booked on a two-hour, forty-minute Lufthansa flight into St. Petersburg. Even with their false identities, Bourne did not want to risk entering Russia through Moscow, where surveillance was always uncompromising. So they would take a train from St. Petersburg to Moscow. It was a long trip, but it couldn't be helped.

Their flight out didn't leave until after ten p.m.; there was time to kill, so to speak. They had a bite to eat and then, exhausted, they went up to their room and, sprawled side by side on the bed, slept like the dead.

———

The rain continued to beat against the window, the lights from the airport control tower flickered in and out of the room like a serpent's tongue. Someone in an adjacent room turned on the TV, a punch line followed by canned laughter seeping through the thin walls. Bourne, awake but unmoving for some time, slammed his fist against the wall, and the sounds ceased.

All at once in this shabby hotel room on the edge of everything, he felt his isolation, something he had lived with and grown used to, as keenly as a knife blade to his throat. He missed Sara more than he had missed anyone for a very long time. Once again, he wondered where she was, hated that he was unable to contact her while she was on assignment for Mossad. He understood as no one else the need for absolute security in the field, but that didn't—couldn't—stop his desire to be with her, to feel her body warm against his.

The phone ringing broke the train wreck of his thoughts, and he snatched the receiver off the console. It was the front desk.

"Yes."

"This is Carolyn, Mr. Winstead. A messenger is here from Tiffany's, sir. He insists on delivering his package to you in person."

"Send him up, Carolyn." *A messenger from Tiffany's* was the code phrase he and Deron had decided on. "Thank you."

"My pleasure, sir."

He woke Mala, the Angelmaker. It was time to go.

———

"We've found a passenger manifest listing," Ellison said into his mobile. "It's one of the names Bourne's been using since his Treadstone days. Paid cash, as expected." He grunted. "The twist is this time it's a mister and missus."

"You're all in place?" Marshall Fulmer said.

"At Dulles International, yes, sir," Ellison replied. "The team is deployed."

"Excellent," Fulmer said. "I'm on my way."

Dirk Ellison put away his mobile, signaled to his team to take their places. He glanced at his watch: 9:45. The international flight that Bourne and his female companion were booked on was scheduled to depart at 10:45; it would begin boarding in fifteen. There was no way Bourne and the woman were getting on that plane. Personally, he thought the woman might very well be that Mossad agent Bourne had been seen with, but, really, it didn't matter to him. Fulmer had been quite explicit: Bourne was the target; nothing else mattered.

Ellison watched the passengers at the gate in the departures lounge with his trained eagle eye—two young people of indeterminate gender sharing everything, a Coke, a burger, and whatever racket that passed for music those people listened to; an elderly threesome of yakking women, gray hair aflutter, hyped up for their first trip abroad; a couple with their three kids, reminding Ellison of the vast hole where his personal life began and ended.

But, hey, he was CIA through and through; second generation, in fact. His father was twice decorated in one of those so very desired secret ceremonies inside HQ that Ellison himself had yet to be invited to. But once he captured Jason Bourne, that would change in a heartbeat. He'd make his father proud of him. As a dedicated CIA agent, he hated taking orders from anyone other than his boss, or *his* boss, but times were changing, cross-agency missions, though despised by all the various mandarins, were now becoming more numerous. He didn't like it, but having made his case to his superior, he knew unequivocally that he had no say in the matter.

However, he had plenty of say in this matter right here, right now, and he was bound and determined to make the most of it. That's why, when he spied the couple coming down from the first class lounge, heading toward the gate as the door opened and the flight was called, he and his team closed in on them from all sides, trapping them in a move from which there was no escape.

32

MUCH TO HIS chagrin, Fulmer was obliged to take Harry Hornden, the freelance journo he had climbed into bed with, on his trip to
the airport. Like it or not, Hornden was now a de facto part of Fulmer's
entourage, sitting in the place of honor, beside Fulmer. Fulmer's nostrils
flared. Was it his imagination or was there a whiff of sulfur coming off
the web scribe

Fulmer sighed, working his butt into the backseat of his custom
Cadillac Escalade in a fruitless attempt to make himself more comfortable. Time was when journalism was a profession to be proud of. He
recalled the era when the CBS News of Douglas Edwards and Walter
Cronkite was the crown jewel of Bill Paley's so-called Tiffany Network.
The news division was an advertising loss leader, but so widely re-
spected and prize-winning it was worth it. No more. In this day and age,
networks could no longer afford loss leaders. Plus, the advent of Rupert
Murdoch's brand of shock-value news upended that American apple-
cart forever.

Now, Fulmer thought sourly, the so-called news was a joke, made
up of people like Harry Hornden, who had opinions in the place of a

journalistic background. And he wasn't even among the worst of them. But they all inhabited their own ring of hell, pulling breaking stories out of their butt holes.

"Marsh," Hornden said now.

Fulmer hated when anyone called him "Marsh," let alone this shmuck, so he grunted by way of reply. Anyway, his mind was elsewhere, already at Dulles, seeing Bourne in a small, windowless room with cuffs on his wrists and ankles. What a story that would be, and, like it or not, Hornden was the perfect journo to break it.

"So there are two men walking down the street," Hornden continued with a certain gleam in his eye. "It's the week before Christmas, bells are ringing, carols coming from outdoor speakers, the scent of free-cut pine trees in the air. One man says to the other, 'I sure don't like this talk of racism all of a sudden.' 'Me, neither,' says the second guy. 'You're not a racist, are you?' the first guy asks. 'Hell, no,' second one says. 'You?' 'Not a bit of it.' 'Good,' the second guy says, 'Let's go get drunk.' 'Capital idea,' the first one says, 'and we can catch us a faggot and roast his chestnuts over an open fire!'"

Hornden laughed so hard tears came to his eyes. At some point, he became aware that Fulmer wasn't joining in his merriment. Wiping his eyes, he nudged Fulmer. "What? You think you're too pure to get a laugh out of that joke?"

"It's not funny. It's not even a joke." Fulmer was straining to look past the building traffic choking the off ramp to Dulles. "Can it now, Hornden. As soon as we get to the airport I've serious business to transact."

Leaning forward, he tapped the new head of his security detail, sitting up front, on the shoulder. Max, his betrayer, had been arraigned and was now sitting in a federal facility, awaiting interrogation. "Louis, please get on the horn and find out what the fuck is going on. I can't afford to be late."

"Already on it, sir." Louis had his mobile to one ear. Now he spoke into it so softly no one could hear what he was saying.

Temporarily mollified, but still on edge, Fulmer sat back in the seat.

"So," Hornden said, "you're as pure as the driven snow. No warts on you, right?"

Fulmer hardly heard him. Whatever Louis had done was working. The traffic was breaking up, and they were pushing their way forward. He caught glimpses of the gleaming shell of the international departure terminal's exterior now.

"Marsh, you're not listening to me." Hornden's voice had turned plaintive, reaching up the scale to unbecoming heights.

Fulmer brushed his words away as he would a bothersome fly. "I told you to can it and I meant it."

"You're choice, Marsh. I mean, you're running the show, right?"

"Right as shit," Fulmer said distractedly.

"But then of course you'll miss out on all the fun."

Fulmer's brow furrowed as he glanced over. "What fun? What are you babbling on about, man?"

Hornden had extracted his mobile from his coat pocket. It was one of those oversize jobbies that people obsessed with selfies were so fond of, Fulmer observed with distaste.

"Well, *this*, for instance." On the screen of the journo's mobile was a photo of Fulmer *in flagrante delicto*. Fulmer was nude, his flabby buttocks high in the air between Gwyneth's widely spread legs. Fulmer's reddened face was visible in the mirrored tabletop, and, to make matters even worse, the lovely and lubricious Gwyneth was grinning lewdly at the camera.

"Where...where did you get that?" Fulmer said stupidly. His mind seemed to have frozen solid, encased in a block of ice.

"This still frame is only the icing," Hornden said with a malicious grin. "Take a gander at the cake, Marsh. I've titled it 'Corpus Delicti,' or 'Caught in the Act.'" And then the video began to play, the whole sordid sexual encounter from smoldering beginning to mortifying end.

———

"How did you do it?" the Angelmaker said, comfortably ensconced in her first class seat.

Bourne was looking out the Perspex window at the passing clouds far below. "Do what?"

"Get us out of the country without a hitch?"

When he turned to her, his smile was lacquer thin. He could not see her the same way, not anymore. "I created a diversion."

She frowned. "What kind of a diversion?"

"I bought two tickets to Istanbul in the name of one of my old Tread-stone aliases and his wife. That sent up red flags in all the right quarters, I have no doubt. That flight was leaving twenty minutes after ours."

She laughed. "Brilliant."

Over their indifferent meal, he said, "Tell me what else you know about Dima Orlov."

She frowned at the piece of unidentifiable meat speared on the tines of her fork. "It isn't much."

"Nevertheless. Everything you know."

The atmosphere between them had subtly altered, as if a breeze from the east had cleared away a cloudbank that had lingered far too long in one place. He heard everything she said through this clear lens. He was no longer obliged to scrutinize every move and expression she made; he already knew what lay beneath her tough reptilian armor.

"Everything I know," she said reflectively while she chewed her bit of meat.

"Your information is all third-hand, I take it."

"No. Not at all. I was friends with Dima's daughter, Katya."

"Past tense."

"Well, yes." She put down her fork; she hadn't eaten much. "Once, we were close—close as mother and daughter. But like many mothers and daughters we had a falling out."

"About what?"

She laughed softly, bitterly. "She accused me of using her to get close to her father."

"How far off the mark was she?"

"Huh. That's the pity of it," the Angelmaker said. "She wasn't off at all."

"You felt nothing for her."

It wasn't a question; she didn't take it as such. "Well, you know me." She gave him a glancing sideways look. "Nice woman, though. Smart, strong-willed. And yet she was inextricably tied to her father."

"Why did you want to get close to Dima Orlov?"

"Keyre sent me. He wanted to do a deal with Dima."

Bourne waited a moment for everything to sink in. "You do realize the irony of that situation."

Another lightning sideways glance. "You mean the 'inextricably tied' bit."

The flight attendant rolled her cart parallel to their seats, took their trays, asked if they wanted dessert, coffee, or perhaps an after-dinner drink. The Angelmaker wanted a brandy; Bourne wanted nothing more than to hear the end of the story.

After the brandy was poured and they were alone again, Bourne said, "It seems to me that in some ways Katya is an older version of yourself."

"I can see how you'd make that mistake." The Angelmaker took a sip of her brandy, set it down on her tray-table. Bourne had already stowed away his.

"Clarify it for me, then."

"Mmm." The Angelmaker bit her lower lip. "Well, for one thing Katya loves her father. For another, she loves him maybe a little too much."

"And you?"

"You're joking, right? You've met my father."

"And your mother?" Bourne asked. "In all the time I've known you, neither you nor your sister ever mentioned her."

There ensued a long silence. The Angelmaker sipped her brandy. The plane began to shudder and the FASTEN SEAT BELTS lights flashed, but they were already buckled up. The turbulence grew worse, and she held onto her glass to keep it from tumbling over.

"My mother. You want to know about my mother?" She knocked back the rest of her brandy, looked around for the flight attendant to get a refill, but they were all sitting down because of the turbulence. "Okay, for the record, she taught me how to say 'Fuck you.'"

"But you were just a little girl."

"There you go, then."

The turbulence departed as quickly as it had arrived. The lights had been lowered, seats had been reclined to the horizontal, mattresses placed, along with quilts covering the passengers. A few read or watched a film, but most were taking advantage of the seat turned bed.

"One sentence can't be the sum and substance of your mother," Bourne said.

"Why are you so interested?" she said sharply.

"I can't remember mine."

She was staring at the blank TV screen ahead of her. "Did it ever occur to you that's a blessing?"

"Not for a moment."

Without another word the Angelmaker unbuckled herself and strode back toward the toilets.

It was several seconds before Bourne realized she had taken her brandy glass with her. Why would she do that? The glass was empty. She could simply be returning it to one of the crew, or . . .

Unbuckling, he followed her down the aisle. She opened the accordion door to the right-hand toilet; she was still gripping the glass. He launched himself along the aisle, at the last minute plucking a fork off a food tray the attendant had yet to clear.

Jamming it into the door, he stopped it from closing completely, kept the Angelmaker from sliding the lock all the way across.

"What are you doing?" he said softly, leaning against the door.

As an answer, he heard the sound of the glass shattering. Any moment now the blood would be spurting out of the opened vein in her wrist.

"Stop it, Mala. Stop it."

Using the tines of the fork as a lever, he worked at prying open the door. He could tell that she had thrown her full weight against him.

"I've no other choice." Her voice was dull, mechanical, as if in her mind she was already dead.

Then, in the sliver of open space, he saw her lift a shard of glass out of the sink, turn it inward. The pale skin of the inside of her wrist rested just below it.

The tines of the fork snapped off.

33

OR MARSHALL FULMER, a day he'd anticipated being filled like a piñata with all kinds of bright, shiny toys, chief among them having Jason Bourne finally, *finally* taken into custody had been, in a painful heartbeat, stood on its head, turned 180 degrees toward the dark side.

First, Hornden shows him the hard evidence of his dalliance with a madam, then even before he has a chance to digest that clusterfuck, that idiot Ellison calls to tell him that, no, the couple he took into custody weren't Bourne and his companion, after all, but a couple about to set off on their twentieth anniversary celebration, of all things! And now where was Bourne—who, Fulmer knew, worked alone? No one knew, certainly not Ellison or any of his crew. Had Bourne even been at Dulles at all?

And Fulmer wouldn't even be thinking of all the ways he could crucify Ellison had it not been for the fact that, considering what Hornden had on him, a major coup like capturing Jason Bourne would have almost made up for him quite stupidly falling into a honey trap.

Running a shaking hand across his face, he told the driver to return to the office. But Hornden said, "Hold on."

He gave the journo a withering look. "What? Why?"

"We need to go to the VIP airstrip." Hornden pointed. "It's that way."

"Fuck you," was all Fulmer could manage, but there was no force, no venom behind it. He sat back in the seat. All the air, all the exhilaration of the now-distant morning had gone out of him.

"Sir?"

He became aware of the driver looking at him in the rearview mirror. "What?" He waved a hand as if the matter were of no import to him. "Oh, do as Mr. Hornden suggests."

Beside him Hornden chuckled. "'*Suggests*,'" he repeated under his breath.

Fulmer considered asking Hornden what they were going to do at the VIP airstrip, but he didn't want to give him the satisfaction. With Hornden, these small, petty victories were all that were left him. Pathetic.

With Fulmer's credentials they passed through the manned gates. Hornden told the driver to pull over to the left and park.

"Okay," he said, opening the rear door, "let's take a walk."

In the darkness of near midnight, the overbright lights on the tarmac elongated their shadows eastward. A light breeze ruffled Fulmer's hair, but Hornden's stayed in place, as if it had been plasticized. Ahead of them, a private aircraft with Dutch insignia crouched, its door open wide in welcome, a rolling staircase set in front of it.

"After you," Hornden said when they reached the foot of the stairs.

No more "Marsh," Fulmer noted. For some reason, this gave him a sense of foreboding.

Stepping into the interior, he saw that it had been retrofitted, seats pulled out, replaced with lounges, desks, flatbed seats, and the like. There seemed to be only one person on the plane; where the crew was he had no idea. The man was slim, tall, saturnine, dark-eyed. Fulmer had seen enough bespoke Saville Row suits and John Lobb shoes to recognize them on the figure who came around from behind a desk and strode toward him with his hand extended.

"Mr. Marshall Fulmer, I have wanted to speak with you for some time, ever since you were a senior senator, in fact." He spoke with a decided Russian accent. "But to be perfectly frank, this meeting was some while in the making."

Fulmer's foreboding ratcheted up to a nauseating level as he took the man's cool, dry hand. *The honey trap?* he asked himself.

"And you are?"

"Oh, pardon me." He gave a little bow from the waist that Fulmer took to be ironic. "Konstantin Ludmirovich Savasin, *Federal'naya sluzhba bezopasnosti Rossiyskoy Federatsii.*" Translation: Federal Security Service, Russian Federation—the successor to the KGB.

Blood drained from Fulmer's face. He felt the floor slipping away from him. As bad as it had been before, he knew that his day had just fallen into the abyss. Now that he was confronted with the head of the FSB, he had no idea how deep the abyss went.

Freeing his hand from Konstantin's grip, he pivoted toward Hornden. "Are you kidding me? You're a Russian agent?"

The journo grinned. "The fun never stops today, does it, Marsh."

Fulmer sank into a seat, head in his hands. "Jesus Christ."

Konstantin gripped his shoulder. "Not to worry, old boy. We won't be asking too much of you."

"Jesus Christ," Fulmer moaned.

"Marshall—may I call you Marshall? Marshall, look at me." Konstantin sighed in a theatrical manner. "Come, come, stand up and take your medicine like a man."

Still in shock, Fulmer slapped his thighs and stood up. His eyes were red-rimmed and there was a tic battering one eyelid as he looked Konstantin in the face.

"You work for me now, Marshall."

Fulmer moaned like a child in pain.

"Please, look on the bright side."

Fulmer's brows knit together. "The bright side?"

"Yes, of course. You are national security advisor for a very different kind of president of the United States."

It was only then that the full import of his situation hit him, and, doubling over, he vomited onto the pile carpet of the aisle.

With a look of distaste, Konstantin stepped back in order to keep his John Lobb shoes pristine. He snapped his fingers. "Mr. Hornden, please be kind enough to inform the crew. Their presence is required immediately to clean up the mess the national security advisor has made."

"At once," Hornden said crisply, pulling out his mobile.

"In the meantime." Konstantin hooked his fingers inside Fulmer's collar, hauling him to his feet. "There is a front cabin. Let us repair there so that we may get on with the business at hand."

Fulmer trudged on feet made leaden by terror and shame. He was in the midst of a nightmare, he kept telling himself. At any moment he would awaken in his bed, the morning sun would be shining, the birds calling to one another.

Sadly, but predictably, that never happened. This *was* a nightmare, but a waking one. And so, without quite knowing how he got there, he found himself sitting opposite the saturnine man in his elegant suit and expensive shoes who just happened to be the head of Russia's most feared security agency.

On the narrow table between them sat a slim notebook computer, a bottle of vodka, its surface already coated in frost, a bucket of ice, and two old-fashioned glasses. Without a word, Konstantin used a pair of silver tongs to transfer ice cubes from the bucket to the glasses, then poured them each three fingers of vodka. He lifted his glass in toast.

"Nasdarovje." He cocked his head. "No? To a long and fruitful association. Still, no?" He shrugged. "Well, then, to your health, Marshall." He clinked the rim of his glass against the one still sitting on the table, for Fulmer had not as yet touched his. He drank, then set his glass down.

"Take a sip, Marshall. This vodka is good—the best. It'll calm your nerves, I guarantee it." When Fulmer still made no move to touch the glass, Konstantin said, "As you wish. Now, down to business. What I want from you is simple. Well, we want to start out easy, don't we? Your orders will get more complicated over time."

Konstantin went at the vodka again. "You're to tell the president and your Pentagon comrades that what you call the Bourne Initiative is nothing more than Russian disinformation."

"But it isn't."

"Of course it isn't, Marshall. Let's not start being naïve this late in the game."

Mention of the Initiative served to focus him. Fulmer's mind was starting to thaw, to come unstuck from the deep freeze into which it had been hurled and held by the day's back-to-back shitstorms—the video evidence of his dalliance; the knowledge that he had done it with... how could he have had such strong feeling for a madam; losing Bourne; and now this...

"Then..."

"This is the start of what you will do for me, Marshall—disseminate disinformation that will give us a leg up on foreign affairs, on alliances with other nations, with negotiations on currently thorny topics with your government."

He lifted up a slim briefcase, snapped it open, laid a file with official Russian Federation, FSB, and, most tellingly, *spetsnaz* stamps on its cover. He laid his hand over the file. "In here are documents—*genuine* documents—from Unit 309, our cyber hacking and disinformation group, backing up your assertion that there is, in fact, no such thing as the Bourne Initiative under that designation or any other."

He pushed the file over. Fulmer didn't even look at it.

"No."

"No?" Konstantin reared back. "What do you mean 'no'? Those photos, that video will ruin you personally and professionally."

Fulmer reached for the glass, tipped it to his lips, then decided against it, set the glass down with the vodka untouched. He needed his mind perfectly clear, not clouded by Russian vodka. Now that he had his wits about him again, his feet on the floor, as it were, he could see a path out of the abyss into which he had been cast. In fact, there was no abyss; it was a figment of the shock that had gripped him.

Pushing the glass away, Fulmer looked up at Konstantin. "No, they won't. Not in this new era. I give it up to Jesus, and all will be well. Oh, some feathers will be ruffled, mainly my wife's, but she'll get over it. As for my new job, just look at the president—he gets away with anything and everything. The American public is different now; it gets its news from social media, it can and will forgive just about anything. Arrogance and repentance in equal measure is a formula they swallow hook, line, and sinker."

He took up the frosty bottle, refilled Konstantin's glass while leaving his own glass still untouched. "So come, *gospodin*, and let us come to—how to put it best?—a more equitable arrangement."

"Boldly played, Marshall. Were I in your position—naturally, I wouldn't be—but if I were, I imagine I'd do the same."

Fulmer looked smug.

Konstantin extracted a manila envelope from his briefcase, slid it across the table.

Fulmer's brows furrowed. "What's this?"

"Open it, Marshall."

Now everything was flipped; Savasin calling Fulmer by his Christian name was grating on him. He hesitated a moment, then snatched the envelope, turned it over, and opened it. Inside, he found a series of eight-by-ten photos. With a trembling hand, he spread them out. A ball of ice formed in the pit of his stomach. He was staring incredulously at a series of photos identical to the ones Hornden had shown him on his mobile device. Except for one terrifying difference: in these, he was making love to a young girl. Black as coal, and clearly under age.

"Tell me, Marshall, I assume you've heard of *kompromat*," Konstantin said in a voice turned silky. "It's an old KGB trick," he went on without waiting for an answer. "We used to hire prostitutes—swallows, we called them—to seduce our targets in honey traps. But, as you have so eloquently pointed out, that methodology is old hat; it's a broken wheel. Times change and so does methodology. We've updated *kompromat*, just as we've updated the KGB to the FSB."

"A devil by any name," Fulmer managed in a hoarse voice.

Konstantin laughed. His fingertip tapped the photos, one after the other. "Be it ever so humble, Marshall. This is your new home. And I— I am your new master. Your control, in the jargon of espiocrats."

He continued to tap the photos. "Would you care to take these with you, Marshall? A clear and present reminder of your *adjusted situation*. No? All right then." He gathered the photos up, slid them back into the envelope, which he deposited in his briefcase.

"Now, I told you that we had updated *kompromat*. I've just shown you one way. Here's another. You are very important to our plans, long term as well as short term. We required an unbreakable lock for you, and Alyosha Orlova provided it."

"What? Who?"

"You know her as Françoise Sevigne." A slow smile spread across Konstantin's face. "You've received some very bad advice lately, Marshall." Opening the laptop, Konstantin brought it out of sleep, pressed several keys, then swiveled it around so Fulmer could see the screen. "Very bad, indeed."

Fulmer was looking at the web site of Fellingham, Bodeys, the company to which Françoise had suggested he move his business. Which he had done forthwith.

He shrugged. "So?"

"So, *this*." Reaching around, Konstantin pressed a key that brought up a list of Fellingham, Bodeys' clients. Among them were the worst of the worst: Robert Mugabe; Viktor Bout, the former world's number one arms trader, now in jail; three heads of the most powerful Mexican and Colombian drug cartels; two ISIS commanders; the Somalian Keyre, who took over after Bout was caught. The list of malefactors, criminals, and terrorists, though short, was as bitter and hard to take as a spoonful of castor oil. "These are very bad people, evil people that your money is keeping company with. Who knows what deals Fellingham, Bodeys is devising for their clients—you included, Marshall. And if you don't comply, we'll send this list and the details of your ill-gotten gains to

Justin Farreng and LeakAGE. We'll do to you what you did to General MacQuerrie, and you know what happened to him."

Fulmer stared at the screen, transfixed by the ramifications of the ingenious trap the Russians had devised for him. The realization suddenly swept through him that the honey trap was merely a way to gain his attention while the real trap closed around him. Good God, Françoise was a Russian spy. Through his disgust and humiliation he felt a vague sense of admiration that they had found him deserving of such meticulous attention and planning.

Konstantin, who seemed to be following Fulmer's thought process via his changing expressions, now said: "You will take the Unit 309 file and run with it, Marshall, convincing the administration to forget all about the Bourne Initiative, giving us time to find out just what the hell that sonuvabitch General Karpov had in mind."

"Why?"

Konstantin's voice was hard as iron. "Because I told you to." Then his tone softened a bit. "But just this once, since you're new to the game, I'll tell you. You're going to help us discredit and destabilize elements within your government and clandestine agencies."

Fulmer went bone-white, as if his flesh had melted away, leaving only his skull. "I can't—I won't do that."

"Oh, you most certainly will." Konstantin smiled with his teeth. "You see, Marshall, you are completely compromised. You have no choice. No choice at all." He raised his eyebrows. "Don't look so downcast, Marshall. We know you harbor great ambitions. Am I on target? Bull's-eye, I'd say. We can and will help you with that, Marshall. In four years you want to run for president. Capital idea, say I! We can imagine nothing better for you. We're patient, you see, very patient. We can wait while you consolidate your power base—with our help, of course. And once you win the nomination, if you continue to play by our rules, we'll win you the election. Triumphant, you will be swept into office like a conquering Caesar. What joy, no?"

He drank more vodka. "In the meantime, there's another service you will do me. And this one is as urgent as the first. Perhaps more so. What I want from you are the Treadstone files on Jason Bourne."

At Bourne's name, Fulmer shook his head. "Impossible. All the Treadstone files were incinerated, as dictated by protocol."

Konstantin sighed. "Marshall, the files weren't destroyed. You know it and I know it. They were ferreted away from prying eyes." He took another sip of the chilled vodka. "You don't know what you're missing." He shrugged again. "Ah, well. Onward. Find the files, copy them, and send them to me via Mr. Hornden." He leaned forward, tapped Fulmer on the knee. "*All* the files. I want to know everything there is to know about Bourne's training, what he was subjected to, how well he stood up under interrogation techniques."

Fulmer shook his head. "Why?"

"Because when I know what he resisted, I'll be able to find that one, single method that will break him."

Finally, Fulmer had something to laugh at.

Konstantin cocked his head. "You find this funny?"

"I do." Fulmer could not stop laughing. He seemed to have lost all control of his emotions, just as he had lost control of his life, which was now in the hands of the enemy. "Do you know how many years it's been we've been trying to catch that bastard, only to have him slip through our fingers time and time again?"

"Just today, as well. So?"

"So what good will the files do you when he can't be caught?"

Konstantin finished off his vodka. "Oh, he can be caught, Marshall, I assure you."

Fulmer shot him a sideways glance; the fog that was blurring his brain anew began to lift once more. "Really?"

"There were three partners in the cyber Initiative. Two of them are dead. The one who is left is named Dima. Dima Vladimirovich Orlov. It just so happens that I have a mole inside Dima's organization. I know that's where Bourne must be headed. To Dima. To find out about the Initiative set up by his friend, that sonuvabitch Karpov."

Konstantin stood. "And when he arrives, you will have already handed over the Treadstone files. I will know how to deal with Jason Bourne, and I will accomplish what has eluded everyone else who has tried and failed to find and trap him."

"Why do you want Bourne, anyway? What's he to you?"

Konstantin peered down at Fulmer as if from Olympian heights. "Just get me the files, Marshall, and all will be well with you, your reputation, and your illegally amassed fortune."

34

CAN I HELP you, sir? Is there something wrong?" The flight attendant, well trained to keep any negative emotion off her face, smiled her plastic smile. "Something I can do for you, sir?" She pointed. "This toilet is free, if you—"

Bourne robed himself in his blandest smile. Move along. *Nothing to see here.* "It's all good, thank you. My wife's a bit indisposed. She needs a bit of help. I know exactly what to do."

"Are you sure, sir? We have—"

"Absolutely sure." His smile brightened. "Happens from time to time." He shrugged. "What can you do."

She nodded, then turned away, returning to the galley area where she and the other first class attendants were chatting, their rest period having begun.

"Mala . . ." Bourne jammed his fingertips around the edge of the door, hauled it open.

"Get in here," she said.

He stepped in, closed the door behind him. Then he took the shard of glass out of her hand—she hadn't yet punctured herself—and dropped it back into the sink.

"What d'you think you're doing?"

She stared at him, her eyes large and questing. "My mother called me Anjelica. I always hated that name—Mala. It was the name my father insisted on, my official name. My mother called me Anjelica," she repeated, more softly now, her voice barely above a whisper. "In secret, when we were alone together. Before, when I was born, she tried to argue with my father, but he beat her for that, too."

He beat her for that, too. There was no point in asking her to elaborate; that sentence said it all.

"Mala—"

"No, don't." She crossed her arms under her breasts. "You have no idea how much I despise myself." She held up a hand to forestall any comment. "Listen to me now." She was trembling slightly, her eyes enlarged with incipient tears. "I have no daughter. Giza doesn't exist. As with all his girls, Keyre was sure to keep me from getting pregnant; the process would spoil our appearance, we would be less than perfect, and that would necessitate us being thrown in the trash, like a piece of rotten meat."

She took a deep, shuddering breath, let it out. "The child—Giza—was his idea. He said I should use the imprisoned daughter card if you started to doubt me. It would, he said, bind you to me in a new and different way."

She produced a rueful smile, tentative and, if he could believe anything about her anymore, frightened. "So, you see, my father was right. I've earned my name—a malediction, a curse."

For a time, Bourne said nothing. Then he gestured at the sink. "Was this fake as well?"

"I...I don't know. Maybe...maybe if you hadn't broken in I would have. What is left of me? I no longer have substance. I no longer have the ability to make choices. And now...now I wonder whether I ever had it."

Grabbing a couple of paper towels, Bourne moistened them, then scooped up the glass fragments, pushed them down into the waste disposal hopper. He ran the water repeatedly until all the glitter had washed down the drain.

"We need to get back to our seats," he said.

"I can't."

"You can," he said, "and you will." He turned her to him. "You have a life to live, Anjelica. A long one."

At the sound of the name her mother had called her, her lips formed a tentative smile. "That sounds good coming from you." The smile never reached her eyes. "Not that you'll believe me. I know I've used up all my credibility with you."

"Come on," he said, reaching for the door. "Someone has to believe in you."

Reaching out, she held his movement in abeyance. "Not you, Jason. Anyone but you."

He glanced down at her hand and she snatched it away.

"Don't you see? I'm like a scorpion. No matter what I say, no matter which way I twist or turn, in the end I'll sting. It's my nature."

"I'll keep that in mind." He opened the accordion door, pressing them up against each other in the process. She flinched away, as if stung or burned, but in the end she followed him back to their seats. As with, it seemed to her, everything else in her life, she had no choice.

———

"Come on now, smarten up, Morgana. You have no choice."

Morgana regarded Françoise with a look of vague bewilderment, which was now calculated, rather than blindly innocent.

"Go with the flow," Soraya had said. And: *"You'll think I've thrown you to the dogs."* She thought that part was behind her, but now she was further along in her brief, burrowing deeper down, and the dogs—the real dogs of war—were heading toward her with teeth bared.

"Why don't you do it, then?"

"It's you he's after. I need to stay out of it."

They were at breakfast the next day, Françoise knocking on her door at daybreak, the sky still in the process of throwing off the veil of night.

Hours before Larry London would wake and come to her with room service breakfast, as was his habit. In a rickety café habituated by local fishermen come in with their catch or on their way out onto the choppy gray water. The stench of fish, both fresh and smoked, was only partially watered down by the fug of cigarette smoke.

"Or seem to stay out of it," Françoise added, as she poured another packet of sugar into her coffee, stirred in cream.

It was all Morgana could do to keep her gorge down. Her breakfast lay before her. It was no more appetizing now than when it had been brought out of the kitchen.

"I'm not saying... I mean, there must be another way out."

"There isn't. You know there isn't." Françoise's voice was clipped, her tone hard, the better to emphasize the finality of her words.

"Okay, well." Morgana's gaze slipped sideways as the door opened to admit a couple more fishermen in their thick rubber slickers and high, gum-soled boots. The fish stink grew stronger than Morgana thought possible. "I'm not saying I'll do it, but what's your plan."

"It's simple," Françoise said, "like all the best plans. The less moving parts the better."

Morgana could agree with that. She nodded. "Fire away." She winced at her choice of words.

"The plan takes advantage of Larry's weakness."

"What weakness?"

"Women. Or hadn't you noticed?"

"It's hard to miss," Morgana said. "I just didn't see it as a weakness."

"Neither does Larry. That's the best part. It's hiding in plain sight."

Françoise took some coffee, made a face, then set the cup down in its saucer. The café was packed and noisy, which is why she'd chosen it for their early-morning rendezvous.

"Larry's always wanted to bed me despite my bad treatment of him back when. I haven't let him, of course, but the key thing here is I haven't cut him off at the knees either. So..."

"So what? You're going to seduce him? How does that help us?"

"Do you know how to handle a handgun?"

"Not really, no," Morgana lied. The moment she discovered that Françoise was a Russian spy, she had quit telling her the truth about anything. The tricky part was to act natural, not to give her former friend the slightest hint of the change in their relationship. She had enough to worry about with Larry ordered to kill her without being afraid Françoise might beat him to it.

Lions to the left of me, lions to the right. Here I am, stuck in the middle with you. She sang this to herself to take the edge off the fear and loathing, the claustrophobic sensation of being trapped.

Françoise tossed her head. "Doesn't matter. You'll be so close to Larry you couldn't miss if you tried."

Morgana's stomach gave a lurch, her heart rate increasing. "What are you talking about?"

"Just this." Françoise leaned over the table, lowering her voice, though in the good-natured din there was no need. "Tonight I'm going to let Larry seduce me. I'll pretend to get a bit drunk. Then I'll lean over the table, like I am now. Only tonight my shirt buttons will be open enough for him to see the tops of my breasts. That's all the invitation he'll need, believe me."

Morgana had trouble breathing, as if the air around her had turned gelid, as if she were submerged beneath a dark and ominous sea. "And then?" She could scarcely get the words out.

"And then you'll come out of the closet with the handgun I will provide and kill him."

"What?"

"One shot to the back of his head." She cocked her hand like a gun. "Blam!"

"That's crazy. Forget it."

"Don't worry, Morgana, I'll make sure he's on top. His back will be toward you." Françoise smiled winningly. "He won't know what hit him, I guarantee it."

Through the smeared windows the sun was burning off the last of the early morning's gray mist.

"Honesty is inefficient," Mala said.

"In our world, at the edge of civilization."

"No, I mean anytime, anywhere. Honesty reveals too much, leaving you feeling defeated."

They were back in their seats. Bourne had drifted off a bit, but it was the kind of surface sleep he'd learned at Treadstone. He made sure he was sensing Mala; if she had left her seat again he would have been right behind her. She had ordered a vodka with plenty of ice, drinking it slowly, methodically, in the way people do when they're determined to get drunk. Bourne wasn't about to let that happen; he'd cut her off before she got halfway there. But he didn't stop her now, sensing that she needed the fortification to tell him whatever it was that was burning its way through her mind.

It was a time of loss for Bourne. Boris was dead, Sara was who knew where, in whatever kind of dangerous situation, and he was sure he was losing Mala, though in what way he could not yet discern. But then what had been their connection? Maybe it had been spun of spider's-web silk, apt to be broken at a moment's notice, or with a wrong turn. Perhaps their connection was an illusion; she wasn't like any other woman he had met or would likely meet. Like the Sphinx in the desert outside Cairo she was a complete enigma. And, quite possibly, therein lay her allure.

Mala stirred beside him, the ice cubes tinkling against the glass as she took another sip. She held the vodka in her mouth a moment, savoring its icy bite before swallowing it.

"Having said that, I'm going to tell you a story. It will be up to you to decide whether or not it's true." She took another sip, settled back in her seat. "For some time after my convalescence, after you left, I had no idea what I was going to do with my life. You had so kindly and generously put my sister into ballet school, and she took to it like a duck to water; her life path was set. But me...?" She shrugged. "I know you believe that I contacted Keyre, that he has some magical or psychic hold over me. I suppose that would have made a good tale, but it's not true. I felt nothing toward him—not hate, not fear, not attraction—nothing at all.

"I needed to get away from the family you put me with. They were nice enough and very helpful to me, but in that house, late at night, or even in the early morning over breakfast, the stench of burning flesh would come to me. I'd have to push my chair back, run to the bathroom and vomit. As if that could rid me of the smell. It couldn't, of course it couldn't. That stench will be with me until the moment of my death."

She pressed the call button, and when the attendant arrived, she shook her empty glass to ask for another. She remained silent until the second vodka arrived and she'd taken several slow and deliberate sips, moving further along the road to getting drunk. Bourne watched her like a hawk.

"So I had to leave," Mala continued as if there had been no interruption. "I missed my mother; I had to find her—it was a kind of fever. I went home to Estonia. I spent six weeks looking for her, but there was no sign of her. It was as if the earth had swallowed her whole. Words are inadequate to express my despair. I was an orphan. Worse, I didn't know whether my mother was alive or dead.

"I wandered, then, to Prague, don't ask me why, then Rome, and ended up in Paris. I was grieving, and more importantly, considering how my life turned out, I was angry—angry at my father for selling us out, at my mother for not stopping him, even Liis, for having a life I did not, could not have."

She pursed her lips, her eyes heavy-lidded, as if these memories still weighed mightily on her. "Paris in the springtime, with the horse chestnuts in bloom and the couples young and old holding hands and kissing as they strolled along the banks of the Seine. What was there for me in Paris, you may ask? I had remembered that my mother spoke to me about Paris when I was little; she even taught me some French. I looked for her there, too, but, of course, it was impossible, like looking for a needle in a haystack. Then, one afternoon in the Tuileries, while I sat on one of those green metal chairs, feeling the sun on my face, I met Françoise. She stepped, rather rudely, between me and the sun, to get my attention, I suppose.

"It was clear from the first moment of our meeting that afternoon, and confirmed soon after as we sat at a café, drinking espressos, that she had meant to meet me. Someone had told her about me, and I imagine you can guess who that someone was.

"As soon as you had placed me with that family and left, Keyre began monitoring me, my movements from city to city, and he had sent Françoise after me. She'd just missed me in Rome, but, despite the lovers all around me, I was comfortable enough in Paris, feeling closer to my mother, hearing French spoken, to give her the chance to catch up.

"Of course, she didn't tell me this right away. She had a way about her—ingratiating without being in the least condescending. Gradually, as we spent more time together, I formed the impression that her background, like mine, was something she wished to forget. That formed a bond, you see. That it was a false bond was something I learned much later, after she had indoctrinated me into her way of life, had trained me. She became my mentor and me her willing acolyte. Under her tutelage, I began to make money—lots of it. I became a go-between, taking a rake-off from both sides. That the deals were shady, that the principals were on the wrong side of the law—often as far on the wrong side as you could get—was of no interest to me. The money was. I was addicted." Her smile was rueful. "You see, Keyre's Yibir magic worked on me, after all."

She was drinking faster now, as if her impending inebriation could save her from herself. Almost finished with her second vodka, she was about to hit the call button like a hospital patient in pain who keeps giving herself intravenous doses of morphine, when Bourne stopped her.

"Go on," he said softly. "Where did it all go wrong?"

Mala closed her eyes for a moment. "I suppose you could say that it all went wrong the moment Françoise came between me and the soothing warmth of the Parisian sunlight. But I know that's not what you meant." She took a breath, stared into the cubes in her glass. "What happened was this: I discovered that Françoise was not what she appeared to be—no, that's not quite right. She was precisely what she appeared to be. On the surface. But underneath, down where it counted, she was someone else. She wasn't French as she purported to be; she was Russian. Her name wasn't Françoise Sevigne, it was Alyosha Orlova."

The name sent a lightning bolt through Bourne. "She isn't, by any chance, related to Dima Vladimirovich Orlov, the man we're going to see, is she?"

Mala nodded. "His granddaughter."

"And Katya, the older woman you were once friends with, is Alyosha's mother."

Mala nodded. Bourne sat very still, thinking that this woman was like an onion—the more layers you peeled away, the more intense the experience.

"Alyosha has been long lost to Orlov; she's the black swan of the family."

Bourne shifted in his seat, as if his mind, working at light speed, made it impossible for his body to remain still. A skein was forming, but he had yet to make out its final shape.

"And that's when you found out that she was working for Keyre."

"Yes and no," Mala said. She seemed calmer now, as if, having broken, the storm or the fever that had gripped her had become a shadow of its former self. "Yes, she was working for Keyre, but at the same time she was working for the Russians. To be more specific, her half brother, Gora Maslov."

Revelation after revelation; strand after strand working itself into a pattern. "So she's the black swan for a good reason. She's the illegitimate daughter of Katya Orlov and Dimitri Maslov. And she's more loyal to the Maslovs?"

"She grew up with the Maslovs but never took the name. I doubt Alyosha knows the meaning of loyalty." Mala glanced at him. "And, yes, I'm fully aware of the irony of that." She ran a hand through her hair. "I should tell you something about Keyre and Gora Maslov: they've been doing business together."

"Gora is Keyre's Russian arms supplier."

"Correct. Until a week ago, that is. Suspecting that Keyre was skimming profits, Gora sent a team in to infiltrate Keyre's cadre. Keyre found out and executed them all. Alyosha was the facilitator linking them, but now that they're the bitterest of enemies, they no longer require her services. I don't know where Alyosha is or what she's up to."

———————

Crouched in the clothes closet in Françoise's hotel room, Morgana lay the compact 9mm Beretta Nano across her thigh. According to plan, Françoise had left the door ajar so Morgana could see a sliver of the bed, but more importantly hear how the plan was progressing and when to emerge.

Morgana had to hand it to the bitch—she'd come up with an excellent plan. As she had said, very few moving parts. The question was whether everything would go according to the plan; there was no trust left inside Morgana when it came to Françoise. She had snapped on latex gloves, had already checked the ammo in the Beretta's magazine to make sure she wouldn't be firing blanks. But what if both Françoise and Larry London were waiting for her to emerge to shoot her to death? But why wait for her to emerge? Which is why she tensed when she heard voices, the door swinging open. Françoise's high laugh. Only now it occurred to her that she was a sitting duck. If they were going to kill her it would be now; stuck in the darkness, amid Françoise's scent and her clothes, there was no escape for her. She lifted the spare pillow she had been clutching, stupidly using it as a shield. Of course it wouldn't stop a bullet, but the gesture was automatic, a very human response to imminent danger.

A line of sweat popped out at her hairline, and the back of her neck felt hot, as if she had come down with a sudden fever. She licked her lips; her mouth was dry, with an unpleasant taste she identified as bile. At any moment she was afraid she might piss herself.

"No you don't," Françoise was saying. "There isn't a man in the world capable of that!"

"Why don't we find out?" Larry's voice was in a deeper register, furred with sexual desire. A good sign; at least the bitch had told the truth about seducing him.

Another high laugh from Françoise, followed by a squeal of delight as the two of them passed through the narrow view afforded Morgana. The bedsprings reacted as the pair launched themselves onto it.

Several moments passed while Morgana heard the rustle and slither of clothes being stripped off, then an excited "Oh!" from Françoise and an answering "Mmmm" from Larry.

The sounds of lovemaking, so much a part of the experience for the participants, vacillated between frightening and ludicrous when heard by an outsider, like Morgana, who cringed as the pace increased.

When she heard Françoise cry out, "Oh, please!" which was their agreed-upon signal, she pushed the closet door open and slowly stood up. As Françoise had promised, Larry was on top, humping away in that animalistic manner endemic to certain men for whom their own pleasure was paramount.

She crossed the pile carpet, silent as a cat, carefully stepping over strewn clothes or sidestepping them altogether. Close up, the grunts and groans seemed even more absurd, the rising and falling of Larry's body, the hard thrust of his pelvis seeming to her a kind of violence that made her shudder.

She was almost close enough now, and she lifted the Beretta, her right arm straight, her left hand clutching the pillow. As she advanced, she felt her heart rate exceeding normal levels. To counteract it, she slowed her breathing. While she had extensive training with guns, she had never killed or even shot at a human being. Now, at the last minute, she felt as if her resolve might fail her. True, she had seen with her own eyes that Larry London had orders from Russia's *spetsnaz* to terminate her, but still the taking of a life, even in self-defense, was no small matter. It was not an act to take easily, or without regret. But she also knew that regret was a shooter's worst enemy—her father had told her as much the first time he had taken her deer hunting and she had missed the clear shot. *"You hesitated,"* he'd said. *"Your hesitation was a manifestation of remorse. You weren't sure you wanted to kill that buck. Morgana, you cannot fire your weapon unless you're sure. When you pull the trigger your mind must be clear, your intent certain. Otherwise you may as well put your weapon away."*

And so now, the Beretta a hand's-span away from the back of Larry London's head, she put aside her qualms, she refused remorse, kicked it into the metaphorical gutter. Leaning forward from the waist, she pressed the muzzle of the Beretta into the pillow, then lowered the pillow against her target's head—for that was how she thought of him now: no name, simply her target.

Nearing orgasm, her target didn't even notice the slight pressure. Taking a breath, she let it out slowly and evenly. Then, with clear eye and mind, she squeezed the trigger.

Larry London's head and, in fact, his entire frame rocketed downward, then rose again like a fish to the hook. There was surprisingly little blood, but a lot of feathers floating like a halo around London's head and shoulders. Morgana felt numb, as chilled as if she had just climbed out of a meat locker. For a moment, she remained still as a statue while her mind caught up with the actions of her body.

Françoise, struggling to shove London's body off her, fixed one eye on Morgana.

"Give me a hand," she said, her voice muffled.

Rage roiled Morgana's gut. As if that rage was a key opening a door, a way out, vivid, intense, and, yes, inevitable, revealed itself to her—the path—the only path—to invert her intolerable situation and escape the lions' den.

"Dammit, Morgana, are you listening to me?"

Morgana blinked. "Yes. Of course."

Elbowing her target's head to one side, she pressed the smoking pillow down onto Françoise's face and pulled the trigger of the Beretta not once, not twice, but three times.

"There." Her voice was a guttural whisper as she placed the 9mm in Larry London's right hand. She stood up straight and tall.

It would be natural to assume that she was observing the scene as if from a distance, outside herself, as if someone else had pulled the trigger four times. She was feeling none of those things. In fact, Morgana had never felt so vibrant, so alive, so in control. Every color throbbed with an intensity new and astonishing to her, the lamplight so brilliant it might have been able to cut glass. She felt the blood rushing through her arteries and veins as if it were a river, wide and deep, and almost intolerably beautiful. She felt her heart so intimately she might have been holding it in her hands.

She had passed beyond the veil, entered a life others never even dreamed of. She'd been blooded; she understood completely that she could never go back, even if she wished to. She was happy here in this new world, exhilarated, exalted. She felt herself initiated, anointed; she was now wreathed in shadows, her work hidden from the world at large. A child of the night.

Good God, she thought, *I've taken to this new life like a fledgling to the air.*

"There you go."

She surely was talking as much to herself now as to Françoise.

35

IF YOU GO from Moscow to Budapest," Bourne said, "'you think you are in Paris.'"

Mala laughed. "Who said that?"

"György Ligeti," Bourne replied, "the Hungarian composer of modern classical music."

Mala stared out the window as the Sapsan bullet train, taking them from St. Petersburg to Moscow, sped at 155 miles per hour across what looked like a frozen landscape. But then the Russian landscape tended to look frozen even in summer.

"He was right."

They had deplaned in St. Petersburg, passing through immigration without incident, which was a relief. Transferring to the Glavny train station was likewise easy enough. However, the only seats available on the Sapsan were in a private conference cabin; they were the most expensive tickets, especially in the current Russian economy, which was no doubt why they had remained unsold. Bourne had snapped them up, again paying cash. In less than four hours the Sapsan, the Russian word for peregrine falcon, would pull into Moscow's Leningradsky Station.

They had had time to buy themselves midweight sheepskin jackets for protection against the chill of late afternoons and evenings.

He was going to continue their conversation, but she had fallen asleep, just like that, from one moment to the next. For her, sleep was a blessing, he understood that, and he closed his eyes. But for him sleep was impossible now. He rose, left his seat vacant, stepped out of the compartment, and went along the aisle to the next car, needing to get away from the reverberations of her memories, which were making him claustrophobic.

He found himself in the first class car, filled mostly with business-men hunched over their laptops and a smattering of American tourists, staring blankly out at the blurred landscape or reading their guidebooks, prepping for their days and nights in Russia's capital.

He was about halfway down the car when he was brought up short as the door at the far end swung open and a man came through. There is a look to FSB agents that goes beyond cheap suits and grim expressions. It's their thousand-yard stare, the look they give you that makes it clear they think you're little people, that your life is virtually worthless, that they already have you in custody.

Without a second thought, Bourne turned around, only to find a sec-ond FSB agent coming toward him from the way he had come. This one opened his coat slightly, revealing his Arsenal Strizh, a full 9mm Para-bellum pistol, the successor to the storied Makarov. Whatever he saw in Bourne's eyes caused him to shake his head. His hand swept out, in-dicating the other passengers in the car. At that moment, Bourne felt the presence of the first agent, the taller and thinner one. The muzzle of his Strizh, hidden by the wings of his open greatcoat, pressed against the base of Bourne's spine.

The stubbier one jerked his head, said, "Let's go," in a Russian accent that told Bourne he came from St. Petersburg.

With Stubby in the lead, they marched Bourne back to the confer-ence cabin.

"Open it and step in," Stubby said. "Just as if nothing's happened."

"Nothing *has* happened," Bourne said, and received a hard poke in the back with the Strizh's muzzle.

"*Svóloch'!*" *Dick!* the agent said from behind.

"*Zatknís'!*" *Shut up!* snapped Stubby, clearly the senior partner.

Bourne opened the door and entered the compartment. Mala was still fast asleep, her torso slumped, her head turned away from the door. The agents stepped in on Bourne's heels.

"Don't wake her," Bourne said.

The taller agent snickered, as if to say he couldn't care less about the woman. "We weren't told about her." He could not keep the salacious tone out of his voice as he eyed Mala.

"Stay away from her," Stubby said in no uncertain terms.

The tall agent tore his gaze from Mala to look at Stubby. He opened his mouth, as if about to say something, but at the last moment apparently decided against it, bit his lip instead.

"I'm going to get him," Stubby said. "Don't do anything stupid."

Taller snickered again. When Stubby was gone, he waved the Strizh in Mala's general direction. "What's her story?"

"What's yours?" Bourne said.

He swung the pistol toward Bourne's knees. "Don't make me, shithead."

He sidled around so as to keep his eye on Bourne while he approached Mala. "She a good fuck?"

"Better than your mother."

Taller's neck and face went beet red. When the color reached his hairline, he touched Mala's foot tentatively with one of his steel-toed shoes.

"I told you not to wake her," Bourne said.

"Who gives a fuck what you say!" Taller drew back his foot and kicked Mala's ankle hard.

Before he knew what was happening, she had swiveled her hips, cocked her left leg and lashed out with a mighty kick to his solar plexus.

Taller made a guttural sound like an animal going to the slaughter. Bourne caught him around the neck, swung him into the table.

"Ack!" Taller exclaimed, even while he jammed his elbow into Bourne's side.

Mala grabbed the pistol out of his grip, but the men were so tightly wound together she couldn't aim properly.

"Don't!" Bourne shouted. "The shot will only bring more FSB."

Then he was too busy dealing with Taller, who had managed to reverse their positions. Now he slammed Bourne against the compartment wall, jammed the heel of his hand under Bourne's chin, pushing upward. Then, using all his weight, he body-slammed Bourne against the wall, over and over. Mala, reversing the pistol, brought the butt down on the back of his head, but he seemed unfazed.

Bourne brought his hands in, used his thumbs to dig into the bundles of nerves just below and behind Taller's ears. That the FSB agent felt. Grabbing him by the front of his jacket, Bourne turned him, rammed his head against the window with such force the glass shattered. Still, Taller wouldn't give up. His hands sought Bourne's neck, his red-rimmed eyes blazed with fury, but when Bourne pressed down on him, the jagged shards of glass punctured the back of his neck. One of them severed the third cervical vertebra from the fourth, and Taller was done. His hands dropped away and all the fire vanished from his eyes as his body went slack.

Before Bourne and Mala had a chance to exchange a word, the compartment door opened and Stubby entered, his right arm holding his Strizh straight out in front of him. Before he had a chance to take in the scene, Mala had stepped forward, wrapped one arm around his, and broke it at the elbow.

Stubby gave a yelp, dropped to his knees. Bourne stepped toward him and Mala aimed Taller's pistol at whoever came through the door next.

"That's enough," First Minister Timur Savasin said. He brushed past Stubby without giving him so much as a glance.

"Is it," Mala said rhetorically. She kept the Strizh aimed at Savasin's head. "I don't think so."

Savasin raised his hands, open palms toward them. "I come in peace," he said.

"That's a sick joke," Mala said, indicating the two agents.

"You certainly did a number on them." He was looking at Bourne, seeking to engage him directly, rather than through his companion, whose identity was a mystery to him. "I apologize for any inconvenience their, um, overzealousness caused you."

"As you can see, the inconvenience was all theirs."

Savasin shrugged. "They're replaceable, I assure you."

"So it goes in the Russian Federation," Mala said.

"Mr. Bourne, since I have no dominion in this compartment, would you be so kind as to ask your companion to lower her gun. This conversation will be somewhat more difficult with a Strizh pointed at my head."

"In a moment, perhaps," Bourne said. "I want to know what the hell this is all about."

"I confess it's a long story," Savasin said.

"I'll bet," Mala said, ignoring Bourne's silent signal to desist.

"Tell me who you are," Bourne said.

"You know very well who I am."

"Even if I do, I want to hear it from your own lips."

"Timur Ludmirovich Savasin, First Minister, Russian Federation."

Bourne crossed to the sofa, sat down on it. "For days now this woman and I have been hunted by *spetsnaz*. On whose orders? Yours?"

"That was a mistake."

"Really?" Mala said. "Jason, let me put a bullet in this lying bastard's brain."

"She'll do it, Timur Ludmirovich," Bourne said. "Killing is like breathing to her."

Savasin licked his lips. "Who is she, Mr. Bourne?"

"The Angelmaker," Mala said.

Savasin started. "I thought the Angelmaker was a bit of fiction, a fairy tale made up by certain people to frighten their competitors."

"If killing them was frightening them," Mala said, "then that's what they did."

Savasin stared at Bourne. "She is who she says she is?"

"Take it to the bank, Timur." He gestured to Mala. "Let's have it."

Without taking her eyes off Savasin, she came to Bourne, handed over the pistol, which Bourne aimed at the first minister. "See if he's carrying—and take his mobile as well."

Savasin closed his eyes for a moment as she put her hands on him. His right hand trembled a bit.

"No weapons," she said, stepping away. "Got his mobile, though. Only the one." She came and sat beside Bourne on the sofa.

"What about Stubby there?" Bourne said.

Savasin looked bewildered "Who?"

"Your man with the broken arm. Looks to me like he's in real pain." He looked at Savasin. "I assume you have more men aboard."

The first minister nodded. Taking the mobile from Mala, Bourne said, "Tell me how to contact them. Let's have them clean up this mess."

———

Ten minutes later, when, save for the broken window and some smeared bloodstains on the floor, a sense of order had been restored to the conference cabin, and the door had been closed and locked against further intrusion, Bourne said, "You said you had a long story to tell." He glanced at his watch. "We get into Moscow in just over an hour. You had better hope you can tell it in that time."

"All right." Savasin nodded. "May I sit down?"

"I think it best that you remain standing." Bourne still had the pistol pointed at him. "Begin, Timur Ludmirovich. Tick-tock."

———

At the same time Bourne, the Angelmaker, and Timur Savasin were hurtling from St. Petersburg to Moscow, Savasin's brother, Konstantin, was on his swift jet winging its way home. He spent the first part of the nine-hour and twenty-five-minute flight reading the Treadstone material Marshall Fulmer had kindly provided. He read the Bourne file three times straight through, then he went back to check certain paragraphs, using a pen with red ink to highlight a number of words and phrases he wished to keep uppermost in his mind.

After a light meal, washed down with a glass of icy vodka, he set the files aside, thumbed the buttons on his seat, lifting his legs and reclining him back. Folding his hands across his belly, he closed his eyes and allowed his mind to traverse the file, to linger over those paragraphs and, especially, the words and phrases he had highlighted in red.

In this fashion he drifted off, and when, an hour later, he awakened, he had his answer. He had identified the weak spot in Bourne's armor. He knew how to drill down to the core of him.

36

I DON'T EVEN know their real names."

"Alyosha Orlova and Nikolay Rozin," Soraya Moore said over the secure line that was a part of the government jet she had sent to pick up her agent in the field and bring her out of the cold. "You did a stellar job, Morgana."

The jet was parked at the airport in Kalmar, where Morgana had boarded it as it was being refueled. The interior was an odd design: only four seats, front and aft. In between, a series of what looked to be storage lockers.

"Have you been back to the hotel?" Soraya asked.

"No. I slept at a friend's."

Soraya's voice became wary. "What friend?"

"Her name's Natalie Soringen."

"I'll have her checked out," Soraya said. She sounded more than a bit annoyed but seemed to put that aside when she said, "You will have no problem at your old hotel."

"I'd assume the place would be swarming, following the murder-suicide."

"I fixed it with Stockholm. There'll be an inquiry, but that will be window dressing. And, best of all, the identities of the deceased will be suppressed."

"I'm impressed. How did you manage that bit of magic?"

"That's why I get the comfy chair." Soraya laughed. "I pointed out to the Swedish powers-that-be that not only were the victims Russian nationals, but they were spies. No one in the Swedish government wants a diplomatic run-in with the Kremlin."

"Let sleeping lions lie."

"That's one way to put it, I suppose."

After a moment's silence, Morgana said, "I don't want to go home."

"What's that? But your brief is done—a more thorough success than I could have imagined. I was tasked with bringing down Alyosha Orlova—Françoise Sevigne, as you knew her. I chose you not only because you were a field neophyte but because Françoise had befriended you. She trusted you; you were one of her scam targets. An important one, I might add."

Morgana was taken aback. "Why didn't you tell me who she really was?"

"I think you can answer that yourself."

Morgana considered a minute. "You wanted all my responses to be genuine. You didn't want to give her a hint anything was amiss."

"Sometimes," Soraya said, "keeping your agent in the field in the dark is the best course of action."

Morgana knew she was right, knew that she had done the right thing, but still she was stung. Soraya had used her, just as Françoise had. But soon enough she realized that the two motivations were light years apart.

"Okay. I understand," Morgana said, "but the reason I got suspicious was I saw Alyosha board a boat docked at the marina here. It's Gora Maslov's boat."

Silence on the line. Finally: "What are you saying, Morgana?" in a measured, cautious tone.

"I want to go after Gora Maslov."

"Wait a minute! You can't just—"

"Look, Alyosha was working for Maslov, that much seems true. I want to know what they were up to."

"But—"

"Don't you?"

"Perhaps. But, with your brief completed, my primary objective now is to get you home safe and sound. I've already subjected you to enough danger."

Soraya Moore was a pro, seasoned at that. She possessed the control's hard, pragmatic line of thought. But she also had something else, Morgana thought, something that drew her to Soraya, that made her want to work for her. It struck her at their first interview, when Soraya put out the first recruitment feelers. She had a heart, and a heart was something very dear to Morgana. She thought she loved Soraya, even though she knew perfectly well you should never love your boss—or, in this case, your control. But then why not? she wondered. Wasn't loyalty at a premium in the world of spies? Something to be held close, something precious.

"I'm the one in the field, Soraya," she said now. "I think I'm better—"

"Stop right there. Morgana, listen to me. I threw you to the lions, it's true. But this was a special circumstance. I had no one else."

"Thanks very much!"

"You misunderstand. I had full confidence in you and what you're capable of. But the truth is you lack training. I can't allow you to remain in the field."

"As you know I'm an ace at all firearms. What you don't know is that my father—"

"A former SEAL. I've read his jacket. He was quite a fine one, brilliant, really."

Now Morgana loved Soraya even more. "Yes. He trained me himself." Another bit of silence. She could almost hear Soraya thinking, recalculating, recalibrating the conversation. "Plus, really, when you think about it, my job at Meme LLC was to solve puzzles—the most difficult puzzles, I might add, puzzles that stumped others in my area of expertise. I find that the field is no different; it's a matter of solving puzzles."

"No, it's very different, Morgana. In the field you're constantly in harm's way."

"I find I like that." This time the silence was tense and brittle. She was about to say, *I'm staying, no matter what you say,* but she felt the wrongness of it. Her mouth could lead her down a bad path with a bad ending. Instead, she said: "But I'll come home." Hearing her father's voice in one ear, she waited a beat before adding, "If that's what you think is best."

Silence. Then: "You're a very clever girl."

"Thank you."

"I took a lot of chances with your brief. What if your friend Françoise didn't come through with her promise? I would have pulled you out of custody. You were never in any real danger as long as you were here in D.C."

"But once I came here, to Kalmar, I was in the real lions' den." Now was the time, she thought, to push it. "What you must understand is that I've become one of them now—a lion. Like my father."

"I appreciate the confidence you've gained, but I fear you're overreaching. You'll be going up against Gora Maslov, a hardened *grupperovka* boss. He'll eat you for breakfast."

"I don't think so," Morgana said, a thrill down her spine: she had won. "I have a way in."

"And what might that be?"

"The point is both Fran—Alyosha and Rozin were deeply interested in the Bourne Initiative, the code for which, I should add, I've not been able to crack. And now I don't think I or anyone outside the Russian team that General Karpov hand-picked to design it will."

"That's of no importance now," Soraya said. "The Bourne Initiative is nothing more than noise, Russian disinformation."

"What? It most certainly is not. The Initiative is real. I've been working on fragments of it and—"

"Getting nowhere, right?"

"Yes, but—"

"All meant for us to chase our tails like idiots. I got this directly from Marshall Fulmer, the new national security advisor, and he ought to know."

"I don't know where he's getting his intel from, Soraya, but I'm telling you it's bogus."

"An intercept of the Russian Unit 309. I've seen the pages, Morgana. They're authentic."

"They're authentic, all right. Authentic disinformation," Morgana said forcefully. "I know those code fragments are real beyond any shadow of a doubt. Do you know how? I found a legitimate zero-day trigger embedded in every one of the fragments I pulled out of the dark net. That's the only thing I was able to decode, but it's vital."

Another silence on the line, longer this time, the tension ratcheted up a couple of notches. "I'm listening. Continue."

"I'm damn good at my job. Don't you think I'd be able to spot fake code, no matter how well put together? No, the Bourne Initiative is real, and it's a ticking time bomb with an unknown target."

"Okay. Let's say you're right. I can't go to the higher-ups and tell them that based on what you've said. Fulmer will swat me down like a gnat. I just got this position; until I prove myself I've got to watch my p's and q's. I can't rock the boat."

"Then don't tell anyone. We'll act together."

"The two of us won't be enough."

"Working alone is essential in this instance."

"So you've said. You sound like the one person I believe can help us without physically interfering with whatever you have in mind with Gora. And he knows Gora. Though he knew his father even better. In fact, he was involved with General Karpov in killing Dimitri Maslov."

"Who are we talking about?"

"Jason Bourne."

Morgana looked around, as if they had just now entered top-secret territory. The interior of the plane was still and serene, no one in her vicinity to overhear her end of the conversation. She returned her attention to Soraya half a world away. "I don't understand."

"Remember a few years back when Bourne was accused of trying to assassinate the former president, and it turned out he'd saved him instead?"

"Sure."

"That was because of me—Sonya and I, who were being held captive."

Morgana gave a gasp. "When your husband was killed."

A small hesitation. "Yes."

"I'm so sorry, Soraya. All over again so sorry."

"Thank you. But to get back to Bourne, he and I go way back. We were in the field together."

"So you're former colleagues."

"More than that. Let's just say I know him more than well."

"Huh!"

Soraya laughed, dry and rough as sand. "Well put."

"I've been wanting to speak with him ever since Mac sent me the first fragment of Initiative code. If anyone knows about the Initiative it's got to be Bourne." Morgana's excitement was ramping up. "You know how to get in touch with him?"

"No, but I know someone who does. A man right here in D.C. by the name of Deron."

"Do you have Deron's number? I'll call him the moment we hang up."

"Deron won't talk to you, let alone tell you how to get in touch with Bourne," Soraya said. "No, Deron knows me. I'll call him."

"I'll sit tight, then."

"Back to the Initiative itself. You don't know what it's meant to do?"

"No."

"Do you know when the zero-day trigger is set for?"

"Yes. Forty hours from now." Morgana took a breath. "Another reason why I need to stay here."

"Bourne may not know this. He needs to."

"Yes."

"Now tell me what you have in mind." Soraya's voice was sharp and

clear, which told Morgana a great deal about her. Unlike the other mandarins who ran various clandestine services whom she had met or had
to deal with, Soraya was flexible. As a former field agent, she knew that
you were sometimes required, or forced, to pivot on a dime in order to
react to or take advantage of the changing situation in the field.

Morgana had had all night to think about a plan and Natalie to talk
it over with. She knew she couldn't get to Gora Maslov on her own.
"Maslov must be involved in the Bourne Initiative. That's why Alyosha
went to see him. Why else would he be here in this Swedish backwater
at the same time as Alyosha and Nikolay, with them presumably helping
me break the code? And if I'm right and they are all in it together, then
he is our chance to get to the Initiative before its inner clock detonates."

Silence on the line, just the hollowness, the faint arrhythmic clicking
of the security programs that shielded their conversation from electronic spying.

"All of this tracks," Soraya said. "The bits of mysterious code you've
pulled off the dark web could be enticements—coming attractions, you
might say. In that event, the Bourne Initiative is going to be auctioned
off to the highest bidder, imminently."

"And I believe Gora will be one of the bidders. Now you can see why
physical backup is the last thing I need. The more of our people here,
the better the chance of Gora becoming suspicious."

"Lord, what have I unleashed in you?"

"The law of unintended consequences, that's what," Morgana said.
"And it's not your doing. Sooner or later I think this was bound to happen."

"I think it's my good luck, then." The sound of what might be Soraya
shuffling papers. "You'll need some form of backup, Morgana."

"I've got you. You're all I need."

Soraya laughed. "You're really a piece of work."

"It's the only way I know how to be now. And for better or for worse,
I have you to thank for that."

Soraya sighed. "Hold on." Several moments passed with only the hollowness and the electronic clicking. When she returned, she said, "Give

me three hours. I'll have a secured Bluetooth earwig and a pair of ear-rings couriered to you from our Stockholm office."

"Earrings?"

Soraya laughed again. "The transmitter for the earwig is in one of them. Don't lose it."

"There are a couple of other things I need, stat."

"Name them." Morgana did. "You'll have them." Then Soraya's tone altered. "And Morgana?"

"Yes?"

"I won't forget this."

"Is that good or bad?" Morgana asked, but Soraya Moore had already disconnected.

———

"I am to use Dima Orlov's name with you, Mr. Bourne."

Bourne sat forward. "Why?"

"He and I are working together."

The Angelmaker laughed. "Dima Orlov working with the first minis-ter?" She shook her head. "I don't think so."

"I'm not here as first minister," Savasin said. "I did not seek out Dima as first minister, but as the brother of Konstantin, who has plans to cap-ture you, Mr. Bourne. Capture you, torture you, then kill you."

"Many have tried," Bourne said.

"Konstantin is a snake. He's ruthless and devious. He lives to create diabolical traps. I beg you not to underestimate him."

"More people have died underestimating their enemy than I care to count." Bourne waved the Strizh back and forth. "I wouldn't concern myself with that."

"But I do, Mr. Bourne. Very much so. Your safety, your knowledge is critical, Dima believes, to finding the codes for the Initiative, for keep-ing them out of the hands of maniacs like Konstantin."

"Of course my help is critical," Bourne said. "According to General

MacQuerrie, Dima Orlov is the one who stole the Initiative right after Boris was murdered."

"What? But that's impossible."

"Why?" Bourne said. "Why is it impossible, Timur?"

"Katya said that he and General Karpov were good friends."

"Maybe that's true," Bourne said, "but the Angelmaker here knows that Boris's death set the two remaining partners against each other. You see, Boris was the peacemaker. Both Dima and MacQuerrie trusted him, but it seems they didn't trust each other. Now only Dima is left, and Dima has the Initiative."

"Then why did he rope me in?" Savasin shook his head. "What does he need me for?"

"Did he contact you, Timur?"

"No. I went to him."

"Why would you do that?" Bourne asked.

"Because my brother..." Savasin's voice trailed off as his thoughts transferred onto another track.

"Konstantin, yes. Dima needs you as protection against the threat your brother presents to him. Konstantin is a threat to you; that's how he roped you in."

"And you," Savasin said. "Why did he send me to find you?"

"Friends close," Bourne said. "Enemies closer."

Bourne lowered the pistol, set it down between him and Mala. He gestured. "Take a pew, Timur. It's true confession time."

———

And so for the first time in his life, including when he was a little boy, Timur Savasin sat down and spoke honestly. He could not remember when he had learned to lie about everything—the moment, or time, was too distant for him to dredge up. But he knew the habit was formed as a response to Konstantin, a kind of protection from the malefic entity his parents had given life to.

And in talking honestly he experienced an enormous sense of relief, as of a terrible weight being lifted from his shoulders, as if his brother had consigned him to the role of Atlas, the weight of the world crushing him every waking moment, from which he had finally freed himself.

"The ironic thing," he said, after he had recounted his meeting with Dima and Katya in great detail, "is after having spent so many years hating and fearing Boris Karpov, I now feel as if I'm moving into his orbit. Konstantin covets General Karpov's position and power, and I know I must do everything in my power to stop him. Karpov was a humanist, Dima and Katya have opened my eyes to that. And now I am eager for the opportunity to understand his friendship with you, Mr. Bourne. Perhaps that is the one good thing that will come out of the dire straits we all find ourselves in, sparked by General Karpov's cyber Initiative, which has come to be known by both the Americans and us as the Bourne Initiative.

"Dima and Katya believe that you are the key to retrieving the codes. They are convinced that Karpov must have left some clue for you that will lead you to it, because it's clear to me that none of the original three partners, two of whom are dead, know what happened to it."

"If, as MacQuerrie believed, Dima hijacked the Initiative, then there is something—some key element—missing from it, and they think I have it," Bourne said.

"Do you?"

"No," Bourne said. "Boris left me his boat, which was sunk by the Americans. That's it."

"Well, that's disappointing."

"When it comes to Boris, people have gotten everything wrong. He would never have created a cyber weapon aimed at the United States. Knowing Boris as I did, I never believed that bit of fiction. What was his aim, then? MacQuerrie said that the code was meant to freeze the security systems of the largest international banks, allowing the three of them access to all the banks' accounts. MacQuerrie believed they were on the cusp of pulling off an electronic theft of unprecedented proportions."

Savasin's eyes narrowed. "I am no novice in reading between the lines, Mr. Bourne. There is something about General MacQuerrie's explanation that doesn't ring true to you."

"Not exactly," Bourne replied. "My sense is this. Boris loved money as much as the next person, more maybe. But he wasn't about to steal from anyone and everyone; that simply went against his grain. So what then? First, I believe Boris was getting ready to leave Russia. He had just gotten married; he had no other family left alive. When he left Russia on his honeymoon, he couldn't be pressured to return. He and his wife weren't coming back.

"So if we accept this scenario, which I do, where was Boris going to get his drop-dead money? He was well off, but not an oligarch by any means; he was unbribable. No, the cyber Initiative was meant to allow him to pick and choose, to take from the terrorist leaders and criminals who were housing their money in those banks whose coffers would be open to him. That plan is Boris Karpov to a T."

"Then he was murdered."

"Which set off a power struggle between the two remaining partners," the Angelmaker said.

"During which someone made off with the codes," Bourne continued. "He or she has them and now means to auction them off to the highest bidder, someone who doesn't have Boris's sense of morality."

Savasin raked his fingers through his hair. "They've created a very deep pit, indeed."

"Add another 'very,'" Bourne said. "MacQuerrie told me that while Boris meant the codes to freeze banks' security software, the Initiative could be directed at the deepest secrets of a sovereign nation."

"Like the United States."

"Or the Russian Federation."

"The stars are aligning." Savasin smiled. "You see, Mr. Bourne, you and I are moving toward the kind of détente you shared with General Karpov for many years."

Mala grunted in clear derision.

"I think it's safe to say," Bourne said, "that we're nowhere close to a détente, Timur."

Savasin nodded, keeping his expression neutral. "As you wish. But now I must tell you something, and from what you've told me the truth of it is unclear. Dima said that there is a timer set into the Initiative."

"A timer?"

"Yes. A zero-day trigger, he called it."

Both Bourne and Mala knew what a zero-day trigger was.

"Did he tell you when the exploit will activate?"

Savasin shook his head. "He claimed not to know. But he also said that the day was close. Very close."

Mala looked from Bourne to Savasin and back again. "There are two things Dima can do with the Initiative if he can retrieve the codes. He can use it for himself, or he can set up an international auction. Can you imagine how much such a cyber weapon would fetch on the clandestine network that terrorist leaders, demagogues, and heads of state of evil intent inhabit?" Her gaze returned to Savasin. "That group would include your Sovereign, First Minister, you know that, right?"

"It would also include my brother," Savasin replied. "He's doing everything in his power to get his hands on the Initiative." Savasin leaned forward, elbows on knees. "To do so, I guarantee that he's going to cross any and all lines he feels he needs to. Sooner or later, Konstantin always gets what he wants."

37

I'M ONLY DOING this for the money." Natalie, the young woman Morgana had spoken to after she had debarked from Gora's boat, swept her blond hair behind her ear. "I have a toddler. She was at my aunt's the night you slept over."

"Spare me," Morgana told her bluntly. "You want your revenge on Gora Maslov. You wouldn't have agreed to meet me otherwise."

They were in Kalmar City Park, standing at the apex of a small but beautiful wooden bridge painted a bright Dutch blue. Below them, in the water of the pond it spanned, water spiders skated across the surface, and now and again, a fish would rise, its mouth agape to scoop up unwary insects flying too low.

Natalie stirred uneasily beside Morgana. "Okay, but there's only so much punishment and humiliation I'm willing to take."

"Think of your toddler at home," Morgana said with evident cynicism. "Do you have an ailing mother, as well?"

Fire erupted behind Natalie's eyes, then just as quickly was extinguished. Her laugh was deep-throated and genuine. "Christ, I can't get away with anything with you."

"Better not to try," Morgana said, her tone lightened considerably by an intimation of friendship. How quickly she had learned from Françoise. It was still difficult to think of her as Alyosha Orlova.

"I like you, Morgana. You're not like other girls I've met."

"I don't believe in playing by the rules," Morgana said, "because they're all made by men."

"Men like Gora." Now Natalie could not keep the bitterness out of her voice. "Corrupt men. Evil men."

The afternoon was waning, the light richer, deeper, the shadows lengthening, so that the children who skipped along the bridge behind them broke out in laughter, running after each other's shadow, as if they could actually be caught. *To be a child again!* Morgana thought. She thought of Peter Pan, whose shadow Wendy had to stitch on him so that he would have one just like everyone else. She felt a bit like Peter Pan now, skimming, like the water spiders, over the atmosphere of Kalmar, seeing the park, the neighboring castle, all the way down to the marina, where Gora's boat basked in the late-day sunlight like a monstrous beast waiting to tear her limb from limb.

"Time to go," Morgana said softly. "He was pleased to hear from you, yes?"

"Insofar as Gora can be pleased, yes, I suppose so. I told him I wanted more money."

"That I'm sure he could understand. And when you told him you might be able to bring a friend this time?"

"He laughed." Natalie spat into the water, scattering the spiders, who must be thinking, What gods are these? "He laughs like a fucking hyena."

They had been through all this before, of course, but Morgana's plan was so acutely calibrated it paid to repeat every step of it multiple times. Plus, it calmed her—like a well-worn prayer before bedtime.

Natalie took Morgana shopping for a dress shorter than any Morgana had ever tried on, let alone worn, heels far higher than any she had ever tried on, let alone worn, and the right pieces of paste jewelry—a bracelet and a necklace just a touch longer than a choker.

"Men like a jewel nestled in the hollow of your throat," Natalie told her. "It reminds them of where their tongue will be in the middle of the night."

When she saw Morgana dressed for the evening with Gora, she said, "You look like ten thousand bucks."

"You mean like a slut."

Natalie shrugged. "Like everything, it's a matter of perspective. I think you're hot; so will Gora."

Morgana lifted the hem of the dress to reveal the small pistol in its chamois holder strapped high up on her inner thigh.

Natalie winked. "Now for the *pièce de résistance*. Makeup!"

The same two goons Morgana had seen when she had spied on Françoise stepping aboard Gora's boat were still at their posts, eyeing everyone who came within fifty paces with undisguised suspicion.

Natalie swallowed the pill Morgana had given her. "This had better work," she muttered under her breath as they strutted down the wooden planks.

"Maybe they won't pat us down," Morgana said, out of the corner of her mouth.

"Right. I think this is nuts, but for the money you're paying me you're the boss."

It was dark; the sun had set more than an hour ago, and lights sparkled along the pier. The water around Gora's boat danced in reflections of the cabin and deck lamps. The sky was a milky gray, the undersides of clouds pale as fish bellies. The goons recognized Natalie, but the one who had hustled her off days ago gave no indication he recalled the incident.

They gestured, and Natalie stood very still. They checked her evening bag, though it was clearly too small to hold a weapon of any serious danger. As they patted Natalie down, quickly and expertly, they flashed glimpses of their Strizh pistols in snug shoulder holsters.

Natalie was clean. Then they turned their attention to Morgana. She spread her legs a little, as if she were bracing herself against the rocking of a small boat.

They found the pistol, of course, and grabbing her by the arm, hustled her onto the deck and into the main salon, Natalie just behind.

One of the goons held up the pistol. "Look what we found," he said in guttural Russian.

"On which one?" Gora said. He had been sprawled on one of a pair of sofas, but now he sprang up. Perhaps deliberately, he was flanked by a pair of marble busts of Roman caesars set on black columns. He wore a cream-colored silk shirt, lightweight slacks, and huaraches. He glared at Natalie. "Is this some kind of payback?"

"It was on the other one," the goon said, handing over the pistol to his boss. "The new girl."

"That so?" Gora turned his attention to Morgana. "What's your name?" he said, switching to English.

"Lana."

He was standing right in front of her now, close enough for her to smell his scent, part cologne, part sweat.

It was emblematic of how he viewed her that he did not ask for her last name; either he didn't care or he assumed she would lie. "Do you know who I am, Lana?"

"I don't care who you are," Morgana said, "as long as I get paid at the end of the session."

"The *session*," Gora said mockingly. "How professional are we?" With his dark brows knit together, his tone hardened as he brandished the pistol. "What the fuck d'you think you're doing, bringing a weapon like this onto my boat?"

"Having a little fun." Morgana's heart was pounding so hard it was giving her a headache.

"Fun?" Gora echoed. "Okay, bitch, I'll show you some fun." He aimed the pistol at Natalie's forehead." His eyes never left Morgana's. "Shall I pull the trigger?"

The point was not to bat even an eyelid. "Go ahead."

"Blow your friend's brains out."

"If that's your pleasure."

A flicker of hesitation passed across Gora's face, like a fleeting shadow, and was gone. His expression hardened like clay in the sun. "If you mean to play chicken with me, you've made a serious mistake." He pulled the trigger.

A spray of water hit Natalie square between the eyes.

The goons looked stunned, Natalie blew water out of her nostrils, and Gora stood still as a statue, while Morgana laughed and laughed until tears came to her eyes. By that time, Gora was laughing, too.

"Jesus Christ," he said. "Jesus Christ." Then, waving a hand: "Some-one fetch her a towel."

He handed back the gun, grips first, and watched Morgana tuck it away in its holster, all the while giving him a good look at her creamy thighs and the tip of the shadowed triangle above.

"Natalie, I've underestimated you," he said as Natalie patted her face with the towel she had been given. "You really know how to choose your friends." He still hadn't taken his eyes from Morgana. His gaze roamed over her body in the way of ancient Roman slave traders; he did every-thing but look inside her mouth at her teeth and gums.

"You know, Lana," he said, "I can see your nipples through the fabric of your dress."

Like all women, Morgana had been subjected to the male gaze, but never like this. It was like being undressed and eviscerated. She had been reduced to a piece of raw meat ready to be devoured, without even a single thought as to its effect on her. In that one moment, Gora had stripped her of her humanity. It hurt—it hurt more than she could have imagined, like a knife slash, the first brick in the wall of domination. She wondered how Natalie managed it without curling up like a flower deprived of the elements it needs to survive and thrive.

"Perhaps it's the trick of the light."

A wicked smile sprouted on Gora's face like a noxious weed. "Right."

Natalie had been completely forgotten. She was old news, used goods, her value greatly diminished. Gora was homing in on the new girl: virgin territory, so to speak.

"Why don't you lift up your skirt again," Gora said. "I'd like to see that pistol wrapped around your thigh."

"You're the man," Morgana replied. "Why don't you do the heavy lifting?"

Gora laughed and reached for the hem of her dress. Morgana stepped back a pace. He came after her, faster this time. As his fingers were about to touch the hem, she swatted them away.

Gora stopped then, looking at her as if through a different lens. "You're not like the others, are you?"

"I am who I am," Morgana said neutrally. "Nothing more, nothing less."

"That's for me to decide."

He held out his hand, and when Morgana took it she felt as if she had put her head between the open jaws of a crocodile. Her skin began to crawl.

Morgana could sense Natalie's jealous gaze, mouth partly open, pearl teeth visible, but she had no idea what she was really thinking. She just prayed to whatever dark gods ruled her new shadowed world that Natalie wouldn't lose her composure, that she would follow Morgana's plan to the letter.

She allowed him to draw her down the wood-paneled corridor, past doorways to the formal dining area, the study he used as an office, several guest cabins.

The master suite was enormous, as plush and well appointed as any five-star hotel suite. It was all polished wood and brass fittings. A crystal chandelier hung from the center of the ceiling, and oriental lamps on hand-carved tables that were built into the wall haloed everything in an intimate glow. The king-size bed was covered in Frette linens, the love seat and two club chairs were covered in moiré silk. The teak deck was covered in an antique Isfahan carpet that quite possibly belonged in a museum. On the walls hung a Marilyn painting by Warhol and an early-career one by Jeff Koons, of the provocateur-artist himself entwined lustfully with his former wife, the former Italian porn star, Cicciolina. It was meant to be erotic, but in Morgana's opinion was just plain crass, which is how she found pretty much all of Koons's work to be. However, the Warhol's garish primary colors and Koons's even more garish subject matter clearly mirrored Gora's idea of setting the mood for a night of Russian debauchery.

Morgana glanced around. No books, not even a bad erotic novel. *Why am I not surprised?* she thought. At last, her gaze alighted on Gora Maslov. Natalie had said that in whatever he does Gora tries too hard, and she was right. This was even reflected in his clothing, which was meant to seem casual, but like the bedroom itself, was a self-conscious attempt at aping the hip-hop mogul of current American culture. It was all she could do not to laugh. But, having absorbed the intel on the Maslovs Soraya had sent with the courier, she knew there was nothing amusing about the family's history of murder, extortion, intimidation, and criminal enterprise. Dimitri, Gora's father, was especially impressive, until he was gunned down in a barber shop, 1930s Chicago gangster style, by Boris Karpov.

It seemed to her now, regarding Gora's vainglorious pose, that the son was suffering under an inferiority complex, trying and failing to live up to his father's image. This was not a good sign. People like Gora tended to be nasty, volatile, aggressive, sometimes violent, beneath their calm, smiling exterior. She needed to be especially careful not to make a false step. This setup could go south in the space of a heartbeat. She took off her heels.

When he grabbed her, Morgana said, "I have to pee."

"He likes to watch me pee," Natalie had told her.

Gora pointed to an open doorway behind her: the bathroom glowing like a jewel box. She turned, headed toward it, acutely aware of him following a pace behind.

When she crossed over the threshold, he said, "Don't you want to close the door?"

"Not especially." She did not bother to put down the seat; instead she turned back toward him, hiked up her dress, and slowly bent her knees. With her legs on either side of the porcelain bowl and her eyes steady on him, she canted she hips slightly forward.

His gaze burned into her. His mouth was half open. She could see a stirring beneath the zipper of his trousers.

"Ready?" she said. "Tell me when."

A little animal noise exploded from the back of Gora's throat.

A high-pitched scream, a loud crash, and the excited voices of the goons raised in explosive Russian curses put an immediate damper on Gora Maslov's erotic fantasy. With a guttural curse of his own, he ran out of the bedroom, down the corridor.

What he confronted was Natalie on the carpet, beside a pool of stinking vomit and the broken shards of one of the busts of Caesar. The other bust—of Augustus, as it happened—looked down upon this plebian mess with true caesarian disinterest.

"What the fuck happened?" Gora shouted.

"I dunno, boss," Goon Number One said.

"She clutched her stomach, staggered, knocked the head off its pedestal, and was sick," Goon Number Two continued.

"Then she collapsed," Goon Number One concluded.

"Is she alive, dead, or in between?" Gora asked.

"Dunno," they both said at once.

"We haven't checked," said Goon Number Two.

"Well, for fuck's sake, do!" Gora shouted. Whatever had sprouted in his trousers had suddenly turned inward like a frightened turtle.

Meanwhile, according to plan, Morgana had moved swiftly and silently on little bare feet down the corridor to Gora's study. She knew she had very little time. She was looking for some proof that linked Gora to the impending auction of the Bourne Initiative, but what form that might take she had no idea.

"Even if you don't think you have time, take in the whole scene," her father had taught her. *"Nine out of ten times whatever you're looking for will get caught in the corner of your eye."*

And so it was. Desk, task chair, laptop, mobile phone and sat phone lying side by side, neat as soldiers on guard duty. The laptop was off, the mobile was guarded by a fingerprint reader, the sat phone had no numbers stored in it. Not a scrap of paper on the desktop, and the drawers contained nothing of value. But a blotch of yellow stuck in the corner of her eye: a Post-it note stuck to the left-side bezel of the laptop's screen. It was curious how many people did that with their most important reminders. So insecure, and yet, like incriminating emails and texts, done all the time.

Moving around behind the desk, she leaned over, took a close look at what was written in the little yellow square: an international phone number and the word *Keyre*. A name? A place? She didn't know. Just below, another international number, this one without a name or a place. Using the mnemonic her father had taught her, she memorized the numbers, figuring they must be extremely important if Gora hadn't stored them in either phone.

"She isn't dead," Goon Number One said as he crouched beside Natalie in the salon.

"Well, that's something," Gora said distractedly. In his mind's eye he was seeing the image of Morgana, her dress raised, her knees bent, her white thighs exposed, asking him, *"Tell me when."* The frightened turtle had vanished, replaced by a snake, slowly stirring. "Get the cleaning materials," he barked at Goon Number Two. "Clean up this mess, then get back to your usual post on the dock. At this late stage I don't want anyone nosing around."

As Goon Number One lifted Natalie's head and shoulders off the carpet, she gave a tiny moan. Her eyelids fluttered.

"Clean her up, too, then get her to bed in one of the guest suites," Gora ordered. "And for fuck's sake get that stink out of here."

Goon Number One wiped Natalie's mouth with the still-damp towel from her water pistol experience, then lifted her in his arms, following his boss down the corridor toward the guest cabins.

"Make sure you get her out of those soiled clothes," Morgana heard

Gora say over his shoulder to Goon Number One. "Wash off all the muck. There'll be something for her to wear in one of the closets."

Morgana was standing in the corridor outside the master suite when Gora saw her.

"What's happened?" she said.

"Nothing. Your friend got sick, that's all."

Morgana's brow furrowed. "How sick?"

"I told you, it's nothing."

Gora reached for her, eager to return to the image in his mind's eyes, but Morgana flew past him, running down the corridor.

"Wait!" Gora cried, and then, seeing that she wasn't listening, "Fuck all." He headed after her.

Morgana entered the room where Goon Number One had laid Natalie on the bed. He was cleaning the muck off the front of her dress, copping a feel of her breasts whenever he had the chance.

Crossing to where Natalie lay, Morgana swatted the goon's hands away. "Get out of here. I'll take care of her."

The goon stood up, looked over at his boss. Gora gestured with his head, and the goon obediently stepped back.

"Nat," Morgana said, bending over the bed. "Nat, what happened?"

Natalie stared up at Morgana, mouthed, *I'm going to kill you.*

Morgana gave her a grin only she could see, before trying to turn her over. Natalie moaned as if she were in great distress. Morgana made a show of putting her ear to Natalie's chest. "Something's wrong, her breathing's labored," she announced in a voice bordering on hysteria. "She might have inhaled some vomit. If her lungs are filling with liquid we'll need to get her to a hospital or she'll suffocate."

"No," Gora said, taking a step toward them. "No hospital."

"All right then. Do you have a pair of large scissors?" she asked over her shoulder.

"What for?" Gora said.

"The zipper is in back. I can't turn her over, she's in too much pain," Morgana replied. "I'll need to cut off her dress to give her some relief."

Gora again gestured with his head, and the goon stepped out of the cabin. Morgana could hear his footsteps receding down the corridor. The idea was to get Gora so agitated that he'd fixate on Natalie, giving Morgana room to execute the last, and most delicate, part of the plan.

Moments later, Goon Number One returned with a pair of kitchen scissors, which he handed to Morgana. "Stay here," she said. "I need your help. Hold her dress away from her so I won't cut her."

Again, the goon glanced at Gora, who nodded, almost wearily. He was done with being the Good Samaritan. All he wanted now was his alone time with Morgana, her dress rucked, her thighs exposed to his avid gaze.

As the goon bent over, pulling Natalie's dress away from her chest, he could not help taking a look down her bodice. That was when Morgana buried the scissor blades into his left side. The goon grabbed her by the throat, callused fingers digging in, trying to rip it out. She struck him hard right above the left kidney with the edge of her hand. He winced, his eyes bloodshot, and she used his own momentum against him, bringing his side back toward her, twisting the scissors in the wound.

Blood spurted, the goon convulsed, and Gora started, unable to see what had happened. Natalie grabbed the goon's Strizh and, when Morgana cast the goon's body aside, pointed it at Gora.

Morgana turned back to Maslov. "Now, Gora, it's time for you to answer some ques—" But she saw Natalie's finger tighten on the trigger, and cried out: "No, no, no!"

She lunged for Natalie's hand, but it was too late. Natalie squeezed the trigger once, twice, three times, just as Morgana had done with Niki, the false Larry London. Gora, eyes open wide, grabbed his chest, staggering back, falling to his knees. His fingers convulsed, trying vainly to stanch the blood pouring out of him. He was staring at Natalie, his mouth, leaking blood, working soundlessly.

"Fuck you, fucker," Natalie spat as he fell over onto his face. She remained rigid, her right arm like a tree branch, in her mind still the weapon aiming at where Gora Maslov had stood a moment ago.

Morgana snatched the Strizh out of Natalie's now compliant hand. As Goon Number Two rushed in, pistol at the ready, having been drawn by the gunfire, she shot him neatly through the heart.

"Dammit, Nat. I told you no deviations."

"I didn't deviate," Natalie said, rolling off the bed. "I meant to kill him from the first." She eyed Morgana. "Why d'you think I agreed to your plan? Just for the money?" Hiking up her skirt, she pulled down her panties, revealing a part of her she'd kept hidden from Morgana: a garden of bruises, deep and dark as secrets. "What's money without revenge?"

38

JASON BOURNE RECEIVED the first call as the Sapsan bullet train was nearing Leningradsky Station in Moscow.

"Hello, Jason, it's your old friend Soraya."

Bourne was standing between Mala and Savasin, so he stepped away down the corridor.

"Soraya, it's really you?"

"It is."

"Where are you?"

"Back in the saddle."

"D.C.? Doing what?"

"Stepping back into the old pond. Now I've been asked to take over Dreadnaught."

"And you said yes."

"I missed the life, Jason. Too much."

"And Sonya."

"Thriving." A pause. "Where are you?"

"Russia. Moscow, to be exact."

"I'm going to give a new operative of mine this number."

"I wish you wouldn't."

"Morgana has been on the Initiative now for over a week. She's a very special person, and she has firsthand intel you need to hear."

"Why don't you relay—"

"You need to hear it from her, complete with her inflections. Take her opinions seriously, will you?" Before he had a chance to answer, she said, "When this is over, come see me in D.C. I guarantee you safe passage."

"No one can do that, Soraya. Not even you."

"Then I'll come to you."

The second call came as they were pulling into the station, readying themselves to disembark.

"Bourne."

"I have very little time, Morgana."

"None of us do." Morgana's voice buzzed in his ear like an insistent fly. "The Initiative contains a zero-day trigger."

"I know."

"Do you also know that there's exactly twenty hours before the Initiative is deployed?" Silence. "I didn't think so." She took a breath. "I still don't know what it's going to be deployed against, but I will tell you that Gora Maslov was involved up to his eyeballs."

Bourne caught the past tense. "Was?"

"He's dead, Bourne."

"You're sure?"

She barked a laugh. "I was there. His half sister, Alyosha Orlova, is dead as well."

"You've been busy."

She took another breath. "Two international phone numbers on a Post-it I found on Gora's boat might be everything you need."

"Tell me."

She recited the first number. "There's a name or a place written after it: Keyre."

"A name. A Somali arms dealer—he filled the vacuum when the authorities caught up to Victor Bout."

"That bad."

"Worse, if that's possible." The train had stopped, passengers were disembarking, dragging their luggage. The ones with briefcases were on their mobiles, talking without seeing. "And the second number?"

"No name." She read off the string of numbers; Bourne memorized them. "That it?"

"One more thing." He heard her breathing down the line and knew she was working herself up to what was most difficult for her. "Alyosha and Nikolay Rozin were also involved in the Initiative, in a way I can't yet work out, except that Alyosha's father was Dimitri Maslov."

Bourne was stepping onto the platform while talking to Morgana. His mind was working overtime, but at the same time his eyes were quartering the platform and, indeed, the entire expanse of the station in his field of vision. He did this unconsciously, as a matter of course, every detail caught in the web of his gaze.

"Soraya was right about you," he said. "Let's keep in touch."

With that he folded away his sat phone. Mala and Savasin were in front of him, the first minister's people grouped at the end of the platform, waiting for them. The remaining two guards who had been on the train with him were busy off-loading the corpses of the two who had been killed during the journey.

The crowd of debarking passengers had thinned, a majority of them shying away from the huddled group of FSB operatives with their long coats and grim faces. The grayness of Moscow hung like a pall over the tracks, and the atmosphere was considerably chillier and sharper, as if the station's HVAC system were pumping out blasts of air imported from Siberia.

Echoes of voices and shoe soles on concrete were dying away like embers losing their inner glow. Steps ahead of him, Mala was taking her time digging a verbal knife between Savasin's ribs. Four repairmen on an electric cart, laden with substantial toolboxes, plus a well-secured rectangle of tempered glass, passed them by, stopped outside the first class car, then clambered in with the slab of glass. Clearly, they had been alerted by the crew to the damaged window and carpet in the conference cabin.

Farther along, at the mouth of the vast station hall, the FSB gang shifted on their feet. Bourne, who had completed his inventory of passenger faces, turned his full attention toward Savasin's greeting committee. His penetrating gaze moved from one face to another, and what he saw gave him pause. One would think that they'd been looking around as he had, the better to pick up any potential threats to the first minister. Such was not the case, however. All of them—Bourne counted seven—were staring fixedly at Savasin.

Bourne checked their surroundings. They were almost at the head of the bullet train, which was on their right. To the left, across the platform, the next track was empty. Two other platforms and three tracks extended further in that direction.

Hurrying to catch up with Timur and Mala, Bourne kept his eyes on the FSB men, who had begun to stir in the manner of bees when their hive is invaded by a human hand. A sudden dull flash of metal, and Bourne had caught Mala by the collar, was swinging her around and down onto the platform. The guns were out now, and he pointed to the gap between the Sapsan and the platform. As Mala wriggled herself into the gap, vanishing beneath the train, the first spray of bullets peppered the side of the train nearest Savasin. Whatever passengers remained ran for cover, and the pair of security guards attracted to the gunshots took one look at the perpetrators and, without a word, melted back into the interior of the station.

Grabbing the first minister, Bourne dragged him down to a prone position, slithered into the gap, hauling Timur into it after him. Behind them, the bristling hive was in motion, as coordinated as bees in flight. Four agents raced down to the front of the Sapsan, while the other three peeled off to patrol the platform on the other side of the train. Two men slid down into the gap, following Bourne, while the remaining two paced along the platform, eyes focused on the gap between the Sapsan and the platform for the slightest sign of movement.

Below the gap, where the Sapsan's narrow undercarriage dwelled, the space widened out, black as pitch, but with room to both hide and maneuver.

Bourne, shadowed and all but invisible, struck the first of the FSB men on the side of the neck, a blow so devastating that the man dropped his Strizh from nerveless fingers. Bourne grabbed him and drew the man into the shadows with him. The second agent made his appearance in the narrow space. When, gun drawn, he crouched down to check out the shadowed area, Bourne shoved his comrade at him. As Bourne had anticipated, the second man shot first and asked questions after. He put a bullet through his comrade's chest before Bourne, emerging from the darkness, grabbed him by the front of his coat, and slammed the heel of his hand into the man's nose. Blood fountained; the man reared back right into Mala's grip. Wrapping her arm around his neck, she twisted hard with her other hand, breaking the man's neck.

"It looks like there was a coup in your absence, Timur," Bourne said as he and Mala armed themselves with the fallen men's weapons.

"My brother," Savasin said with active distaste.

"Going after the first minister," Mala said. "That takes brass stones."

Bourne waved them to silence as he got down on his stomach. They followed suit, and the three of them made their wriggling way between the rails, where there was enough clearance for their prone bodies but not much more. Bourne went as fast as he could, knowing that the gunshot would bring the others converging on the spot the explosion came from.

In fact, he was counting on this. There were five remaining FSB agents. Having all of them in a group was much more to his liking than having them spread out over the station. Having worked their way halfway down the Sapsan, he tapped Savasin on the shoulder, mouthed for him to stay where he was. Then he signed to Mala, who snaked her way to their left, toward the platform on the far side of the train.

Bourne himself rolled to his right, moving toward the gap between the train and the platform. On the verge of being able to get to his feet, he paused, watching for moving shadows, listening for hushed conversations, or even single voices.

When, after five minutes of the only form of surveillance available to him, he discerned that at least the spot he had chosen was clear, he picked his way forward into the gap. Again, he paused to listen; again he heard nothing but the normal noises attributable to engines, steel wheels, sighing hydraulics, and, every once in a while, the conversation of the repairmen coming through the broken window in the conference cabin.

Working his way backward, he headed for the front of the train.

39

IVAN WAS NEARING the end of the line. He'd been working on trains more or less his whole adult life—actually even before that. His father had worked on the trains in Moscow, though of course he'd never even dreamed of anything like the Sapsan. But the Sapsan had been Ivan's baby from the moment it had rolled into the yard at Leningradsky Station. He'd had to spend a week in a stuffy glass box of a classroom where he was taught every aspect of the Sapsan's workings, then another week working hands-on in the yard. That was how he came to love the Sapsan, and he thought of his father every time his gnarled hands touched the sleek outer shell or the even sleeker innards.

Unfortunately, Ivan thought as he surveyed the destruction of his most luxurious conference cabin, he was saddled with a trio of near-idiots. They were young, it was true, but they were also lazy, un-teachable, and almost always high on some illegal substance that Ivan refused to acknowledge, let alone identify.

It was not always thus, he thought with an inward sigh. When he came up through the ranks the youngsters were enthusiastic, eager to learn an honorable trade. No more. Nowadays, the young ones were infected by modern-day culture. Clubbing, whoring, and hanging out drinking, smoking, and making mischief were their off-hours avocations. Useless carbuncles on the ass of decent society, that's what they were, Ivan thought sourly as he directed Fool Number One to scrub out the carpet with a solution he had concocted to take out vomit and bloodstains from the special carpet in first class without affecting the color.

He ordered Fool Number Two to vacuum up the shards of glass from the blown-out window. Luckily, there weren't many of them, as the blow had come from the inside, but those that were there were bloody, and they all donned thick rubber gloves to protect themselves. Fool Number Three was in charge of making sure the pane of glass didn't strike any hard surface or topple over. Nevertheless, as Ivan picked his way over to the blown-out window he kept an eagle eye on Fool Number Three, the youngest, rawest, and highest of the trio.

Possibly that was why he didn't sense the Angelmaker until she was in his face. She grabbed the front of his uniform, pulled him hard against the chrome frame of the window, and put a forefinger across her lips in the universal sign for silence. Then she grinned at him, though all his terrified mind registered was her bared teeth. He had the irrational thought—though considering what was going on in the world today it was hardly impossible—that she was going to tear into his throat with those sharp, white teeth.

Instead, she drew him to one side while a man with the watchful, steely eyes of someone who saw and understood everything at first glance climbed in through the open space where the window had been. It was a long window; there was plenty of space. When the man looked at Ivan, Ivan's guts turned to water, and he felt an urgent need to piss. Then the man smiled at him, not in the feral way the woman had, but rather it was the smile of a comrade, an old hand with whom you could share a cold vodka and a cigarette at the end of a long day. He asked the woman to let go in perfect, fluid, Moscow-inflected Russian. He looked Russian, too. Ivan relaxed somewhat.

As for the three Fools, only the youngest one, mouth gaping open, noted the man's appearance. The other two were too occupied in trying to attend to their duties to notice, let alone care.

"What's your name?" the man said.

"Ivan Ivanovich," Ivan said, blinking like an owl in sunlight.

"Well, Ivan Ivanovich, my name is Fyodor Ilianovich," Bourne said, using a legend he'd employed before in Moscow. "I'm very pleased to meet you."

Ivan stared at him as if mesmerized. He did not know what to say. He suddenly longed for a glass of strong tea, or better yet, a vodka. Even a cigarette would do, he thought, but none of these amenities were on offer.

Bourne turned, and so did Ivan, gaping at two more figures clambering through the opening. One was the woman with the feral smile. The other was a figure out of the newspapers and state TV. Ivan goggled. It couldn't be!

And yet Fyodor Ilianovich confirmed his tentative identification. "May I introduce Timur Ludmirovich Savasin, First Minister of the Russian Federation. First Minister, this is Ivan Ivanovich, an upright citizen, and I trust a patriot, of the Russian Federation."

If I didn't see it with my own eyes, Ivan thought, *I wouldn't believe it. What on earth is the First Minister doing climbing through the window of my carriage?*

"Of course, of course!" Ivan said, coming out of his brief stasis. It was totally lost on him that no one bothered to introduce the woman with the feral smile. In point of fact, he was relieved. "Of course a patriot, First Minister."

"Ivan Ivanovich, it is an honor to meet a true patriot of Mother Russia such as yourself," Savasin said in his most formal voice.

Ivan all but passed out. To his utter chagrin, he was sweating profusely. "The honor is all mine, First Minister, I assure you."

Savasin smiled. "I—we—need your help."

"Anything, First Minister," Ivan said. "I am entirely at your service."

And so it was that Ivan Ivanovich, nearing the end of the line, experienced the greatest day of his life—notwithstanding it being an experience he swore never to tell anyone, not even his wife and three sons. Twenty minutes after they had crawled through his window he was leading the first minister, Fyodor, and the woman with the feral smile out of the first class carriage and into the electric cart. All of them were wearing train yard workman's uniforms and caps, stripped off Fools One, Two, and Three, who had been bound and gagged virtually naked, and thrust into the bathroom, under his benign and—he had to admit it!—amused gaze. Ivan locked them in himself with his master key that opened every door on every train and in the train yard itself. After thirty years on the job, he had amassed any number of privileges.

One of the trio, he could not tell which, but he imagined it to be the woman with the feral smile, glanced behind them, where five men in trench coats, holding pistols in their hands, frowning deeply like old men at a comrade's funeral, stood on the platform, discussing God alone knew what. Ivan did not want to know, just as he did not want to know the nature of the first minister's current difficulty. His heart was filled with the opportunity—call it a gift!—he had been given to do his duty as a citizen and—his chest swelled with pride at the thought—as a patriot. He had never in his life felt more Russian, not when he had gotten married, not during the occasions of the births of his three sons, nor the wedding of the eldest. These were all beautiful moments in a man's life, to be sure, but they were shared by almost every man. But this moment, this one was special. It was unique in his life—shared with no other. Only Ivan Ivanovich. And he would remember it and bask in its glory until his last dying breath.

"Come see me when this is all over," Savasin told the old man as he let them off on the far side of the train yard, a place so vast the station itself was barely a smudge on the near horizon. Ivan Ivanovich smiled shyly, brushed some soot off the first minister's lapel, and gave them a military salute. And that was how Bourne, Savasin, and the Angelmaker left him.

They made their way through a gap in the cyclone fence the old man had pointed out to them. Daylight was dying, the last glimmers of sun sparking off the tops of Moscow's tallest buildings, turning them to molten gold. A strong north wind had sprung up, sending the temperatures plummeting by at least ten degrees. Scattered clouds rushed by overhead, except for a gathering in the west, like birds seeking out the last rays of the sun before Moscow slipped into darkness.

Across a narrow service road a municipal parking lot spread out like an old lady with too much weight. And like that old lady, the tarmac was cracked and pockmarked by time and harsh weather.

It took them some time to find a car they could break into. Muscovites still maintained the habit of taking their steering wheels with them when they parked, to ensure their vehicles would still be there when they returned. But at last Bourne found one intact, broke in, and hot-wired the starter. Savasin climbed into the passenger's seat and, without a word of protest, the Angelmaker occupied the backseat. It was the first minister who knew Dima's new address and the best route to get them there unnoticed. They did not speak about the incident at Leningradsky Station. Savasin was sunk in gloom. Bourne felt it best not to disturb him, and the Angelmaker, uncharacteristically, refrained from mocking Savasin's humiliation. Seeing with their own eyes how his own FSB had been turned against him, acting on orders from an older brother who, though in an inferior post, somehow wielded more power than he did seemed punishment enough.

40

"ONLY TWO DEAD?" Konstantin's glance bounced off the pair of corpses lying on the Sapsan platform of Leningradsky Station and up to the remaining five men. "Bourne must be losing his touch."

"Two dead is an unacceptable number, sir," Viktor, the leader of the *spetsnaz* squad, said. "These are my people."

Konstantin's eyes glittered, and his voice crackled with harsh energy. "No, Captain, you and everyone else in the FSB are *my* people. Never forget that."

Viktor stared stoically at Konstantin, perhaps in silent rebuke, perhaps not. Konstantin elided over it; the captain and all these men were beneath his notice. So far as he was concerned every member of *spetsnaz* was cannon fodder. On the front line, in enemy territory, theirs not to reason why.

Besides, Konstantin had more important matters to attend to than standing around with the little people. Turning his back on the captain and what was left of his detail, he said, "Scrape the remains off the platform, Captain. The sooner the better. The Sapsan's next departure has been delayed far too long as it is."

"*And fuck you too,* sir," Viktor muttered under his breath as he watched Konstantin blur into the haze of the station.

———————

"We're being followed," the Angelmaker said, half turned so she could look out the rear window.

"For about a mile now," Bourne replied.

"Well?" Her voice was like a newly sharpened stick. "What do you propose to do about it?"

This barbed exchanged brought Savasin out his self-imposed exile from the real world.

"Nothing."

"Why the hell not?" the Angelmaker said.

Bourne smiled. "Patience."

They were still on the Outer Ring Road, more than five miles from the address Savasin had given Bourne. With a jolt, the first minister looked around, their location snapping into place. "Bourne, we're nowhere near the exit we need to get to Dima's."

"That's the point," Bourne said, as he swung off the Outer Ring Road. He sped down the off ramp and onto the tangle of city streets.

"They're still on us," the Angelmaker reported.

Bourne said nothing, concentrating on the road ahead. He was looking for an anomaly: a detour, a construction site, an abandoned warehouse. Instead, he found a trestle train crossing.

"Hang on," he said tightly, as he turned the wheel hard to the right. The car rattled down the tracks.

Savasin's eyes opened wide, his mouth hung open in stupefaction. "I don't think this is a good idea."

"Nobody asked you, your highness," the Angelmaker snapped.

When Mala had started to call the first minister "your highness" Bourne had not a clue. Perhaps when they had been walking and talking together on the platform in Leningradsky Station.

The car behind them had turned onto the road that paralleled the tracks. Bourne could see its shadow flickering between the pine trees. Night had fallen, as suddenly as if an immense cloak had been thrown over the city. Lights burned, but dimly, as they were on the far outskirts where factories, power stations, and slums huddled against one another as if in an attempt to keep warm. The air was filled with soot and oil particulates; the pines were black with it. And then the moon, made hazy by the thickened atmosphere, lost its shape, vanishing altogether in the gathering clouds. It began to snow, a gray shower in the twin beams of the headlights, reminding Bourne of the photos he'd been shown during Treadstone training of the houses surrounding Auschwitz and Buchenwald half obscured by the pall of gray ash pluming from the tall brick chimneys of the crematoriums.

Bourne increased his speed, even as the snow began to come down first in veils and then in sheets, inflicting multiple compressions on visibility. It was no longer possible, for instance, to be sure they were still being paralleled by the following vehicle. Then, all at once, a powerful spotlight pierced the snow and the pine needles. It swung back and forth like a maddened eye, before picking them out. It flickered, its dazzling light dancing off the side of their car, then leaving them in utter darkness for long moments at a time.

Savasin appeared mesmerized by the blinding light.

"How did they pick up our trail?" the Angelmaker asked.

Bourne was too busy at the moment to give either of them attention. He was fully concentrated on the dimly glowing ball of light that hovered four feet above the tracks. It grew brighter as it rushed toward them. And then, as the Angelmaker cranked down her window, over the howling of the gusting wind they heard the distinct *clickety-clack* of the oncoming train, felt the strong push of the air it drove before it.

"Bourne, what the hell are you doing?" Savasin shouted in clear distress. "You're going to get us all killed!"

Leaning forward, the Angelmaker clamped down on Savasin's shoulders, said, "Shut up, your highness. Let him do what he does best."

The train was almost upon them now. The engineer must have seen them, finally, because he let out a blast on his air horn, and then, seeing that the car ahead wasn't turning, sounded the horn again and again, until the searchlight from the car running parallel to them swung to illuminate the train so the occupants could see what was coming.

This was the moment Bourne had been awaiting. He turned the wheel hard over left. For a heart-stopping instant the car stalled as the tires hit the left-side rail. Then he gunned the engine and the car, bouncing upward, ran over the rail, and they were off the track, crunching down over the narrow cinder bed, still in danger of being clipped by the front of the train, which was so close now it loomed over their heads like a fire-breathing demon, a solid wall of flashing steel and grinding wheels.

Then they were in the woods, jouncing between spindly pines, churning the gray snow to slush, the almost bald tires slipping and sliding until Bourne guided them beyond the far tree line, onto a country track that eventually led them to paved road. Fifteen minutes later, they arrived at a crossroad with signs enough to orient Savasin.

"That way," he said, pointing to their right.

Instead of heading in that direction, Bourne pulled over onto the verge, though there was no traffic visible in either direction. He got out, leaned into the Angelmaker's open window, and said, "Your turn."

She dutifully got out, went around to slide behind the wheel. Bourne opened the front passenger's door, told Savasin to get in the back. Then he took his place beside the Angelmaker.

"Now," he said to Savasin, "direct us to the closest metro station that will get us nearest to Dima's place."

"The Kapotnya Oblast has no nearby metro stop," Savasin said. "No municipal buses, either."

"Just get us closest you can then," Bourne said.

Savasin considered a minute, then said to the Angelmaker, "Go left."

And then, as if to himself, "We're just inside the Outer Ring Road, eastern Moscow. We need to travel south, but not too far."

He directed them to the Domodedovskaya metro station.

"This is where you and I get off, Timur." Bourne turned to the Angelmaker. "Considering how far we've been followed, it will be more secure if we split up. Take the car. Change it for another, if you deem it wise. You know Dima's address. Meet us there."

The Angelmaker nodded. "Take care of yourself. And do me a favor, keep his highness in line." With that, she was off, a thick cloud of exhaust trailing after her.

Bourne led Savasin down the steps. The Domodedovskaya station was Brutalist modern. It had none of the opulent charm of the metro stations in and around the Inner Ring Road, where a magical mystery tour of old czarist Russia, post–World War II exuberance, lit by bulbous chandeliers, awaited the gawking tourist.

They took the metro in a leisurely northeasterly direction, emerging in the Alma-Atkinskaya station, in the Brateyvo District, across the Moskva River from Kapotnya. The Alma-Atkinskaya station was even more modern, having an almost space-age look. But that was to be expected from the newest of Moscow's outlier stations.

Out in the gray night, the snow continued to fall, blurring the ranks of identical gray modern residential high-rises, and haloing the light from the occasional sodium light that wasn't smashed.

Bourne saw the car first—a black Zil, with a long snout and blacked-out windows. They shot first—two men pointing pistols through zipped-down windows. Pulling Savasin down behind the bulk of the station's entrance that emerged from underground like a boil spoiling to be lanced, Bourne squeezed off three shots, two of which hit their mark. The hostile fire ceased as quickly as it had begun. The driver put the Zil in gear but made the mistake of flooring the accelerator. The Zil began to skid sideways on the thin coating of ice concealed by the snow. That error in judgment allowed Bourne to fire three times at the driver's side of the windshield; the third trigger pull told him the magazine was empty.

The Zil screamed as if it felt pain, and Bourne was running hard toward the car, Savasin fast on his heels. The Zil, driverless, was still making tight circles when Bourne wrenched open the driver's door and hauled the dead man out. One bullet had struck his chest, the other his head.

Launching himself forward, Bourne gained control of the car, stopped it long enough for Savasin to scramble in beside him. Bourne went through the clothes of the two shooters, looking for identification, found none. The two men exchanged clothes with the dead shooters. Blood spatters aside, the new outfits suited them better. Plus, the overcoats made them instantly warmer.

Abandoning the Strizh on the backseat, Bourne grabbed the shooter's pistol. Then he turned to Savasin, who had turned up his collar against the rising wind.

"Shit," Bourne said.

Savasin, knotting his tie, said, "What is it?"

"The Angelmaker asked how they were able to follow us." Bourne picked up the train worker's coat that the first minister had been wearing, pulled out a pin with a gleaming head from the underside of the collar.

"What the hell is that?" Savasin asked, alarmed.

"A miniature GPS tracker," Bourne said. Dropping the pin, he ground it beneath the heel of his shoe.

"That fucking Ivan Ivanovich," Savasin said.

"It looks as if your brother has been one step ahead of us."

"But how the hell would he know we'd run into Ivan Ivanovich?"

"He didn't," Bourne said. "But thinking ahead like a chess master, Ivan Ivanovich was just one of his plans. If we escaped his men— which we did—we'd seek out someone who could help us, someone in uniform who could lead us to other uniforms we could put on. The shattered window was his good fortune. The men in uniforms were more or less right in front of us."

A string of Russian curses exploded from Savasin's mouth. Then he said: "He'll pay for this."

"Forget Konstantin for the moment." Bourne checked his watch. "We need to get to Dima as quickly as possible."

Savasin pointed to the section of the Outer Ring Road. "Head north. Good thing I know all the shortcuts in Kapotnya."

If Morgana was right, they had sixteen hours until the zero-day trigger of the Bourne Initiative was engaged.

41

SORAYA, CONNECTED TO Morgana via her wireless earwig, made all the arrangements. A car was waiting for Morgana and Natalie. However, Natalie asked to be let off before the car got to the airfield where the Dreadnaught jet was standing by.

"But you can't stay here," Morgana said. "It's far too dangerous. You've been seen boarding Gora's boat multiple times. The police are going to be looking for you."

"I can't leave my son, Morgana."

"Then that wasn't a line."

Natalie smiled. "No. I'm not going anywhere without Karl." She squeezed Morgana's arm. "Don't look so alarmed. This is my country. I know how to get around. I know how to evade the police." She laughed. "I've been doing it almost all my life."

"This is different," Morgana said. "You know it is. Three people dead, my God. I'll take you and Karl back to the States with me."

"So I can do what, exactly?" Natalie shook her head. "Thanks, but no thanks. Sweden's my home. I'm not leaving."

With her hand on the door handle, she turned back. "Morgana, I know I fucked up." Her brows knit together. "Why aren't you angry with me?"

"I know what Gora did to you, how far he pushed you, how he humiliated you."

Natalie bowed her head. "Thank you." And she was out the door, walking down the street before Morgana had a chance to say anything more.

As it turned out, it was just as well Natalie didn't want to come back to D.C. with her. Inside the Dreadnaught plane, as it was readying to take off, Soraya's voice buzzed in her ear. "Sat phone. Now."

"Change of plans," Soraya said when Morgana had dialed in on the sat phone. "I hope you're not homesick, because you're not coming back to Washington, at least not right away. Things are still too hot and everything is happening so fast now I haven't had a chance to smooth the way for your return."

The plane had taxied to the head of the runway. The engines were revving up.

"Where are you sending me?" Morgana asked as she strapped herself in.

The plane hurtled down the runway and lifted off. With a hum of hydraulics, the wheels retracted.

"Somalia," Soraya said. "I want you to keep an eye on the arms dealer, Keyre, whose mobile number you found on Gora's boat. There's been an awful lot of chatter surrounding him all of a sudden. The storage lockers are filled with a wide range of arms and electronic listening devices; use anything you need. I want to know what's going on."

"Will do."

"And Morgana. Keep your distance, at all costs. I can't overemphasize the danger this man represents."

"I hear you."

"I mean it," Soraya said before signing off. "Keyre's a fucking nightmare."

The filthy air enveloped them, soot fell from the sky and turned the snow black before it hit the ground, cinders crunched under their soles, and evil-smelling eruptions belched from the immense smokestacks of hapless Kapotnya. As Bourne and Savasin picked their way along the sidewalks, the sky was so low it was impossible to tell whether it was composed of clouds or smoke. The sunless afternoon had slid unnoticed into turbulent twilight. Street lights—those that worked—cast a dim and fitful illumination on the sulphurous atmosphere.

Vehicles crawled slowly forward, then stopped for long minutes. The hellacious traffic had forced them to abandon the Zil. The sidewalks were bloated with people making their way home. Old men sat on icy stoops with their heads in their hands, exhausted simply by breathing. Teenagers zigzagged through the crowds, picking pockets or selling the latest iterations of cheap and dangerous drugs. No music, no car horns tonight, only small noises that constituted a deathly silence.

Bourne let Savasin lead the way. He was torn between needing to get to Dima as soon as possible and his instinct to continually scan the immediate vicinity for Konstantin's people, although how Savasin's brother could know where they were now that he had crushed the life out of the GPS, he could not imagine. Still, several times he guided the first minister into a doorway to observe the pedestrians coming up from behind them. He found nothing suspicious, and each time they continued their journey, hurrying now, shouldering their way through the crowds, stepping into the gutter when their way was blocked by knots of people too dense to push through without drawing attention to themselves.

"Next block," Savasin announced. "Ekaterina, Dima's daughter, gave me instructions on how to approach and enter the building." He pointed to their left, and they turned a corner. "It has a back entrance, of course, but there's also a side entrance, a small door, painted green, that the concierge uses on occasion. This way."

The side street, too narrow for vehicles of any sort, was nearly deserted, and they picked up their pace. It was faced by blank brick walls, nearly black from the soot and the dismal weather.

Bourne saw the green door coming up on their right. It was, indeed, narrow, hidden by shadows, so that it was easy to miss. Savasin stepped up to it, turned the crusty handle. Nothing happened; the door remained closed.

"Ekaterina didn't give you a key?"

Savasin shook his head. "She said it would be open."

Moving the first minister aside, Bourne examined the door. It was made of metal, much dented and as beaten up as a boxer. Here and there slashes of red could be seen, vestiges of an earlier coat of paint. An old lock was rusted into uselessness. Putting his shoulder to the door, he slammed into it once, twice, and with a soft shriek it gave grudging way. It was a poor fit for the frame, the bottom flange scraping the concrete floor of the gloomy hallway within.

Here, Bourne held them up. They stood, silent, deep in the shadows, while he accustomed himself to the cluster of small sounds—the boiler, water running through the pipes, floorboards creaking, the wind whistling through cracks in the windowpanes. It was like listening to a living thing. The building breathing in its own particular rhythm. Then a baby crying, a violin playing a soft, sad melody, a burst of laughter, quickly throttled. Footsteps on the stairs disappearing behind the sound of a closing door. Now no one on the stairs.

"Top floor," Savasin whispered as they emerged from the service area, reaching the vestibule.

Bourne did not bother to turn on the thirty-second light to illuminate their way. Instead, he indicated to Savasin to follow his lead in slipping off his shoes. Carrying them in one hand, they ascended to the first floor, where Bourne kept them still as he listened. The baby had stopped crying, but the violin was scraping away, occasionally hitting sour notes that made Savasin wince.

Bourne held them again on the landing to the third floor. The violin was louder now, obviously coming from one of the third-floor apartments. The melody, such as it was, had started all over again from the beginning, note for note the same as before.

Halfway up to the top floor, Bourne halted them again. He wished he were alone; he did not like dragging Savasin around with him, but he'd needed him to get to Dima Orlov. Now, not so much.

He began again to ascend, but when the first minister began to follow him, he put an arm out. "Wait here," he whispered.

"After coming all this way, after everything Konstantin has thrown at me to stop me, there's no way I'll be left standing on the threshold."

Bourne studied him for a moment. The young violinist hit the same sour note. "You have the Strizh you took from the gunman?"

"Sure." Savasin nodded, slipping it out to show Bourne. "But why would I need it? We're in the one place in all of Moscow safe from my brother."

Bourne said nothing, climbing up the last of the stairs, the first minister on his heels. Savasin had told him to expect the presence of the mountain-size protector named Cerberus and, as they reached the final landing with its riot of thick foliage, its magnificently turned wooden doors banded in iron and sporting the eagle bas-relief in the center of each door, wings spread, talons to the fore, Bourne saw that he hadn't exaggerated. Cerberus was the largest human being he had ever come across. The guard dog's raisin eyes regarded Savasin, lit up dully with recognition, then turned his attention on Bourne. He grunted.

"Hold that thought," Bourne said. Taking out his sat phone, he dialed the second number Morgana had dictated to him over the phone, the one she found along with the one for Keyre's mobile, the one without attribution.

He had noted that the number had a Russian prefix, as well as one of the very new Moscow exchanges created due to the proliferation of mobile phones. They heard a phone ring behind the decorative doors— a very distinctive melody, Ravel's "Pavane for a Dead Princess."

"I know that melody," Savasin said before it cut out abruptly. "It's Dima's favorite."

"No, it isn't," Bourne said, hearing the voice at the other end of the line say, *"Gora?"*

Bourne waved to Cerberus, who opened the doors, allowing them entrance to the Orlovs' vast atelier-apartment.

"I told you not to use this number unless—" Ekaterina broke off as she and Dima watched in shock as Bourne strode toward them, his sat phone against his cheek.

"Not Gora," he said with a millimeter-thin smile. "Gora's dead, Ekaterina." He pointed the Strizh at her heart. "This is the end of the line—for you, your father, for the auction, for the Bourne Initiative."

He heard Savasin's warning shout at the same time the immense blur came hurtling toward him.

How can someone so big move so fast? he wondered. Cerberus slammed into him, sending him tumbling across the floor. As his right shoulder struck the wooden boards, the Strizh flew out of his hand, skittering just out of reach. No matter, the mountain was upon him, battering him with fists as big and destructive as medieval maces. Bourne felt his left side go numb with the pounding he was taking. He tried to get to his knees, but Cerberus slapped him with the back of his hand. Bourne recoiled, and to the sound of splintering wood, he crashed into the stack of frames waiting to be assembled.

Giving him no respite, Cerberus closed in. Bourne got in three or four quick blows, which, astoundingly, appeared to have no effect whatsoever. Cerberus was bent over him, his raisin eyes filled with red rage: Bourne had threatened his mistress. Dimly, Bourne could make out Ekaterina calling her guard dog off, but he was beyond hearing, beyond anything but the simple principle of destruction.

His massive hand closed around Bourne's neck, squeezing so hard Bourne thought his eyeballs would pop out of his head. His breathing was labored, his heart was racing too fast; black spots appeared before his eyes, clouding his vision. His left side was still numb, useless. All he had was his right hand and, even as his world closed in to a pulsing red spot and his lungs strained for oxygen that wasn't coming, it scrabbled at his side, found a length of frame and, with the mitered end upward, with his last reserves of strength, drove it through Cerberus's throat, severing his spinal cord at the spot between the second and third cervical vertebrae.

All the air seemed to come out of Cerberus along with his blood. He deflated like a balloon stuck with a vandal's knifepoint.

Bourne rolled him off and scrambled to his feet as best he could. His training allowed him to go into *prana*, using long, slow breaths to reoxygenate his system. Not that it mattered. The violin melody from downstairs was gone. In the ensuing silence Konstantin Savasin appeared seemingly out of nowhere, surrounded by two of his men, trench-coated and armed with short-barreled Uzis. One of them had disarmed the first minister who, with his arms behind his back, looked white as a sheet.

"Taste." Konstantin, suave, slim, and saturnine, sauntered toward Bourne. "There's no accounting for it." He turned to his brother. "When you lie down with dogs, dear brother, you're sure to get fleas."

Responding to a hand signal, his other man came toward Bourne, the muzzle of the Uzi pointed at his midsection.

"Keep still," Konstantin admonished, seeing Bourne's muscles tense. "The thing will cut you in half in about three seconds." He shrugged. "Besides, from the look of you, I doubt you have much fight left in you."

At that, his man slammed the metal butt of his Uzi into Bourne's chin, and Bourne went down like a sack of cement. The last he knew a booted foot was closing in on the side of his head.

Then the silence of a vast and unfathomable night.

42

WHEN BOURNE AWOKE it was to see Ekaterina Orlova's face hovering over him like a full moon in all its glory.

"Usually," she said, in her smoky voice, "it's the last person to speak who's the mole. Isn't that the way it works in your world, *gospodin* Bourne?" She nodded. "But here, in *my* world, I'm the first to speak with you. I, the mole. The one who's made the alliances my father was too old or too hidebound to make himself. He couldn't see how much the world had changed, how much faster it was going to change. Like all old people, he's not a fan of change."

Her smile was like that of a badger—territorial and belligerent. And like a badger she had small, sharp teeth. She eased herself down onto a straight-backed chair, and Bourne realized he was similarly seated, save that his wrists were tied behind his back, his ankles strapped to the front chair legs. It was a metal chair, very heavy, which he discovered when he tried to rock it back and forth without success.

"I had a choice, you see—between the two brothers. Once Boris was gone, my father's power crumbled into so much sand. We could not stand alone; he did not understand that." She shrugged. "Who knows?

Maybe he didn't choose to understand. His fire is banked low; most days he's content to cozy up to his plants and his painting. Pasture work, if you catch my drift. So I chose the stronger of the brothers. Konstantin has plans and, with the Somali's help, the wherewithal to implement them. Plans poor Timur Ludmirovich could not even comprehend." She pursed her lips. "He tries, poor dear, but, well, we both know his elevator's not going too high."

Her laugh sent shivers down Bourne's spine, not that Bourne could feel them. The numbness on his left side had spread to his spine—not a good sign.

"Actually, much as I liked Boris, his death was an unexpected blessing. We were slated to make a great deal of money when the cyber weapon he'd had made shut down the ten targeted banks worldwide. Now, however, there is far more money to be made by going to auction. Including us, there are fifteen entities—individuals, governments, rogue military entities, industrial conglomerates—drooling to get their hands on it."

He was split in two now. Part of him was listening carefully to every word Ekaterina said while the other part was working on repairing whatever the hell Cerberus had done to him.

"One of those is, of course, Konstantin. He wants the Bourne Initiative so that he can present it to the Sovereign, thereby cementing his power in the Federation for a very long time." She wrinkled her nose, leaned close enough for him to smell her stale breath. "The fly in the ointment, and where I come in, is that Konstantin and the Somali, Keyre, are at war. Konstantin was stupid enough to have underestimated Keyre, delivering a shipment of Kalashnikovs of which some were defective. He claimed innocence, of course, but Keyre didn't believe him. Then, several weeks ago, Konstantin blundered again. Responding to actionable intel that it was Keyre who had taken the Initiative and was trying to short-circuit the auction, he had Gora send a cadre of men into the Somali's camp to steal the Initiative. Big mistake. Keyre caught them and beheaded them all. He sent the heads back to Konstantin packaged in dry ice via DHL."

Having been partially revived by his inner self, the outer self be-stirred, albeit creakily. "So Konstantin had become a liability."

"In the medium term," Ekaterina confirmed. "But as for now, he still serves an important purpose." She reached out, drew her fingertips along Bourne's cheek. "One piece is still missing: whatever it is Boris left you regarding the Initiative. We all think the coding is complete, but we can't be sure until you tell us."

"Why don't you ask the coders?"

"Why don't I? That would be so simple." Ekaterina rested her elbows on her knees. "Unfortunately, life's never simple. The fact is I don't know what group of hackers Boris dug up on the dark web and paid to build this cyber weapon, and neither does anyone else." She pointed a finger at him. "That leaves you."

"I can't tell you anything," Bourne said between thickened lips. "Boris didn't leave me anything."

"Liar!" She was in his face now. "He left you his boat. You were on it. You must have searched it, don't tell me you didn't."

"Of course I did, but if he left anything for me I didn't find it."

The disconcerting smile again, more teeth showing this time. "Sorry, *gospodin*, but no one believes you."

"It's the truth, whether you believe it or not."

"I don't. None of us does. Which is where Konstantin comes in." She rose. "I'll leave you to his not-so-tender mercies." The smile turned crooked, like the expression on a jack-o'-lantern. "Are you familiar with the fizzy drink trick? You will be soon enough."

Her laugh drifted after her as she left the room and closed the door. It was only then that Bourne realized that he was in a small, window-less room off to one side of the atelier. The door was reinforced metal and had a peephole at eye height. He barely had time to register these details before Konstantin and one of his men entered. The man was carrying a funnel and a case of thirty-two-ounce bottles of soda. He put the case down by the left side of Bourne's chair, then stood at attention. He held the funnel as if it were his Uzi: it had a long, curved snout.

"Wicked looking thing, isn't it?" Konstantin said. "I don't really like to use it. Court of last resort. But that's where you find yourself, Bourne. And time is rapidly running out."

He sat down in the chair Ekaterina had vacated, a buff-colored folder on his lap. "I'm not going to ask you nicely the way Katya did because I know you won't answer. So we'll just start the process further along the line."

"I know this trick," Bourne said. "It won't work."

"Oh, I know," he said, grinning like a jackal. "But one has to have a bit of fun now and then." He picked up the folder, waved it in front of Bourne's face. "In any case, I've read your file."

"What file?"

"Your Treadstone file, *gospodin* Bourne." Konstantin fluttered the folder like a fan. "I know every bit of your training."

"You're lying. All Treadstone files are buried so deep—"

Opening the folder, Konstantin read out several lines to verify his claim, then he closed it with a slap of his palm. "One has to have friends in high places." He shrugged. "Otherwise what's the point."

He gestured with his head. "Vlad."

Vlad took a rubberized bung out of his pocket. It was an obscene shade of pink. He pried open Bourne's jaws and crammed it into Bourne's mouth, even as Bourne shook his head violently from side to side. The moment the rubber came in contact with his saliva it expanded, filling his mouth so completely he had only his nose to breathe through.

Vlad inserted the end of the funnel into Bourne's left nostril, pushing it down through his sinuses. Bending, he drew up a bottle of soda from the case, unscrewed its top.

"Here we go, Bourne," Konstantin said. "We're dropping you into the Marianas Trench. Be sure to let me know how you like it."

Vlad tipped the bottle, poured the carbonated water into the funnel. That was hellish enough, when the carbon dioxide hit the back of Bourne's throat and burned its way down his esophagus and into his stomach, but Vlad kept pouring.

Bourne jerked and twisted. His insides felt as if they were being fried and then turned inside out. His head felt as if it were about to explode. All this was experienced by the outer part of him, while the inner part, the one that had been busy limiting the damage Cerberus had done to him, worked assiduously to bring feeling back first into his spine and then to his left side. He had been trained well. The only way to survive articulated interrogation was to wall off a part of your mind so securely that nothing could breach its defenses. That accomplished, one form of torture was pretty much like the next, or the one before it, for that matter. Whatever agonizing indignities were perpetrated on the body, that part of the mind remained safe, keeping you sane in the face of a thousand dark paths to insanity.

Bourne's body gagged, got hold of itself, gagged again. The other Bourne, the inner one, stared up at the ceiling, turning it into blue sky with birds wheeling freely. And Vlad kept pouring, and Bourne kept gagging so vociferously that once the bung bulged out of his mouth before Vlad rapped it back in with his knuckled fist. More fizzy water, more agony. Bourne's eyes watered; the whites turned red. He was drenched in sweat, and the muscles in his extremities trembled uncontrollably. And still, Bourne's gaze never wavered from the birds high above. As they breathed, he breathed. As they lived, he lived. They spoke to him, soothed him, circling, circling...

43

U NTIL FROM FAR away he heard Konstantin say:
"Enough."

And then, "Unplug him, Vlad. Bring him back to the surface."

When Bourne came to, Timur Savasin was standing in front of him. He had no memory of vomiting up an entire bottle of soda, but the evidence was all around him. The floor, his shoes and socks, the bottoms of his pants legs were sopping wet.

Konstantin clucked his tongue. "Look at you, Bourne. Back from the dead, yes, but looking the worse for wear. Did you enjoy your little vacation?"

It was then that Bourne saw Konstantin had a gun pressed against the side of his brother's head. "So now to the finale," he said. "Or, rather, I should say the starting line." He tilted his head. "Your Treadstone file revealed your one weak spot, Bourne. You're a humanist. You actually care about human lives." He pursed his lips. "Which makes you some kind of conundrum I'm at a loss to explain." He shrugged. "Well, I suppose some mysteries aren't meant to be solved. No matter. The point here is that if you don't tell me what Boris Karpov left you, I'm going to blow my brother's brains all over your face. How's that for a succinct message?"

"Okay, let's have a talk," Bourne said through the cotton of his swollen lips. "There's no reason to kill your brother."

"Oh, there are any number of reasons, Bourne, but at the moment I have no time to enumerate them. The auction is almost upon us." He removed the gun from the side of his brother's head. "Go ahead. Tell me what Karpov left you regarding the workings of the cyber weapon."

Of course, Bourne had nothing. He was playing for time in order to keep Timur alive. He was about to open his mouth, to tell Konstantin some nonsense that, knowing Boris's MO as well as he did would make some sense, when the sound of a gunshot hammered them from the other side of the door.

Konstantin started. "Go see what the fuck is happening out there," he told Vlad.

But before Vlad could get to the door, two more shots exploded. Then nothing. No one inside the room moved. The harsh noise of their breathing was the only sound. Then, a knock on the door, not urgent but relaxed, as if a neighbor had come to ask for a cup of sugar.

Konstantin gestured silently for Vlad to see who it was. Obediently, Vlad put his eye to the peephole, only to be hurled backward by the bullet that, having shattered the glass of the peephole, penetrated his eye and lodged itself in his brain. As he slammed against the rear wall, Timur took advantage of the shock to wrestle the handgun out of his brother's hand. Konstantin punched him full in the face, and he staggered back. With a snarl of fury Konstantin launched himself after him, grabbing his gun hand, lifting it above their heads.

A fifth gunshot shattered the door's lock, and the Angelmaker stepped inside the room.

"Jesus Christ," she said, seeing Bourne, "what the hell did they do to you?"

Bourne gave her a lopsided grin. "Not enough." He gestured with his head at the two antagonists. Konstantin and Timur were locked in a death grip, neither one giving any quarter.

"Now that's what I call sibling rivalry."

"Get me out of here," he said.

"In a minute." The Angelmaker appeared fascinated by the two brothers locking horns.

"They'll kill each other," Bourne said.

"That's what I'm counting on."

"Mala. Cut me loose."

"You'll stop them."

"I will."

"They're like a pair of Siamese fighting fish."

"Mala!"

She shrugged and, with a knife, cut through his bonds front and back.

Konstantin drove his fist into his brother's solar plexus, doubling him over, and tried to wrest the gun from Timur. Bourne raised himself off the chair, got halfway to where the brothers were struggling, went down on one knee. He waved the Angelmaker back, rose of his own accord, closed with the two brothers. He wrenched the gun out of their shared grip. Reversing it, he smashed the butt into Konstantin's face, shattering cheekbone and eye socket. Konstantin moaned, sank to his knees. Bourne dropped him with a massive blow to his right ear. He lay unmoving.

"Christ, that was close," Timur said, the relief clear on his face. Then, as Bourne grabbed his arms, "Wait, what are you doing?"

Bourne pushed him into the chair he had occupied.

"Now that's better." Grinning, the Angelmaker bound his wrists and ankles.

"What is this?" Timur said. "I led you here, I gave you my trust, now you tie me up?"

"I've no intention of letting you get your hands on the Initiative," Bourne told him.

"I'll kill you for this!" he shouted. "Both of you!"

Bourne turned the gun on him. "Think hard, First Minister. Do you really want to threaten us?"

"He did kill your brother," the Angelmaker pointed out.

"Now your path is clear," Bourne said. "I suggest you make the most of it." Before Timur could reply, he stuffed the rubber bung into his mouth.

"Someone's sure to come by," Bourne said.

"Sooner or later," the Angelmaker added. "And if not?" She shrugged.

As they crossed the room, Bourne swept up the folder that contained his Treadstone file, slid it inside his shirt.

"What was that?" the Angelmaker asked.

Bourne had questions of his own. "What about Dima and Ekaterina?"

"What about them," she said tersely.

"Dead or alive?"

"Do you really care?"

"Ekaterina told me she was running the auction."

"That's what she said, on the point of death," the Angelmaker said with distaste. "It was a surprise. My money was on Dima. She told me that he was the one who made contact with Konstantin."

Bourne reacted. "Then who has the Initiative?"

"Ekaterina wouldn't have kept it here," the Angelmaker said. "Too insecure."

"That leaves Keyre."

"It always comes back to him, doesn't it?"

Bourne stood at the open doorway. He was never so happy to get out of anywhere. At that moment, the Angelmaker turned back to the curled body of Konstantin Savasin. She leaned over. "You dead yet? Well, just to make sure..." Flexing her right knee, she stamped down hard on his neck.

The sound of vertebrae cracking was not a pleasant one. Except, possibly, to her.

44

SOMALIA. THE HORN of Africa. A gleaming citadel on the oceanic edge of a poverty-stricken, burnt-out landscape. Before, there had been nothing but fishermen and the maimed remnants of constant war, until hunters of another sort, led by the Yibir magus, Keyre, arrived. Pitching their tents, they set about creating a port, first of all, and then the warehouses to house the bounty brought in by Mexican and Colombian cartel drug money. Then the warlords of African and Mideast nations got wind and wanted to join the party. After them traipsed the Russian *grupperovka,* oligarchs, and elite Kremlin *siloviki,* the Eastern European mafiosi, the deeply corrupt politicos and greedy merchant bankers from Western Europe and, last and best of all, all manner of quick-buck merchants, including a smattering of crafty espiocrats from the United States. And like everything the United States stuck its snout into, the sky then became the limit—for Keyre and everyone else enjoying the fruits of his illegitimate labors. Now there was peace. Keyre's peace. Now there was prosperity. Keyre's prosperity. Now the war was exported all over the world. The killing, carpet-bombing, gassing continued, only not here in Keyre's haven.

Bourne and the Angelmaker arrived very early in the morning. Bourne had slept the whole way. Under the names Arnold and Mary Winstead, the fictitious couple whose passports Deron had had made for them before leaving D.C., they had taken a commercial flight from Moscow to Istanbul. Before leaving Russia, Bourne had phoned Abdul Aziz, a longtime friend and importer-exporter with connections all over the Middle East and Africa.

Zizzy, as he was known to his friends and family, was more than happy to accommodate Bourne's requests. In Istanbul, they had transferred to the private airstrip reserved for VIPs and visiting dignitaries, where Zizzy had one of his company's jets standing by, along with a doctor and nurse to treat Bourne. When he heard that Bourne was injured, it was all Bourne could do to keep Zizzy from getting on the plane himself. But he did meet his friend and female companion at the private airstrip to see for himself that his friend wasn't on death's door. "Because," he said, his usually sunny face an aggrieved mask, "then, my friend, I would have no choice but to take you straightaway to my home where both the doctor and my wife would nurse you back to health."

By the time Zizzy's plane touched down in Somalia, Bourne had been treated, filled with fluids of various sorts, shot full of antibiotics, and, with a shot of morphine, sent off to slumberland while doctor and nurse worked to patch him up.

A salmon-pink slash heralded the rising of the sun. Having danced across the Arabian Sea from the southern tip of Kerala Province in India, a warm onshore breeze ruffled their hair. Apart from a low bank to the west, the sky was almost cloudless. The sun was going to be merciless.

A jeep, battered and dusty but with a full tank of gas, was waiting for them, courtesy of one of Zizzy's trading partners in Mogadishu. It took them just over an hour to reach the area. That left no more than two hours to get to Keyre and somehow stop the Bourne Initiative's zero-day trigger from self-actualizing.

The perimeter of the citadel had expanded even since the last time they had been here. Cranes and earthmoving machinery were hard at work among the pyramids of sunbaked bricks, sandstone, sacks of dry concrete, and various tile roofing materials.

They were stopped at the main gates. As the Angelmaker negotiated with the guards, Bourne caught a glimmer in the corner of his eye, a quick shard of light from the rising sun glancing off a metallic or glass surface. He might have thought nothing of it, but it was out past the perimeter of the cyclone fencing and the Uzi-toting guards who patrolled ceaselessly, day and night. He might have mentioned this to the Angelmaker, but he didn't. Instead, as they passed through the perimeter into the citadel itself, he said, "Keyre has done nothing but lie to me. He told me that the Maslovs were the ones he was doing business with."

"They are."

"But he also told me that Gora and Alyosha sent the thirteen men to infiltrate this village. In fact, it was Konstantin Savasin who sent the men. It was Konstantin he was at war with."

"Who told you that?"

"Ekaterina Orlova."

"And you believe her?"

"She had no reason to lie."

"And Keyre does."

"It's a way of life with him."

They passed supply depots with doors open as men on forklifts filled them with barrels of oil and other liquids used in construction and demolition. They passed immense generators housed in concrete structures, open-topped for venting, food halls, barracks, even a parade ground of earth pounded flat, with a flag flying from a forty-foot pole in the center and, where in more peaceful settings decorative fountains might be, four anti-aircraft weapons at the corners. Keyre's quarters were, of course, in the center of the compound.

To her credit, the Angelmaker made no attempt at refutation, so Bourne continued. "Keyre also lied about not knowing anything about the Bourne Initiative. He knows almost everything about it, since he's running the auction."

"Again Ekaterina."

"Yes."

"She was quite the chatty Kathy with you, wasn't she?"

Bourne gave her a grim smile. "She was trying to recruit me."

"She was the easy way."

He nodded. "And Konstantin was the hard way."

"You survived both."

"With your help."

"Then bravo to both of us." She turned off the ignition. "I don't think Keyre was lying to you about one thing: he doesn't know how real this thing he's about to auction off is. If it's the real deal or a bust."

"He'd run an auction without knowing the real value of the item?"

The Angelmaker barked a short, unpleasant laugh. "For the right amount of money Keyre would sell anything to anyone."

They arrived at the center of the citadel: a two-story building larger than any of the other residential structures, even though its sole occupant was Keyre. He required a good bit of room—for his offices, his library, his study, and, of course, the laboratory—the place, originally in a humble tent, where he had worked on Mala and would have on Liis if Bourne hadn't violently intervened.

Bourne was concentrated on the coming confrontation with Keyre and, to some extent, on the enigmatic woman about to get out from behind the jeep's steering wheel. But at the back of his mind hovered the sun-bright glimmer out beyond the citadel's perimeter.

Inside, Keyre stood, arms folded across his chest, in a large, round room Bourne had not seen before, so modern Bourne couldn't believe it existed in the bleak, war-scarred countryside of Somalia. Clad in pure white marble, it must have cost a fortune to build. A high, domed ceiled was pierced by an oculus through which sunlight moved during the course of the day. The room was centrally located. There were four doors, mirroring the placement of the four anti-aircraft guns around the parade ground. Through one open door, Bourne could see a table that looked suspiciously like the one he had seen in the tent where Keyre had worked on Mala years ago. Another, a solid mahogany door slightly ajar, led to a vast bedroom suite. The third was fully open, revealing a modern kitchen of white tile and stainless-steel appliances, gleaming beneath overhead lights. The fourth door was closed. It was made of metal, like that of a bank vault. Arrayed around the walls were flat-panel screens, showing various points around the perimeter of the compound. Below them were banks of terminals.

Keyre welcomed them like conquering heroes. Naturally, he was overjoyed when Bourne told him the good news. "So it's for real!" He rubbed his hands together. "And even better, some of the Russian participants are out of the picture. I haven't heard from either Gora or Alyosha."

"You won't be hearing from Ekaterina, either." Bourne turned to the Angelmaker. "But then I'm thinking you already know this."

"Yes," Keyre acknowledged. "The Angelmaker told me that Ekaterina and her father are out of the picture completely."

Bourne returned his attention to Keyre. "She shot them dead. Which, I'm assuming, was why you insisted she come along with me. You knew the path you set me on would lead to Ekaterina and Dima."

Keyre raised a forefinger. "Knew, no. But I suspected as much. For some time now, my lines of communication with the Russians have been somewhat, how shall I put it, sketchy."

"Which was why you needed me. You knew my close knowledge of Moscow and its people in certain circles."

"Like Karpov."

"Like Karpov," Bourne acknowledged. "But I was right about Boris. He himself would never have conceived of such a cyber weapon as you described to me. It was meant instead to enrich him and his two partners. But after his death the Initiative was hijacked, its purpose redirected." Bourne stared at Keyre. "Who could have done that, do you imagine?"

"If I'm to be honest, Bourne, I thought it was Konstantin."

"The Russian *silovik* who ordered thirteen Somalis turned by *spetsnaz* to steal it from you?" Bourne shook his head. "I don't think so."

Keyre cocked his head and, without missing a beat, said, "Did you ask him?"

"I was too busy killing him." Bourne flexed his hands at his sides. "So, let's count the people who *didn't* hijack the Initiative: Konstantin, his brother Timur, Dima Orlov, Ekaterina Orlova. I knew Gora Maslov—"

"I'd heard he was shot to death by one of his whores."

"Gora was too stupid to think of it," Bourne went on. "And as for Alyosha, she's dead, too."

Keyre raised his eyebrows. "Really? Now that *is* a surprise."

Bourne refused to be sidetracked. "So that leaves who exactly, Keyre? You. Only you. You hijacked the Initiative. You've had it all the time. You just wanted me—and Mala—to avenge the insult the Russians—particularly Konstantin—visited on you."

Keyre blew a contemplative puff of breath between his lips. "A fanciful tale, Bourne." He gestured with the flat of his hand. "But just for the fun of it, let's assume everything you've told me is true. What now?" His eyes sparked. "Will you attempt to wrest the Initiative away from me? Will you try to stop the auction?" He was almost laughing.

"You're hoping for that," Bourne said.

Keyre nodded. "Indeed I am."

"Actually, those aren't the first things on my mind," Bourne said. "The Initiative has a zero-day trigger."

Keyre's eyes narrowed. His smile was gone now. "What do you mean?"

"Remember Morgana Roy, the cybersecurity expert you mentioned who worked for General MacQuerrie? When she told me that there's a trigger built into the Initiative's root code it got me to thinking. Why would Boris want such a thing? I mean, if he was going to sell it—which I know he wasn't—or if he was going to use it as a cyber weapon— which I know he wasn't—a zero-day trigger would make no sense. In either case, it wouldn't be needed. In fact, it would become a detriment. An unnecessary race against time. But if he had it designed to take down the cyber-infrastructure of international banks, a zero-day trigger is logical. Boris must have known that the banks initiate a certain number of the largest international transfers in bulk at a certain time each week. That's when the theft on an unimaginable scale would take place."

"So that's what it was created for. Thievery." Keyre laughed. "That Karpov. I've got to hand it to him. Brilliant man. But, you know, so am I. Yes, I hijacked the Initiative. And I also redesigned it. It wasn't too difficult if, as I did, you had the entire coding. So. First, I set up the auction idea. But then the Sovereign contacted me. He wanted the Initiative because he had something big cooking. Something very big indeed. He offered me money, lots and lots of money. But he also offered me something even more valuable than money. Can you guess?" Keyre's eyes danced merrily. "He offered me and my shipments safe passage in the ports beyond even my reach." He shrugged. "It was an offer I couldn't refuse, especially when he added that he wanted me to rid him of"—Keyre snapped his fingers—"what word did he use? Oh, yes. He wanted me to rid him of several 'unstable' individuals. You see, your friend Karpov's betrayal of him hit home. The Sovereign no longer trusted anyone around him. He wanted them gone."

"Including Konstantin."

"Yes."

"Which suited you perfectly."

"It did."

"So you sent the Angelmaker to bring me to you."

"Well. Yes. But first through neutral intermediaries I had your whereabouts transmitted to the Russians and Americans."

"We could have been killed," Bourne pointed out.

"No, no, Bourne. I had too much faith in you. And in the Angelmaker. I knew she'd bring you to me."

"So no auction."

"A ruse. I kept it going for cover."

Bourne frowned. "Cover for what?" He checked his watch. "The zero-day trigger will activate in twenty-three minutes."

"Ah, well, that. I'm sure you've heard the news stories about the Russians massing along the borders of the Baltic States. Well, instead of shutting down the banks, as Karpov planned, the Initiative will freeze NATO's communications and defense infrastructure. Once that happens, the Russians will cross the borders into Latvia, Estonia, Lithuania. Then it will be Sweden and Finland's turn. By the time NATO figures out a way around the Initiative, the Russian putsch will be a fait accompli."

"Keyre, you can't do this. Even for you—"

"But my dear Bourne. It's already done. At least it will be in, what, nineteen minutes."

And, as it turned out, Bourne was right in having the glimmer stuck in his consciousness like a splinter, because at that moment twin explosions rocked the camp as the generators blew, plunging the citadel into an electrical and electronic abyss.

Center. Breathe. *"Timing is everything,"* her father, the angel on her shoulder, said in her ear. Aim. Squeeze the trigger. *Ka-boom!*

Chaos.

But before that... Morgana had staked out Keyre's citadel for some hours, familiarized herself with the daytime and nighttime peregrinations of the guards, as well as their shift changes. She lay on her belly, peering through the powerful eyepieces of the military-grade field glasses she'd found on the plane and stuffed into a backpack, along with everything else she thought she'd need, and finally she saw the Angelmaker exit a jeep. In this one instant, remembering Mac's recitation of her kills in just the past five years, ending with *"She's a menace,"* her decision was made for her.

She watched as the Angelmaker entered Keyre's building with Jason Bourne. Her blood was running hot, and she had wanted to fire then and there, but the timing was off. With no way to ensure that all the guards would be pulled off of their posts, she needed to wait until they were in the right positions. She had already calculated how long it would take her to reach the area of cyclone fence she had targeted, and she factored this in.

When the time was right, *Ka-boom!*

And amid the chaos she scooped up her backpack and ran. She was through the fence, the wire-cutters left behind, and inside Keyre's citadel without attracting any attention. The twin explosions had caused more chaos than she had anticipated.

She ran toward her target.

Last lap, she thought. *Do or die.*

She was on her way.

45

WHAT DID YOU DO?" Keyre growled.

Bourne spread his hands.

"He didn't do anything," the Angelmaker said. "I was with him the whole time."

"Maybe you were, maybe you weren't." Keyre glared at her. "Maybe the two of you cooked this up together.

"I'm not blind." In a blur, he reached out, grabbed the Angelmaker's upper arm, brought her to him. "I see the way you look at him. I know how you feel about him."

Bourne, who knew how dangerous she could be, was appalled at the slackness in her the moment Keyre touched her. Her eyes grew soft and dreamy, her head tilted back slightly, exposing the pale flesh of her throat, as if to a lover. She bent backward, as if about to swoon. Bourne had never seen her like this, and it frightened him. It looked to him as if in Keyre's grip she had lost all control.

He lunged at her, trying to wrest her from the Somali, but she wouldn't help him work her loose.

Keyre bared his teeth, the lips drawing back, exposing black gums, in an atavistic expression, revealing all the history and power of the Yibir. "Don't you get it yet, Bourne? Look, look. She doesn't want to come."

He was right, but that didn't stop Bourne from chopping down on Keyre's wrist. As his hand dropped away, Bourne wrapped an arm around the Angelmaker's waist and dragged her away. She fought him.

"I hate you, I hate you, I hate you!" she cried, in eerie echo of the first time he had come to save her. It was as if they had all stepped back in time, as if the present was replaying the past in perfect synchronicity: Keyre laughing, Mala squirming and shouting, and him doing his best to contain the anger and panic of her younger self. In this unstable state, he half expected her to call out for him to find Liis and save her.

Perhaps to forestall her, he whispered into her ear: "You told me you had a daughter, that Keyre was holding her hostage. What else have you lied to me about?"

"That's what I do. I lie," she said, pointedly not answering him. "I warned you about my scorpion nature."

He had no answer for her. With a sickening lurch, he saw no path through the thorny forest of her inscrutable nature. She was drawn to Keyre like a flame, she always would be. He kept trying to save her, but only she could save herself from the Yibir mesmerism, and he honestly didn't know whether she possessed the inner strength.

Time seemed to slip away from him. He saw Keyre coming toward him, he felt Mala's breath against his cheek, the heaving of her body, the flailing of her limbs, as if she had lost her coordination. He saw Keyre's fist coming toward him, he saw the gleaming Damascus blade held in it, but they seemed to have no meaning for him. Not until the razor-sharp edge sliced into the meat of the arm he held around Mala.

With a shock, fire rode up his arm. His shoulder felt like it had been dislocated. As if from a great distance, he saw it drop away from Mala, he felt the blood as if it were someone else's blood. He became aware of Mala yanking the gun from him, saw her take a staggering step back, her arms held out straight in front of her, both hands wrapped around the weapon's grips. Strangely, Keyre didn't continue his attack, but stood his ground three paces from Bourne, as if rooted to the spot. Blood dripped from the tip of the knife, which was now pointed at the floor. Dimly, Bourne wondered whether the blade was coated with a drug that was now in his system.

"You see how it is now, Bourne," the Yibir magus said. "It won't be me who doles out justice, it will be the Angelmaker."

"Mala," Bourne heard himself say. "Her name is Mala."

"I'm afraid not, Bourne," Keyre said, a note of genuine pity in his voice that pierced Bourne more deeply than if Keyre's knife had found his heart. "Mala died a long time ago." He pointed toward his laboratory. "She died, upon the same table that sits now in the middle of that room. All my paraphernalia is the same, in fact, it's in the exact same spot the old tent occupied. Just the surroundings have changed."

His expression was enigmatic; it was as if he had sunk inside himself, as if that essential part was hidden from Bourne, maybe from Mala as well.

"Mala is dead, Bourne. You've never accepted that fact. Mala died and in her place I created the creature you see before you: the Angelmaker." He inclined his head toward her. "It will be the Angelmaker who will dispense justice to you."

Mala had swung the gun in his direction. Her expression was as unreadable as was Keyre's. Her eyes seemed to be looking inward, or perhaps through him. What was she, in fact, seeing? What Keyre wanted her to see? If so, Bourne knew he was finished. One thing Konstantin had been right about. He'd read Bourne's Treadstone file, and he had gleaned the essential information. Bourne could not kill Mala, perhaps not even at the point of death. Part of him loved the part of her he still believed to be alive, despite Keyre's contention otherwise.

"Kill him," Keyre said. "Kill him now."

And then from out of the depths of Bourne's unconscious came the one last try to save them both. "Anjelica," he said to Mala. "Your mother called you Anjelica. I'm calling you Anjelica, because that's who you are. Anjelica didn't die here years ago. She's here now. She is you."

Mala blinked.

"Anjelica."

A small smile, perhaps of recognition, lit her face. Her lips parted as if to reply to him, and then she pitched forward onto her face, felled by a gunshot that had come from directly behind her. Locked as they were in their own world of fatal consequences, neither Bourne nor Keyre had heard Morgana's stealthy entrance into the building. And until the gunshot, Mala had blocked Keyre's view of her.

Both he and Bourne shouted at the same time, in shock and grief, perhaps, but the sounds, like those of an animal, were indecipherable. As they went at each other, Bourne felt a rage, pure and powerful, rise up within him. Now she was gone. Bourne knew she was gone without having to kneel beside her, check her pulse, or listen for her breath. She lay as she had fallen, deathly still, nothing more than a husk now, and perhaps, at last, at peace.

Bourne soon found that there was no good way to fight Keyre. He was as slippery as an eel, seemingly as immune to the blows Bourne rained on him as if he were made of stone. As for Morgana, she was trying her best to get a clear shot at Keyre, without success. Meanwhile, Keyre's returned blows were taking their toll on Bourne. In his weakened state, he knew he couldn't hold out for very long. He needed to end the struggle quickly or face defeat and death.

With lightning speed he went through his options, none of which seemed to him to give him much of a chance. But there was one, though the riskiest of the bunch, which might see him through. With the next strike from Keyre, he doubled over, moaning in pain. Taking the bait, Keyre doubled down on his attack, which built to such a frenzy that he completely disregarded his defense.

That was where Bourne got him. From his knees, Bourne drove a fist upward and, with the Somali bent over him, his knuckle struck Keyre squarely in the sternum, shattering it. In shock, Keyre seemed to freeze for a moment. And in the moment, Bourne acted. Rising from his penitent's position, he buried his fist in Keyre's side. Ribs went, at least two, possibly three, stove in by the power of the blow. The third strike caught Keyre's left kidney. The fourth and fifth, as well.

Bourne grabbed a handful of the Somali's hair, dripping sweat, and, using the massed tips of his fingers, drove the shards of Keyre's sternum inward, into his organs. Blood poured out of Keyre's mouth, his eyes turned upward, as if beseeching his unknown Yibir gods for a surcease that did not come. Bourne was in no mood for mercy. Taking Keyre's head in his hands, he slammed his face into his raised knee.

Keyre dropped like a stone and lay in a widening pool of his own blood.

At the sound of pounding boot soles, Bourne turned to see a pair of guards run into the room. Morgana shot them both before they could fire. Bourne and Morgana's eyes locked again, and a strange mixed message passed between them. She had killed Anjelica, but then the Angelmaker had been about to kill him. It was her nature, as she had told him. The nature of the scorpion. He nodded to her, and she nodded back.

He looked down at Mala's body, the surprised expression on her face. Her eyes were as blank as those of the Sphinx. What had she thought at the end? he wondered. He thought of her tortured life, both when she was with Keyre and after. He had never left her; he'd been a poison in her blood that no amount of figurative transfusions could defeat.

In the end, despite all of his help, Keyre had owned her, body and soul.

"Bourne!" Morgana cried.

The sharpness of her voice broke the spell, and he told her how Keyre had altered the Initiative to shut down NATO to accommodate the Russian Sovereign.

"That's it then," she said in despair. "Even if we were to somehow get through to someone high up in NATO, even if the person would believe us, it would be too late."

"But there must be a way," Bourne said. "Boris wouldn't have had the Initiative constructed without a fail-safe. A key. A way to shut down the zero-day trigger in case of emergency."

She looked up, a gleam of hope in her eyes. "If he left it with anyone, he left it with you. He must have. You two were thick as thieves; you were the only one he trusted. You must have it."

"Everyone seems to think I do," Bourne said. "But I don't."

"All right then. But to have even the remotest chance I have to get a look at the completed code."

He nodded. "This way."

Bourne led her to the only metal door in the room. Fireproof. "I'll bet anything what we need is behind here."

It occurred to her then that the complete code had been her holy grail from the moment she had been given her slightly hysterical orders from Mac. She had hit a wall and had decided to take a different route altogether; the route her father would have had her take. But all the while, like an itch she couldn't scratch, her failure at piecing together the Initiative never left her mind. It had increased in stature, like a myth, like fabled El Dorado. Now she fairly shook at the thought of actually seeing the finished code.

"We have less than ten minutes to find the Initiative and to somehow defeat the zero-day trigger, and, look, there's no lock." She could not keep the despair out of her voice. "There's not even a handle." She pointed. "Just this rectangle affixed to the surface."

"It must be the locking mechanism."

"But there's no keypad. How—?"

Bourne touched the plate. His fingertip made an impression, just as it would on a haptic mobile phone or laptop screen.

"Good God," Morgana said. "How can we possibly know what to input? There are no numbers, no letters, nothing but a blank screen."

"Quiet," Bourne said. "I'm thinking,"

"Well, think quickly," she said. "We're at seven minutes and counting."

The trick was to put himself in Keyre's mind. A horrible thing to have to attempt, but it had to be done. He turned back to look at his corpse. What would the Yibir have used to gain entrance, something no one else could possibly know? How could he know? How could anyone know? His gaze drifted inevitably to Mala. So many names, so many identities.

Without warning, he was thrown back to their night on Skyros, the blackness, the turbulence of the storm, how he had traced the runes on her back, committing them to memory, even as she turned away, as if she were ashamed of them. He froze.

The runes.

Tentatively, he touched the screen again, and then ever more authoritatively began to trace out the shape of the scars on Mala's back.

"What the hell are you doing?" Morgana said, but it was clear that she was fascinated.

"Keyre was a Yibir magus." Bourne was halfway through now. "He scarred Mala—the Angelmaker—with these runes." He was done. He held his breath.

The door clicked open, and they rushed through. They found themselves in a dimly lit room, windowless and claustrophobic. Apparently it had its own generator, because all the electronics were working. On a semicircular table was a powerful desktop surrounded by two laptops. Four screens showed different areas of the citadel and the port. It was clear from them that the explosions had morphed into fires that had spread to the neighboring buildings. As they watched, transfixed, a warehouse of war matériel went up in a ball of fire and black smoke. Keyre's men were swarming all over that section of the compound in a frantic effort to keep the rest of the stored weapons and ammo from going up and destroying the entire village.

The laptops were open but their screens were dark. Perhaps they were waiting patiently for the auction that would now never come. The desktop screen was on and active.

"It's the Initiative!" Morgana cried. "I recognize the bits of it I've tried and failed to decipher."

"But you discovered the zero-day trigger," Bourne said.

Setting her backpack down, she perched on the mesh task chair. "Yes.

That much I was able to decode." She turned to him. "D'you really think there is a fail-safe?"

"Knowing Boris, I do. He was meticulous about such things. He made sure he accounted for every contingency." He stared at the screen, his mind racing. "It would be logical if the fail-safe was in the same bit as the zero-day trigger, wouldn't it?"

Morgana's fingers were racing across the keyboard. "It would. But then why didn't I see it before this?"

Bourne glanced at his watch. "Three minutes left."

Morgana, half bent over the keyboard, her fingers a blur, kept combing through the code of the cyber weapon. "Honestly, I'd need hours, if not days to find it. Unless, of course, someone knew the key code."

"I've told everyone under the sun I don't have it. Boris didn't leave me anything."

"Nothing?" Morgana lifted her fingers from the keyboard, rocked back and forth in despair. "Ninety seconds. I'll never be able to stop it."

"Well, his yacht, but that's at the bottom of the Mediterranean now. You can be sure that I searched it thoroughly before it was sunk."

She picked her head up. "What was the name of the boat?"

"What? Why?"

"You said he left you the boat." She turned to him. "What if the boat is the key?"

Bourne's heart started to race. "*Nym*," he said. "Boris's boat was named *Nym*."

As she turned back to the keyboard, he spelled it out for her.

"N-Y-M," she repeated back as if to herself. "Fifty-three seconds. Here goes."

She typed in the letters. Nothing happened.

"Shit," she said.

"What is it?"

"I must have entered the key in the wrong place." Her fingers frantically worked the keyboard, and then—

Everything stopped.

"There," Morgana said.

The screen went dark.

"Got you, you sonuvabitch."

For Morgana that was the end of her second successful brief for Soraya Moore. But for Bourne, there was one more thing left to do. Much as he wanted to, he couldn't carry Mala's body out of the citadel, even amid such chaos, so he did the next best thing.

In Keyre's laboratory, he stared at the table with its old bloodstains, now almost black as pitch. How much pain and suffering had this table seen—not only Mala's, but all the young girls who had come before her.

Searching through the magus's supplies he came upon a can of flammable liquid. What he had done with it, how he had applied it judiciously to his "girls" Bourne could not—and would not—imagine.

Standing in the doorway, even with her phone against her cheek, briefing Soraya, bringing her up to date in hushed tones, assuring her she had made a copy of the code and then destroyed the fail-safe-locked original, Morgana sensed his great sorrow. She did not pretend to understand his relationship with the Angelmaker, nor why he could feel anything for her at all. But it wasn't her place to understand, and she did not judge him.

She watched silently as he doused the table with the liquid, then ran a thin line of it across the lab's floor to where the Angelmaker's body lay. There were a number of devices that created a flame in the lab, but Bourne deliberately chose the most primitive of them—long wooden matches.

Scraping the head of one along the side of the box, he watched the flame flare up. He wished he were the kind of person who believed in God; he wished he knew a prayer.

He composed his own. "Good-bye, Anjelica," he whispered. "You will be remembered."

Then he threw the match onto the center of the glistening table.